epic!

COSMIC

PIZZA PARTY

Nick Murphy • Paul Ritchey

Illustrated by

Bea Tormo

Andrews McMeel
PUBLISHING®

Cosmic Pizza Party created by Nick Murphy, Paul Ritchey, and Bea Tormo

Andrews McMeel Publishing
a division of Andrews McMeel Universal
1130 Walnut Street, Kansas City, Missouri 64106

www.andrewsmcmeel.com

Epic! Creations, Inc.
702 Marshall Street, Suite 280
Redwood City, California 94063

www.getepic.com

21 22 23 24 25 SDB 10 9 8 7 6 5 4 3 2 1

Paperback ISBN: 978-1-5248-6733-1
Hardback ISBN: 978-1-5248-6807-9

Library of Congress Control Number: 2020950784

Design by Dan Nordskog and Wendy Gable

Made by:
King Yip (Dongguan) Printing & Packaging Factory Ltd.
Address and location of manufacturer:
Daning Administrative District, Humen Town
Dongguan Guangdong, China 523930
1st Printing — 3/1/21

To my wife, Rebecca,
and our son, Desmond--
wanna order pizza tonight?
--Nick

Mom--thanks for all the
bedtime (and daytime) stories.
--Paul

To Fran--I love and respect you
even though you like pineapple
on your pizza.
--Bea

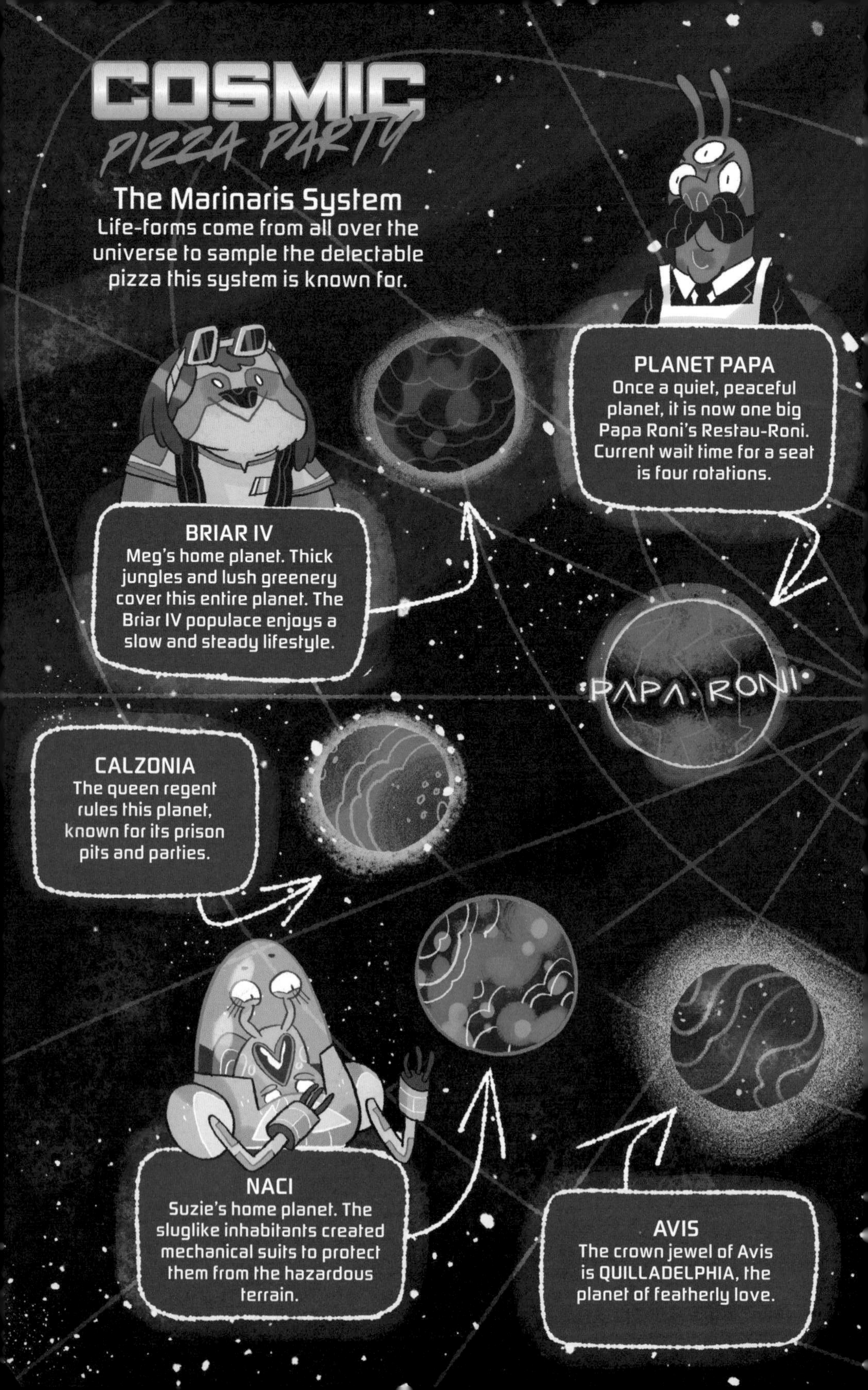
COSMIC
PIZZA PARTY
The Marinaris System
Life-forms come from all over the universe to sample the delectable pizza this system is known for.
PLANET PAPA
Once a quiet, peaceful planet, it is now one big Papa Roni's Restau-Roni. Current wait time for a seat is four rotations.
BRIAR IV
Meg's home planet. Thick jungles and lush greenery cover this entire planet. The Briar IV populace enjoys a slow and steady lifestyle.
PAPA·RONI
CALZONIA
The queen regent rules this planet, known for its prison pits and parties.
NACI
Suzie's home planet. The sluglike inhabitants created mechanical suits to protect them from the hazardous terrain.
AVIS
The crown jewel of Avis is QUILLADELPHIA, the planet of featherly love.

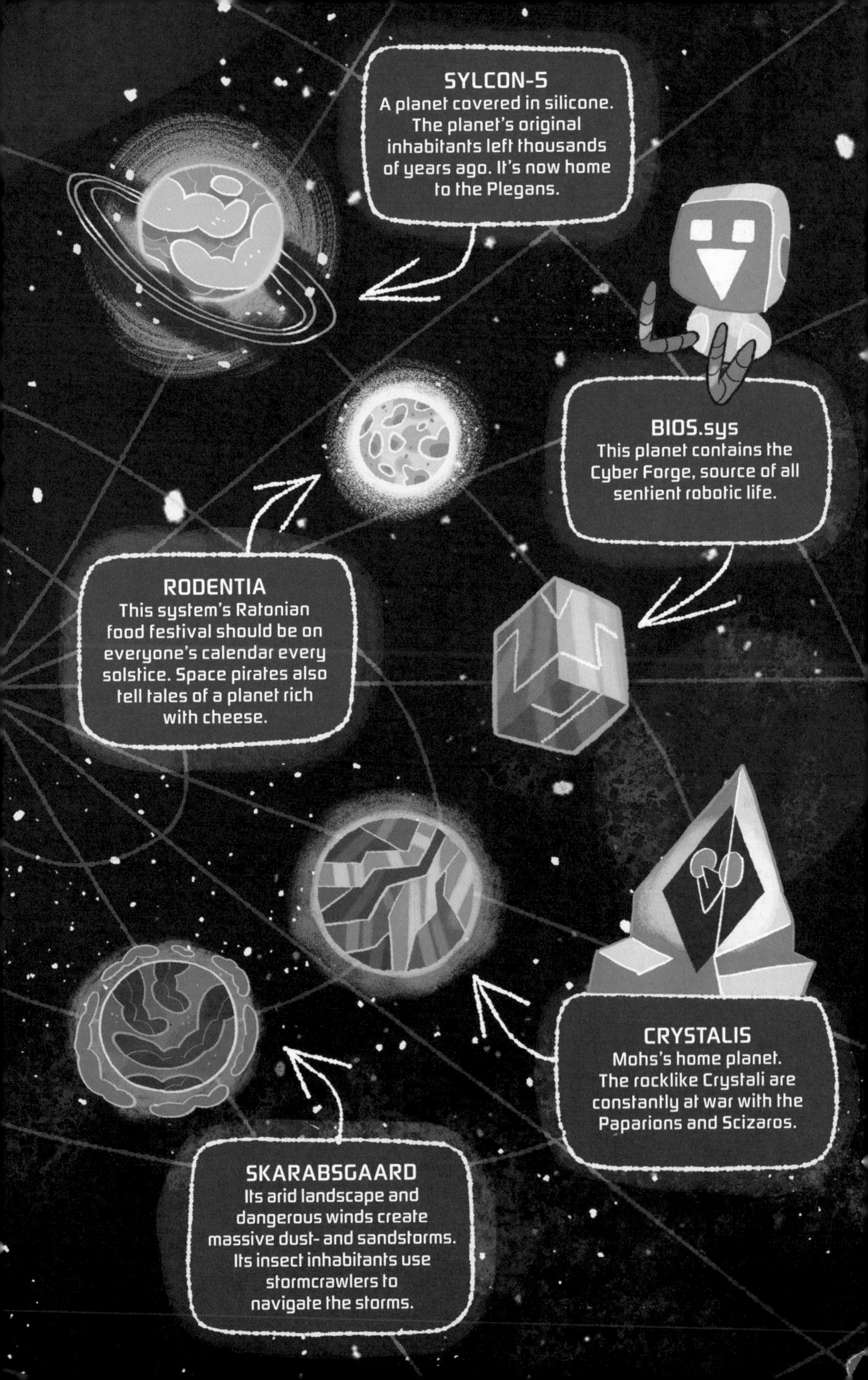
SYLCON-5
A planet covered in silicone. The planet's original inhabitants left thousands of years ago. It's now home to the Plegans.
BIOS.sys
This planet contains the Cyber Forge, source of all sentient robotic life.
RODENTIA
This system's Ratonian food festival should be on everyone's calendar every solstice. Space pirates also tell tales of a planet rich with cheese.
CRYSTALIS
Mohs's home planet. The rocklike Crystali are constantly at war with the Paparions and Scizaros.
SKARABSGAARD
Its arid landscape and dangerous winds create massive dust- and sandstorms. Its insect inhabitants use stormcrawlers to navigate the storms.

CHAPTER 1
Nothing to Cheese At

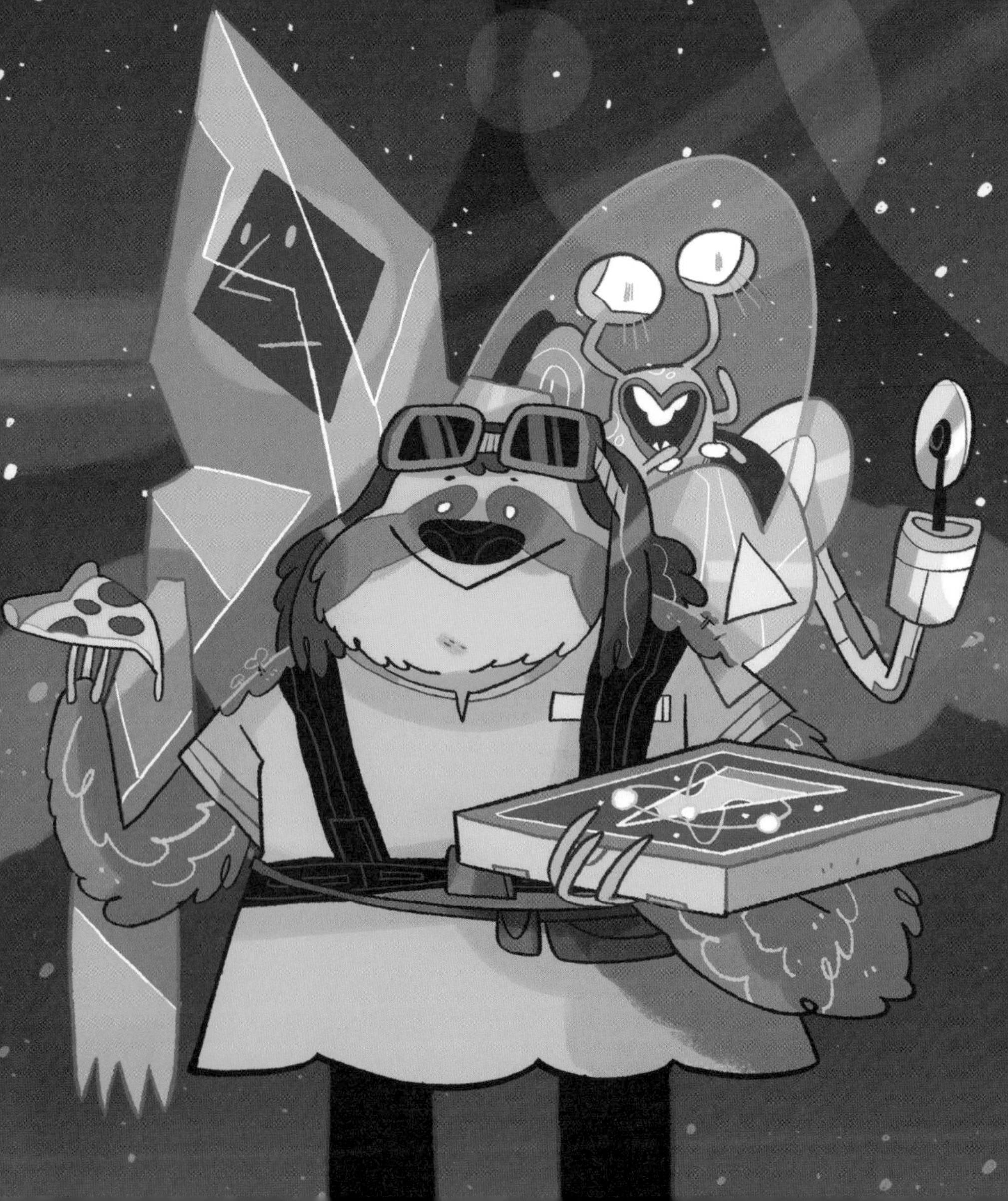

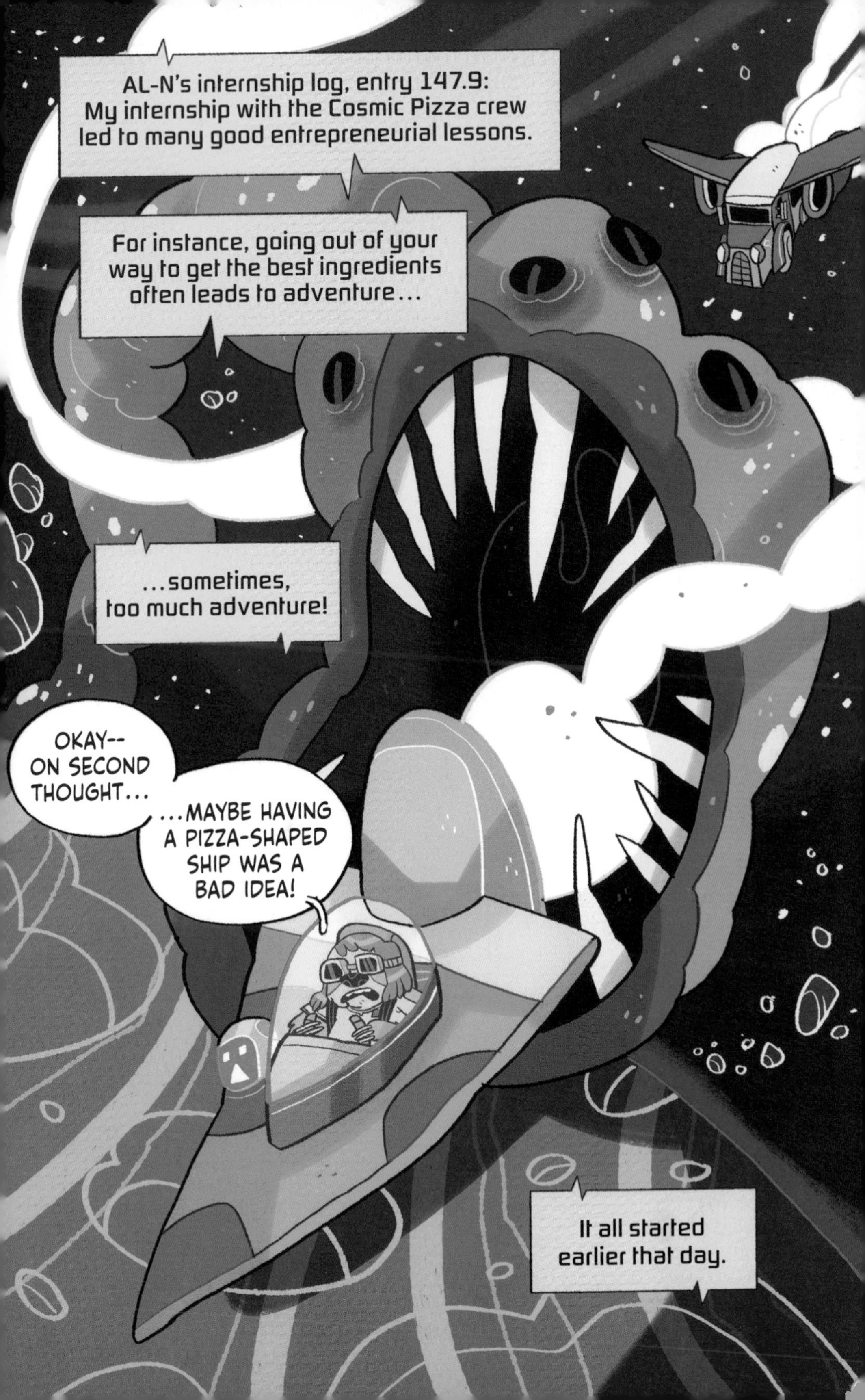
AL-N's internship log, entry 147.9: My internship with the Cosmic Pizza crew led to many good entrepreneurial lessons.
For instance, going out of your way to get the best ingredients often leads to adventure...
...sometimes, too much adventure!
OKAY-- ON SECOND THOUGHT...
...MAYBE HAVING A PIZZA-SHAPED SHIP WAS A BAD IDEA!
It all started earlier that day.

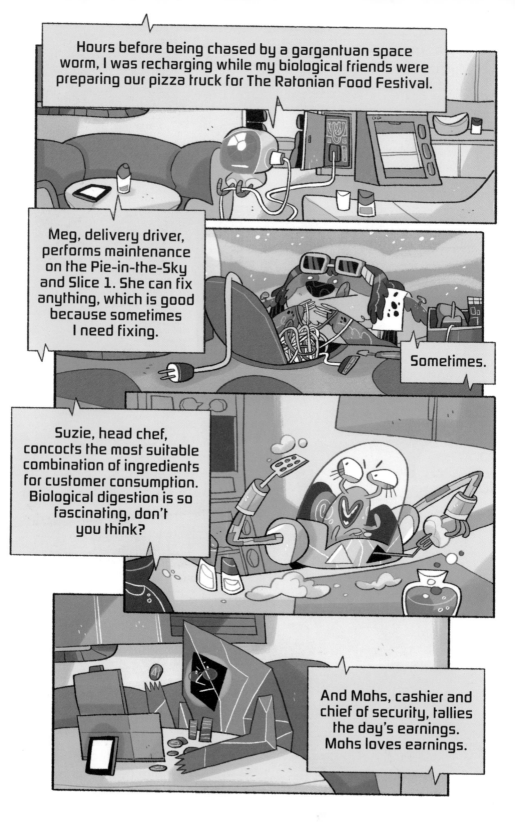

Hours before being chased by a gargantuan space worm, I was recharging while my biological friends were preparing our pizza truck for The Ratonian Food Festival.

Meg, delivery driver, performs maintenance on the Pie-in-the-Sky and Slice 1. She can fix anything, which is good because sometimes I need fixing.

Sometimes.

Suzie, head chef, concocts the most suitable combination of ingredients for customer consumption. Biological digestion is so fascinating, don't you think?

And Mohs, cashier and chief of security, tallies the day's earnings. Mohs loves earnings.

2

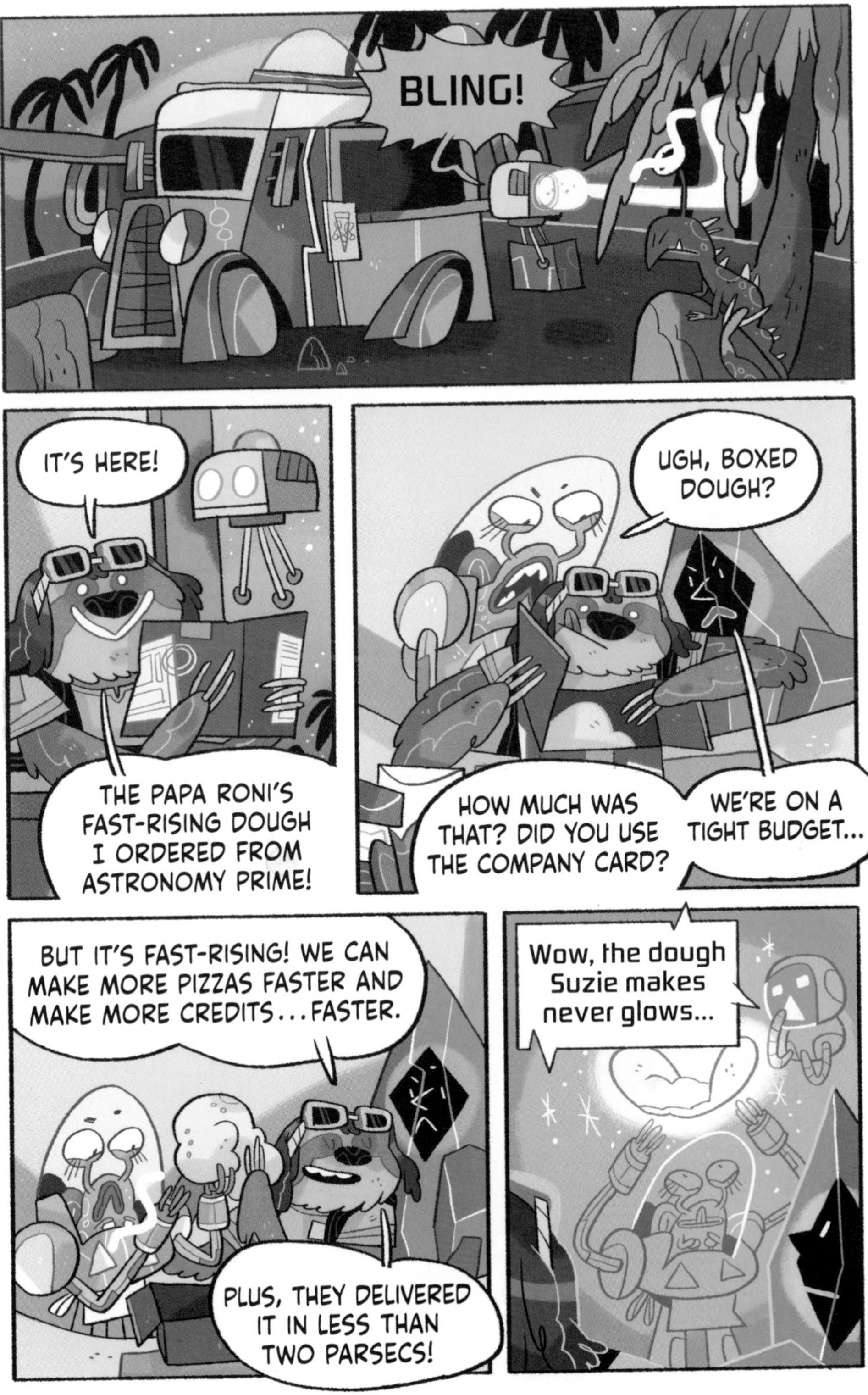

BLING!
IT'S HERE!
THE PAPA RONI'S FAST-RISING DOUGH I ORDERED FROM ASTRONOMY PRIME!
UGH, BOXED DOUGH?
HOW MUCH WAS THAT? DID YOU USE THE COMPANY CARD?
WE'RE ON A TIGHT BUDGET...
BUT IT'S FAST-RISING! WE CAN MAKE MORE PIZZAS FASTER AND MAKE MORE CREDITS . . . FASTER.
PLUS, THEY DELIVERED IT IN LESS THAN TWO PARSECS!
Wow, the dough Suzie makes never glows...

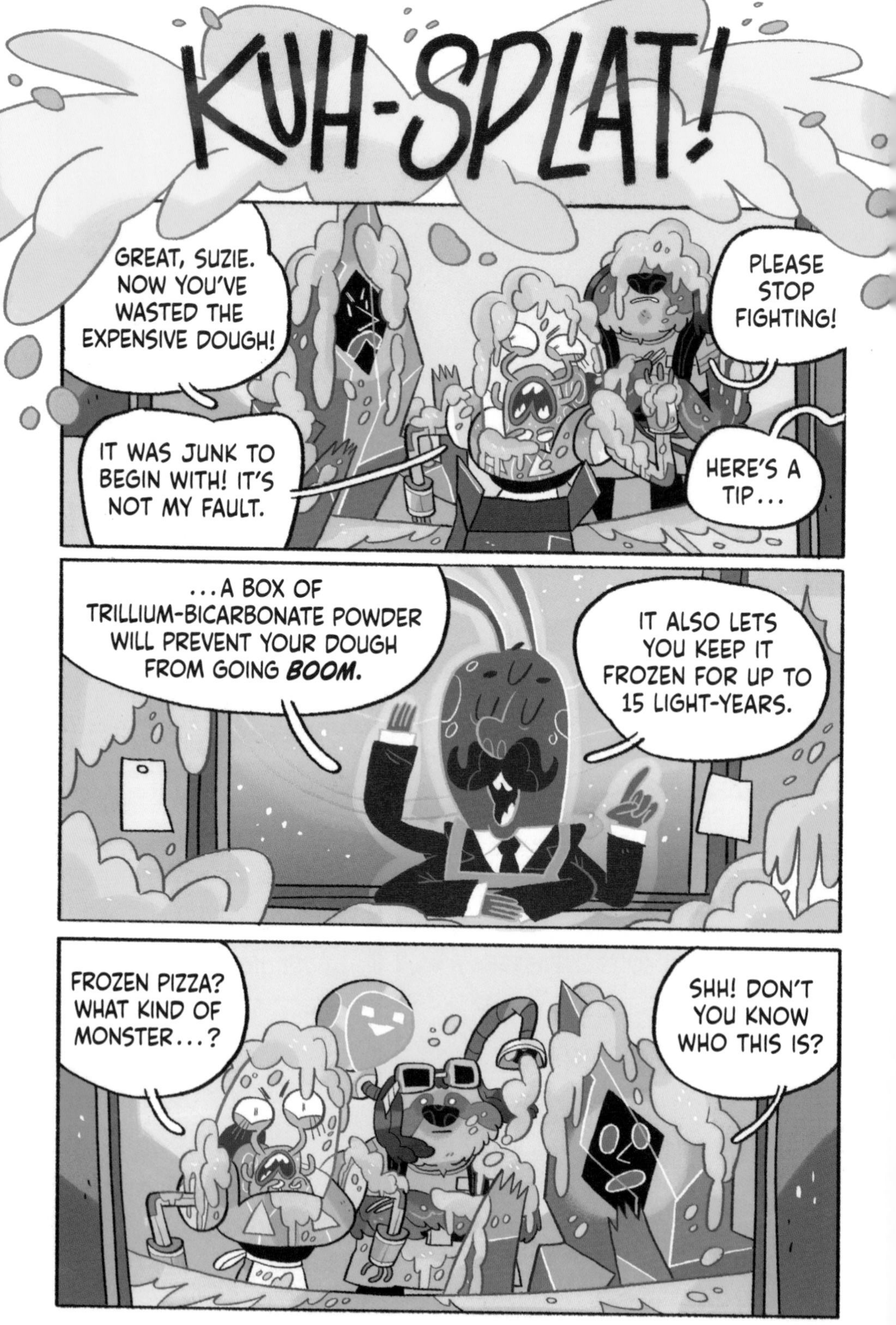
KUH-SPLAT!
GREAT, SUZIE. NOW YOU'VE WASTED THE EXPENSIVE DOUGH!
PLEASE STOP FIGHTING!
IT WAS JUNK TO BEGIN WITH! IT'S NOT MY FAULT.
HERE'S A TIP...
...A BOX OF TRILLIUM-BICARBONATE POWDER WILL PREVENT YOUR DOUGH FROM GOING ***BOOM***.
IT ALSO LETS YOU KEEP IT FROZEN FOR UP TO 15 LIGHT-YEARS.
FROZEN PIZZA? WHAT KIND OF MONSTER...?
SHH! DON'T YOU KNOW WHO THIS IS?

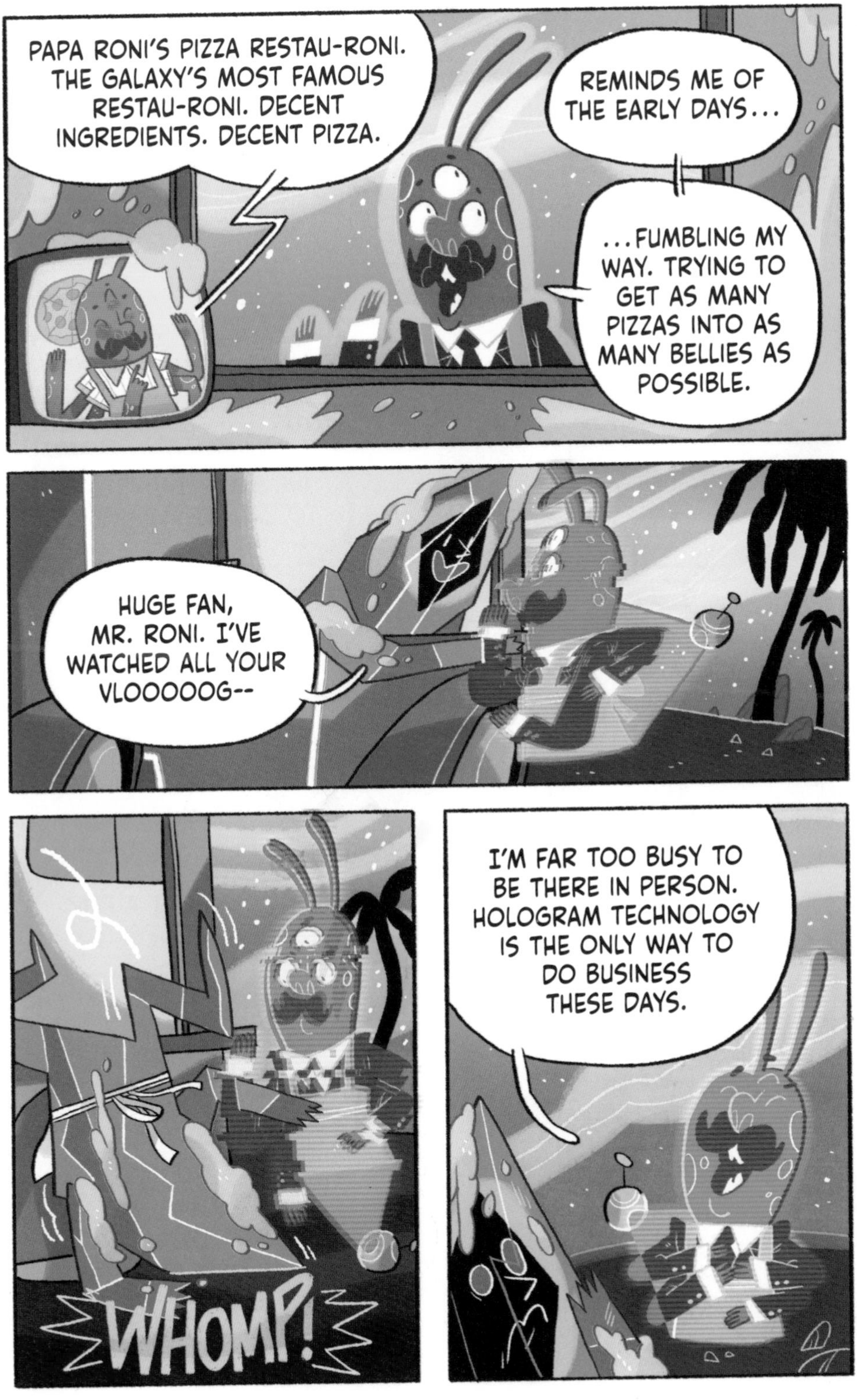
PAPA RONI'S PIZZA RESTAU-RONI. THE GALAXY'S MOST FAMOUS RESTAU-RONI. DECENT INGREDIENTS. DECENT PIZZA.
REMINDS ME OF THE EARLY DAYS...
...FUMBLING MY WAY. TRYING TO GET AS MANY PIZZAS INTO AS MANY BELLIES AS POSSIBLE.
HUGE FAN, MR. RONI. I'VE WATCHED ALL YOUR VLOOOOOG--
WHOMP!
I'M FAR TOO BUSY TO BE THERE IN PERSON. HOLOGRAM TECHNOLOGY IS THE ONLY WAY TO DO BUSINESS THESE DAYS.

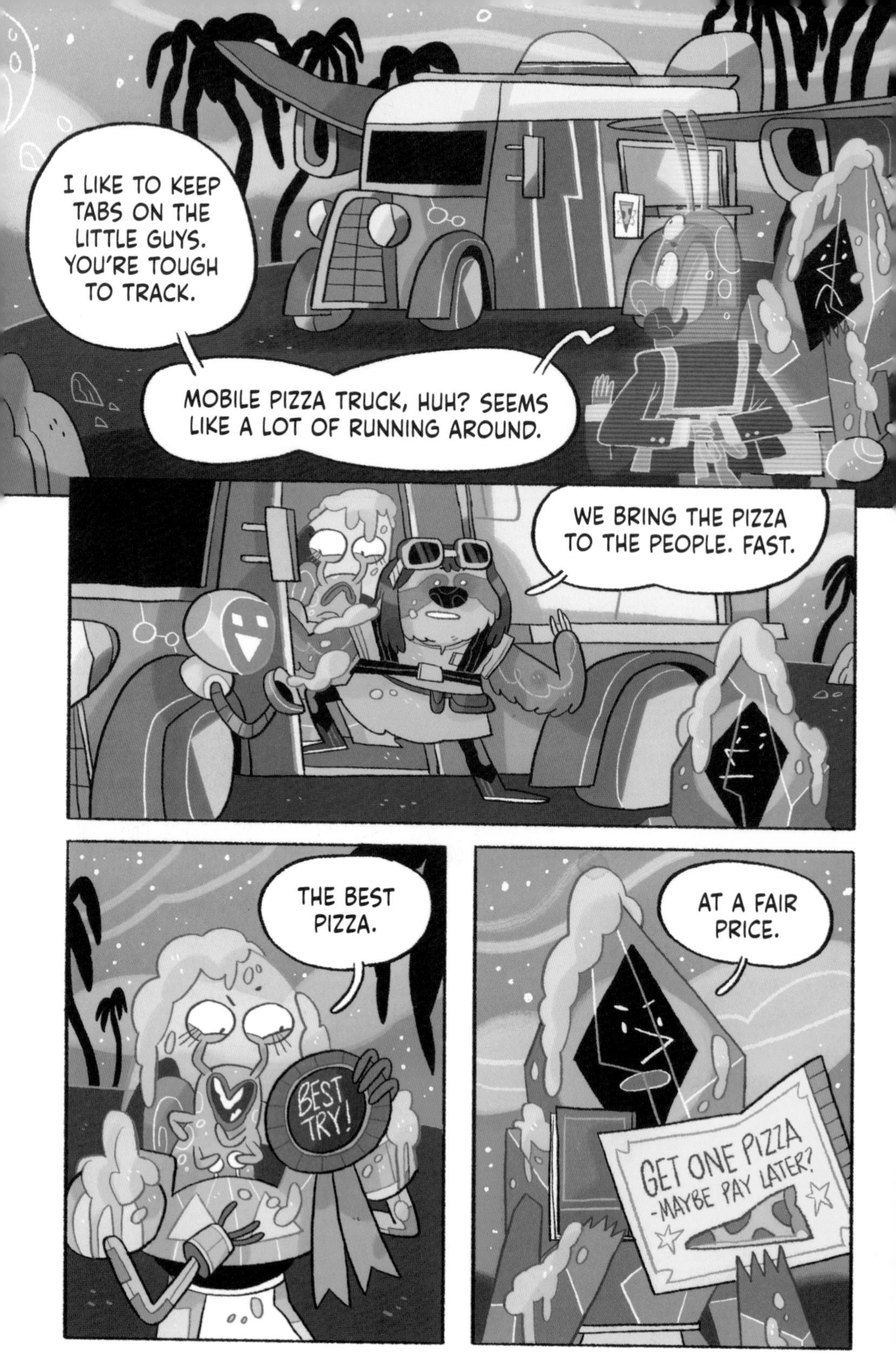

I LIKE TO KEEP TABS ON THE LITTLE GUYS. YOU'RE TOUGH TO TRACK.
MOBILE PIZZA TRUCK, HUH? SEEMS LIKE A LOT OF RUNNING AROUND.
WE BRING THE PIZZA TO THE PEOPLE. FAST.
THE BEST PIZZA.
BEST TRY!
AT A FAIR PRICE.
GET ONE PIZZA -MAYBE PAY LATER?

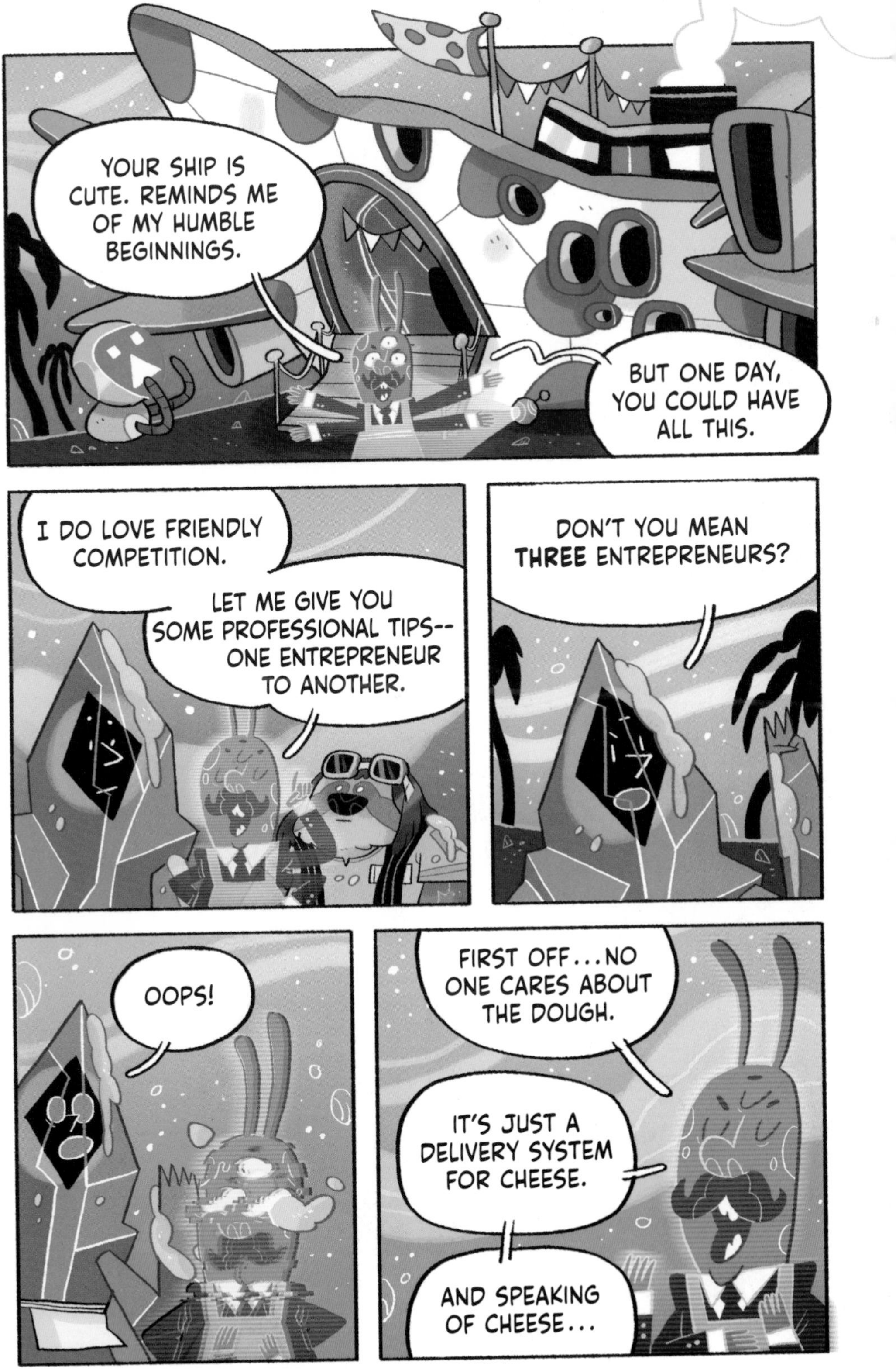
YOUR SHIP IS CUTE. REMINDS ME OF MY HUMBLE BEGINNINGS.
BUT ONE DAY, YOU COULD HAVE ALL THIS.
I DO LOVE FRIENDLY COMPETITION.
LET ME GIVE YOU SOME PROFESSIONAL TIPS--ONE ENTREPRENEUR TO ANOTHER.
DON'T YOU MEAN THREE ENTREPRENEURS?
OOPS!
FIRST OFF...NO ONE CARES ABOUT THE DOUGH.
IT'S JUST A DELIVERY SYSTEM FOR CHEESE.
AND SPEAKING OF CHEESE...

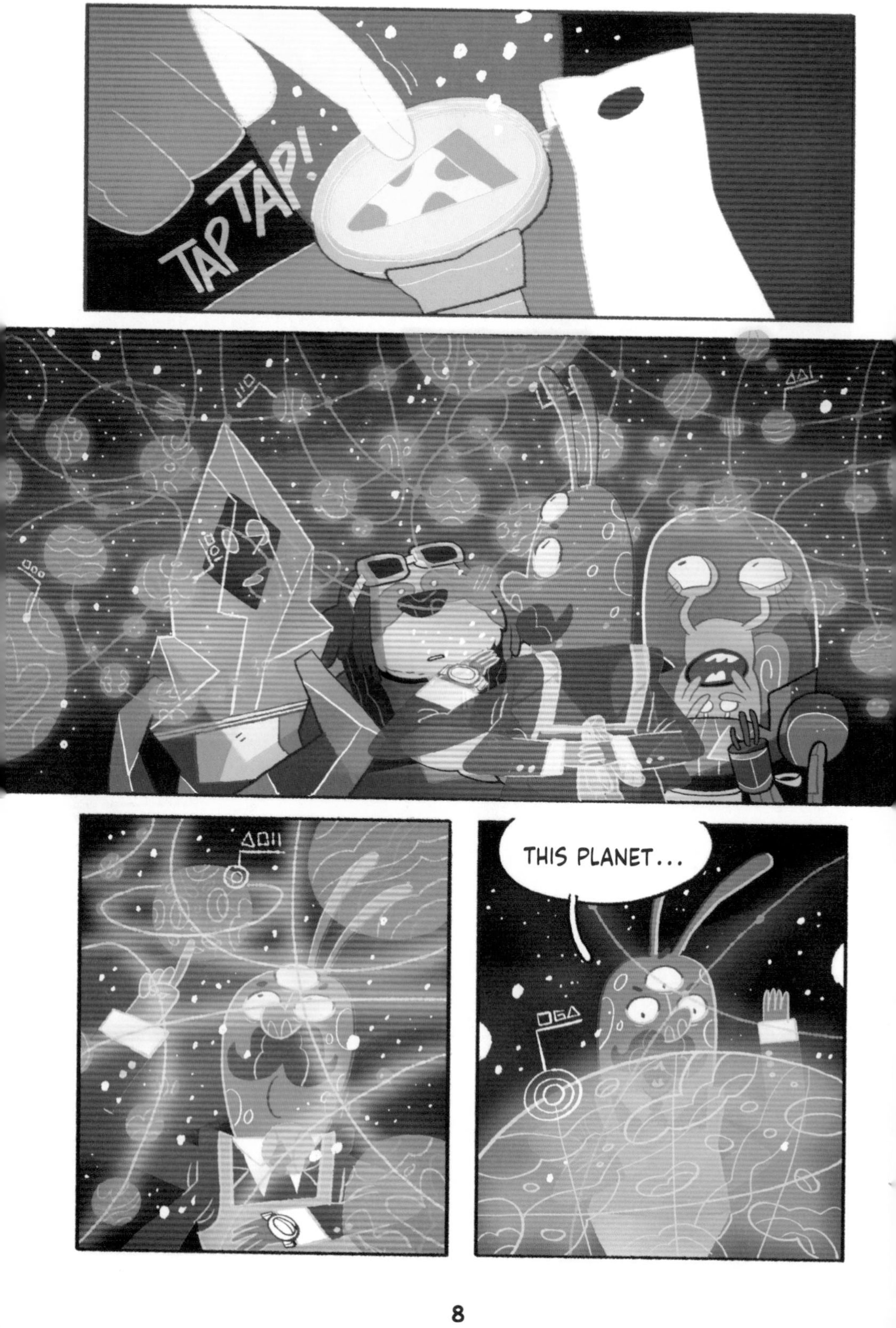
TAP TAP!
THIS PLANET...

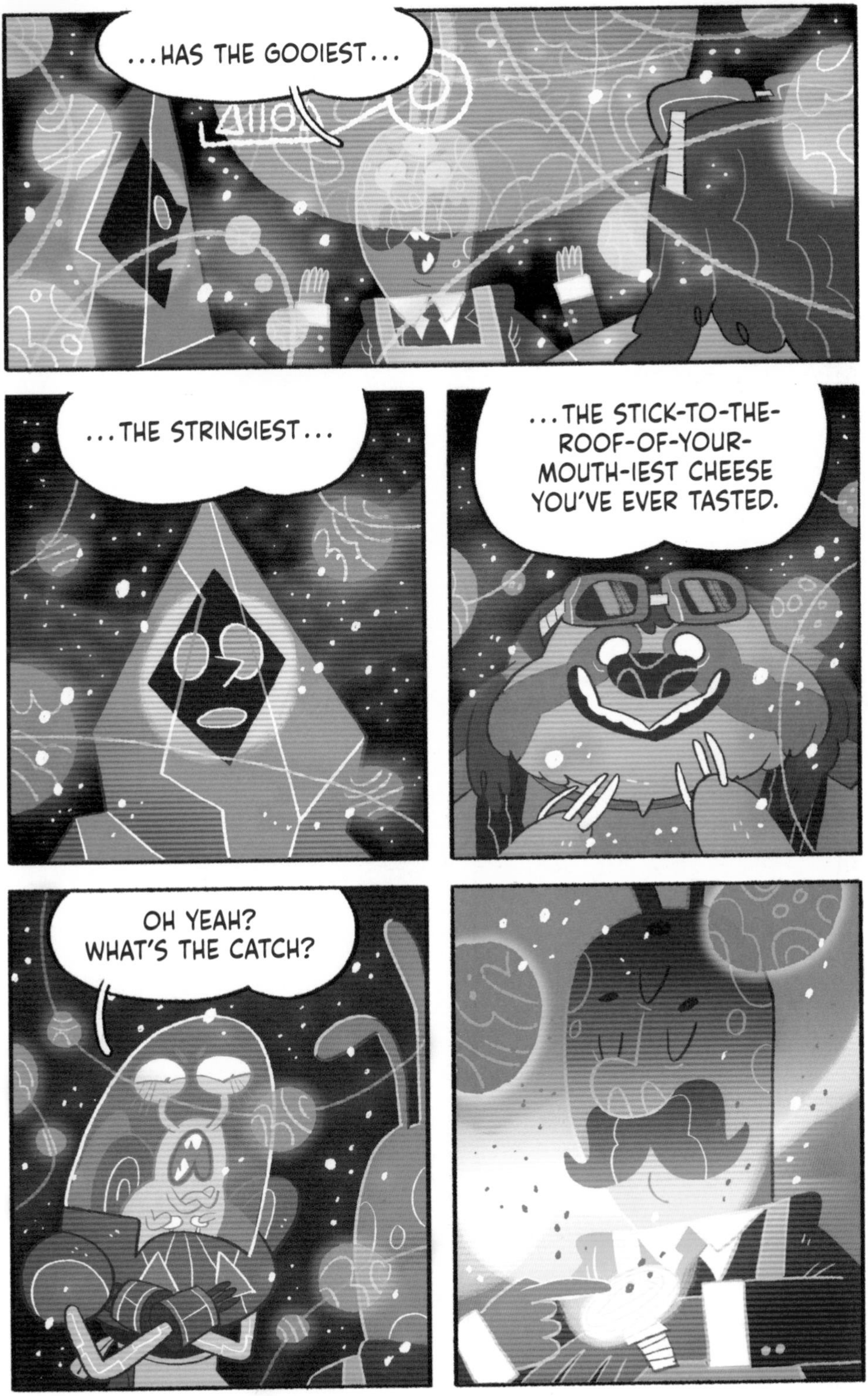
...HAS THE GOOIEST...
...THE STRINGIEST...
...THE STICK-TO-THE-ROOF-OF-YOUR-MOUTH-IEST CHEESE YOU'VE EVER TASTED.
OH YEAH? WHAT'S THE CATCH?

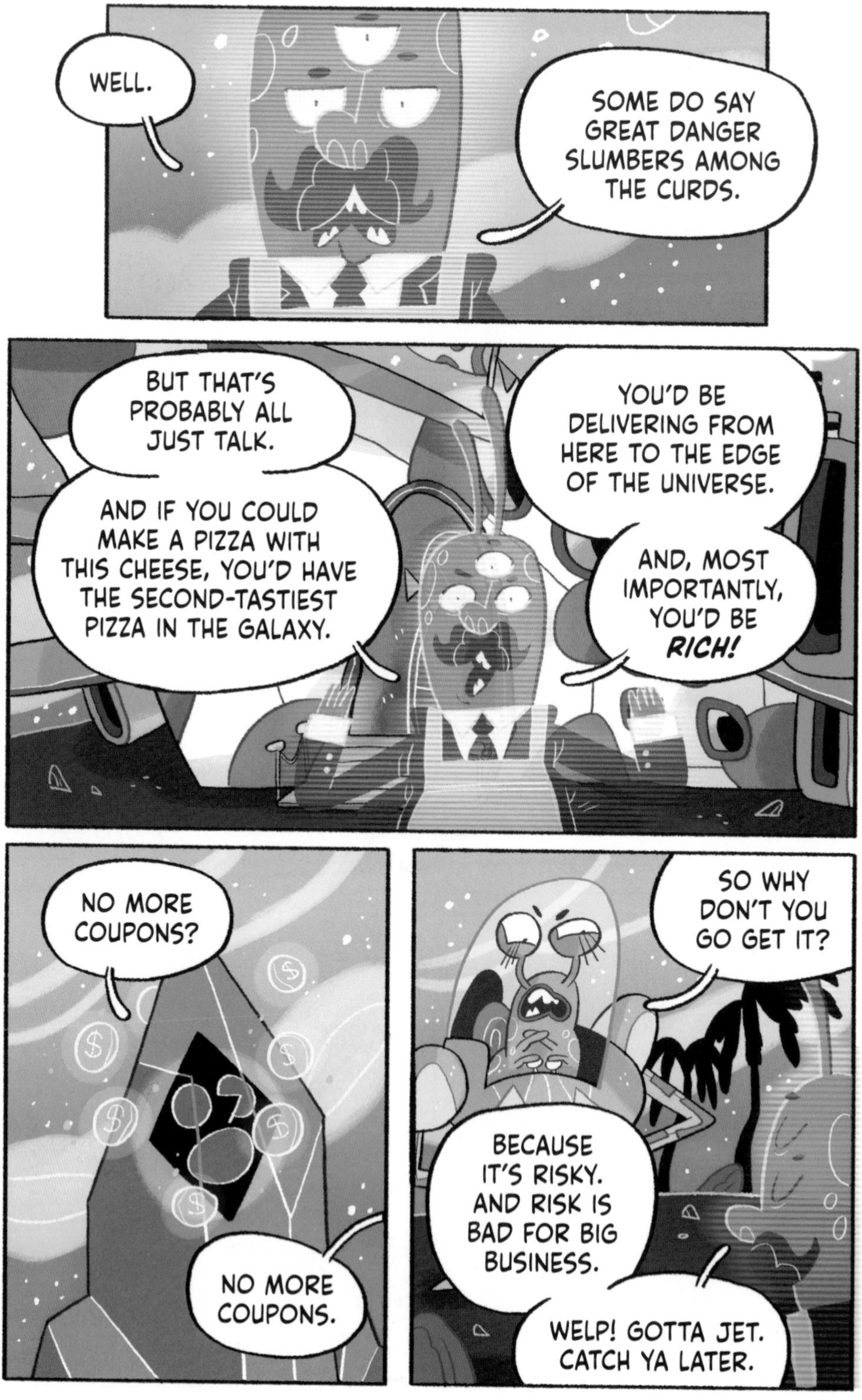
WELL.
SOME DO SAY GREAT DANGER SLUMBERS AMONG THE CURDS.
BUT THAT'S PROBABLY ALL JUST TALK.
YOU'D BE DELIVERING FROM HERE TO THE EDGE OF THE UNIVERSE.
AND IF YOU COULD MAKE A PIZZA WITH THIS CHEESE, YOU'D HAVE THE SECOND-TASTIEST PIZZA IN THE GALAXY.
AND, MOST IMPORTANTLY, YOU'D BE *RICH!*
NO MORE COUPONS?
NO MORE COUPONS.
SO WHY DON'T YOU GO GET IT?
BECAUSE IT'S RISKY. AND RISK IS BAD FOR BIG BUSINESS.
WELP! GOTTA JET. CATCH YA LATER.

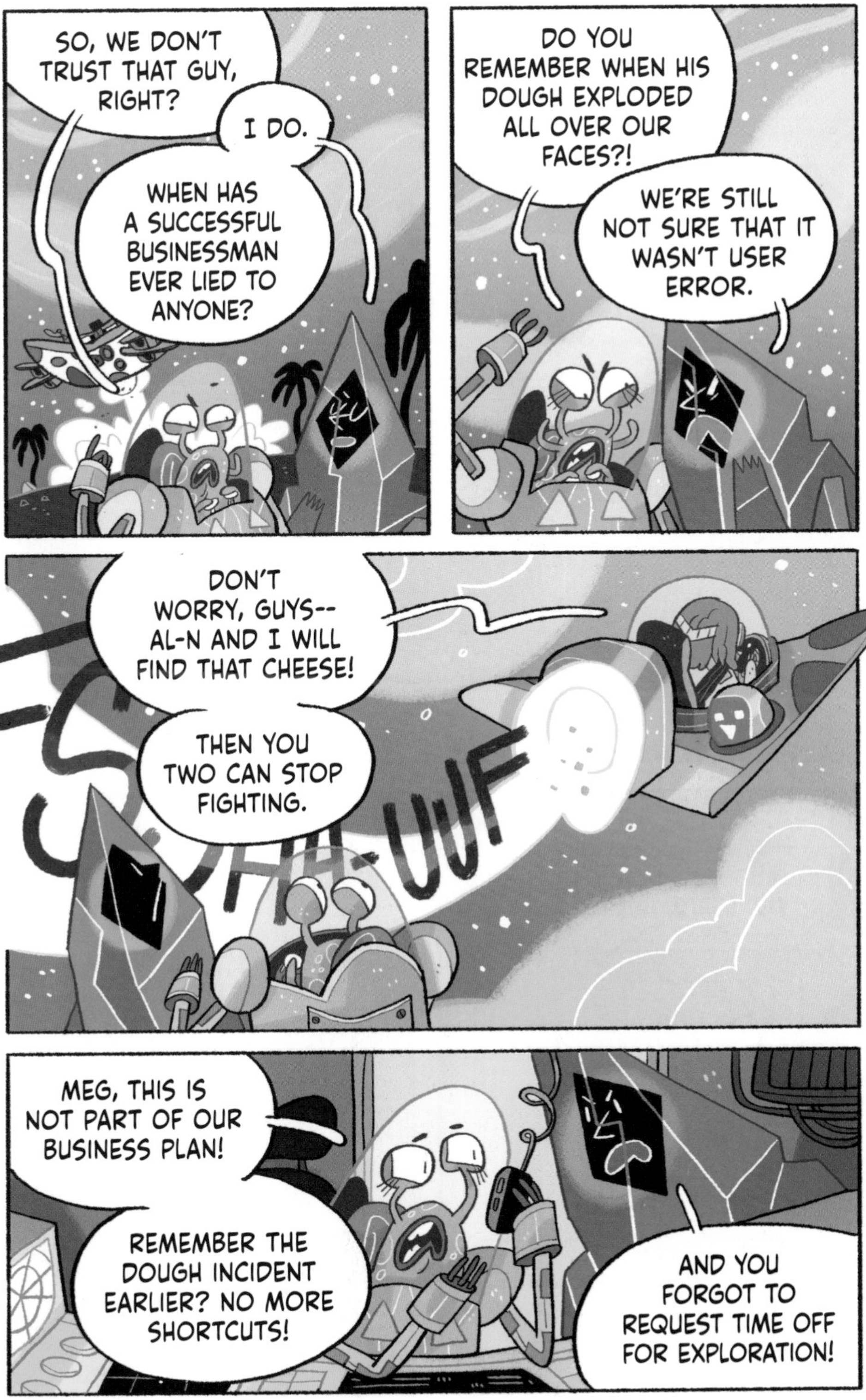
SO, WE DON'T TRUST THAT GUY, RIGHT?
I DO.
WHEN HAS A SUCCESSFUL BUSINESSMAN EVER LIED TO ANYONE?
DO YOU REMEMBER WHEN HIS DOUGH EXPLODED ALL OVER OUR FACES?!
WE'RE STILL NOT SURE THAT IT WASN'T USER ERROR.
DON'T WORRY, GUYS-- AL-N AND I WILL FIND THAT CHEESE!
THEN YOU TWO CAN STOP FIGHTING.
MEG, THIS IS NOT PART OF OUR BUSINESS PLAN!
REMEMBER THE DOUGH INCIDENT EARLIER? NO MORE SHORTCUTS!
AND YOU FORGOT TO REQUEST TIME OFF FOR EXPLORATION!

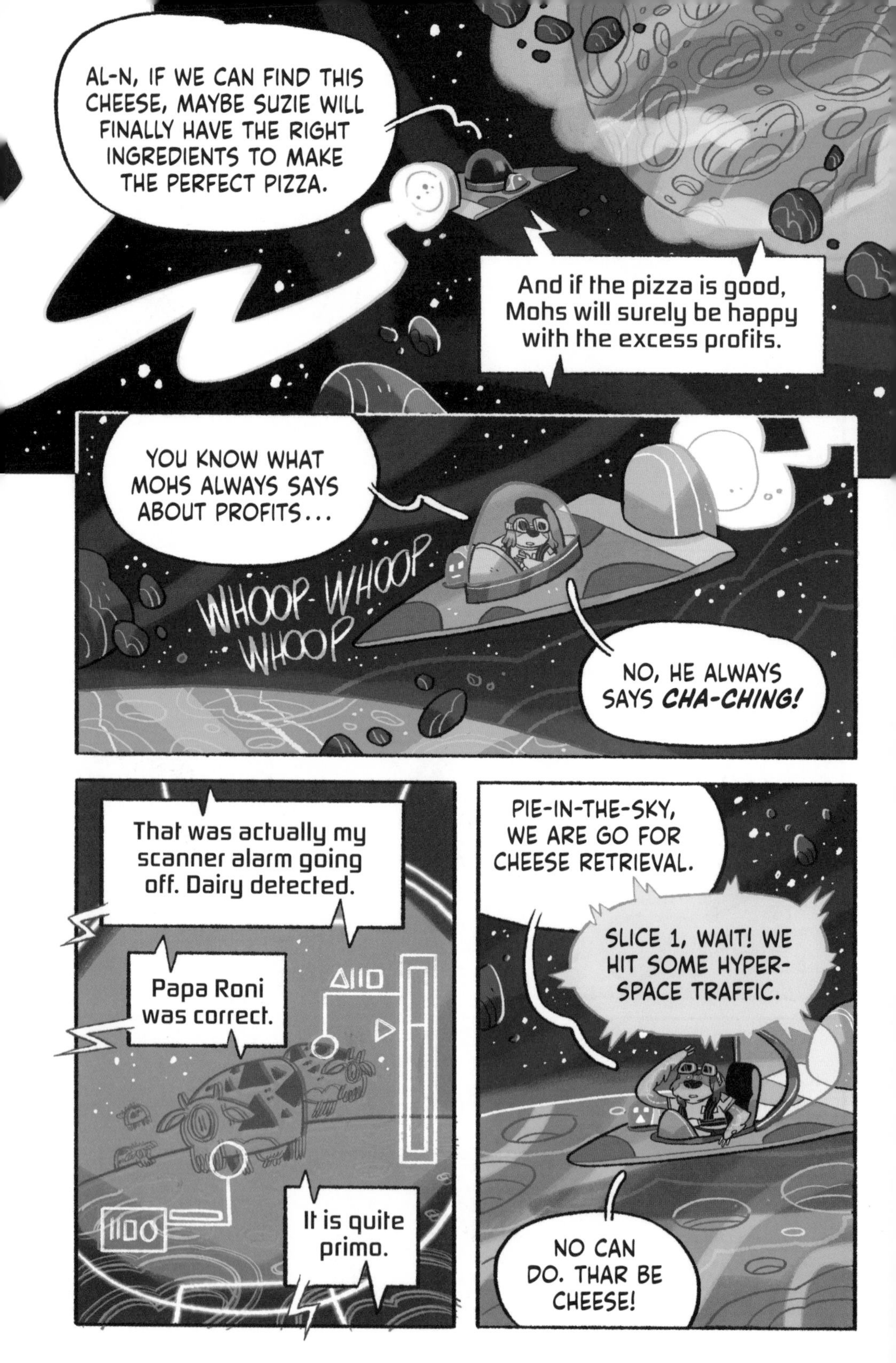
AL-N, IF WE CAN FIND THIS CHEESE, MAYBE SUZIE WILL FINALLY HAVE THE RIGHT INGREDIENTS TO MAKE THE PERFECT PIZZA.
And if the pizza is good, Mohs will surely be happy with the excess profits.
YOU KNOW WHAT MOHS ALWAYS SAYS ABOUT PROFITS...
WHOOP-WHOOP WHOOP
NO, HE ALWAYS SAYS CHA-CHING!
That was actually my scanner alarm going off. Dairy detected.
Papa Roni was correct.
It is quite primo.
PIE-IN-THE-SKY, WE ARE GO FOR CHEESE RETRIEVAL.
SLICE 1, WAIT! WE HIT SOME HYPER-SPACE TRAFFIC.
NO CAN DO. THAR BE CHEESE!

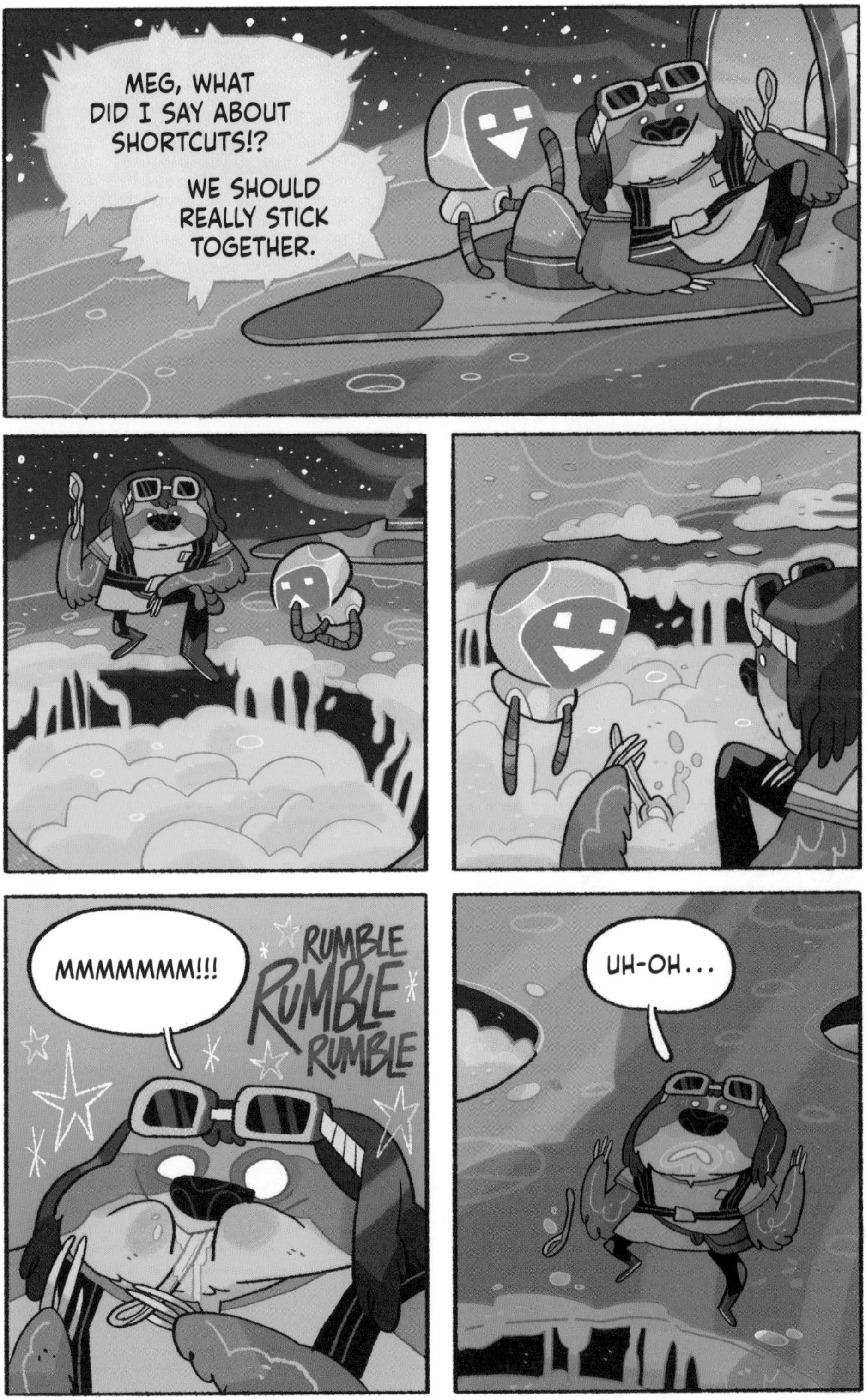
MEG, WHAT DID I SAY ABOUT SHORTCUTS!?
WE SHOULD REALLY STICK TOGETHER.
MMMMMMM!!!
RUMBLE RUMBLE RUMBLE
UH-OH...

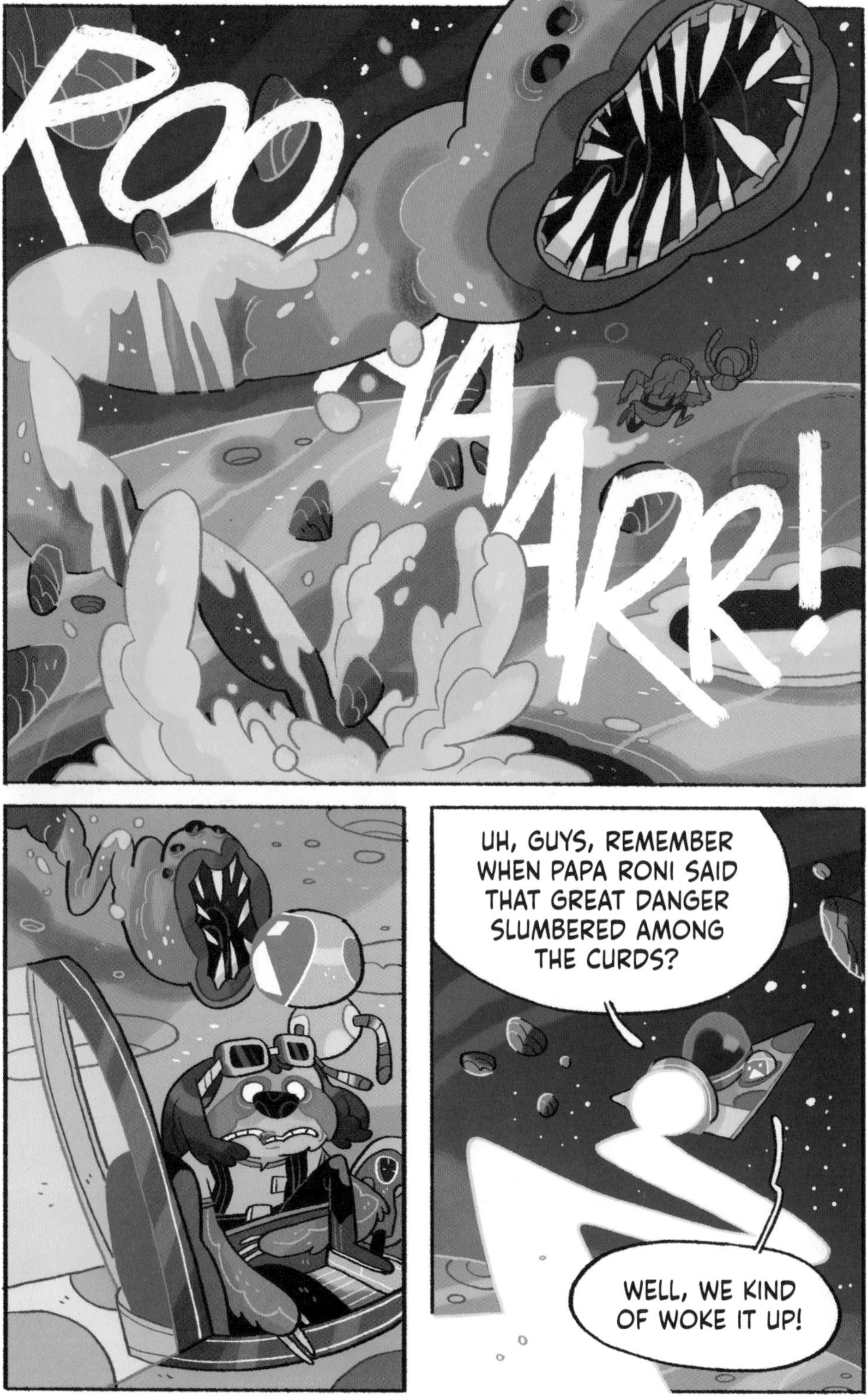
ROOAARR!
UH, GUYS, REMEMBER WHEN PAPA RONI SAID THAT GREAT DANGER SLUMBERED AMONG THE CURDS?
WELL, WE KIND OF WOKE IT UP!

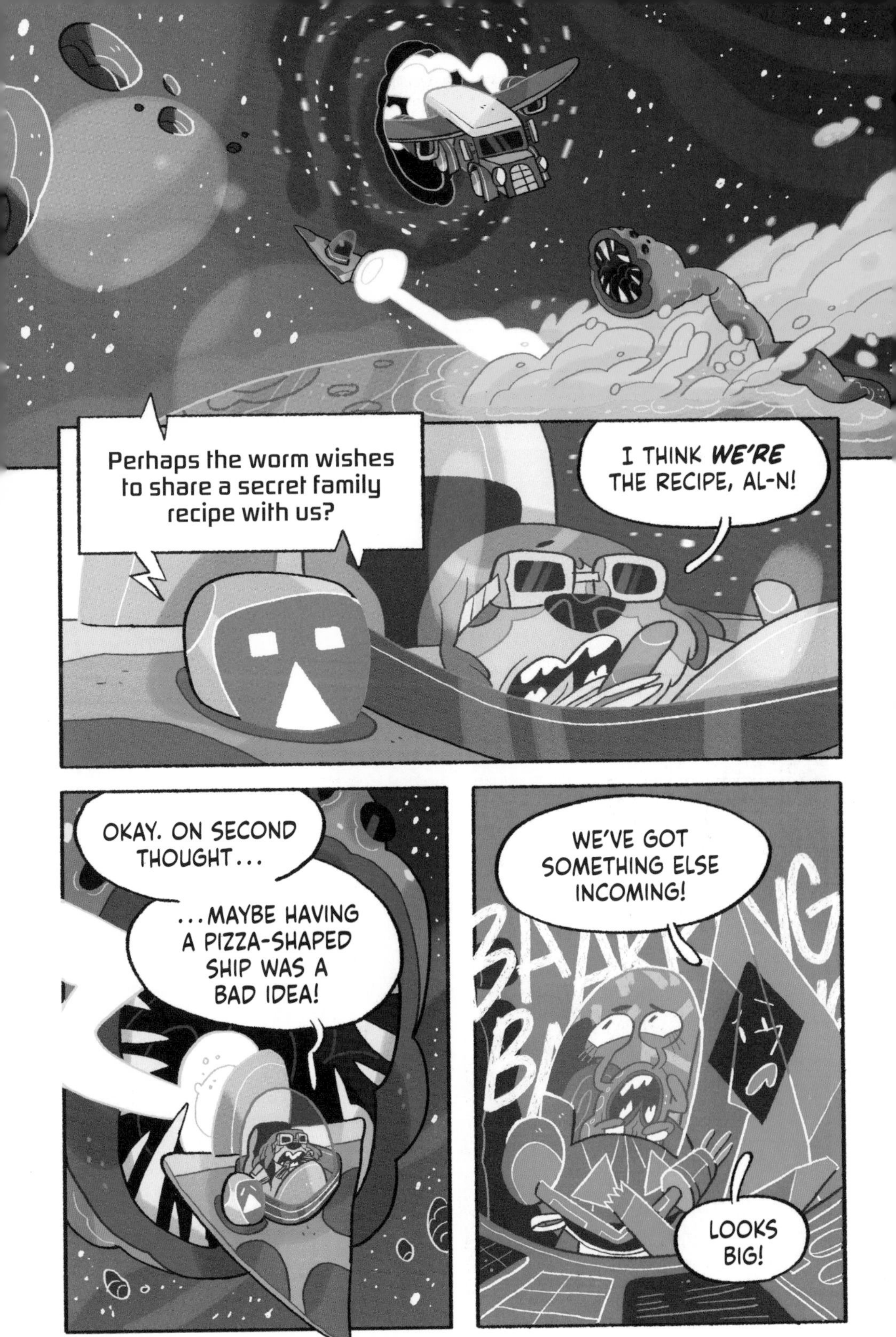
Perhaps the worm wishes to share a secret family recipe with us?
I THINK ***WE'RE*** THE RECIPE, AL-N!
OKAY. ON SECOND THOUGHT...
...MAYBE HAVING A PIZZA-SHAPED SHIP WAS A BAD IDEA!
WE'VE GOT SOMETHING ELSE INCOMING!
LOOKS BIG!

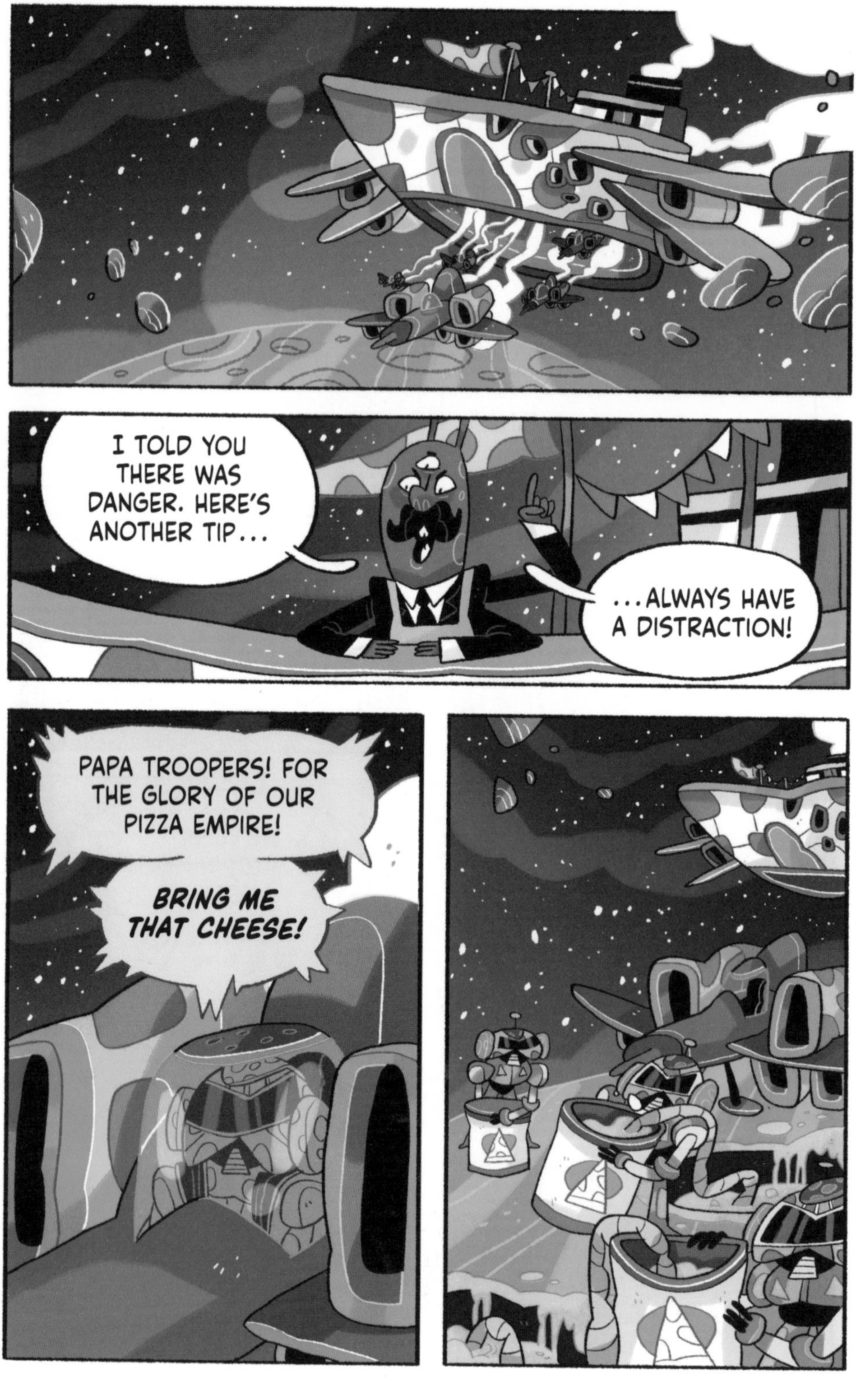
I TOLD YOU THERE WAS DANGER. HERE'S ANOTHER TIP...
...ALWAYS HAVE A DISTRACTION!
PAPA TROOPERS! FOR THE GLORY OF OUR PIZZA EMPIRE!
BRING ME THAT CHEESE!

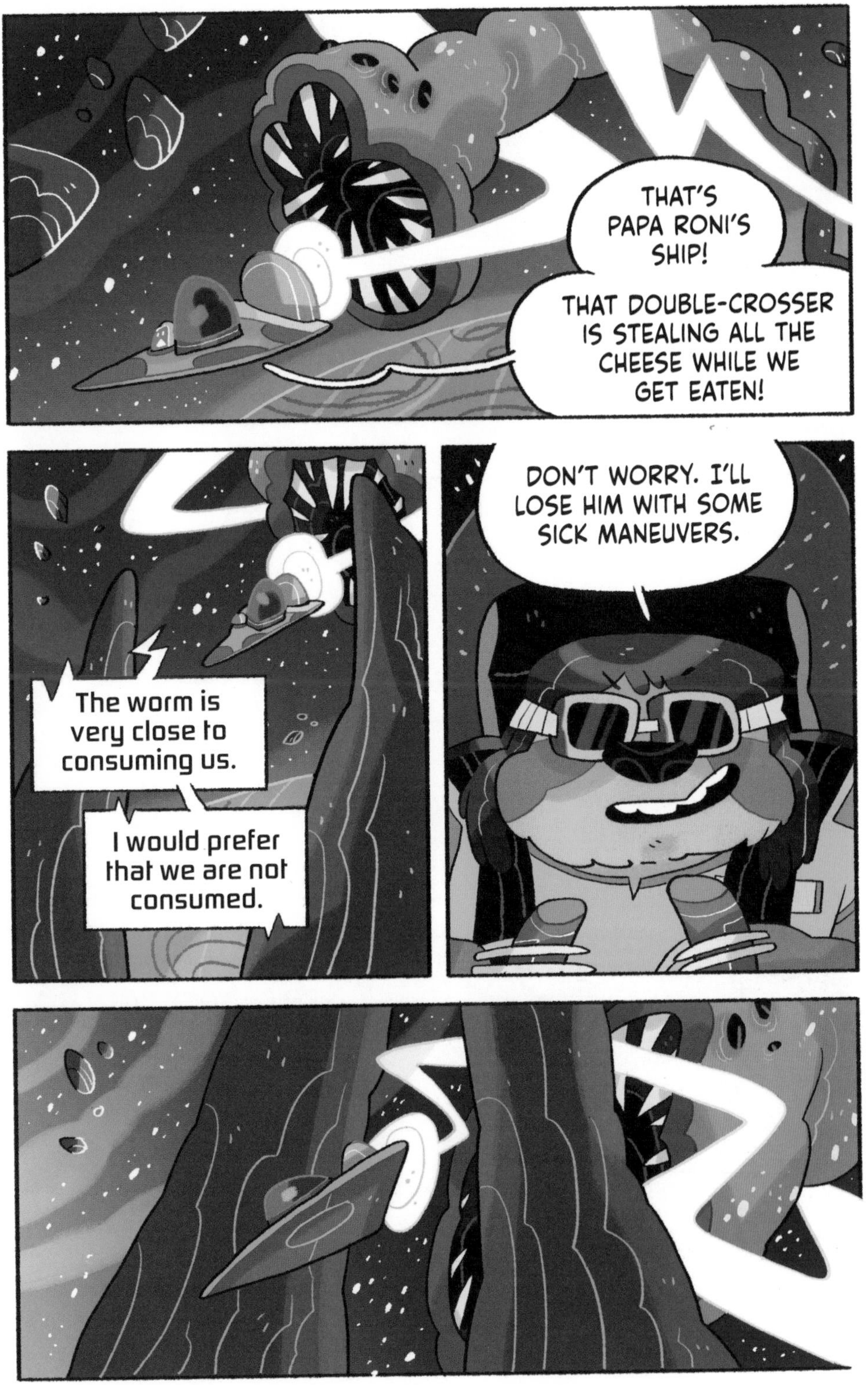
THAT'S PAPA RONI'S SHIP!
THAT DOUBLE-CROSSER IS STEALING ALL THE CHEESE WHILE WE GET EATEN!
The worm is very close to consuming us.
I would prefer that we are not consumed.
DON'T WORRY. I'LL LOSE HIM WITH SOME SICK MANEUVERS.

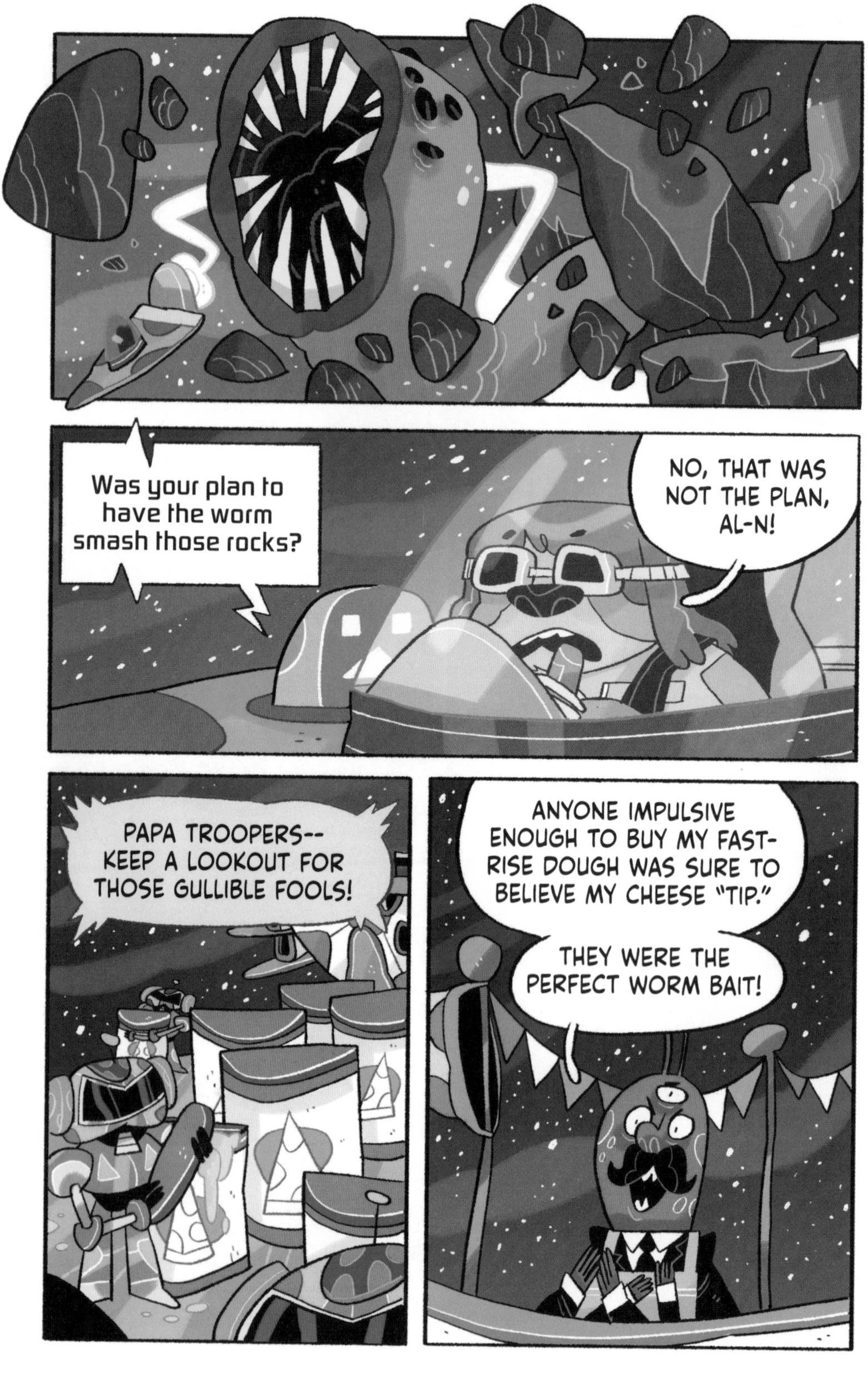
Was your plan to have the worm smash those rocks?
NO, THAT WAS NOT THE PLAN, AL-N!
PAPA TROOPERS-- KEEP A LOOKOUT FOR THOSE GULLIBLE FOOLS!
ANYONE IMPULSIVE ENOUGH TO BUY MY FAST-RISE DOUGH WAS SURE TO BELIEVE MY CHEESE "TIP."
THEY WERE THE PERFECT WORM BAIT!

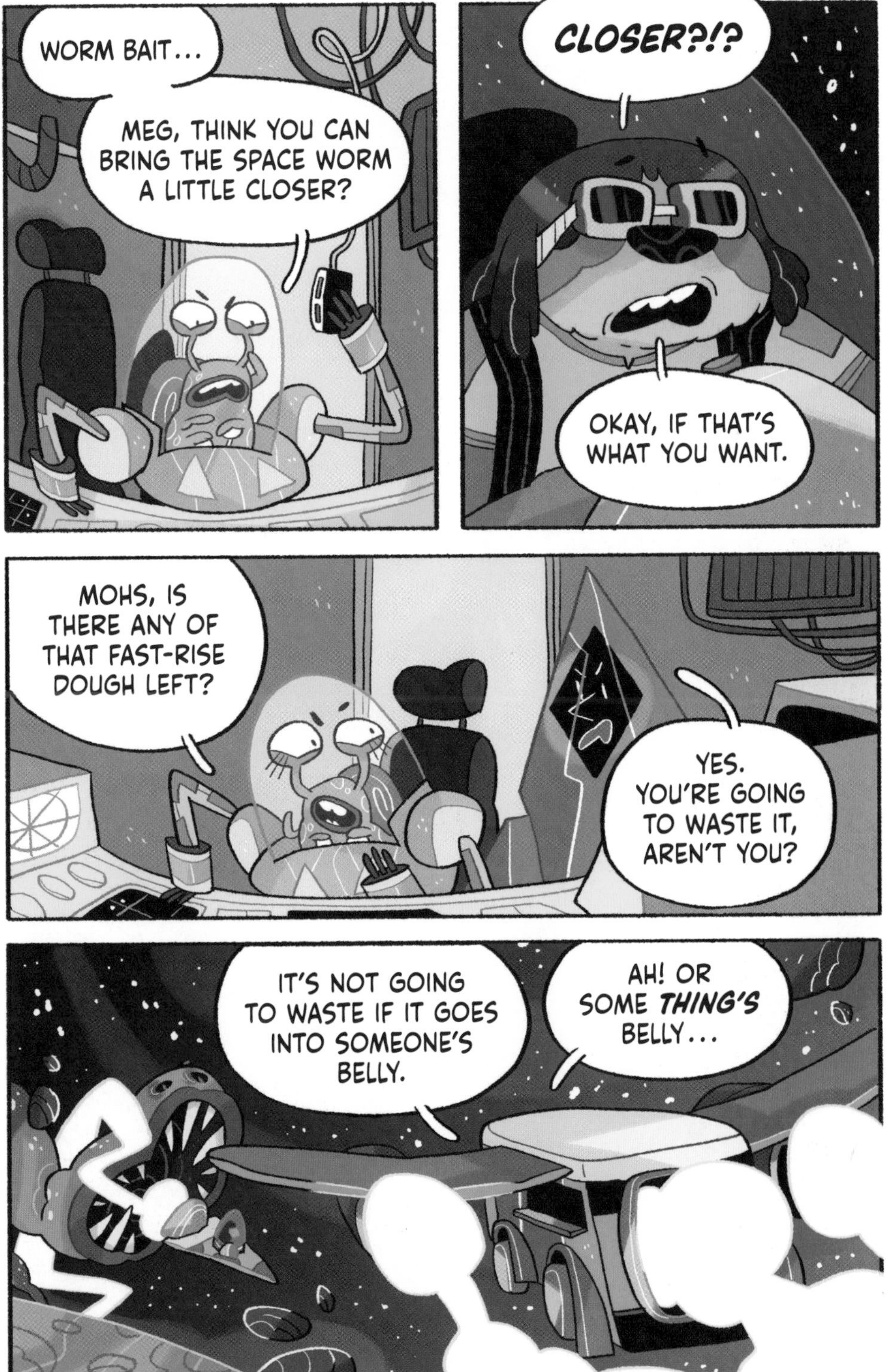
WORM BAIT...
MEG, THINK YOU CAN BRING THE SPACE WORM A LITTLE CLOSER?
CLOSER?!?
OKAY, IF THAT'S WHAT YOU WANT.
MOHS, IS THERE ANY OF THAT FAST-RISE DOUGH LEFT?
YES. YOU'RE GOING TO WASTE IT, AREN'T YOU?
IT'S NOT GOING TO WASTE IF IT GOES INTO SOMEONE'S BELLY.
AH! OR SOME *THING'S* BELLY...

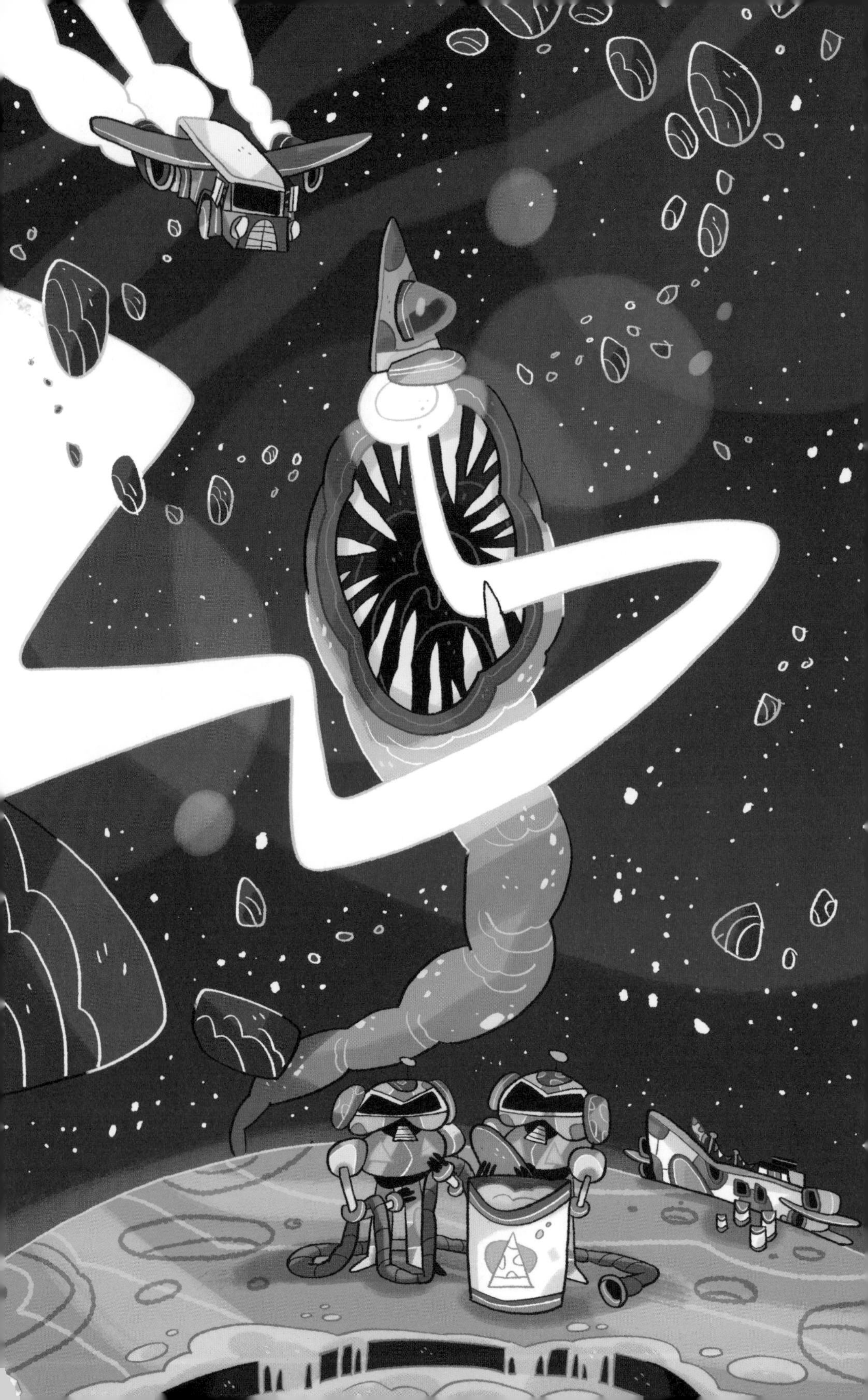

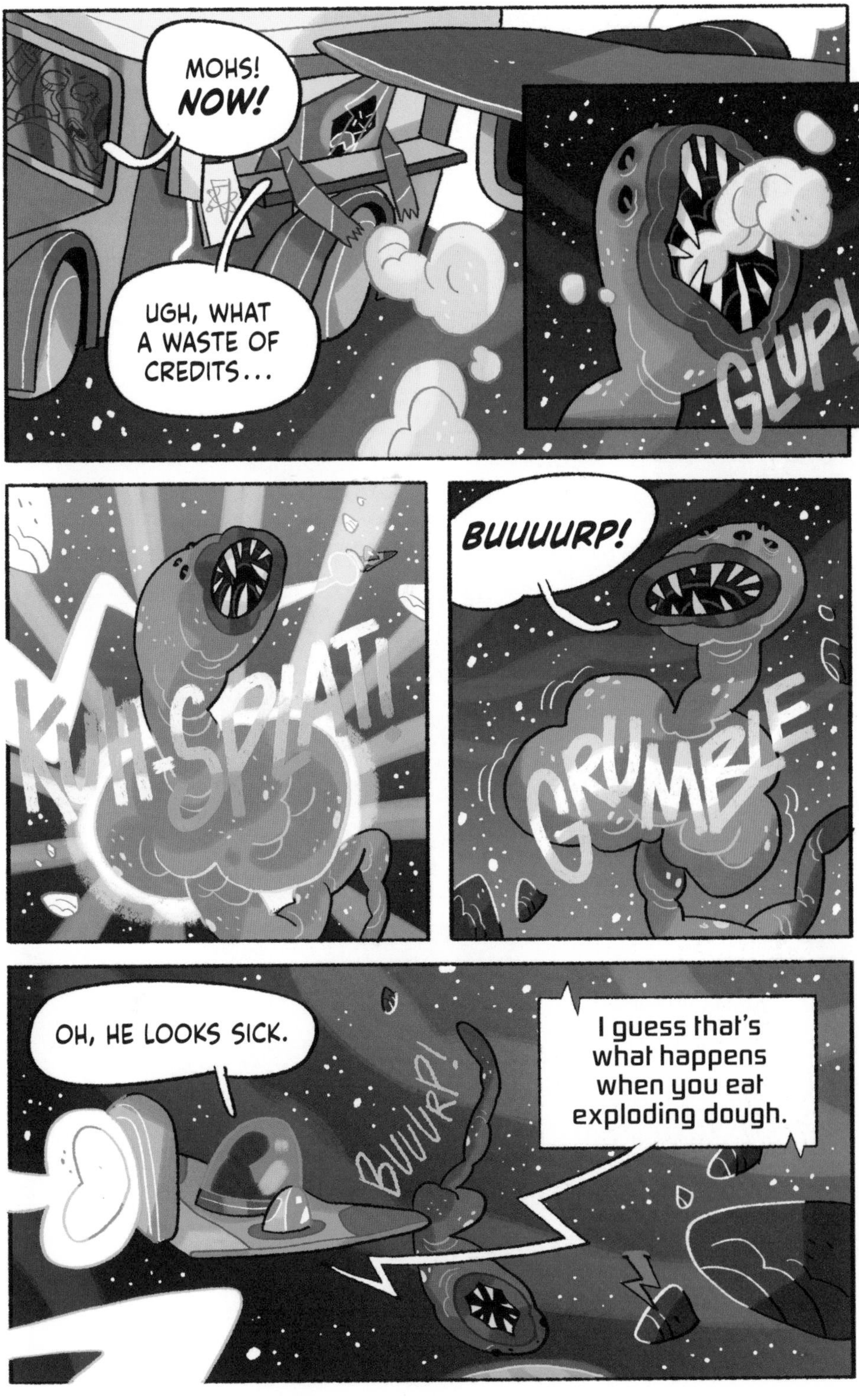
MOHS! NOW!
UGH, WHAT A WASTE OF CREDITS...
GLUP!
KUH-SPLAT!
BUUUURP!
GRUMBLE
OH, HE LOOKS SICK.
BUUURP!
I guess that's what happens when you eat exploding dough.

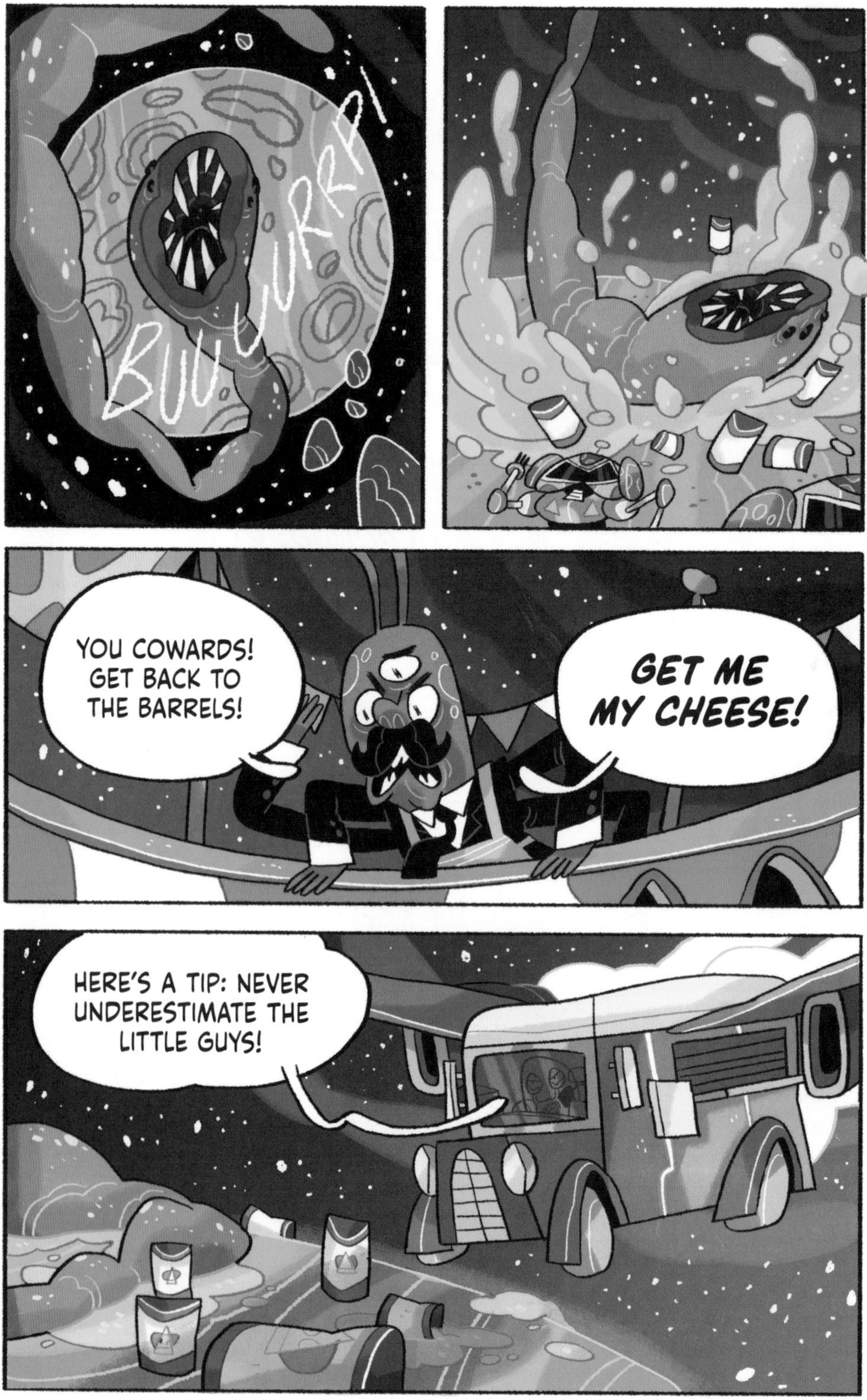
BUUURRP!
YOU COWARDS! GET BACK TO THE BARRELS!
GET ME MY CHEESE!
HERE'S A TIP: NEVER UNDERESTIMATE THE LITTLE GUYS!

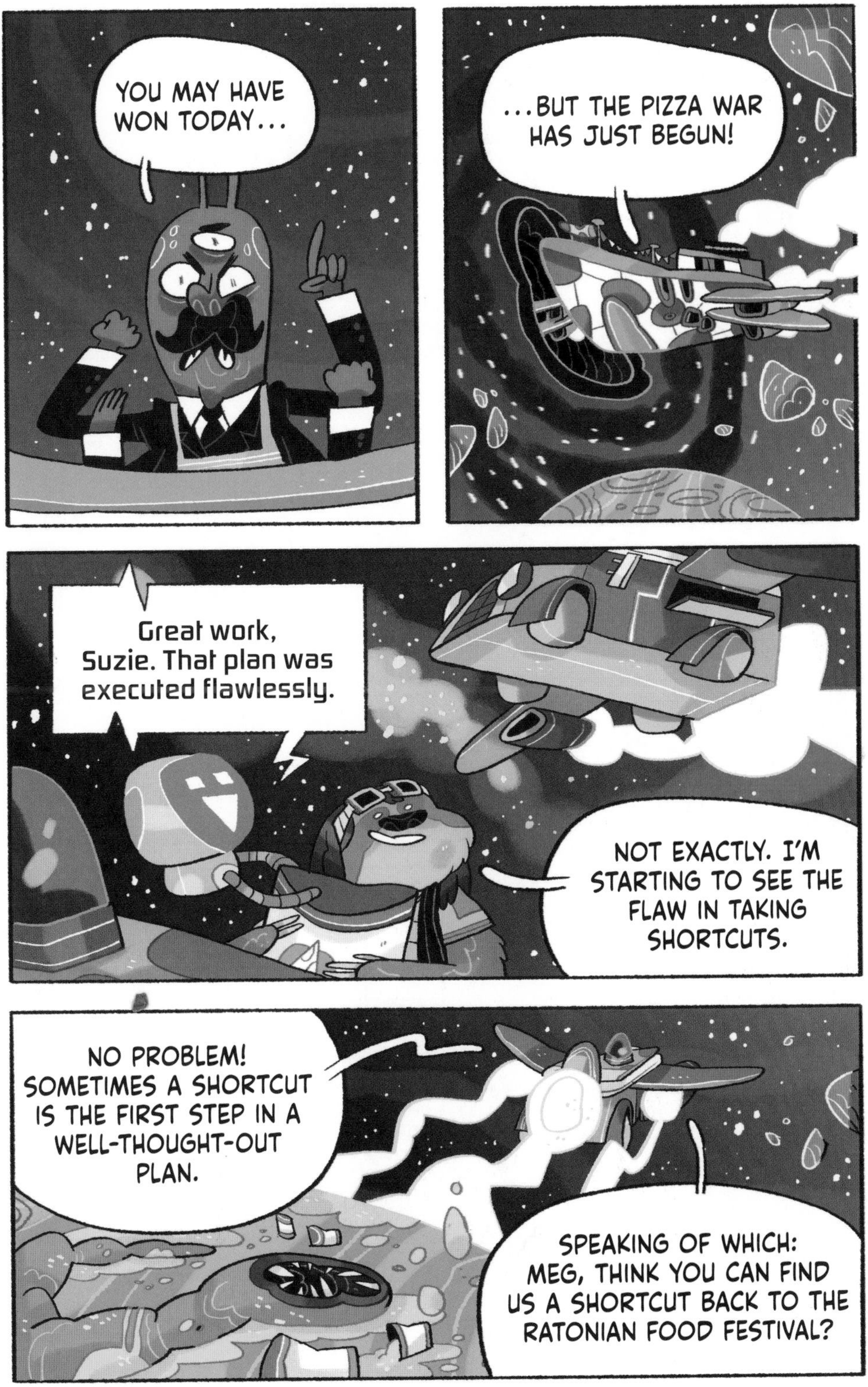
YOU MAY HAVE WON TODAY...
...BUT THE PIZZA WAR HAS JUST BEGUN!
Great work, Suzie. That plan was executed flawlessly.
NOT EXACTLY. I'M STARTING TO SEE THE FLAW IN TAKING SHORTCUTS.
NO PROBLEM! SOMETIMES A SHORTCUT IS THE FIRST STEP IN A WELL-THOUGHT-OUT PLAN.
SPEAKING OF WHICH: MEG, THINK YOU CAN FIND US A SHORTCUT BACK TO THE RATONIAN FOOD FESTIVAL?

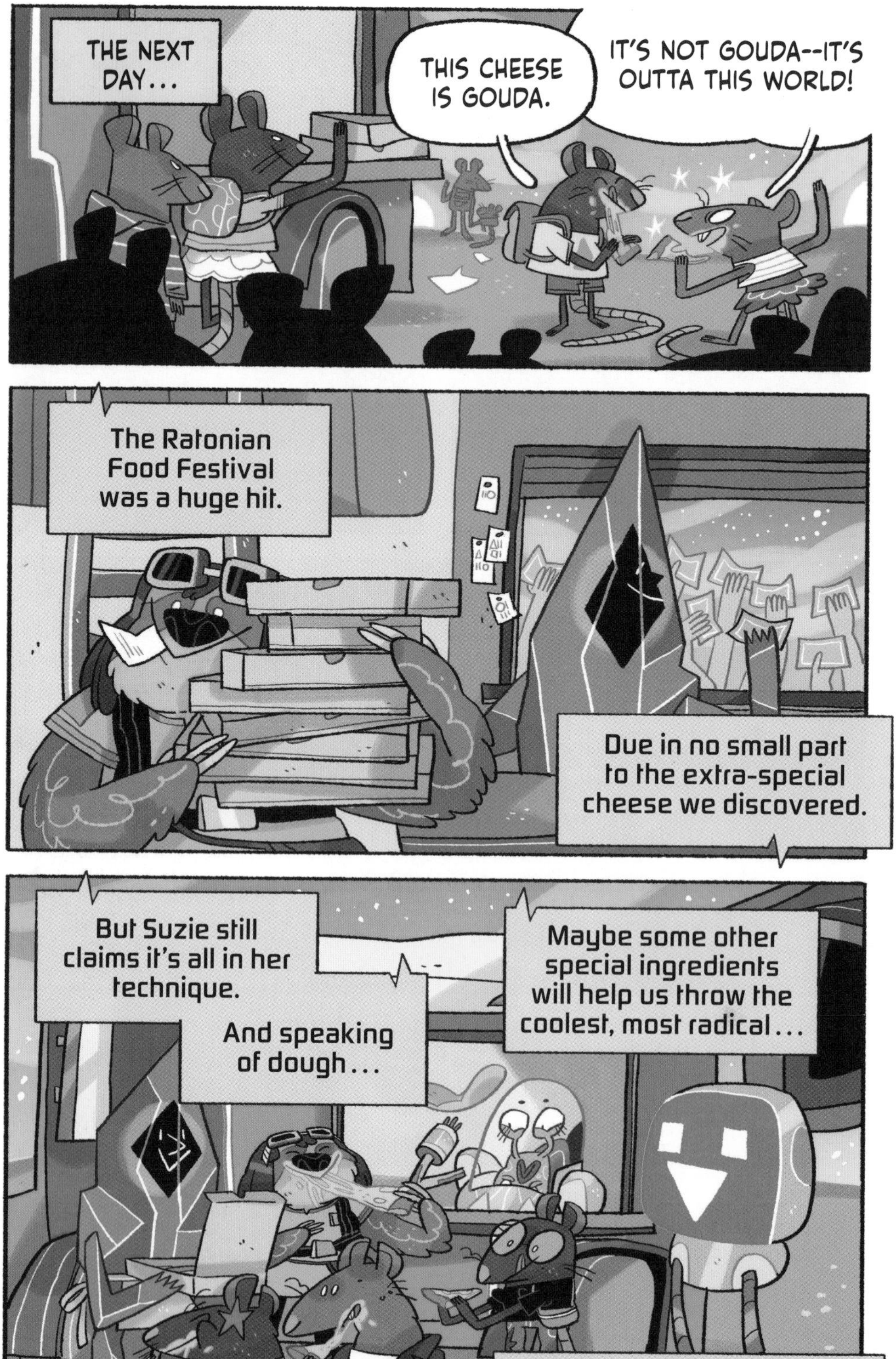
THE NEXT DAY...
THIS CHEESE IS GOUDA.
IT'S NOT GOUDA--IT'S OUTTA THIS WORLD!
The Ratonian Food Festival was a huge hit.
Due in no small part to the extra-special cheese we discovered.
But Suzie still claims it's all in her technique.
And speaking of dough...
Maybe some other special ingredients will help us throw the coolest, most radical...
...COSMIC PIZZA PARTY!

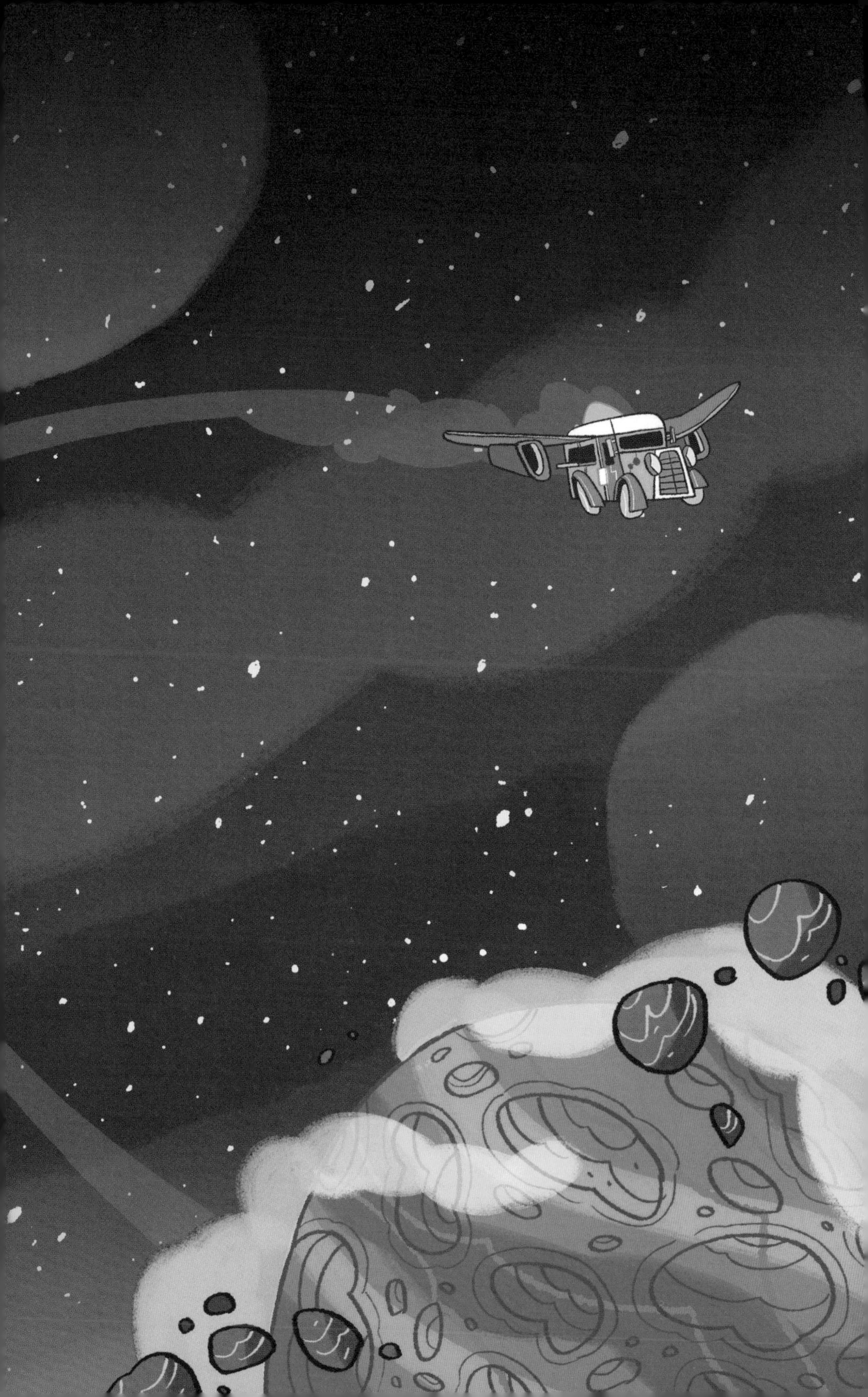

CHAPTER 2
Pizza Power-Up

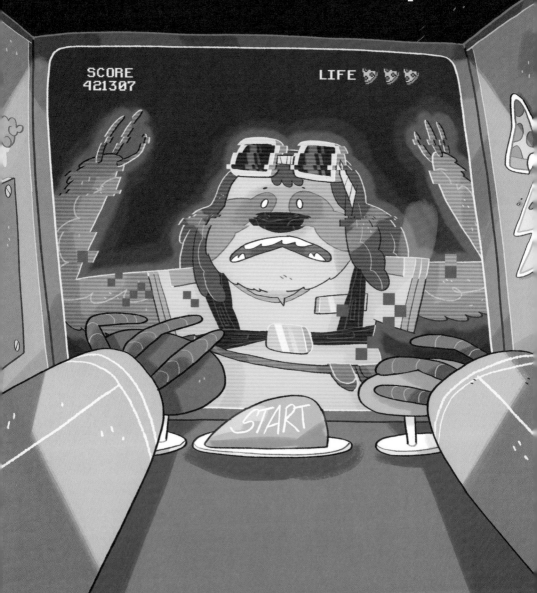

SCORE
421307

LIFE

START

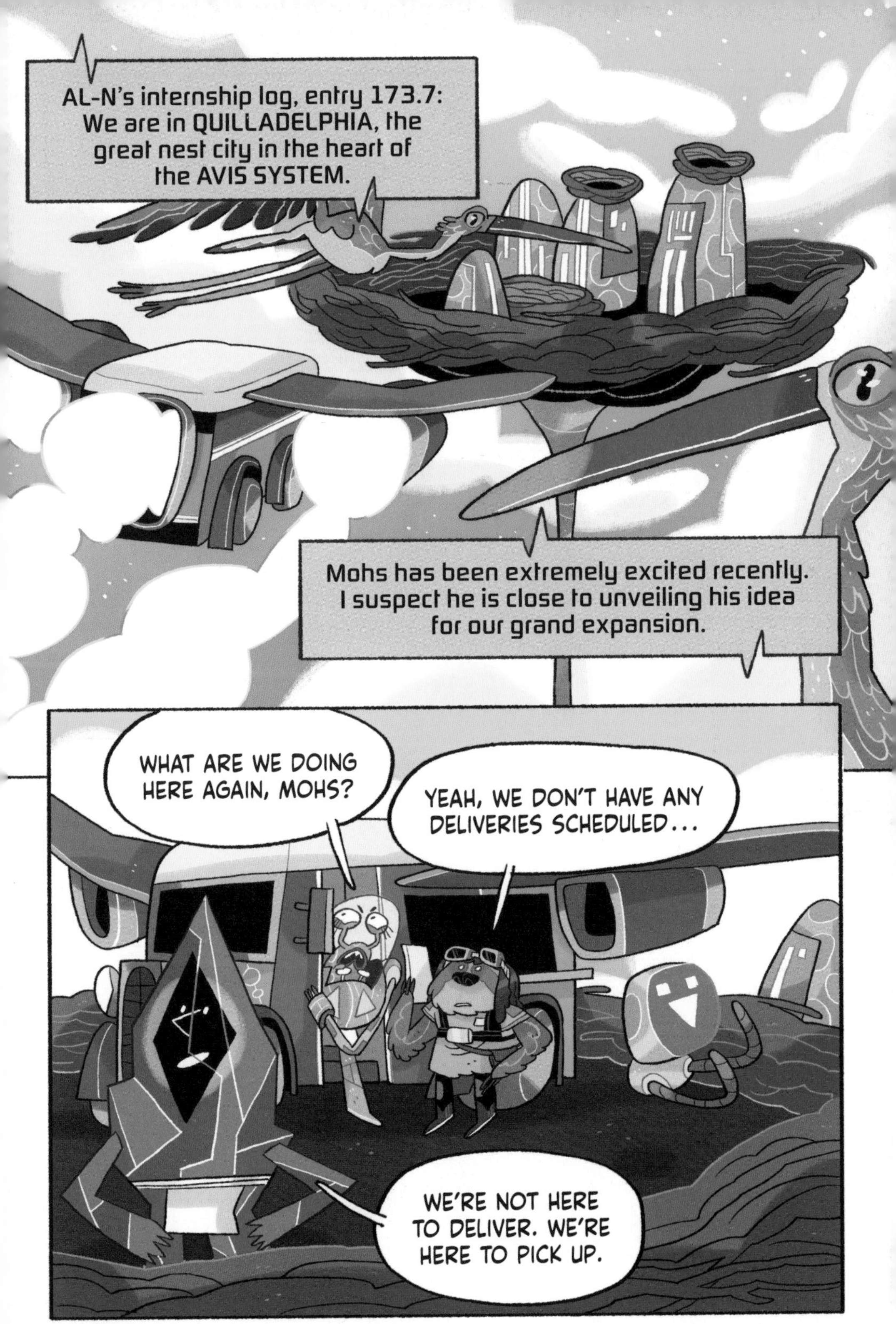
AL-N's internship log, entry 173.7: We are in QUILLADELPHIA, the great nest city in the heart of the AVIS SYSTEM.
Mohs has been extremely excited recently. I suspect he is close to unveiling his idea for our grand expansion.
WHAT ARE WE DOING HERE AGAIN, MOHS?
YEAH, WE DON'T HAVE ANY DELIVERIES SCHEDULED...
WE'RE NOT HERE TO DELIVER. WE'RE HERE TO PICK UP.

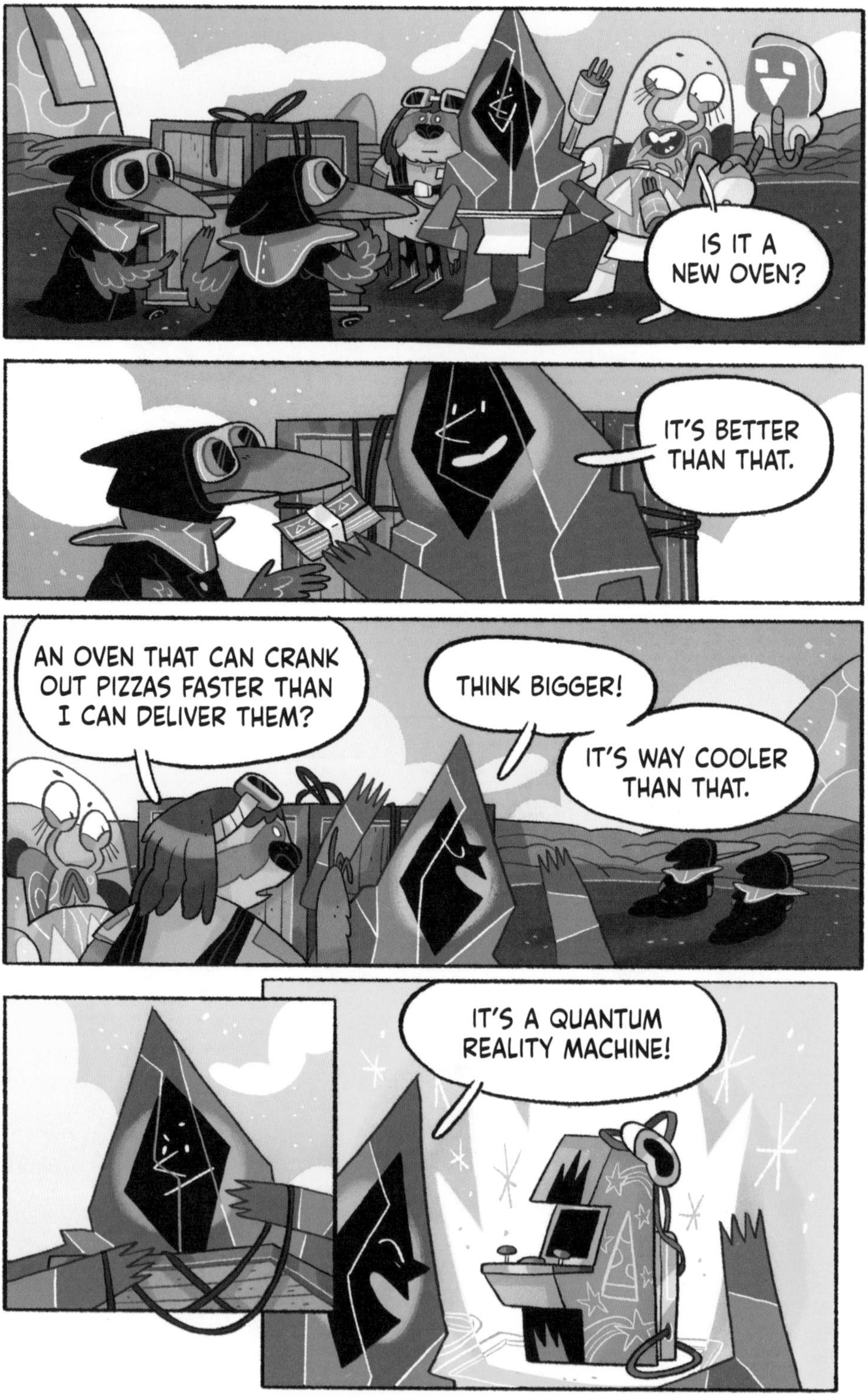
IS IT A NEW OVEN?
IT'S BETTER THAN THAT.
AN OVEN THAT CAN CRANK OUT PIZZAS FASTER THAN I CAN DELIVER THEM?
THINK BIGGER!
IT'S WAY COOLER THAN THAT.
IT'S A QUANTUM REALITY MACHINE!

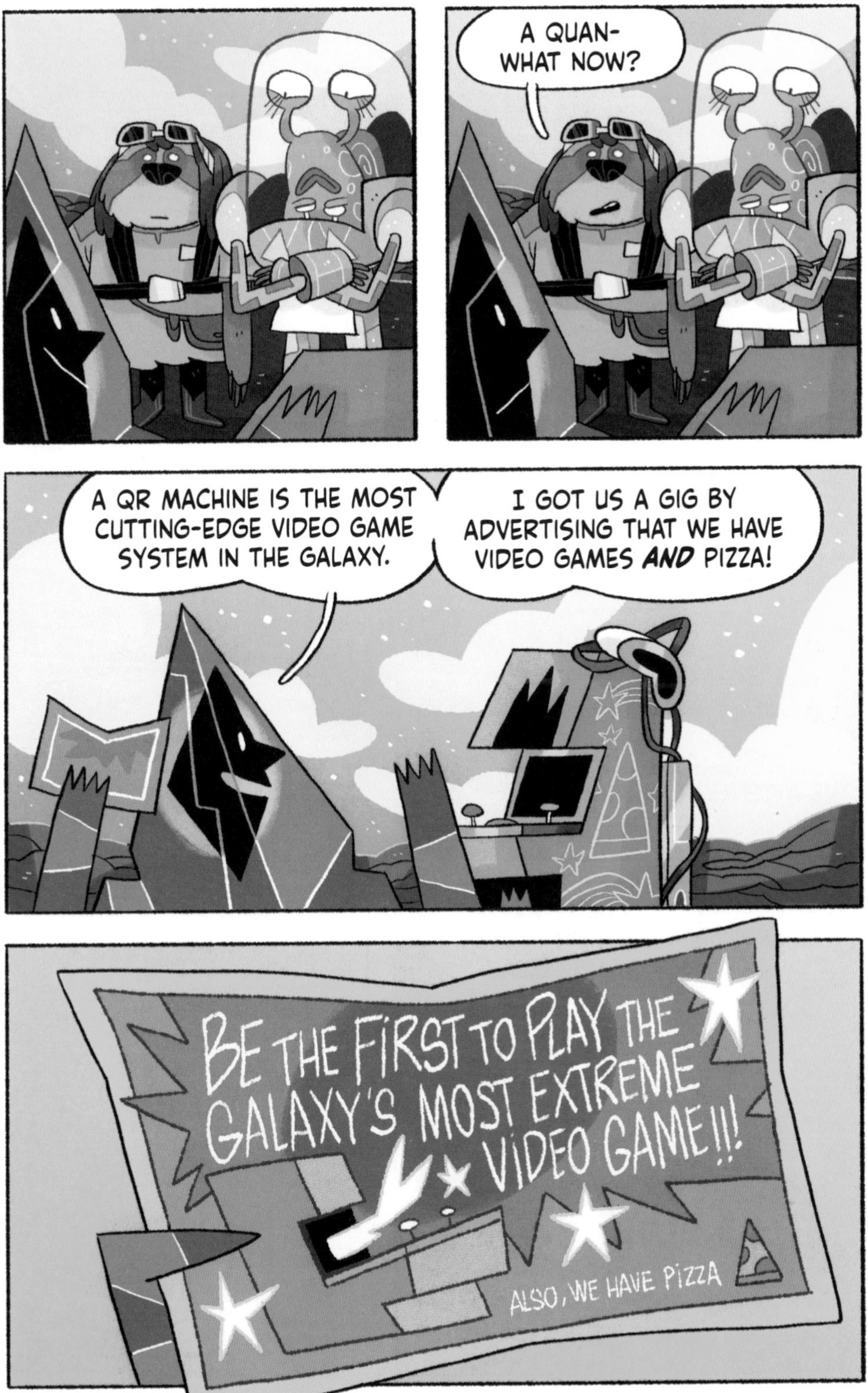
A QUAN-WHAT NOW?
A QR MACHINE IS THE MOST CUTTING-EDGE VIDEO GAME SYSTEM IN THE GALAXY.
I GOT US A GIG BY ADVERTISING THAT WE HAVE VIDEO GAMES **AND** PIZZA!
BE THE FIRST TO PLAY THE GALAXY'S MOST EXTREME VIDEO GAME!!!
ALSO, WE HAVE PIZZA

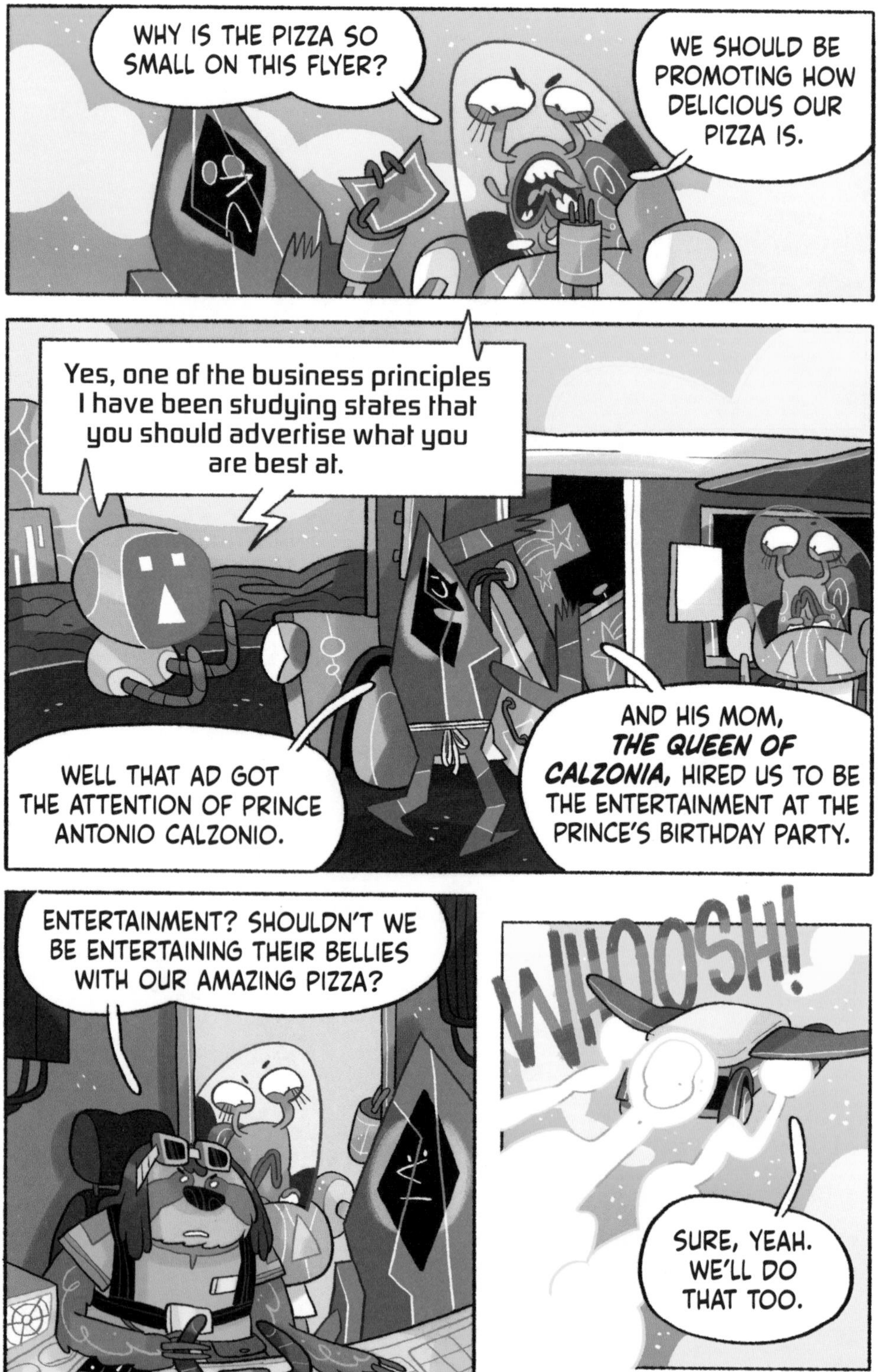
WHY IS THE PIZZA SO SMALL ON THIS FLYER?
WE SHOULD BE PROMOTING HOW DELICIOUS OUR PIZZA IS.
Yes, one of the business principles I have been studying states that you should advertise what you are best at.
WELL THAT AD GOT THE ATTENTION OF PRINCE ANTONIO CALZONIO.
AND HIS MOM, THE QUEEN OF CALZONIA, HIRED US TO BE THE ENTERTAINMENT AT THE PRINCE'S BIRTHDAY PARTY.
ENTERTAINMENT? SHOULDN'T WE BE ENTERTAINING THEIR BELLIES WITH OUR AMAZING PIZZA?
WHOOSH!
SURE, YEAH. WE'LL DO THAT TOO.

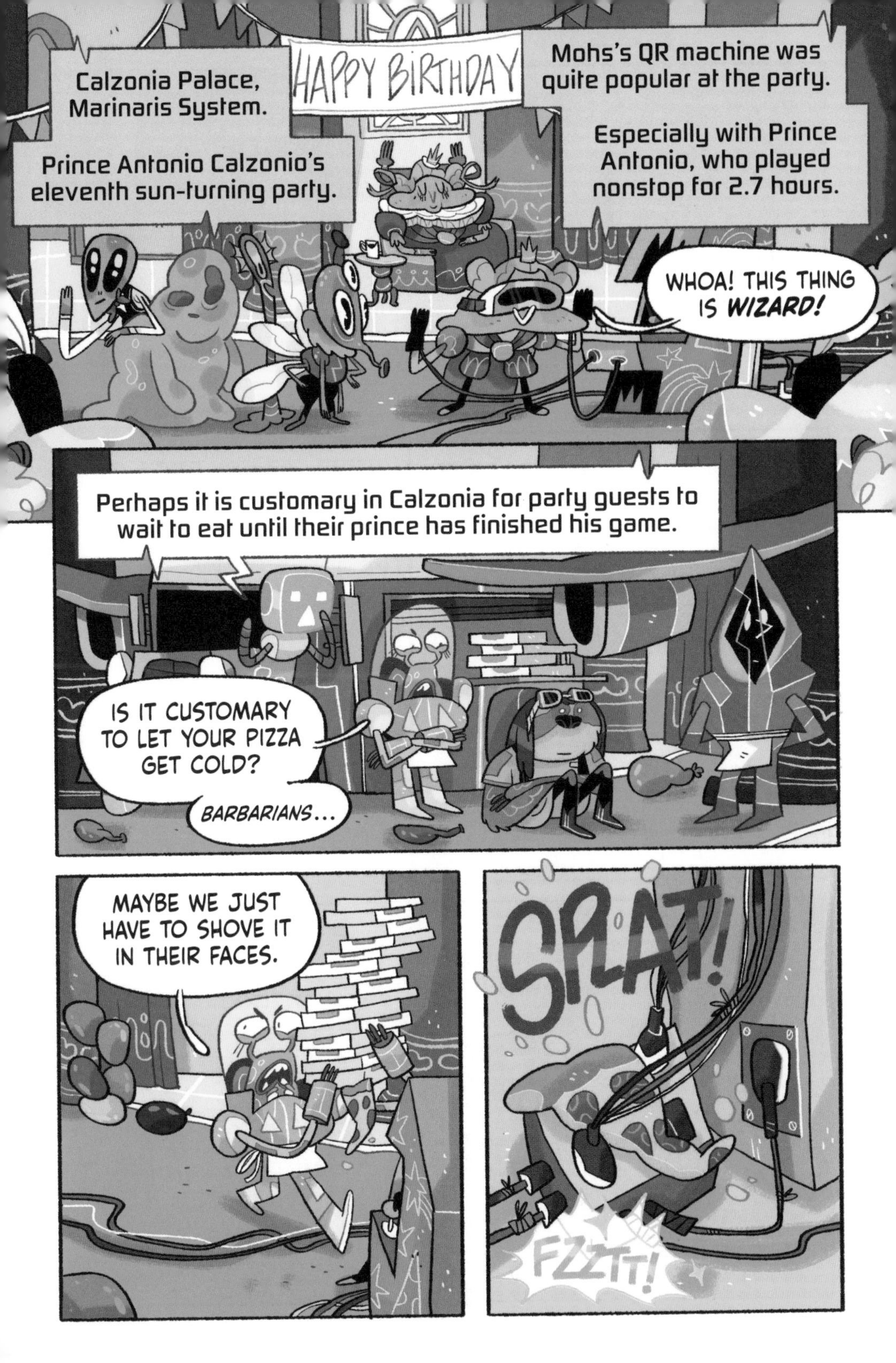
Calzonia Palace, Marinaris System.
Prince Antonio Calzonio's eleventh sun-turning party.
HAPPY BIRTHDAY
Mohs's QR machine was quite popular at the party.
Especially with Prince Antonio, who played nonstop for 2.7 hours.
WHOA! THIS THING IS WIZARD!
Perhaps it is customary in Calzonia for party guests to wait to eat until their prince has finished his game.
IS IT CUSTOMARY TO LET YOUR PIZZA GET COLD?
BARBARIANS...
MAYBE WE JUST HAVE TO SHOVE IT IN THEIR FACES.
SPLAT!
FZZTTT!

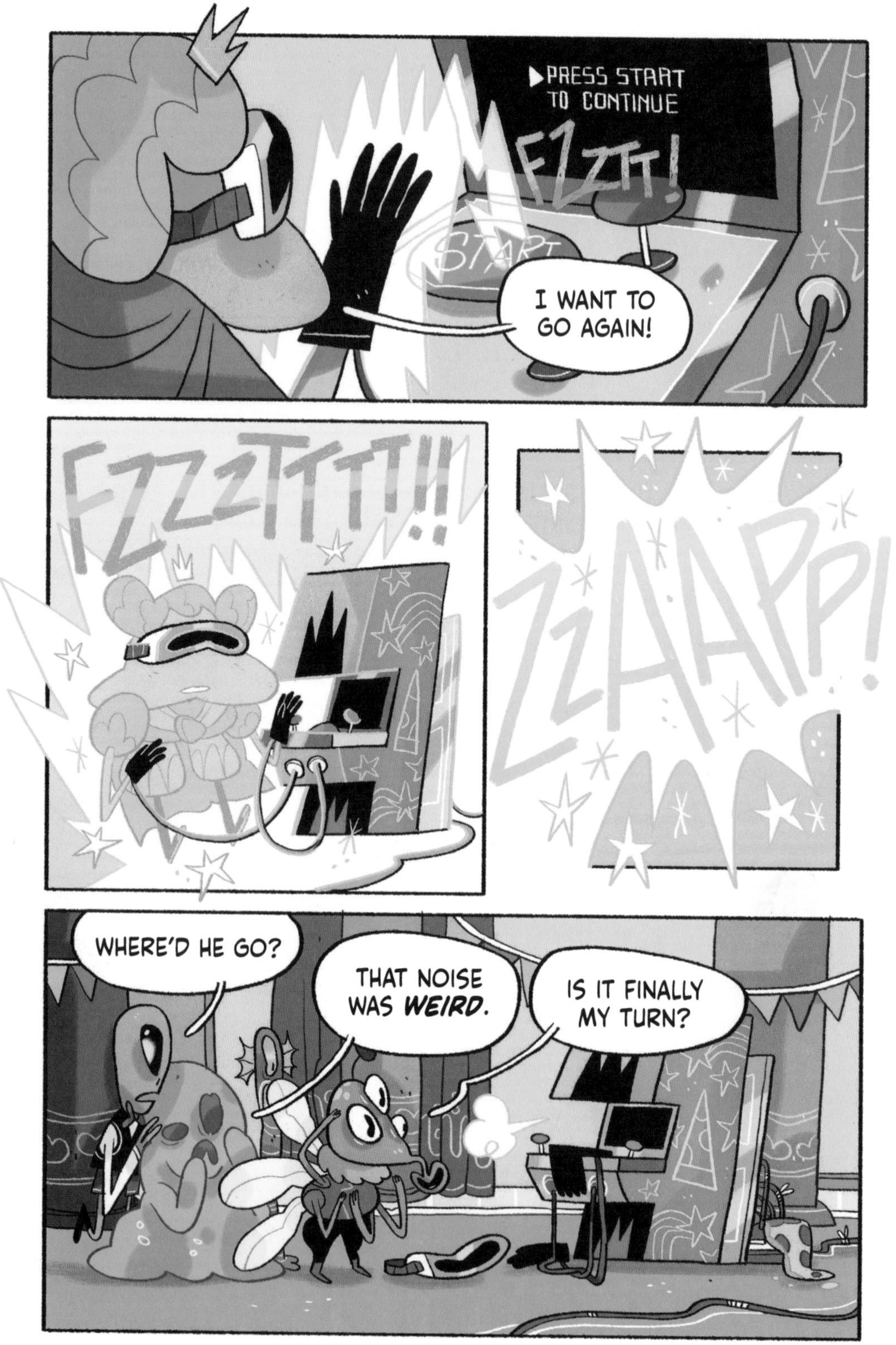
▶PRESS START
TO CONTINUE
FZZTT!
START
I WANT TO GO AGAIN!
FZZZTTTT!!
ZZAAPP!
WHERE'D HE GO?
THAT NOISE WAS ***WEIRD***.
IS IT FINALLY MY TURN?

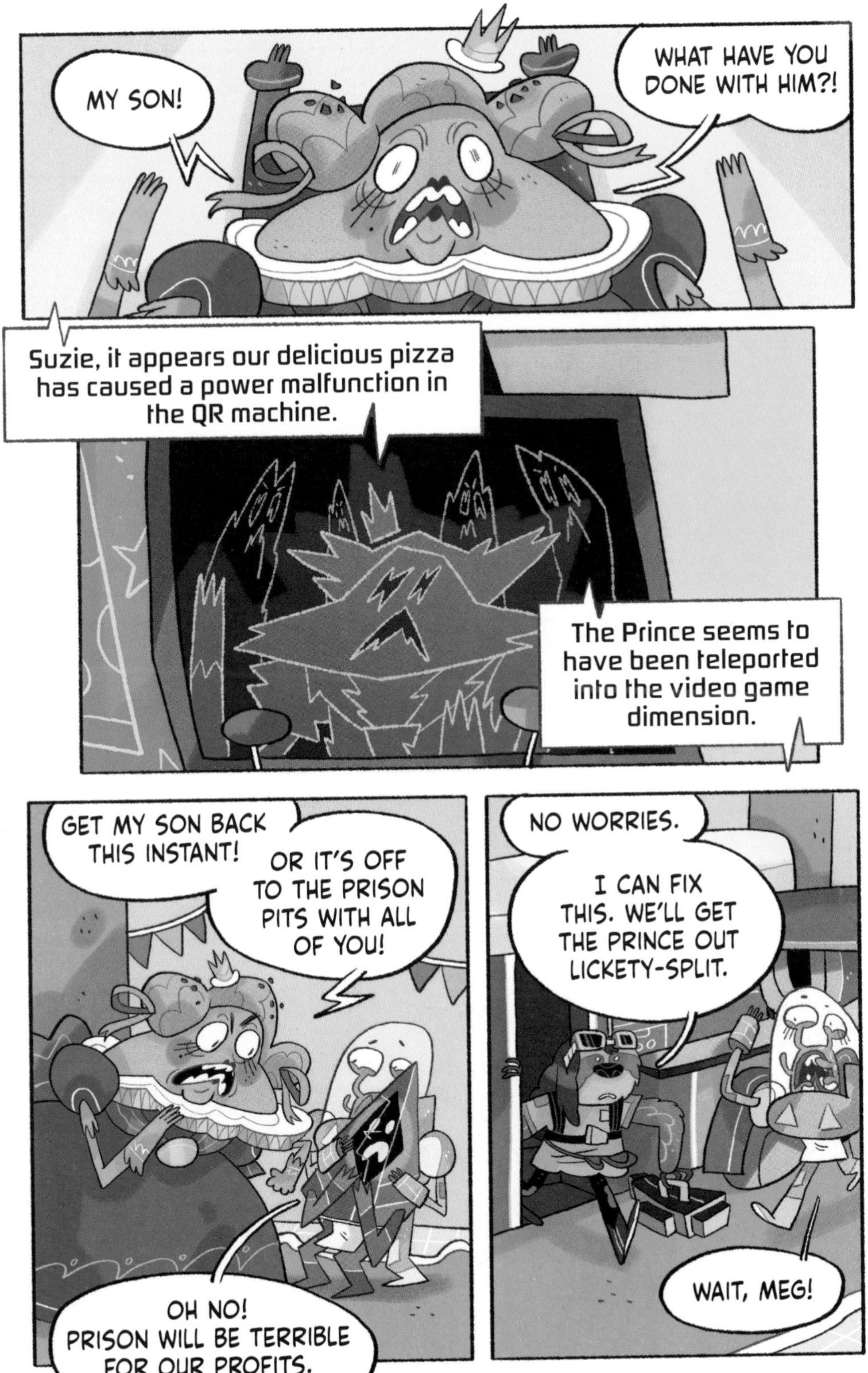
MY SON!
WHAT HAVE YOU DONE WITH HIM?!
Suzie, it appears our delicious pizza has caused a power malfunction in the QR machine.
The Prince seems to have been teleported into the video game dimension.
GET MY SON BACK THIS INSTANT!
OR IT'S OFF TO THE PRISON PITS WITH ALL OF YOU!
OH NO! PRISON WILL BE TERRIBLE FOR OUR PROFITS.
NO WORRIES.
I CAN FIX THIS. WE'LL GET THE PRINCE OUT LICKETY-SPLIT.
WAIT, MEG!

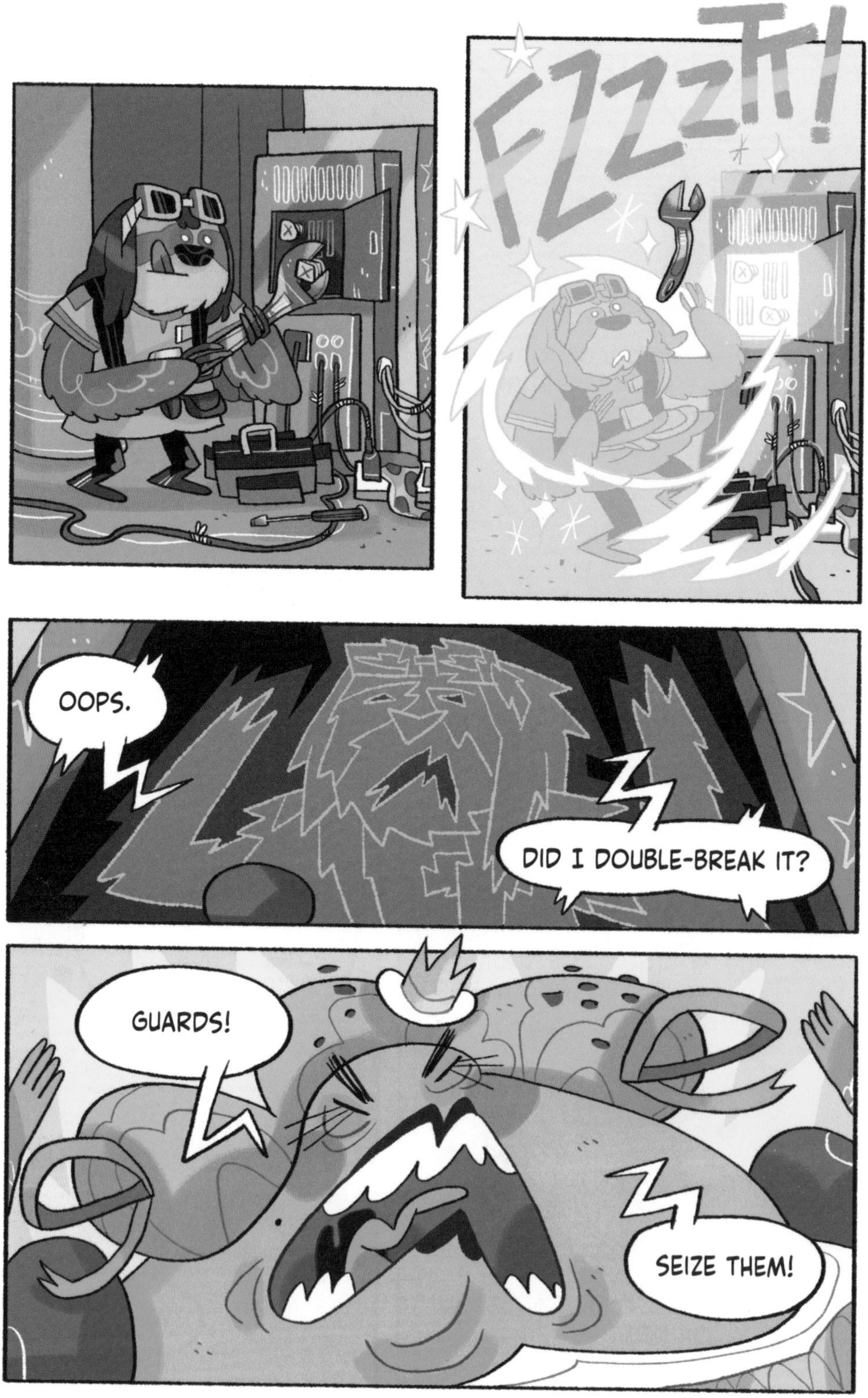
FZZZRR!
OOPS.
DID I DOUBLE-BREAK IT?
GUARDS!
SEIZE THEM!

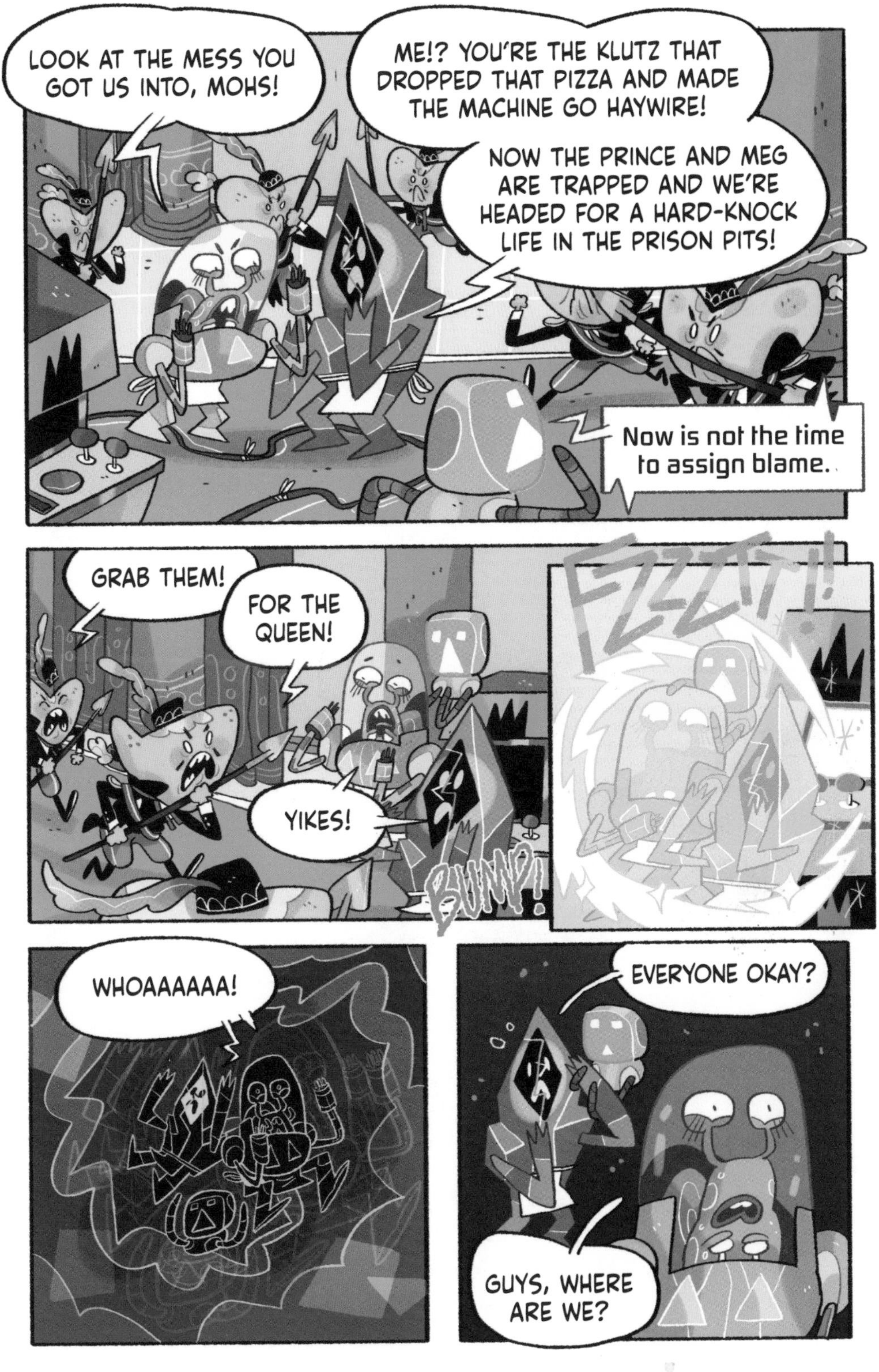
LOOK AT THE MESS YOU GOT US INTO, MOHS!
ME!? YOU'RE THE KLUTZ THAT DROPPED THAT PIZZA AND MADE THE MACHINE GO HAYWIRE!
NOW THE PRINCE AND MEG ARE TRAPPED AND WE'RE HEADED FOR A HARD-KNOCK LIFE IN THE PRISON PITS!
Now is not the time to assign blame.
GRAB THEM!
FOR THE QUEEN!
YIKES!
BUMP!
FZZZTT!!
WHOAAAAAA!
EVERYONE OKAY?
GUYS, WHERE ARE WE?

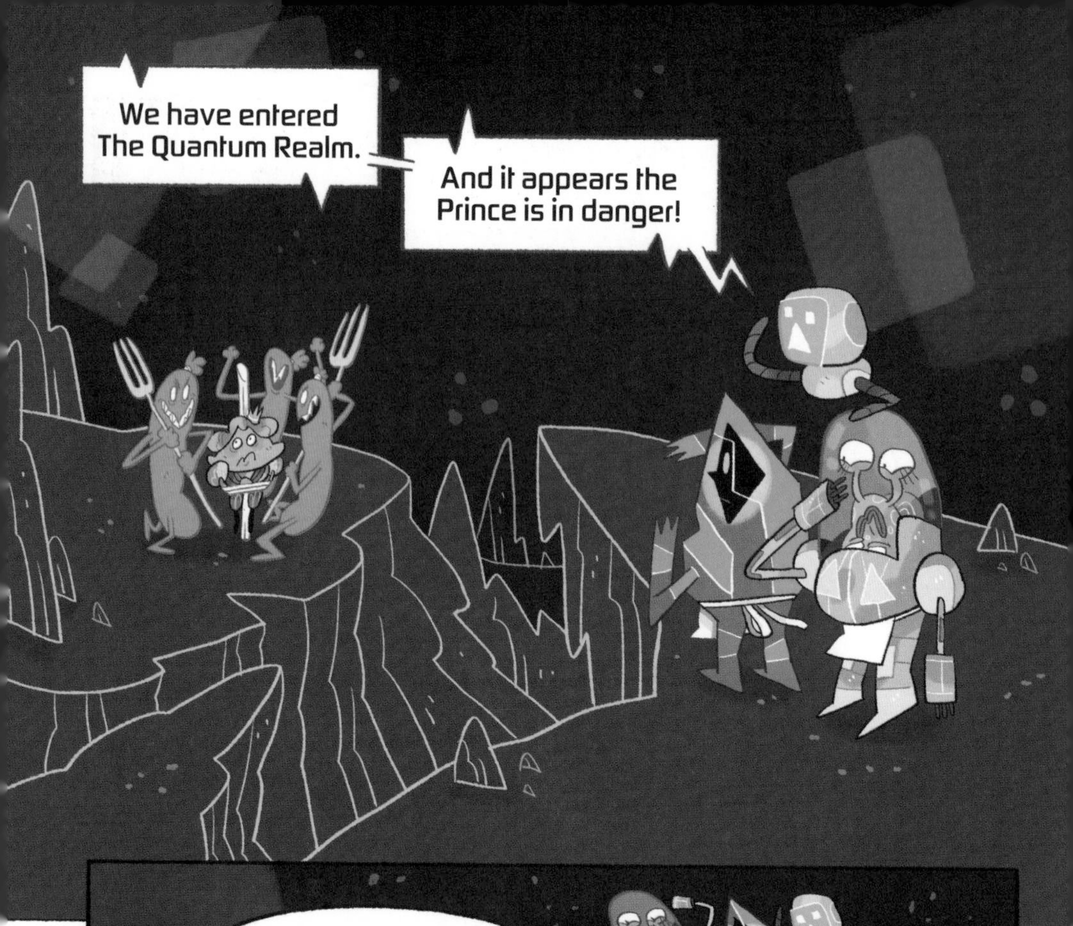
We have entered The Quantum Realm.
And it appears the Prince is in danger!

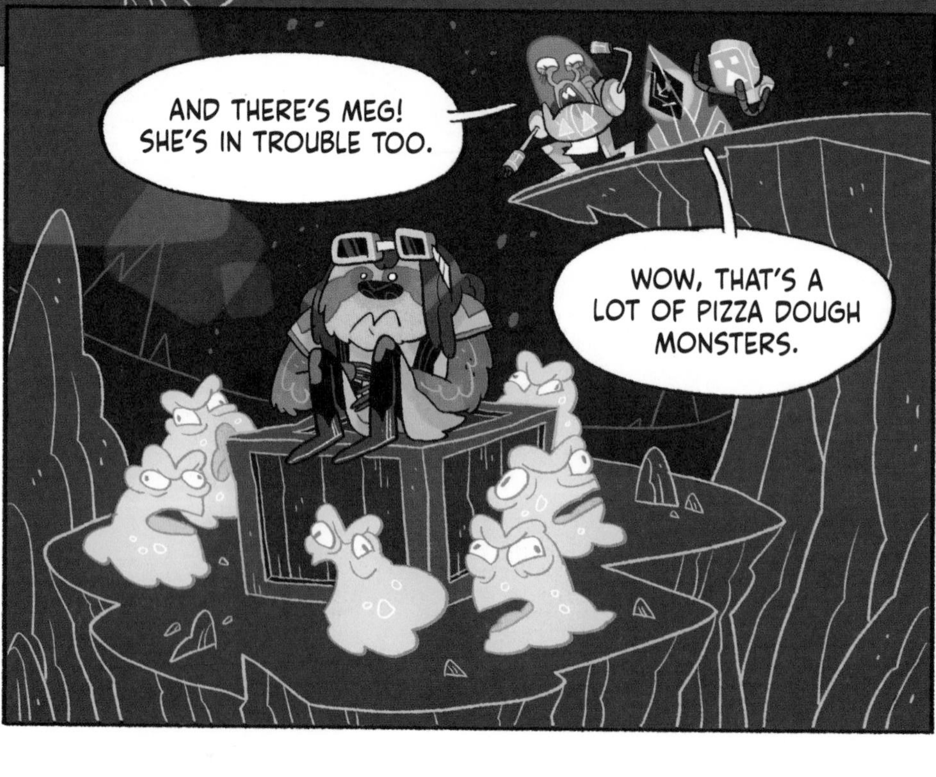
AND THERE'S MEG! SHE'S IN TROUBLE TOO.
WOW, THAT'S A LOT OF PIZZA DOUGH MONSTERS.

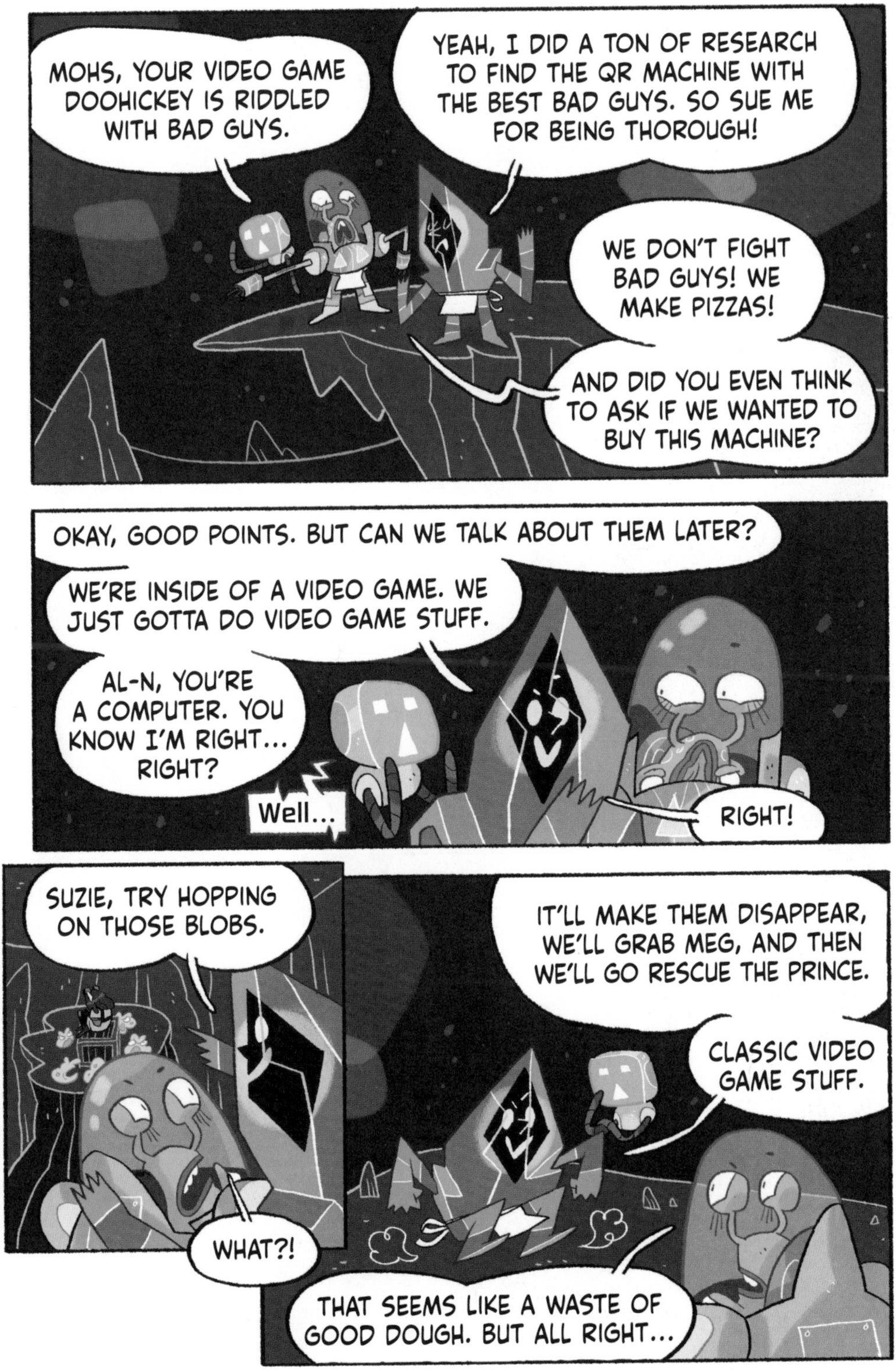
MOHS, YOUR VIDEO GAME DOOHICKEY IS RIDDLED WITH BAD GUYS.
YEAH, I DID A TON OF RESEARCH TO FIND THE QR MACHINE WITH THE BEST BAD GUYS. SO SUE ME FOR BEING THOROUGH!
WE DON'T FIGHT BAD GUYS! WE MAKE PIZZAS!
AND DID YOU EVEN THINK TO ASK IF WE WANTED TO BUY THIS MACHINE?
OKAY, GOOD POINTS. BUT CAN WE TALK ABOUT THEM LATER?
WE'RE INSIDE OF A VIDEO GAME. WE JUST GOTTA DO VIDEO GAME STUFF.
AL-N, YOU'RE A COMPUTER. YOU KNOW I'M RIGHT... RIGHT?
Well...
RIGHT!
SUZIE, TRY HOPPING ON THOSE BLOBS.
WHAT?!
IT'LL MAKE THEM DISAPPEAR, WE'LL GRAB MEG, AND THEN WE'LL GO RESCUE THE PRINCE.
CLASSIC VIDEO GAME STUFF.
THAT SEEMS LIKE A WASTE OF GOOD DOUGH. BUT ALL RIGHT...

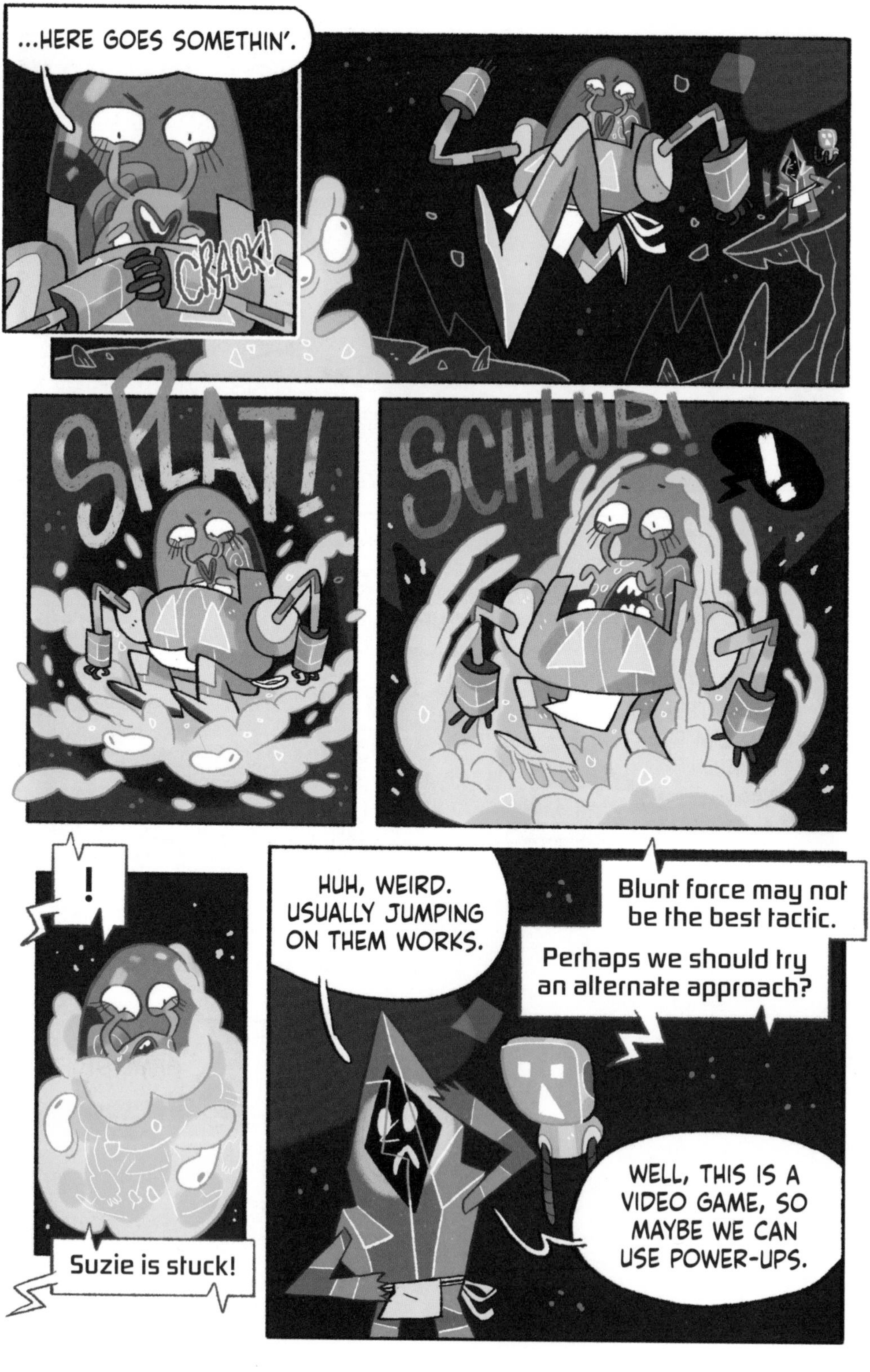
...HERE GOES SOMETHIN'.
CRACK!
SPLAT!
SCHLUP!
!
!
HUH, WEIRD. USUALLY JUMPING ON THEM WORKS.
Blunt force may not be the best tactic.
Perhaps we should try an alternate approach?
Suzie is stuck!
WELL, THIS IS A VIDEO GAME, SO MAYBE WE CAN USE POWER-UPS.

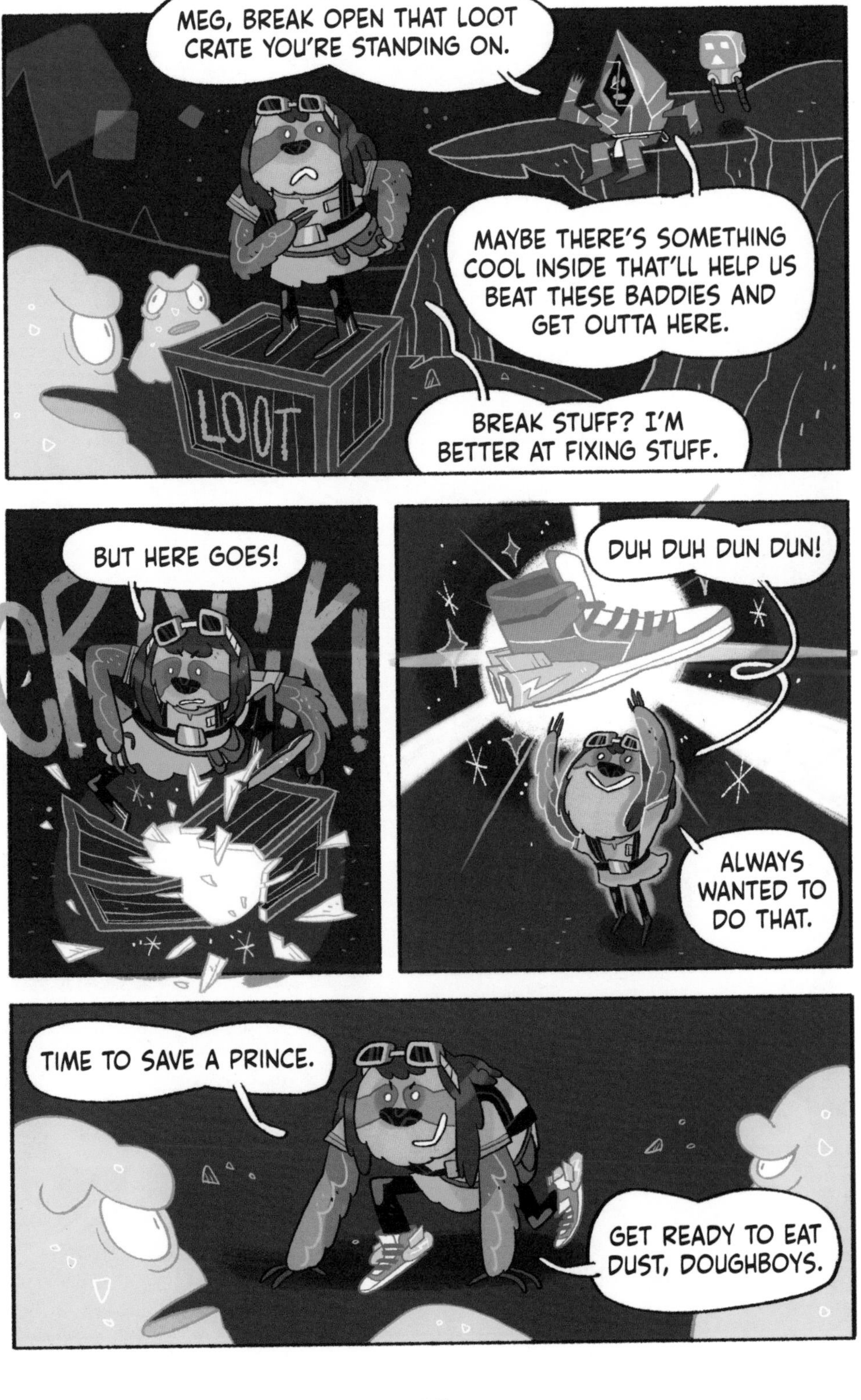
MEG, BREAK OPEN THAT LOOT CRATE YOU'RE STANDING ON.
MAYBE THERE'S SOMETHING COOL INSIDE THAT'LL HELP US BEAT THESE BADDIES AND GET OUTTA HERE.
LOOT
BREAK STUFF? I'M BETTER AT FIXING STUFF.
BUT HERE GOES!
DUH DUH DUN DUN!
ALWAYS WANTED TO DO THAT.
TIME TO SAVE A PRINCE.
GET READY TO EAT DUST, DOUGHBOYS.

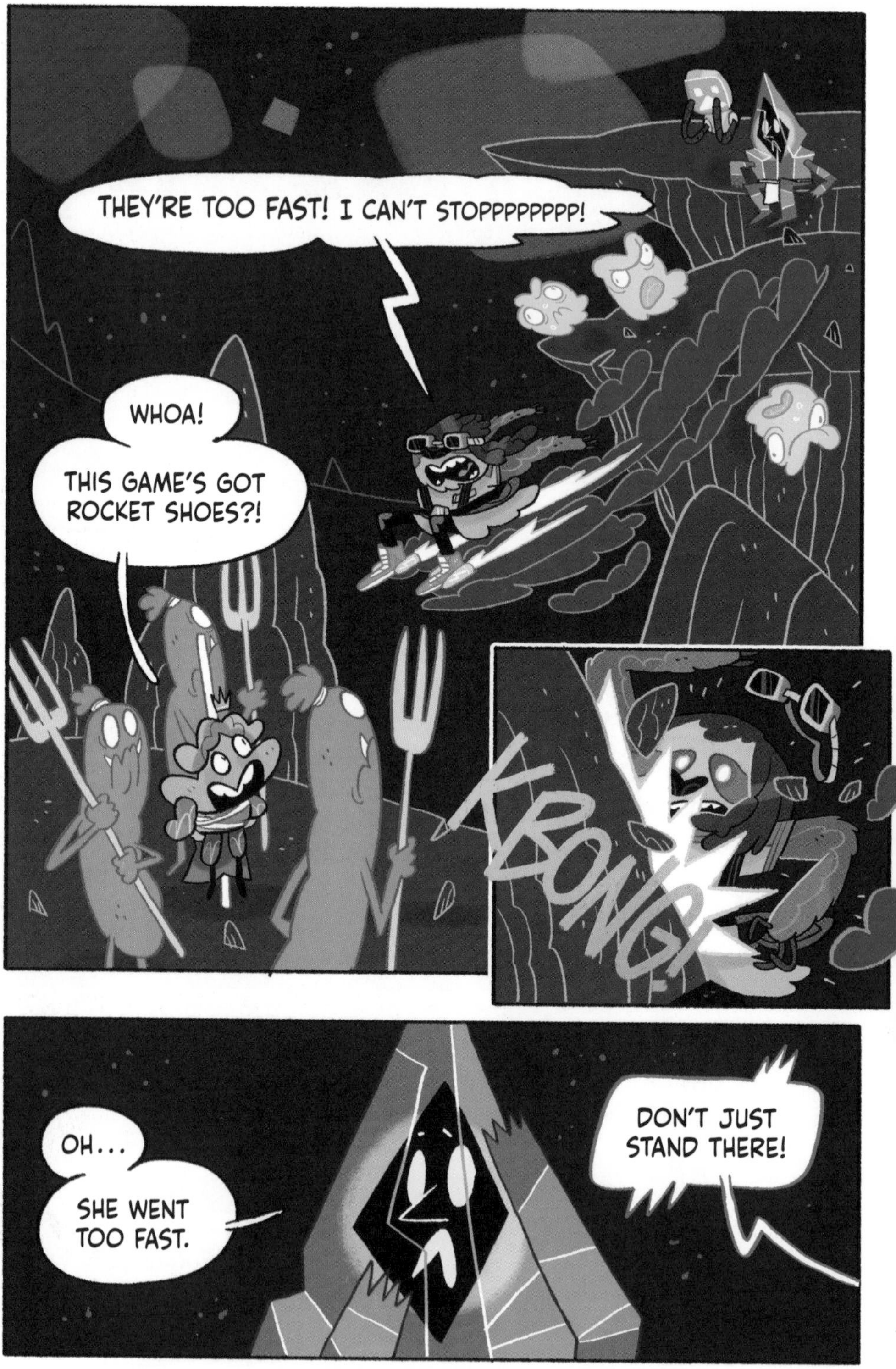
THEY'RE TOO FAST! I CAN'T STOPPPPPPPP!
WHOA!
THIS GAME'S GOT ROCKET SHOES?!
KBONG!
OH...
SHE WENT TOO FAST.
DON'T JUST STAND THERE!

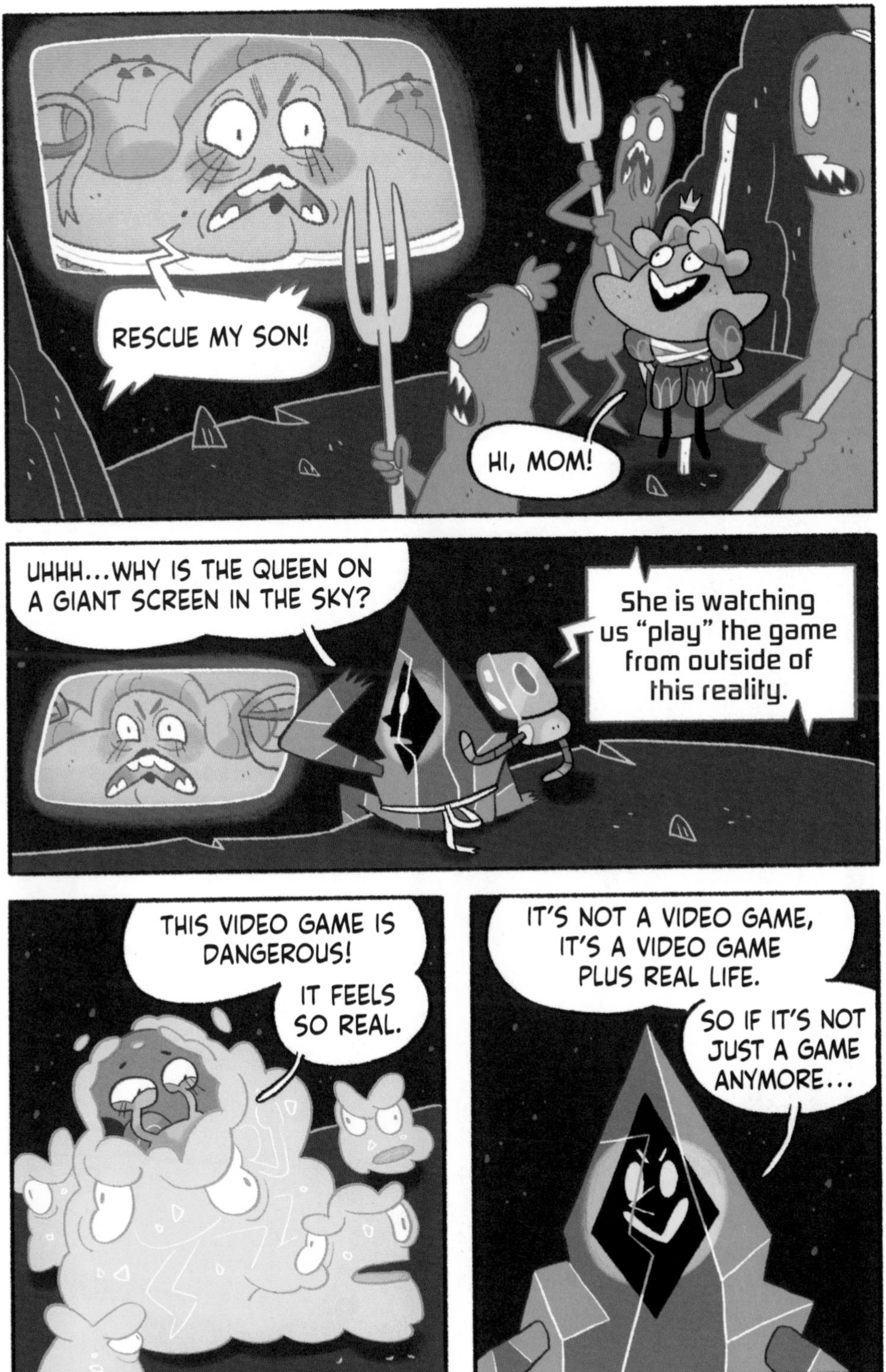
RESCUE MY SON!
HI, MOM!
UHHH...WHY IS THE QUEEN ON A GIANT SCREEN IN THE SKY?
She is watching us "play" the game from outside of this reality.
THIS VIDEO GAME IS DANGEROUS!
IT FEELS SO REAL.
IT'S NOT A VIDEO GAME, IT'S A VIDEO GAME PLUS REAL LIFE.
SO IF IT'S NOT JUST A GAME ANYMORE...

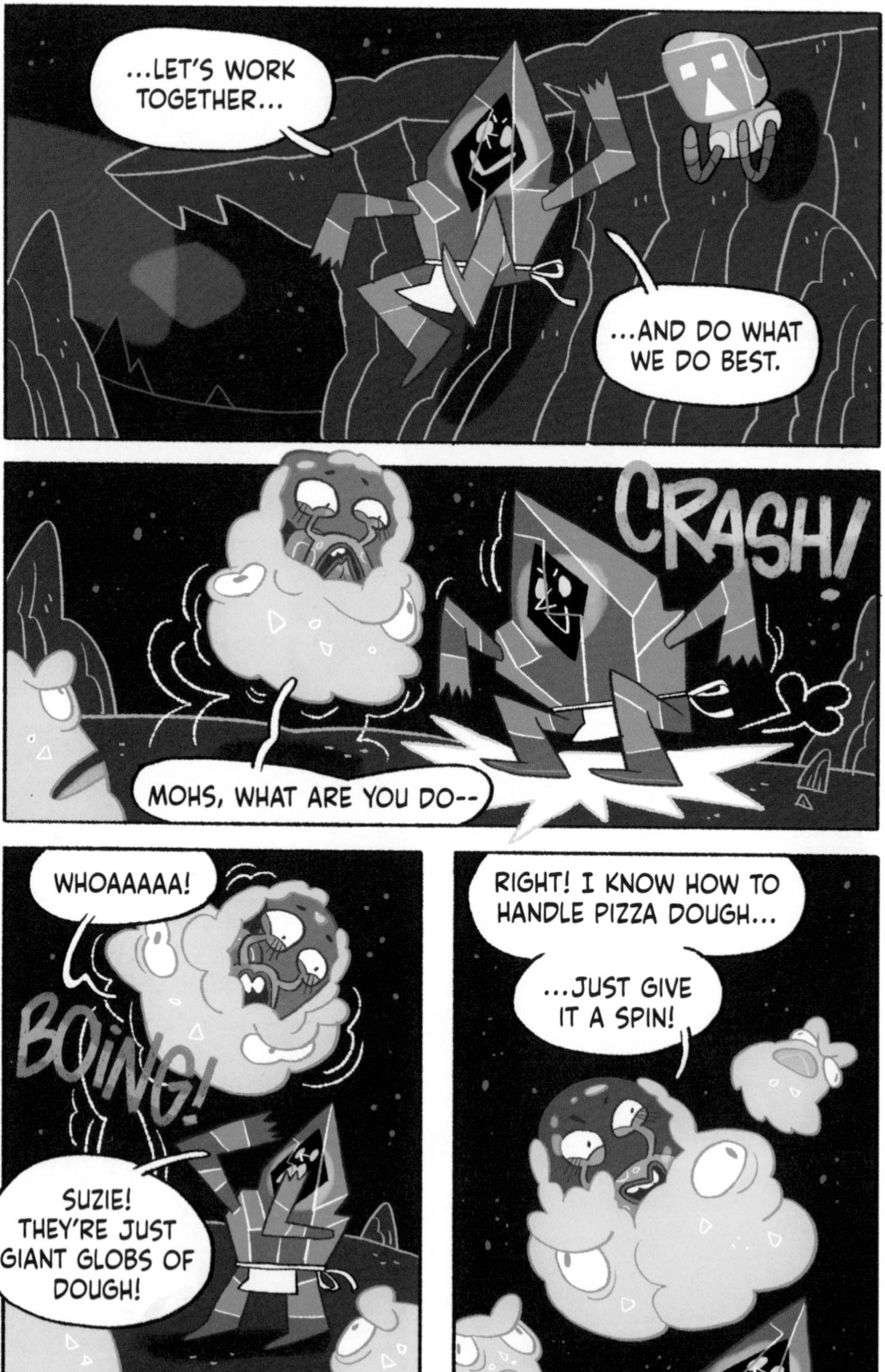
...LET'S WORK TOGETHER...
...AND DO WHAT WE DO BEST.
CRASH!
MOHS, WHAT ARE YOU DO--
WHOAAAAA!
BOING!
SUZIE! THEY'RE JUST GIANT GLOBS OF DOUGH!
RIGHT! I KNOW HOW TO HANDLE PIZZA DOUGH...
...JUST GIVE IT A SPIN!

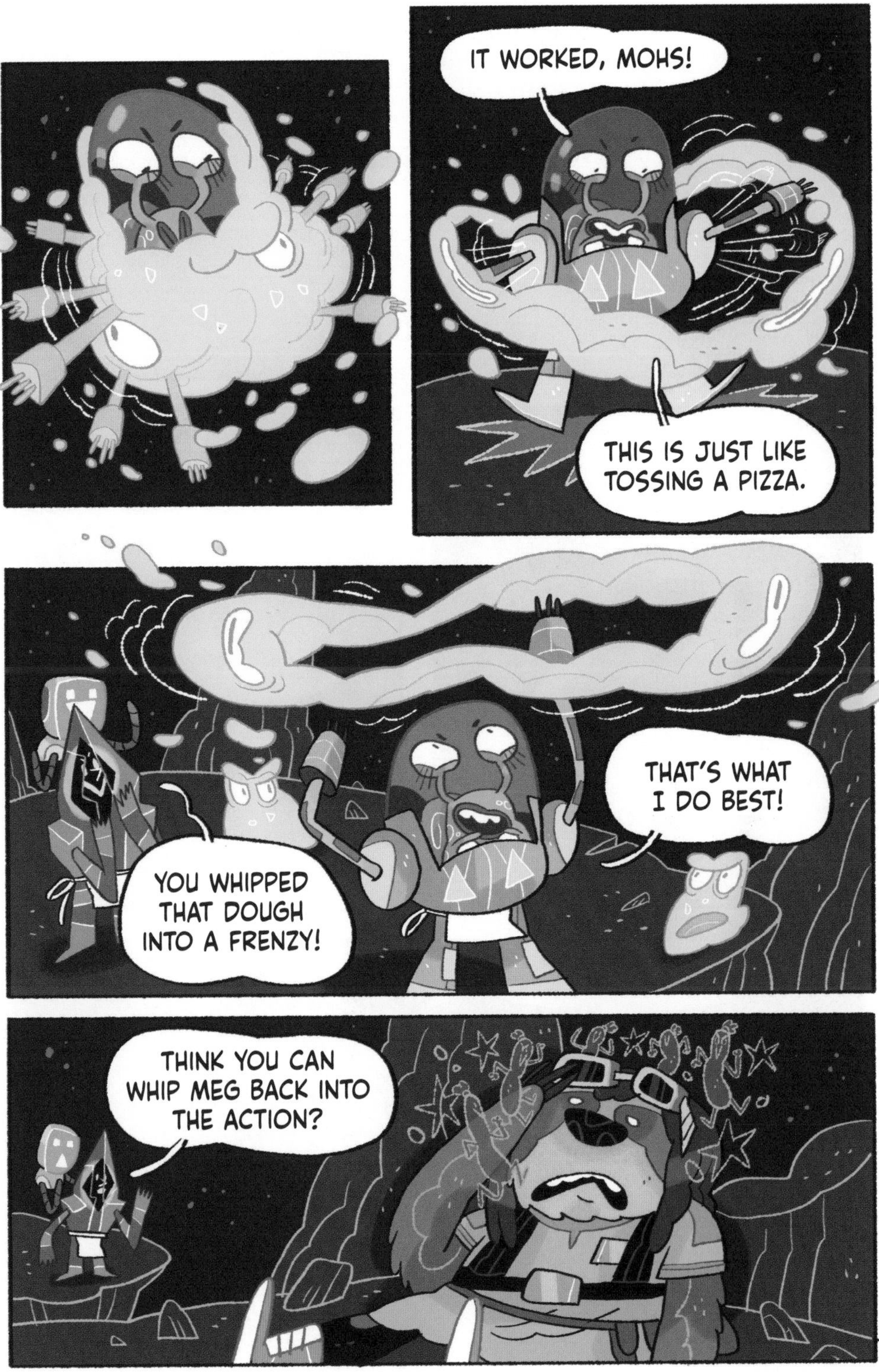
IT WORKED, MOHS!
THIS IS JUST LIKE TOSSING A PIZZA.
YOU WHIPPED THAT DOUGH INTO A FRENZY!
THAT'S WHAT I DO BEST!
THINK YOU CAN WHIP MEG BACK INTO THE ACTION?

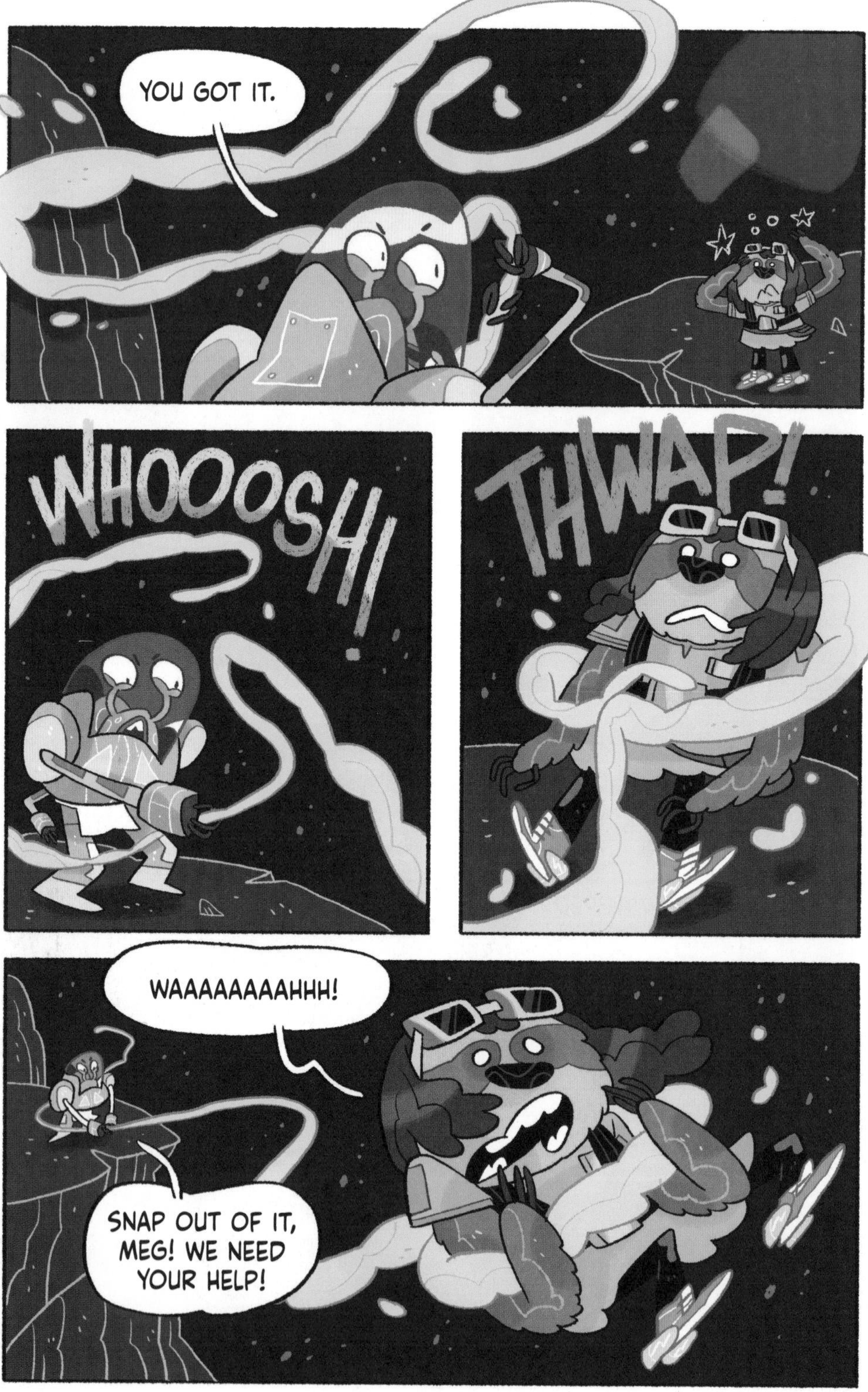
YOU GOT IT.
WHOOOSH!
THWAP!
WAAAAAAAAHHH!
SNAP OUT OF IT, MEG! WE NEED YOUR HELP!

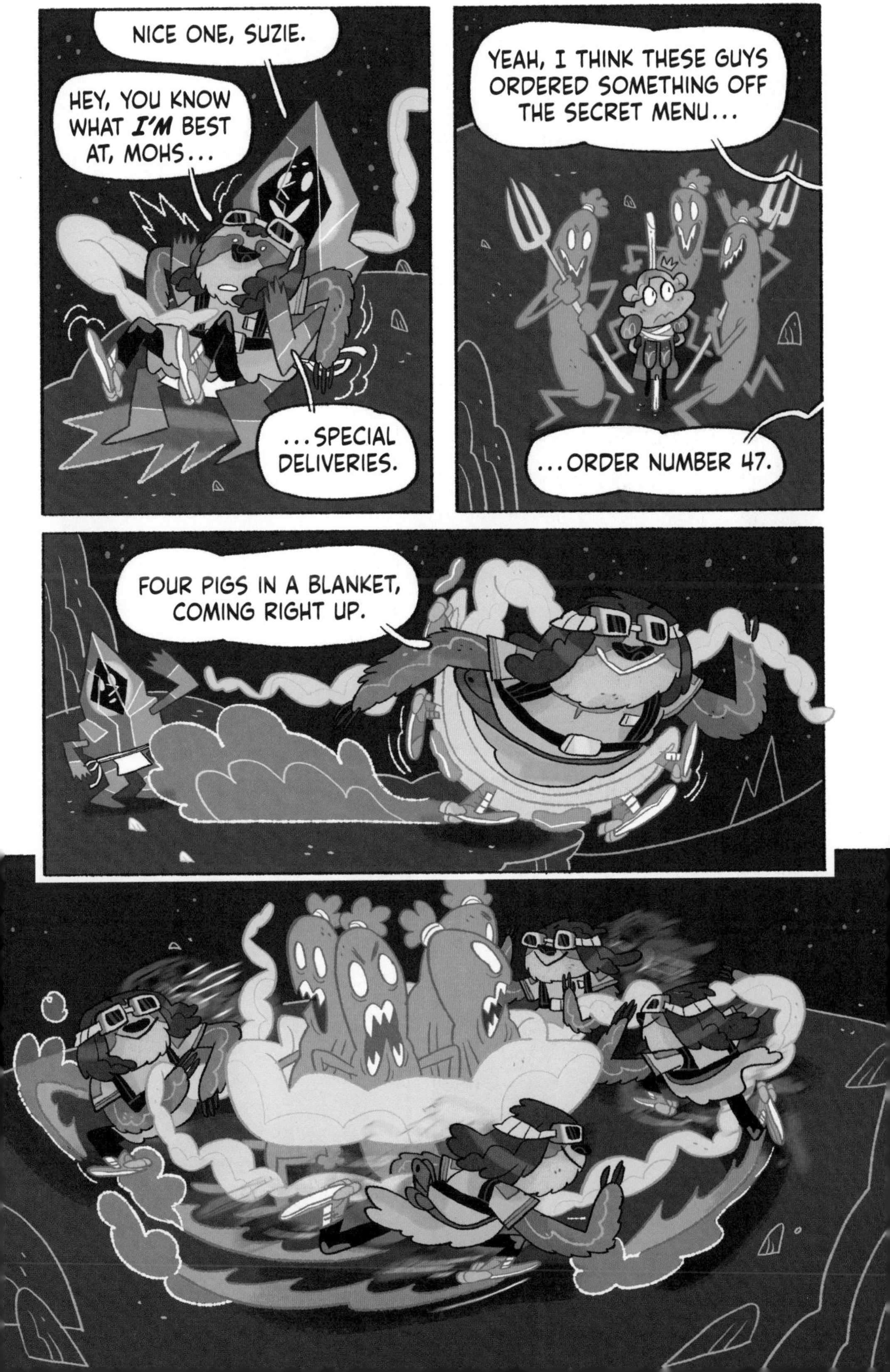
NICE ONE, SUZIE.
HEY, YOU KNOW WHAT *I'M* BEST AT, MOHS...
...SPECIAL DELIVERIES.
YEAH, I THINK THESE GUYS ORDERED SOMETHING OFF THE SECRET MENU...
...ORDER NUMBER 47.
FOUR PIGS IN A BLANKET, COMING RIGHT UP.

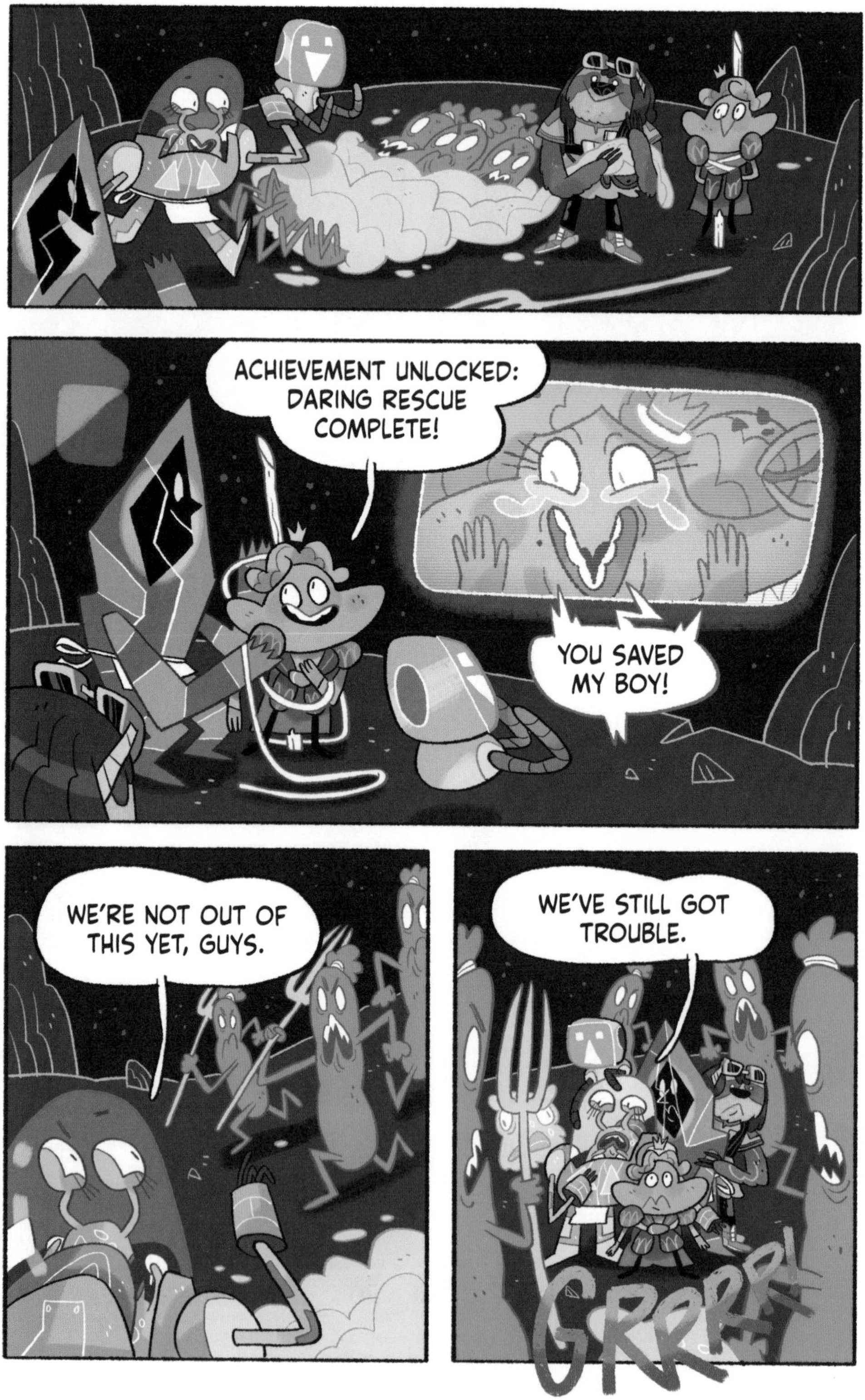
ACHIEVEMENT UNLOCKED: DARING RESCUE COMPLETE!
YOU SAVED MY BOY!
WE'RE NOT OUT OF THIS YET, GUYS.
WE'VE STILL GOT TROUBLE.
GRRR!

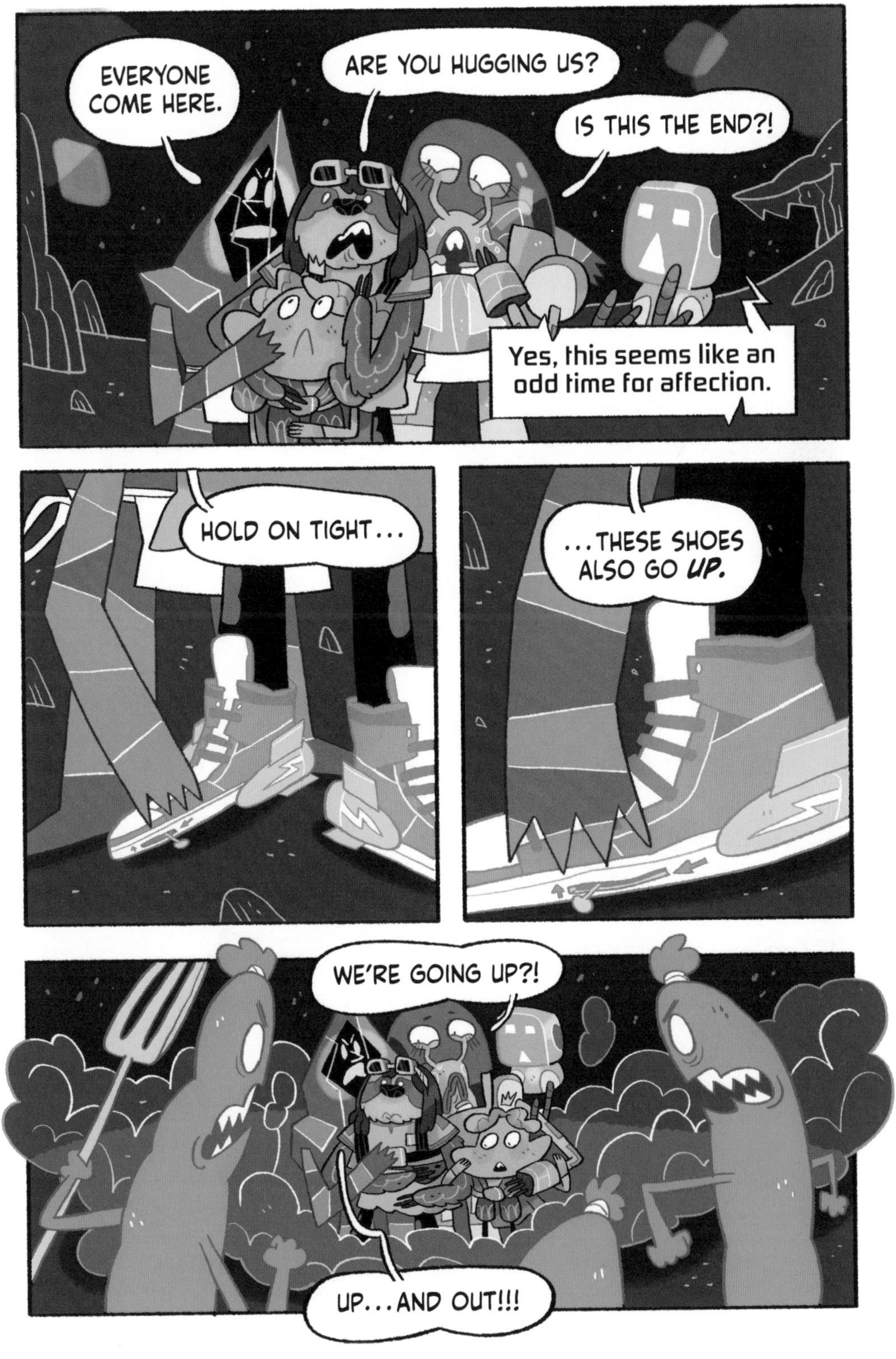
EVERYONE COME HERE.
ARE YOU HUGGING US?
IS THIS THE END?!
Yes, this seems like an odd time for affection.
HOLD ON TIGHT...
...THESE SHOES ALSO GO UP.
WE'RE GOING UP?!
UP...AND OUT!!!

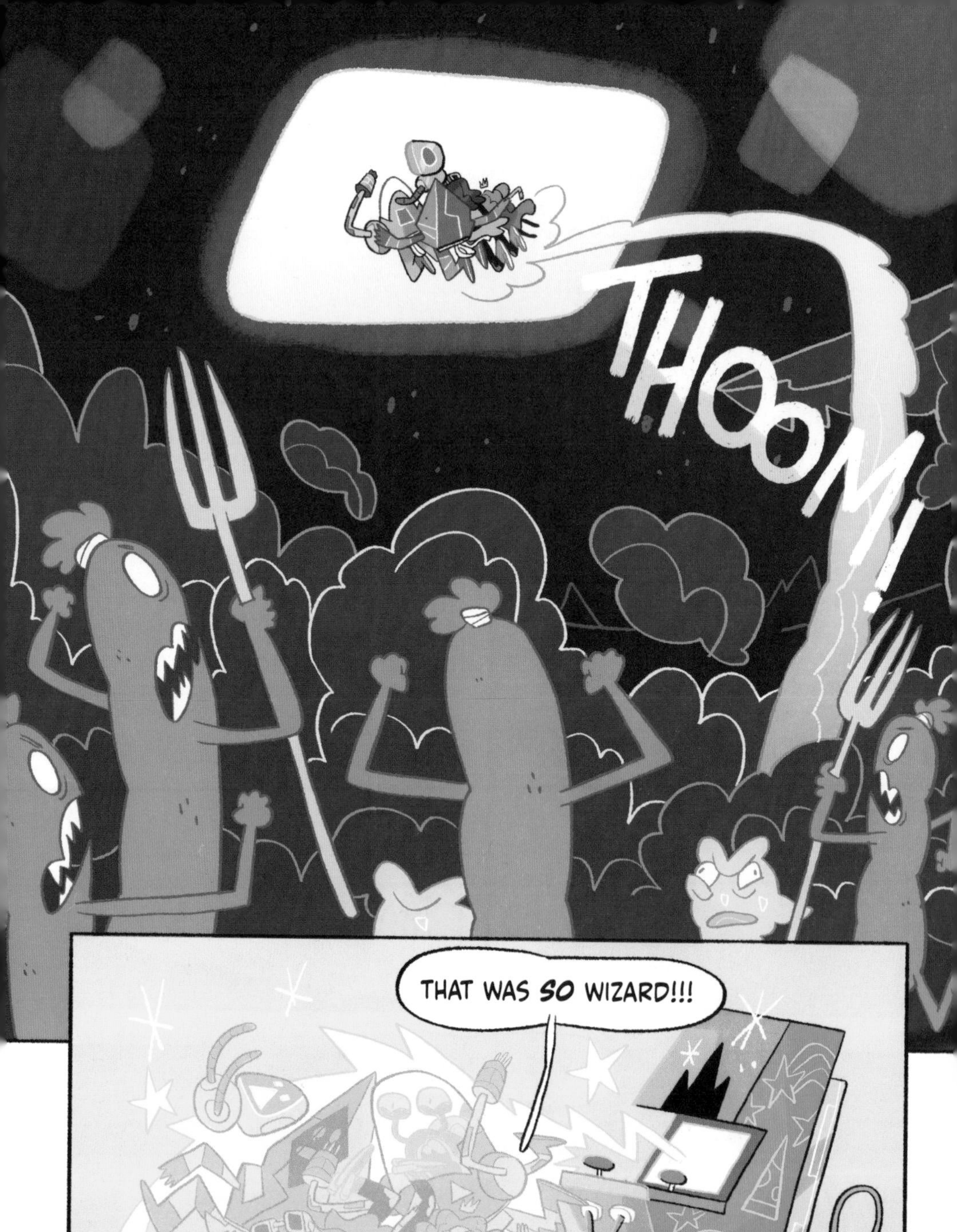
THOOM!!

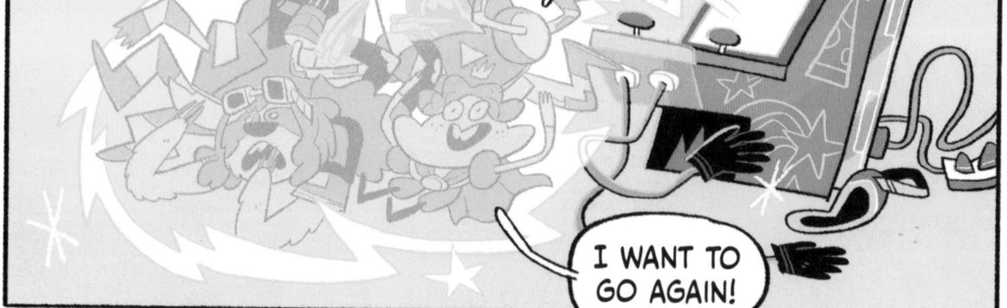
THAT WAS SO WIZARD!!!
I WANT TO GO AGAIN!

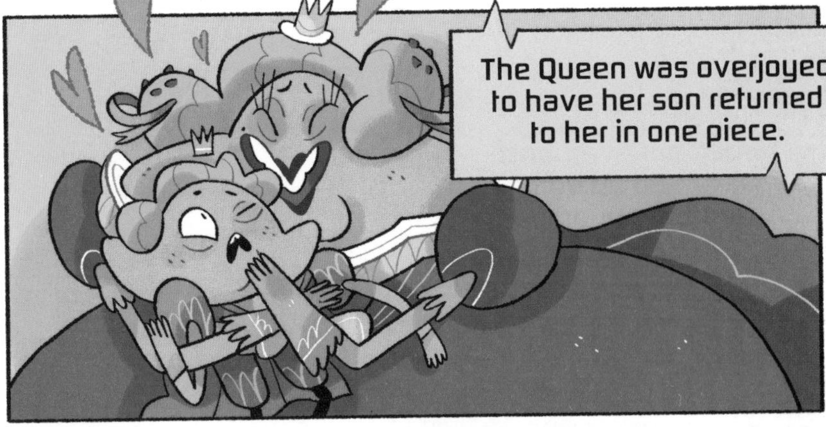
The Queen was overjoyed to have her son returned to her in one piece.

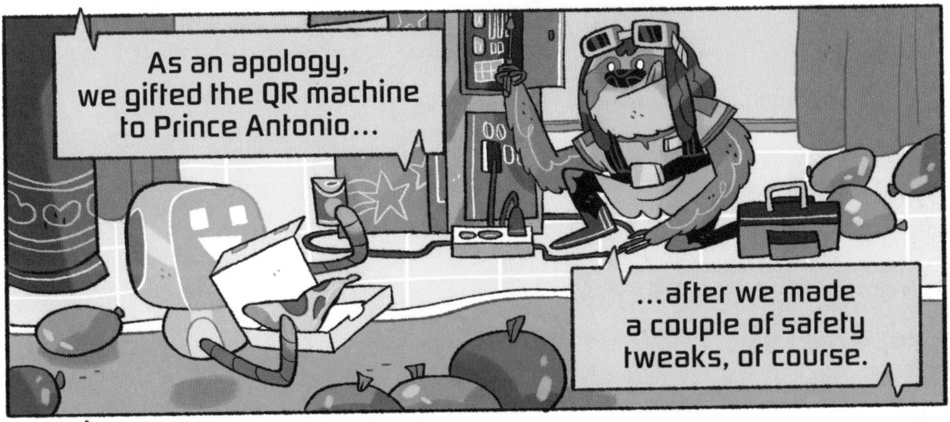
As an apology, we gifted the QR machine to Prince Antonio...
...after we made a couple of safety tweaks, of course.

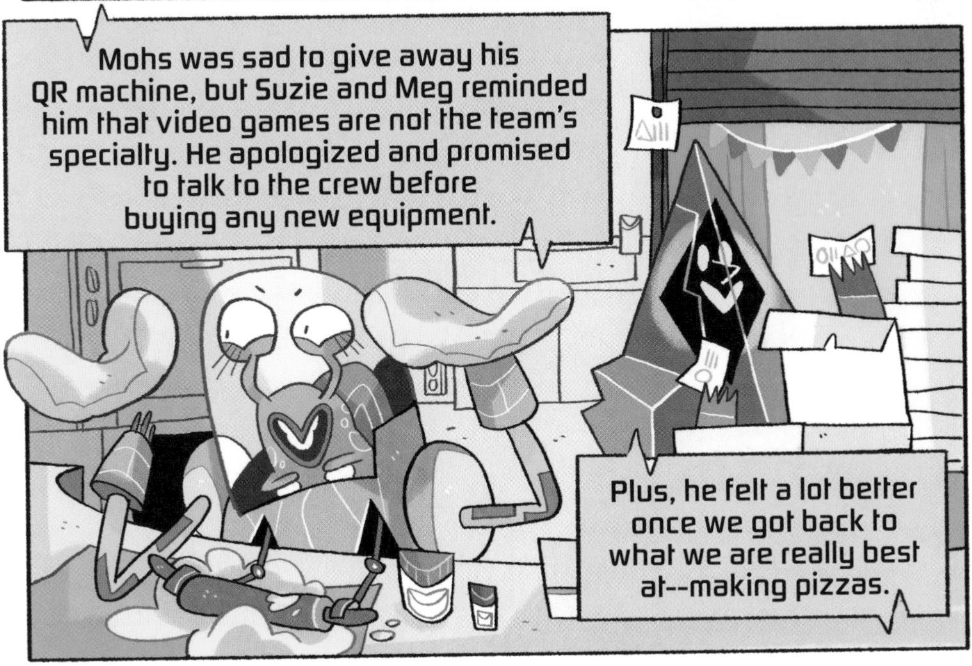
Mohs was sad to give away his QR machine, but Suzie and Meg reminded him that video games are not the team's specialty. He apologized and promised to talk to the crew before buying any new equipment.
Plus, he felt a lot better once we got back to what we are really best at--making pizzas.

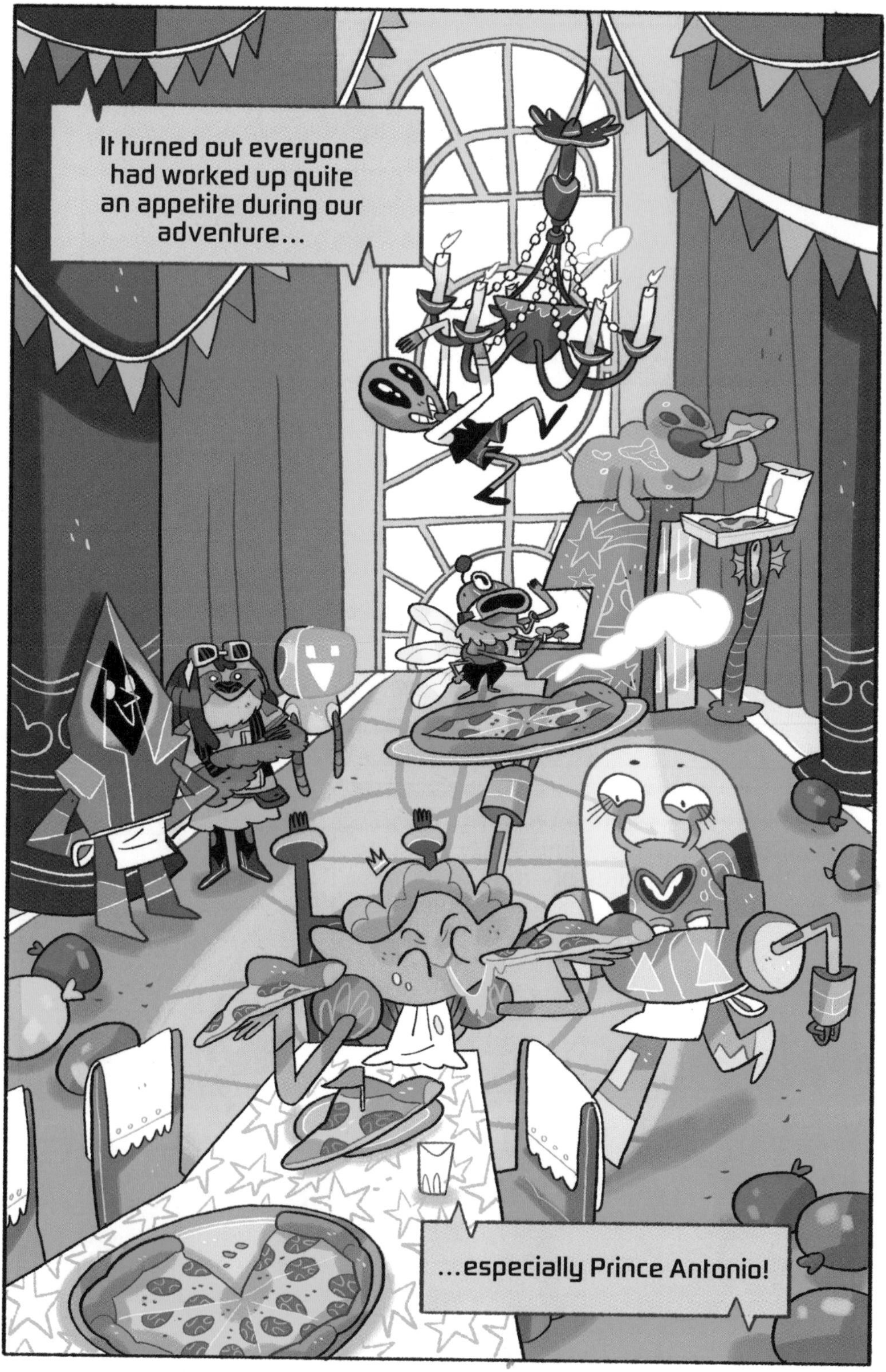
It turned out everyone had worked up quite an appetite during our adventure...
...especially Prince Antonio!

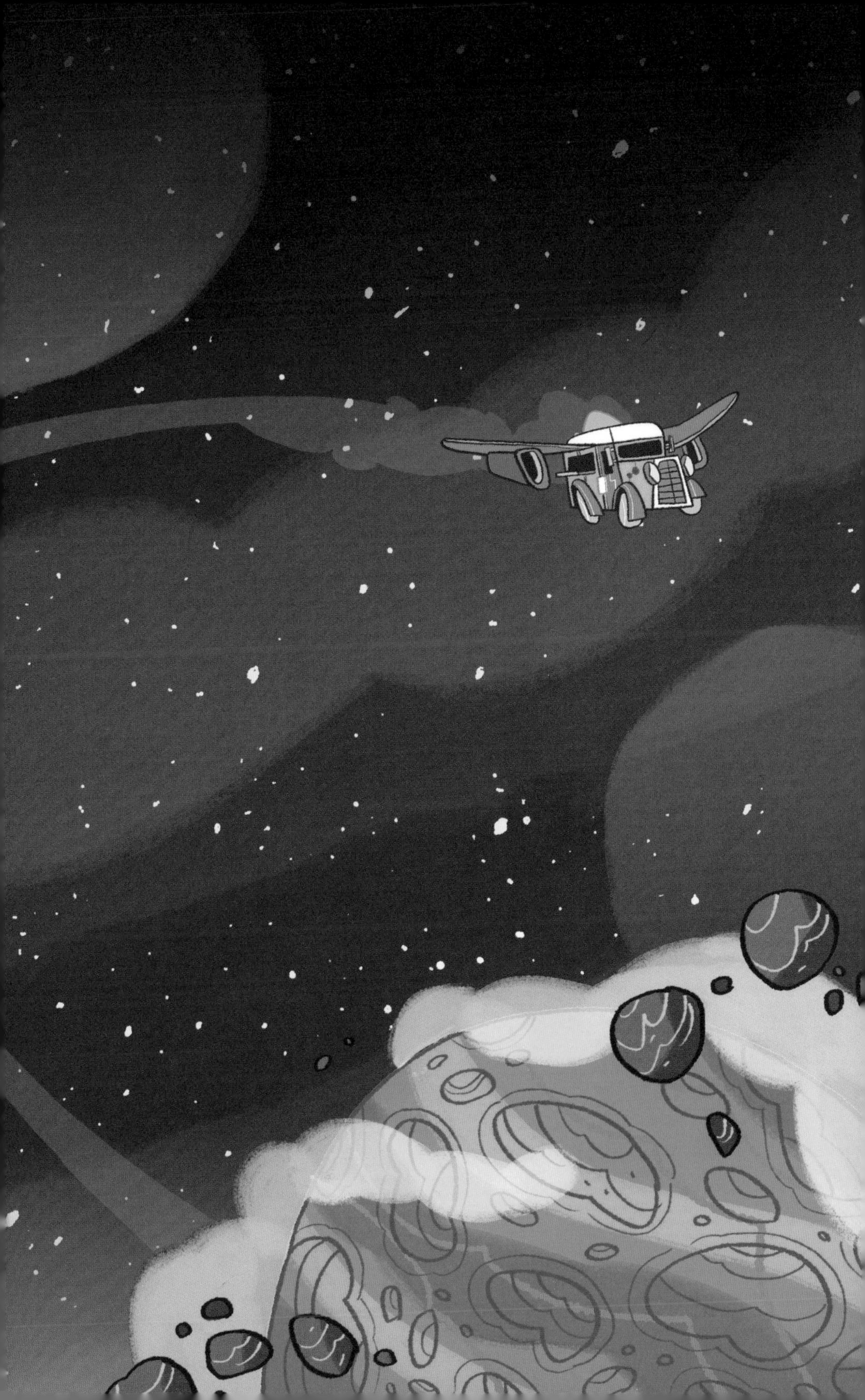

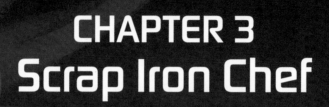

CHAPTER 3
Scrap Iron Chef

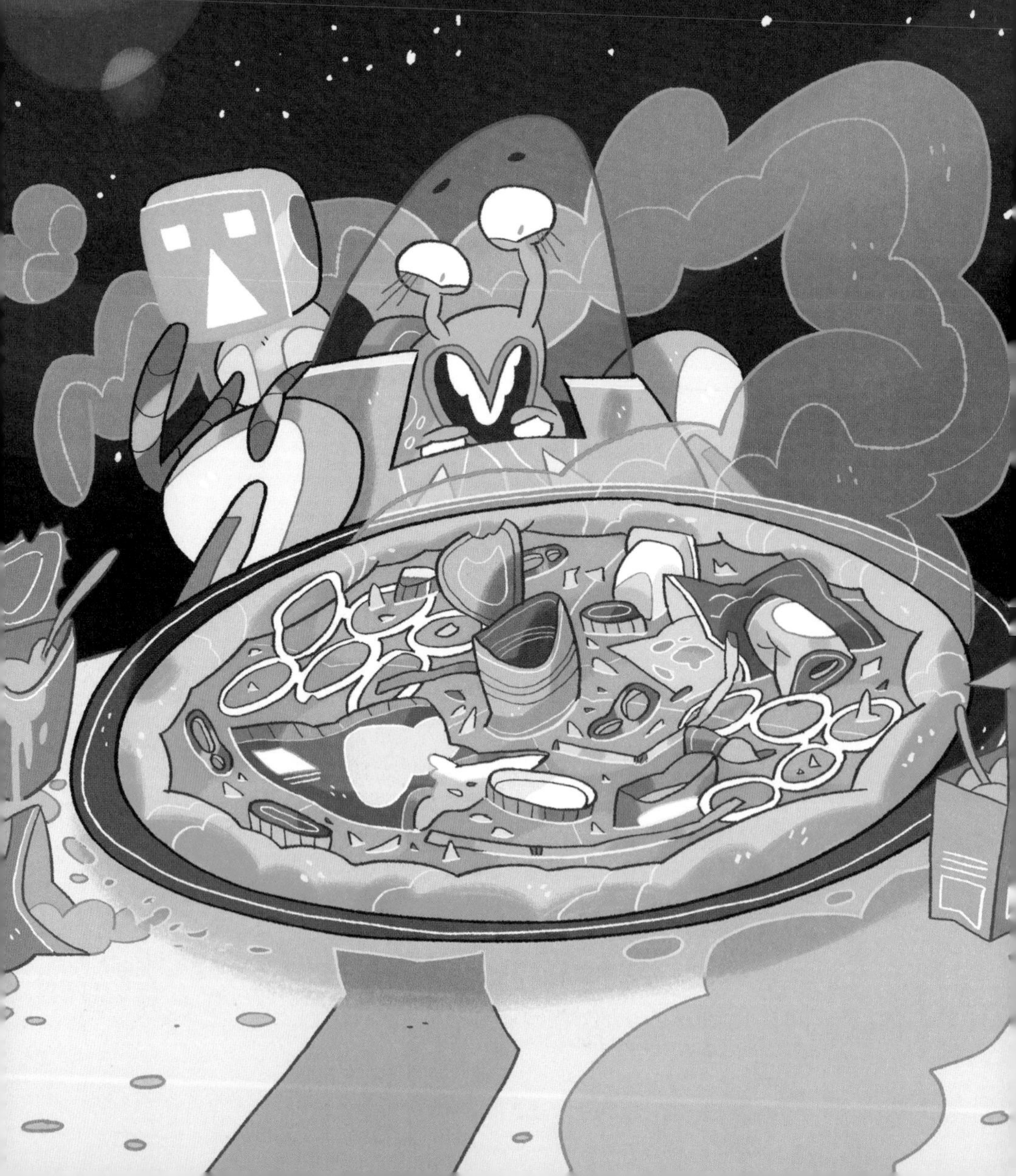

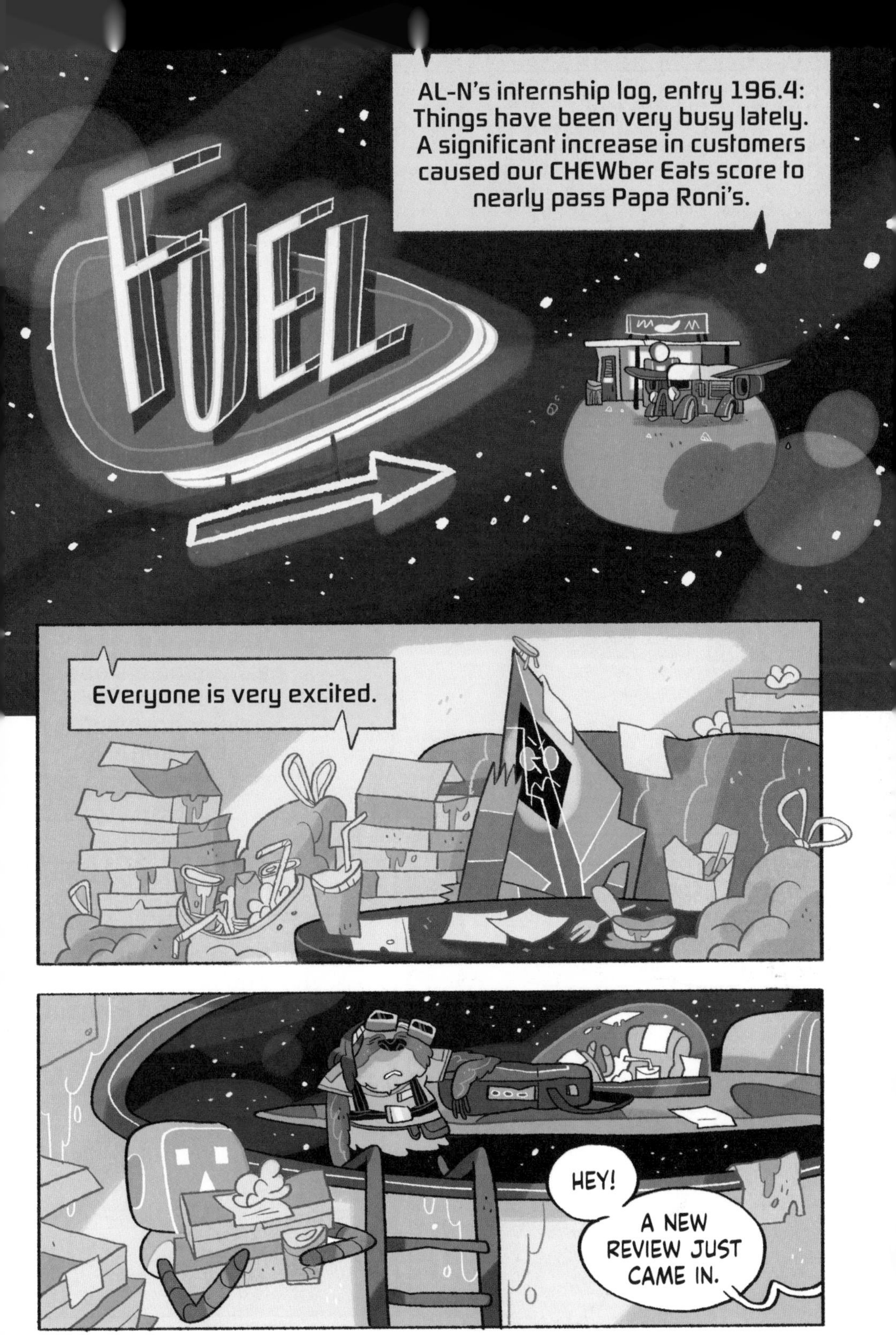
AL-N's internship log, entry 196.4: Things have been very busy lately. A significant increase in customers caused our CHEWber Eats score to nearly pass Papa Roni's.
FUEL
Everyone is very excited.
HEY!
A NEW REVIEW JUST CAME IN.

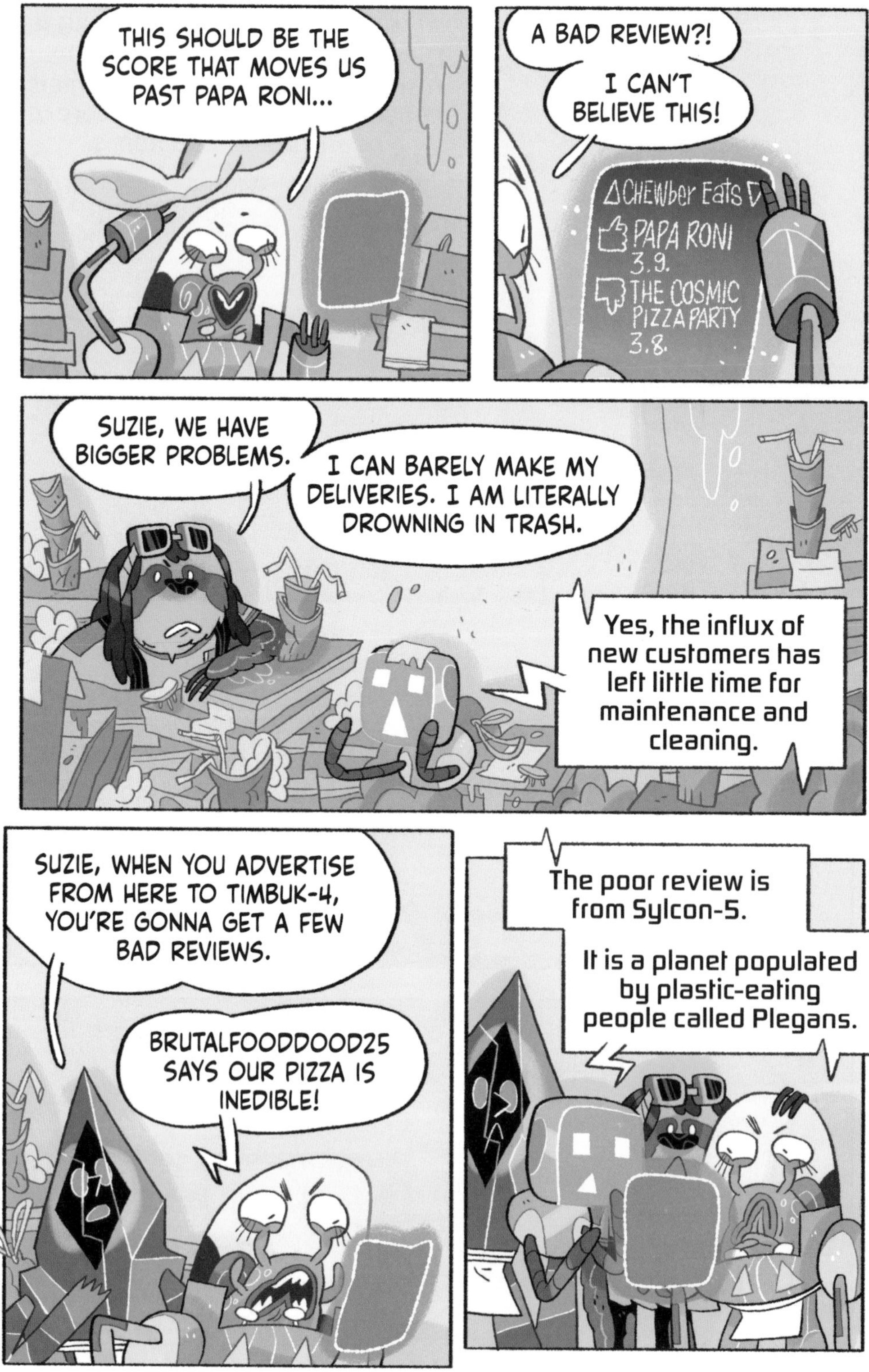
THIS SHOULD BE THE SCORE THAT MOVES US PAST PAPA RONI...
A BAD REVIEW?!
I CAN'T BELIEVE THIS!
CHEWber Eats
PAPA RONI 3.9.
THE COSMIC PIZZA PARTY 3.8.
SUZIE, WE HAVE BIGGER PROBLEMS.
I CAN BARELY MAKE MY DELIVERIES. I AM LITERALLY DROWNING IN TRASH.
Yes, the influx of new customers has left little time for maintenance and cleaning.
SUZIE, WHEN YOU ADVERTISE FROM HERE TO TIMBUK-4, YOU'RE GONNA GET A FEW BAD REVIEWS.
BRUTALFOODDOOD25 SAYS OUR PIZZA IS INEDIBLE!
The poor review is from Sylcon-5.
It is a planet populated by plastic-eating people called Plegans.

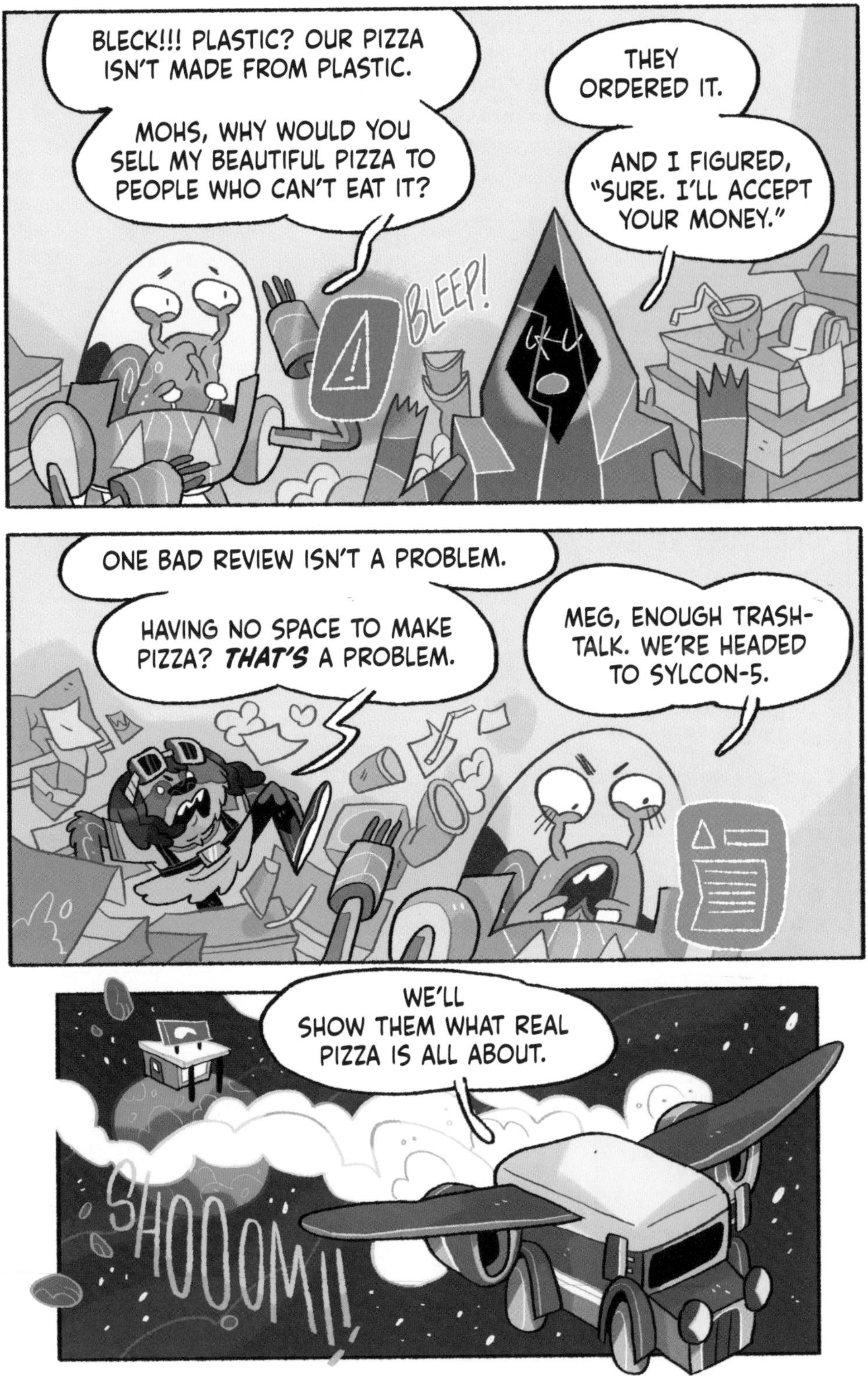
BLECK!!! PLASTIC? OUR PIZZA ISN'T MADE FROM PLASTIC.
MOHS, WHY WOULD YOU SELL MY BEAUTIFUL PIZZA TO PEOPLE WHO CAN'T EAT IT?
BLEEP!
THEY ORDERED IT.
AND I FIGURED, "SURE. I'LL ACCEPT YOUR MONEY."
ONE BAD REVIEW ISN'T A PROBLEM.
HAVING NO SPACE TO MAKE PIZZA? *THAT'S* A PROBLEM.
MEG, ENOUGH TRASH-TALK. WE'RE HEADED TO SYLCON-5.
WE'LL SHOW THEM WHAT REAL PIZZA IS ALL ABOUT.
SHOOOOM!!

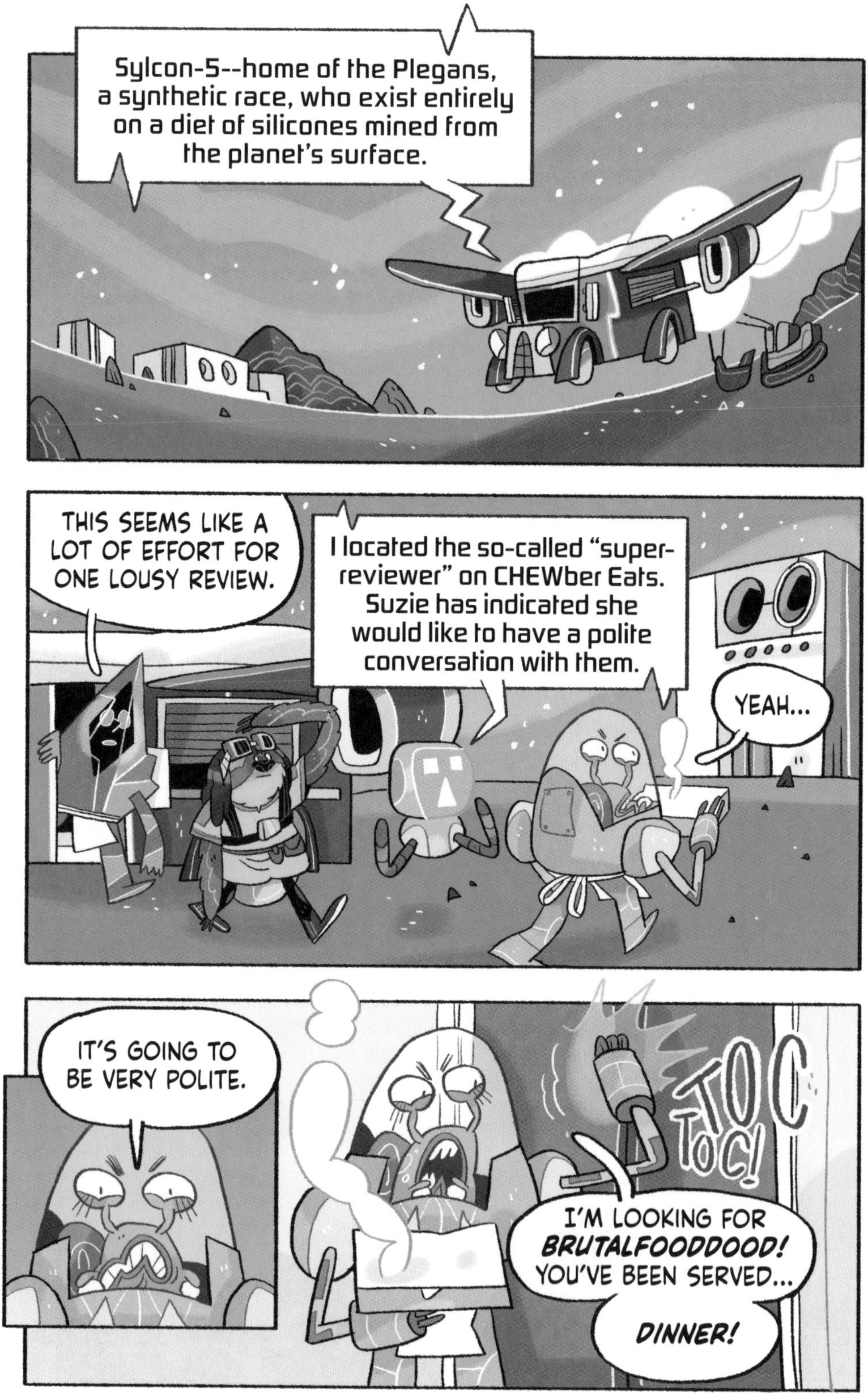
Sylcon-5--home of the Plegans, a synthetic race, who exist entirely on a diet of silicones mined from the planet's surface.
THIS SEEMS LIKE A LOT OF EFFORT FOR ONE LOUSY REVIEW.
I located the so-called "super-reviewer" on CHEWber Eats. Suzie has indicated she would like to have a polite conversation with them.
YEAH...
IT'S GOING TO BE VERY POLITE.
TOC TOC TOC!
I'M LOOKING FOR BRUTALFOODDOOD! YOU'VE BEEN SERVED...
DINNER!

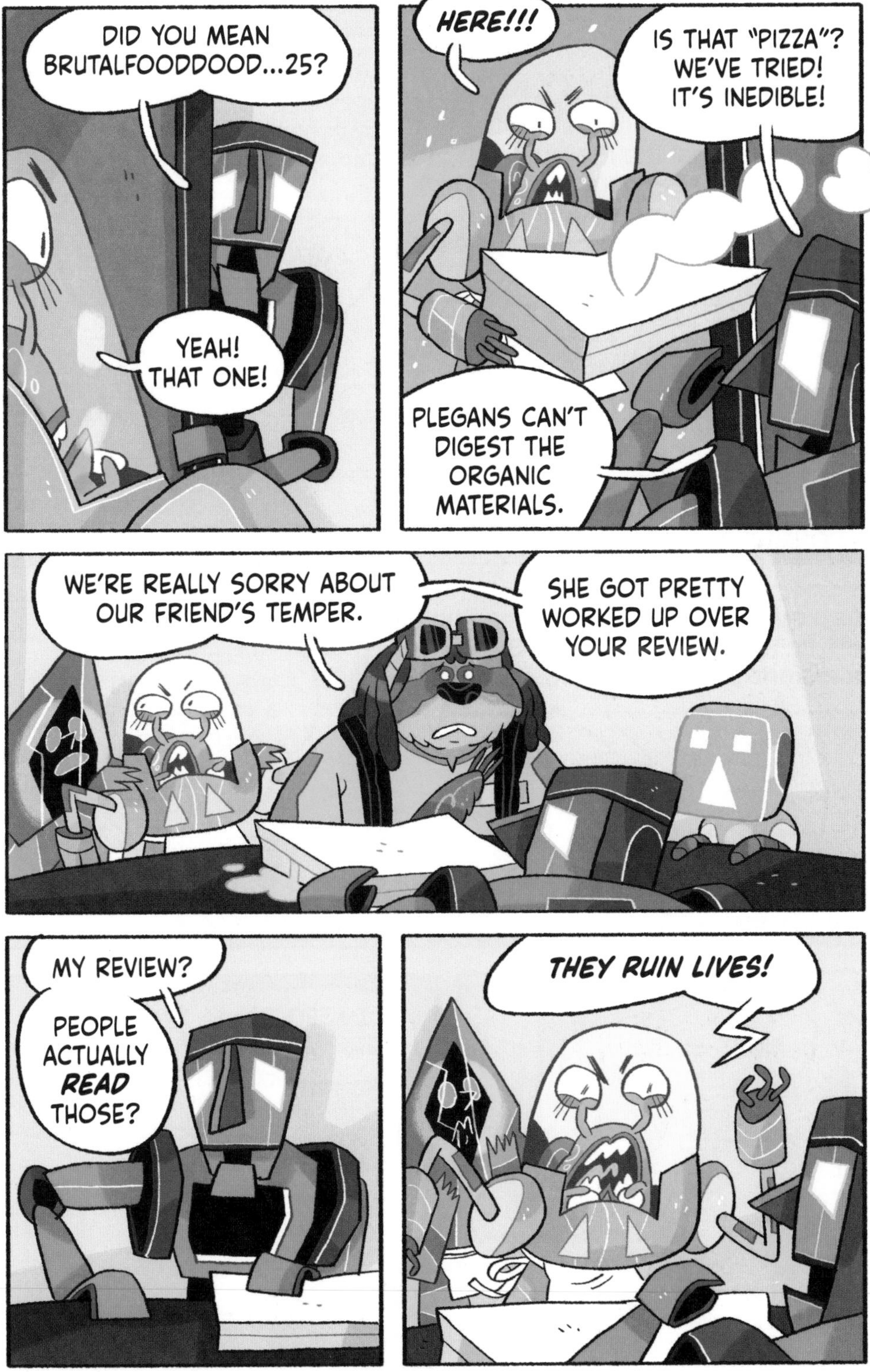
DID YOU MEAN BRUTALFOODDOOD...25?
YEAH! THAT ONE!
HERE!!!
IS THAT "PIZZA"? WE'VE TRIED! IT'S INEDIBLE!
PLEGANS CAN'T DIGEST THE ORGANIC MATERIALS.
WE'RE REALLY SORRY ABOUT OUR FRIEND'S TEMPER.
SHE GOT PRETTY WORKED UP OVER YOUR REVIEW.
MY REVIEW?
PEOPLE ACTUALLY READ THOSE?
THEY RUIN LIVES!

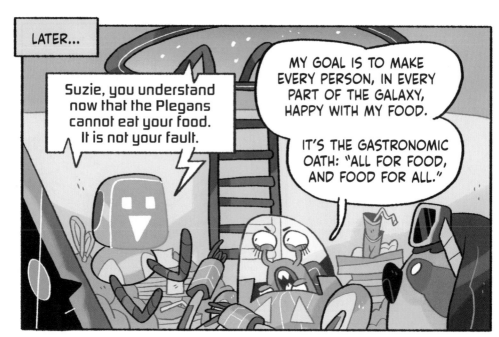

LATER...

Suzie, you understand now that the Plegans cannot eat your food. It is not your fault.

MY GOAL IS TO MAKE EVERY PERSON, IN EVERY PART OF THE GALAXY, HAPPY WITH MY FOOD.

IT'S THE GASTRONOMIC OATH: "ALL FOR FOOD, AND FOOD FOR ALL."

As a synthetic being, I am sympathetic to the Plegans' complaints. But I also understand Suzie's desire to please them.

WELL, MAYBE WE FOCUS ON A PROBLEM WE CAN SOLVE?

LIKE CLEANING UP OUR SHIP.

FST...UH-UUFF

RIGHT, SUZIE?

SUZIE!?

I NEED TO CLEAR MY HEAD.

58

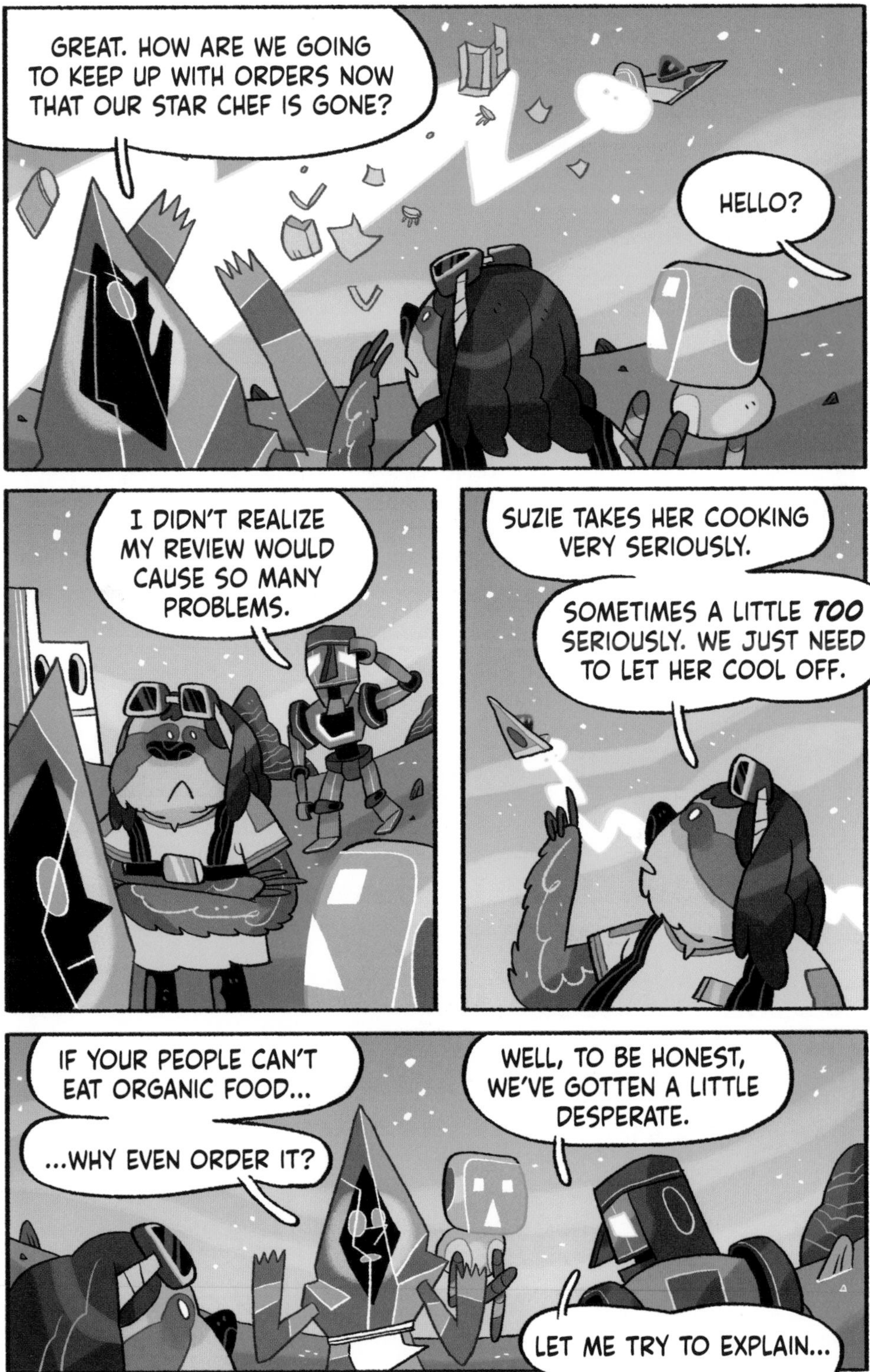
GREAT. HOW ARE WE GOING TO KEEP UP WITH ORDERS NOW THAT OUR STAR CHEF IS GONE?
HELLO?
I DIDN'T REALIZE MY REVIEW WOULD CAUSE SO MANY PROBLEMS.
SUZIE TAKES HER COOKING VERY SERIOUSLY.
SOMETIMES A LITTLE ***TOO*** SERIOUSLY. WE JUST NEED TO LET HER COOL OFF.
IF YOUR PEOPLE CAN'T EAT ORGANIC FOOD...
...WHY EVEN ORDER IT?
WELL, TO BE HONEST, WE'VE GOTTEN A LITTLE DESPERATE.
LET ME TRY TO EXPLAIN...

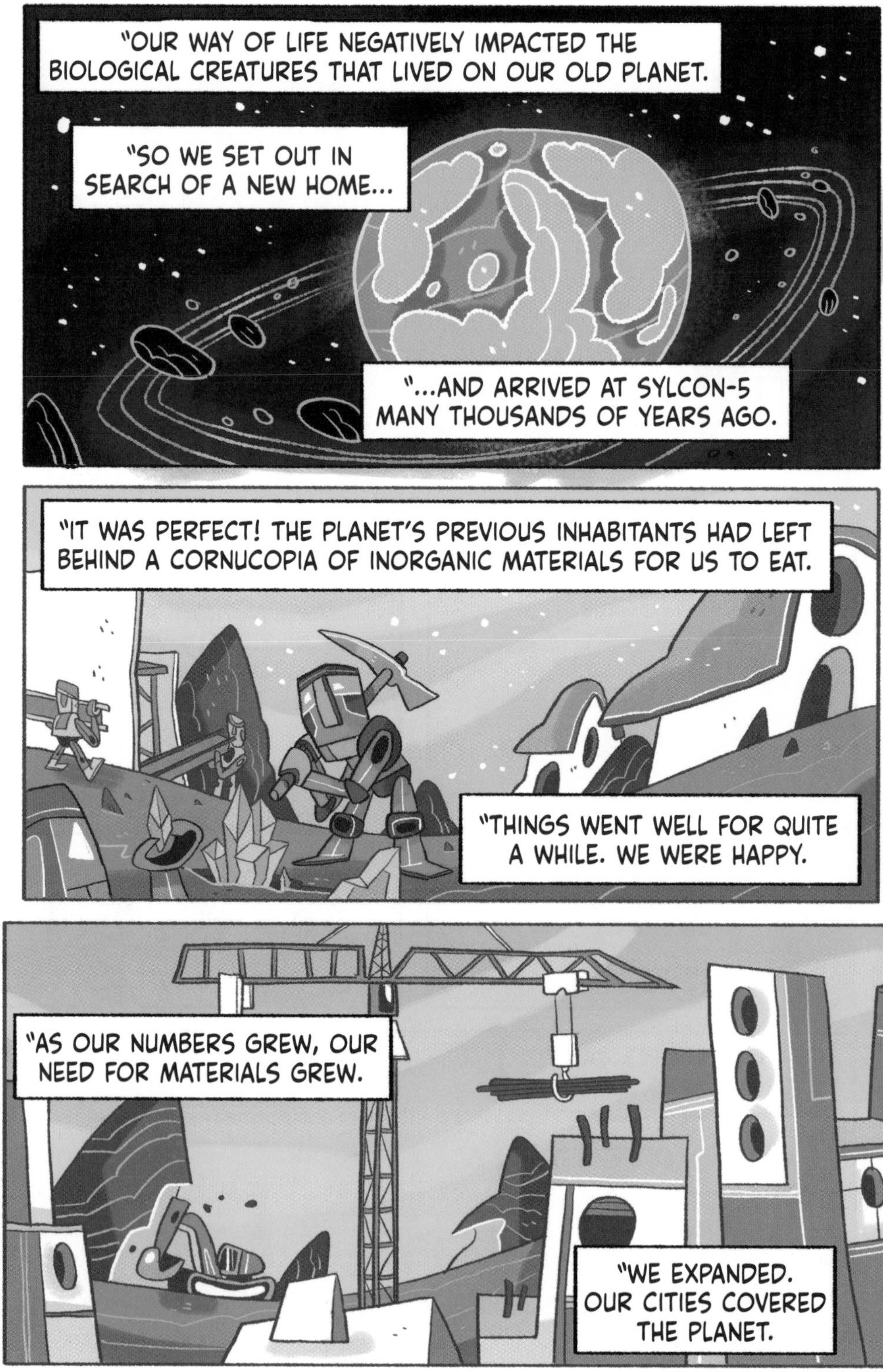
"OUR WAY OF LIFE NEGATIVELY IMPACTED THE BIOLOGICAL CREATURES THAT LIVED ON OUR OLD PLANET.
"SO WE SET OUT IN SEARCH OF A NEW HOME...
"...AND ARRIVED AT SYLCON-5 MANY THOUSANDS OF YEARS AGO.
"IT WAS PERFECT! THE PLANET'S PREVIOUS INHABITANTS HAD LEFT BEHIND A CORNUCOPIA OF INORGANIC MATERIALS FOR US TO EAT.
"THINGS WENT WELL FOR QUITE A WHILE. WE WERE HAPPY.
"AS OUR NUMBERS GREW, OUR NEED FOR MATERIALS GREW.
"WE EXPANDED. OUR CITIES COVERED THE PLANET.

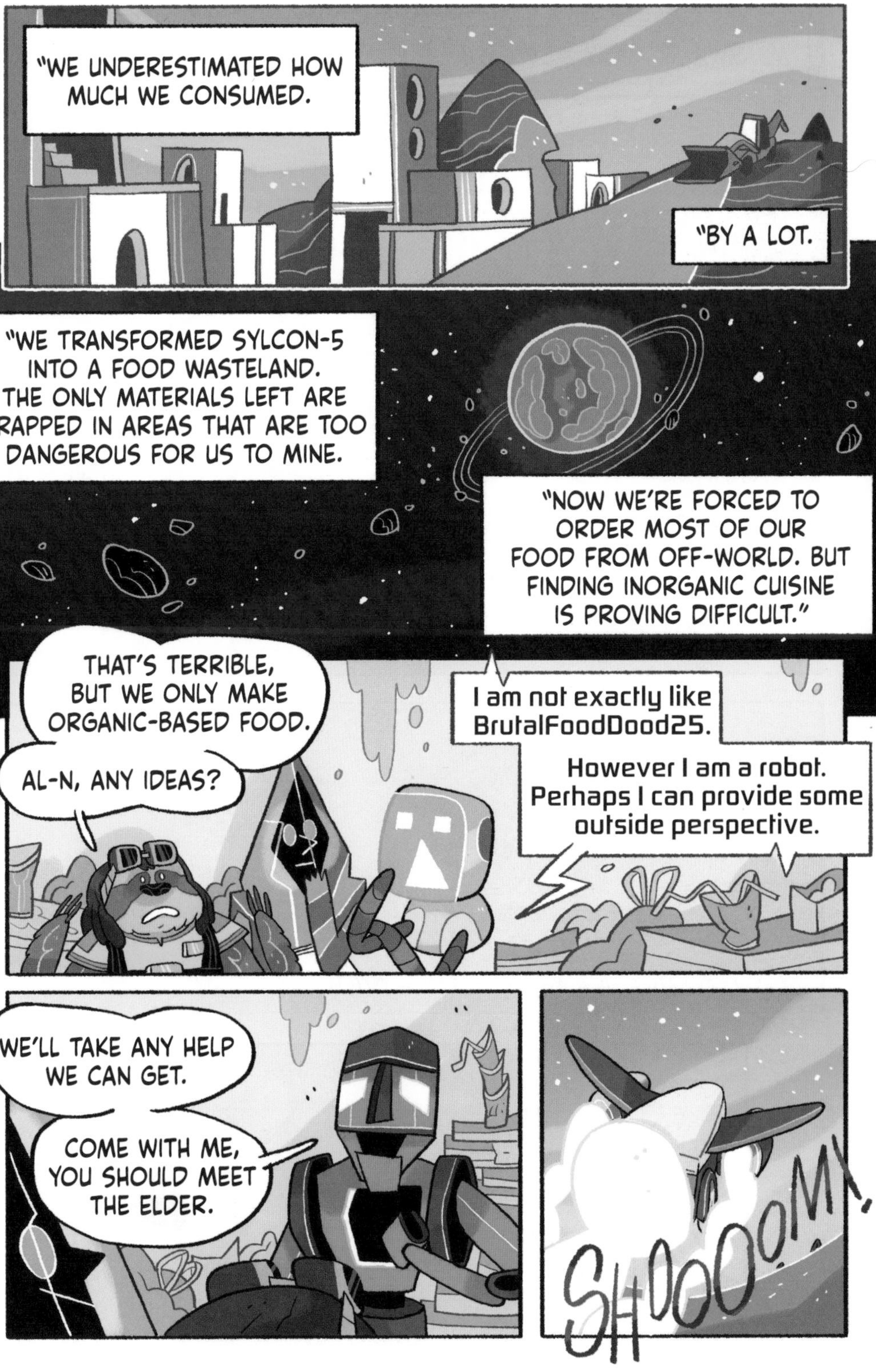
"WE UNDERESTIMATED HOW MUCH WE CONSUMED.
"BY A LOT.
"WE TRANSFORMED SYLCON-5 INTO A FOOD WASTELAND. THE ONLY MATERIALS LEFT ARE TRAPPED IN AREAS THAT ARE TOO DANGEROUS FOR US TO MINE.
"NOW WE'RE FORCED TO ORDER MOST OF OUR FOOD FROM OFF-WORLD. BUT FINDING INORGANIC CUISINE IS PROVING DIFFICULT."
THAT'S TERRIBLE, BUT WE ONLY MAKE ORGANIC-BASED FOOD.
AL-N, ANY IDEAS?
I am not exactly like BrutalFoodDood25.
However I am a robot. Perhaps I can provide some outside perspective.
WE'LL TAKE ANY HELP WE CAN GET.
COME WITH ME, YOU SHOULD MEET THE ELDER.
SHOOOOM!

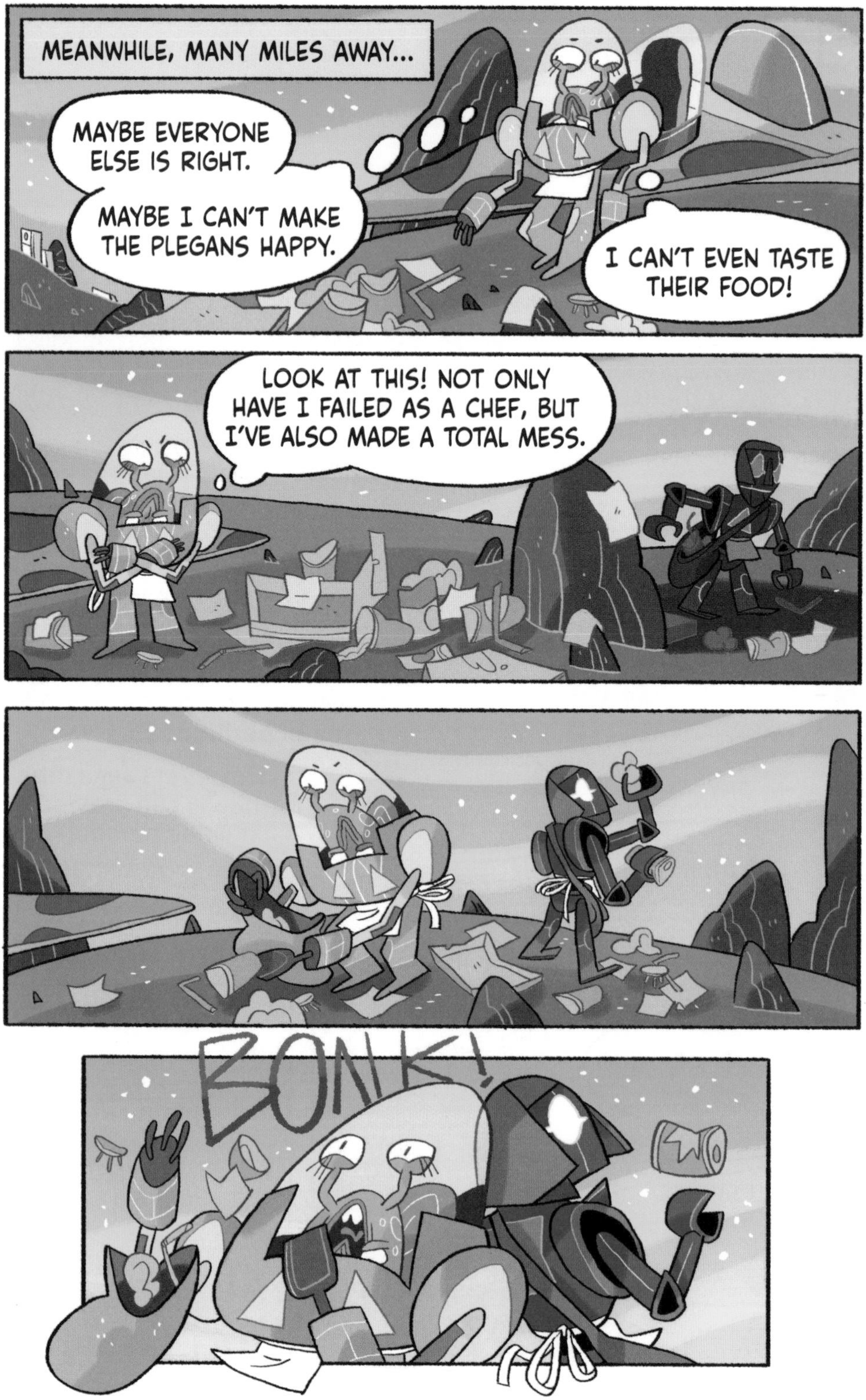
MEANWHILE, MANY MILES AWAY...
MAYBE EVERYONE ELSE IS RIGHT.
MAYBE I CAN'T MAKE THE PLEGANS HAPPY.
I CAN'T EVEN TASTE THEIR FOOD!
LOOK AT THIS! NOT ONLY HAVE I FAILED AS A CHEF, BUT I'VE ALSO MADE A TOTAL MESS.
BONK!

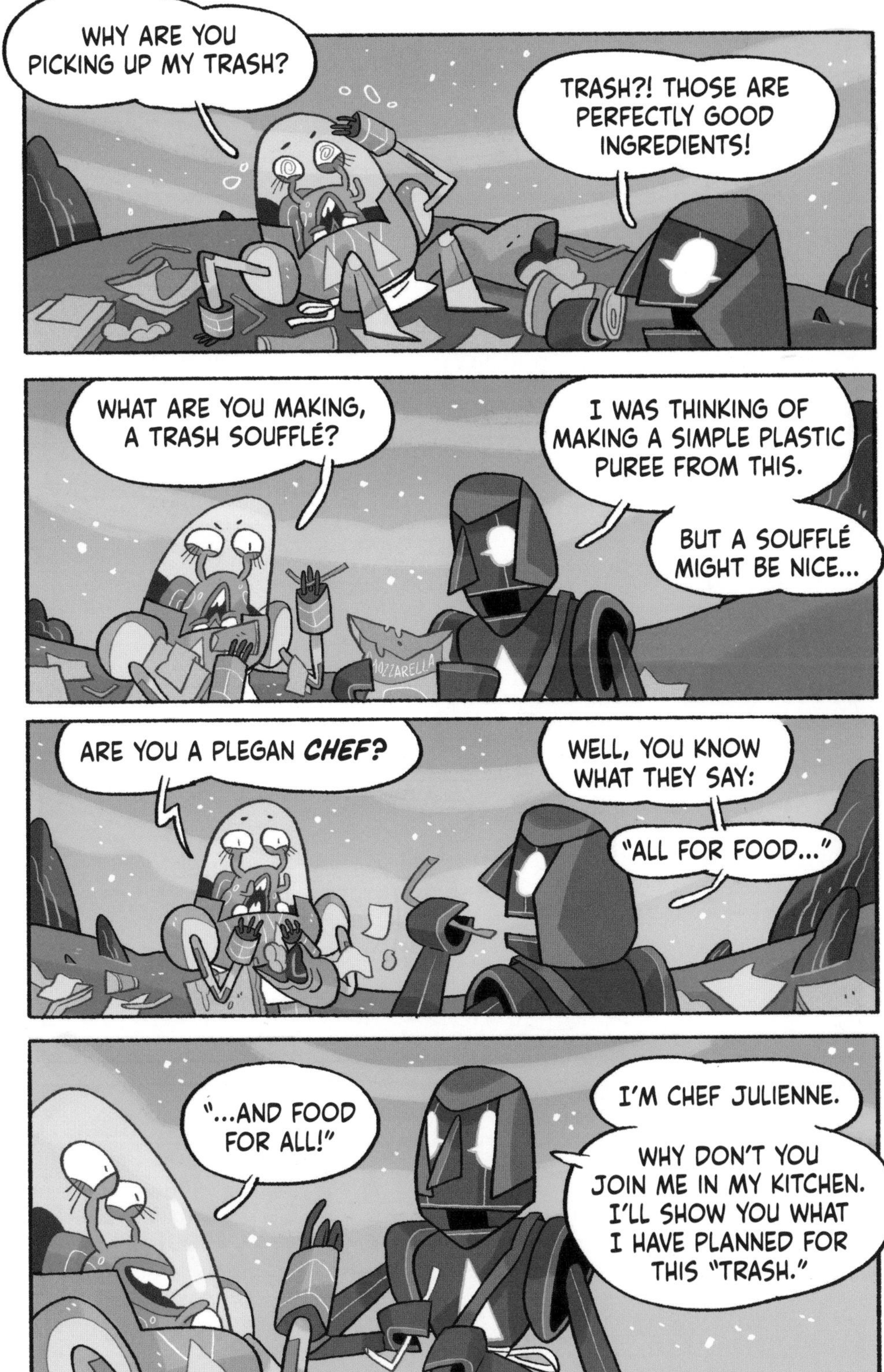
WHY ARE YOU PICKING UP MY TRASH?
TRASH?! THOSE ARE PERFECTLY GOOD INGREDIENTS!
WHAT ARE YOU MAKING, A TRASH SOUFFLÉ?
I WAS THINKING OF MAKING A SIMPLE PLASTIC PUREE FROM THIS.
BUT A SOUFFLÉ MIGHT BE NICE...
MOZZARELLA
ARE YOU A PLEGAN ***CHEF?***
WELL, YOU KNOW WHAT THEY SAY:
"ALL FOR FOOD..."
"...AND FOOD FOR ALL!"
I'M CHEF JULIENNE.
WHY DON'T YOU JOIN ME IN MY KITCHEN. I'LL SHOW YOU WHAT I HAVE PLANNED FOR THIS "TRASH."

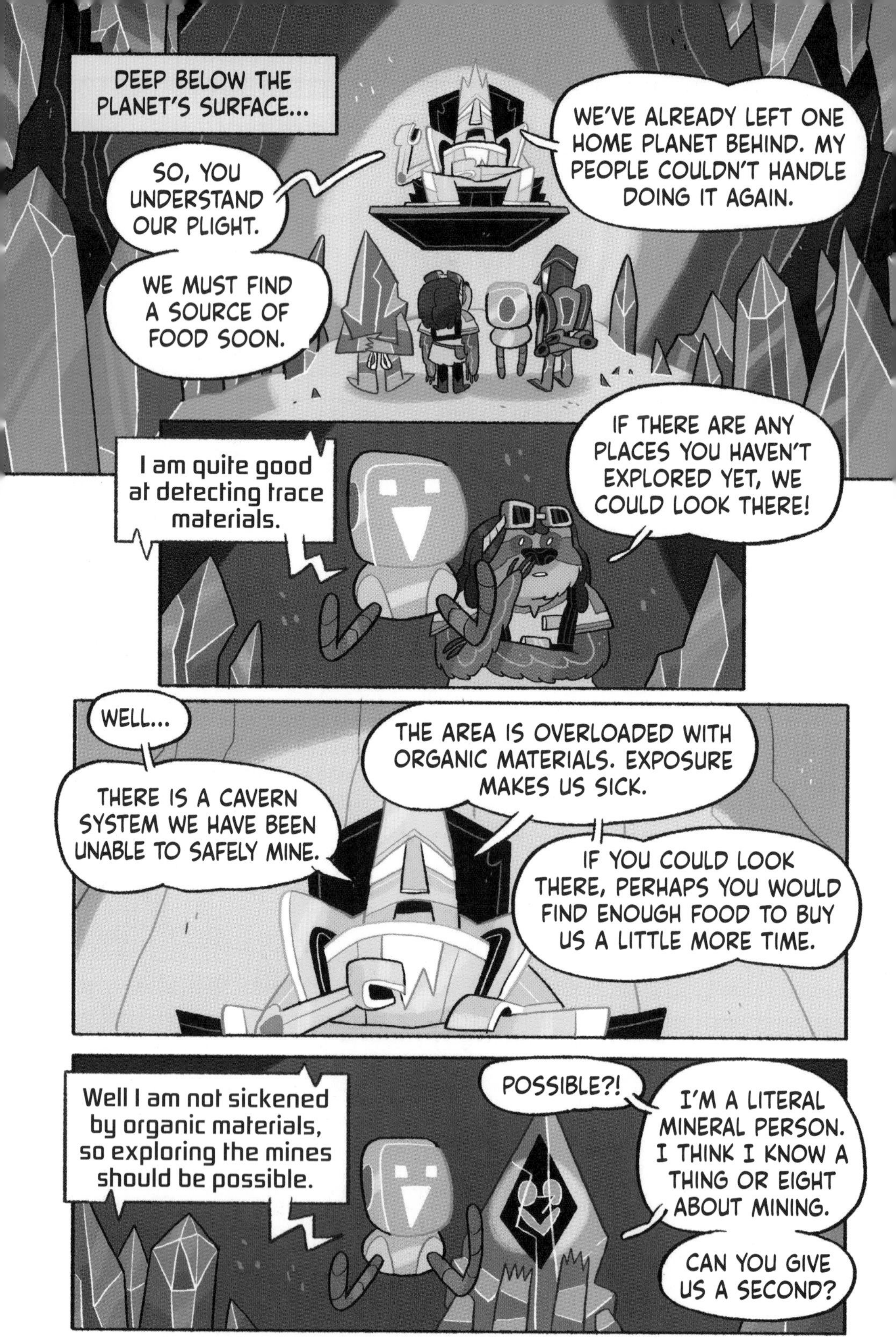
DEEP BELOW THE PLANET'S SURFACE...
SO, YOU UNDERSTAND OUR PLIGHT.
WE MUST FIND A SOURCE OF FOOD SOON.
WE'VE ALREADY LEFT ONE HOME PLANET BEHIND. MY PEOPLE COULDN'T HANDLE DOING IT AGAIN.
I am quite good at detecting trace materials.
IF THERE ARE ANY PLACES YOU HAVEN'T EXPLORED YET, WE COULD LOOK THERE!
WELL...
THERE IS A CAVERN SYSTEM WE HAVE BEEN UNABLE TO SAFELY MINE.
THE AREA IS OVERLOADED WITH ORGANIC MATERIALS. EXPOSURE MAKES US SICK.
IF YOU COULD LOOK THERE, PERHAPS YOU WOULD FIND ENOUGH FOOD TO BUY US A LITTLE MORE TIME.
Well I am not sickened by organic materials, so exploring the mines should be possible.
POSSIBLE?!
I'M A LITERAL MINERAL PERSON. I THINK I KNOW A THING OR EIGHT ABOUT MINING.
CAN YOU GIVE US A SECOND?

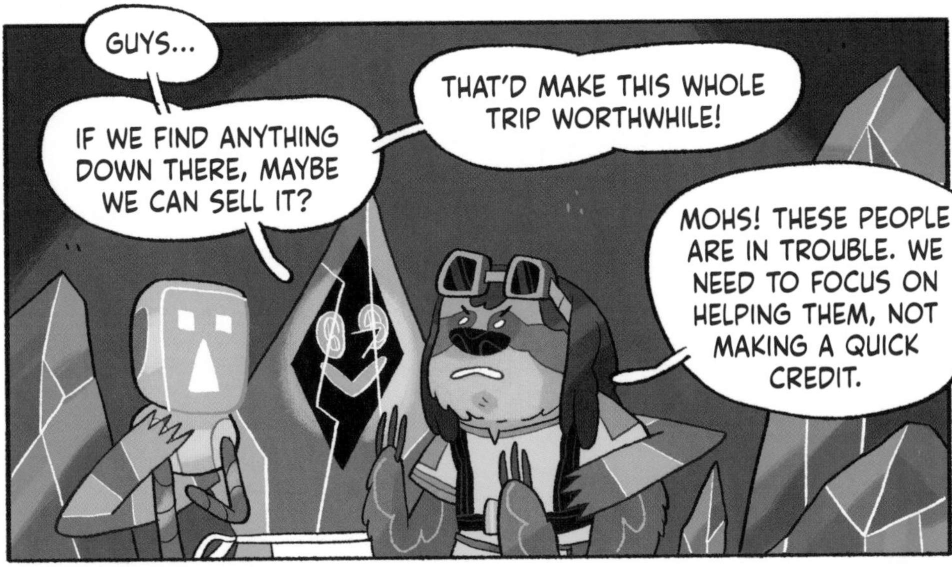
GUYS...
IF WE FIND ANYTHING DOWN THERE, MAYBE WE CAN SELL IT?
THAT'D MAKE THIS WHOLE TRIP WORTHWHILE!
MOHS! THESE PEOPLE ARE IN TROUBLE. WE NEED TO FOCUS ON HELPING THEM, NOT MAKING A QUICK CREDIT.

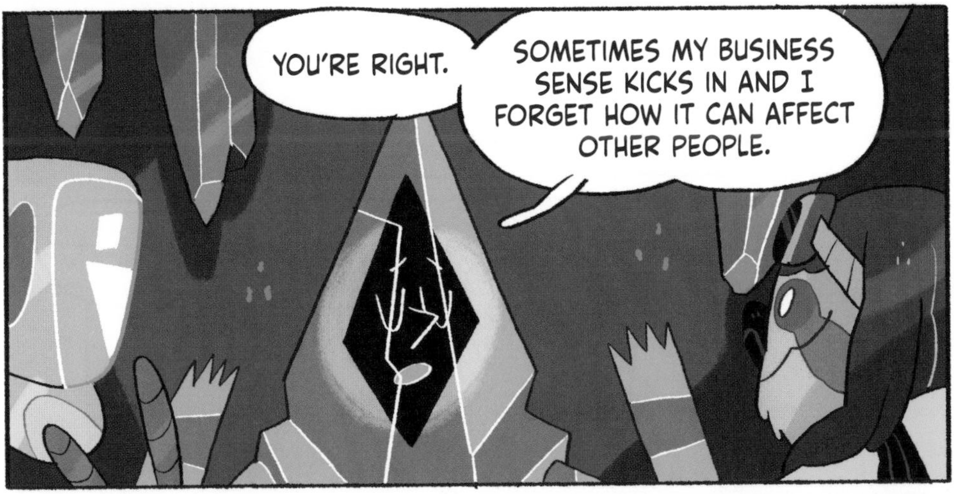
YOU'RE RIGHT.
SOMETIMES MY BUSINESS SENSE KICKS IN AND I FORGET HOW IT CAN AFFECT OTHER PEOPLE.

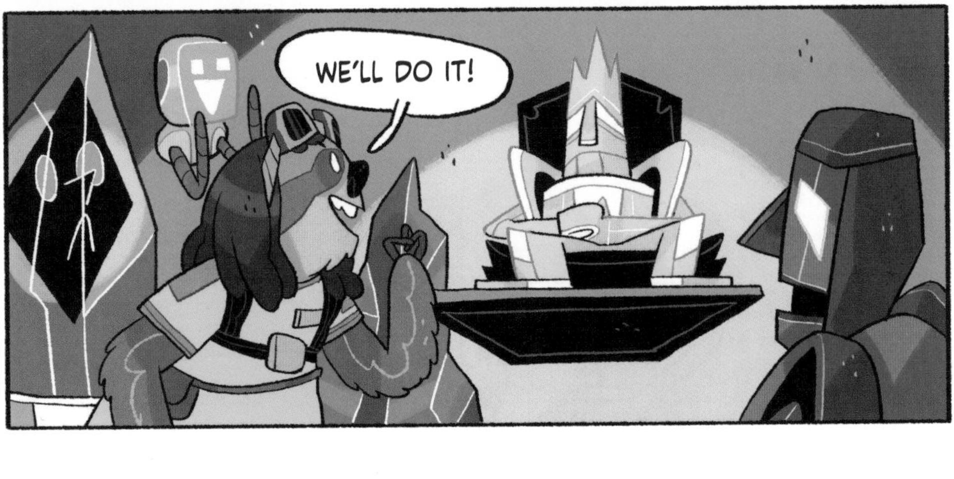
WE'LL DO IT!

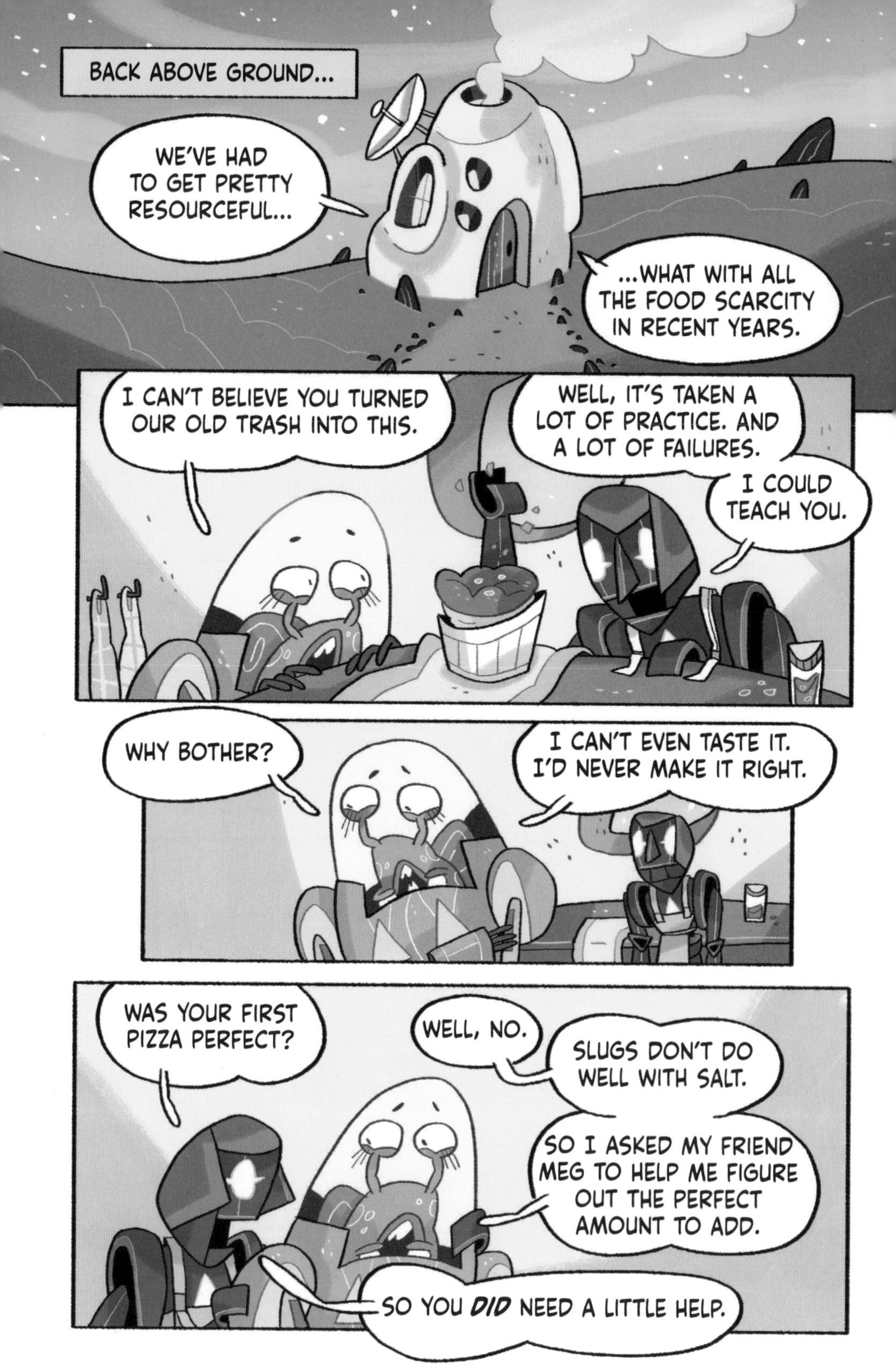
BACK ABOVE GROUND...
WE'VE HAD TO GET PRETTY RESOURCEFUL...
...WHAT WITH ALL THE FOOD SCARCITY IN RECENT YEARS.
I CAN'T BELIEVE YOU TURNED OUR OLD TRASH INTO THIS.
WELL, IT'S TAKEN A LOT OF PRACTICE. AND A LOT OF FAILURES.
I COULD TEACH YOU.
WHY BOTHER?
I CAN'T EVEN TASTE IT. I'D NEVER MAKE IT RIGHT.
WAS YOUR FIRST PIZZA PERFECT?
WELL, NO.
SLUGS DON'T DO WELL WITH SALT.
SO I ASKED MY FRIEND MEG TO HELP ME FIGURE OUT THE PERFECT AMOUNT TO ADD.
SO YOU *DID* NEED A LITTLE HELP.

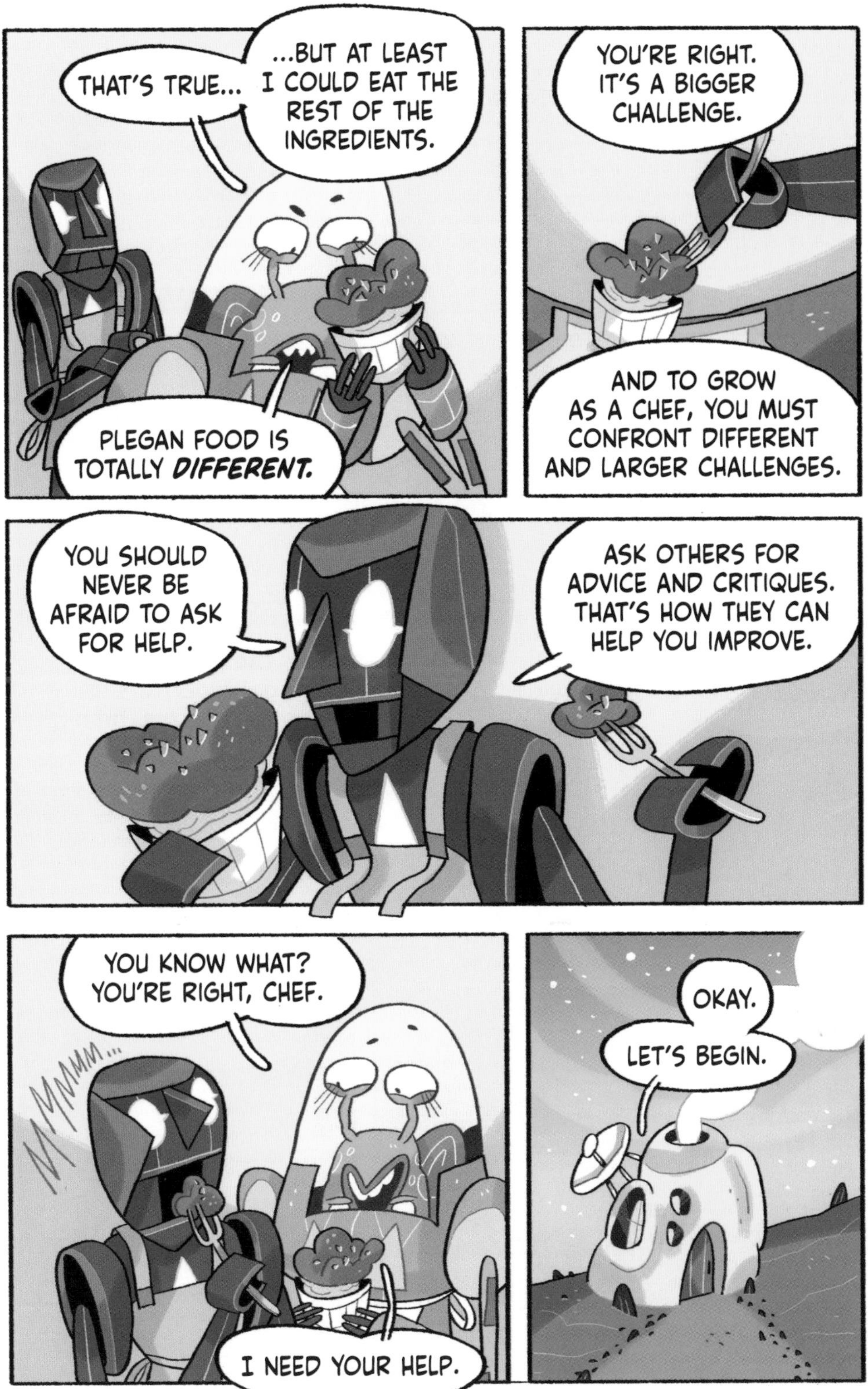
THAT'S TRUE...
...BUT AT LEAST I COULD EAT THE REST OF THE INGREDIENTS.
PLEGAN FOOD IS TOTALLY *DIFFERENT.*
YOU'RE RIGHT. IT'S A BIGGER CHALLENGE.
AND TO GROW AS A CHEF, YOU MUST CONFRONT DIFFERENT AND LARGER CHALLENGES.
YOU SHOULD NEVER BE AFRAID TO ASK FOR HELP.
ASK OTHERS FOR ADVICE AND CRITIQUES. THAT'S HOW THEY CAN HELP YOU IMPROVE.
YOU KNOW WHAT? YOU'RE RIGHT, CHEF.
MMMMM...
I NEED YOUR HELP.
OKAY.
LET'S BEGIN.

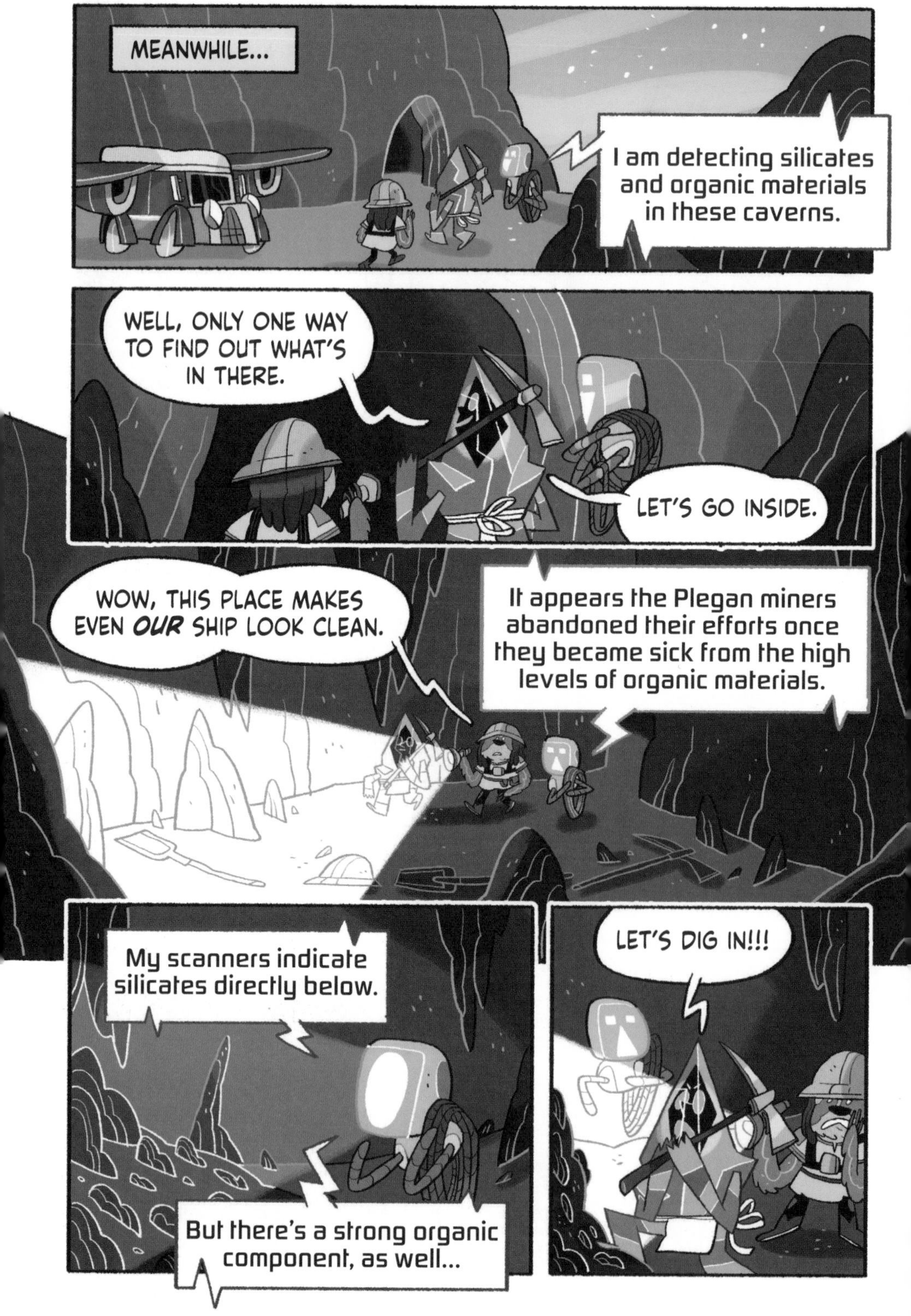
MEANWHILE...
I am detecting silicates and organic materials in these caverns.
WELL, ONLY ONE WAY TO FIND OUT WHAT'S IN THERE.
LET'S GO INSIDE.
WOW, THIS PLACE MAKES EVEN *OUR* SHIP LOOK CLEAN.
It appears the Plegan miners abandoned their efforts once they became sick from the high levels of organic materials.
My scanners indicate silicates directly below.
But there's a strong organic component, as well...
LET'S DIG IN!!!

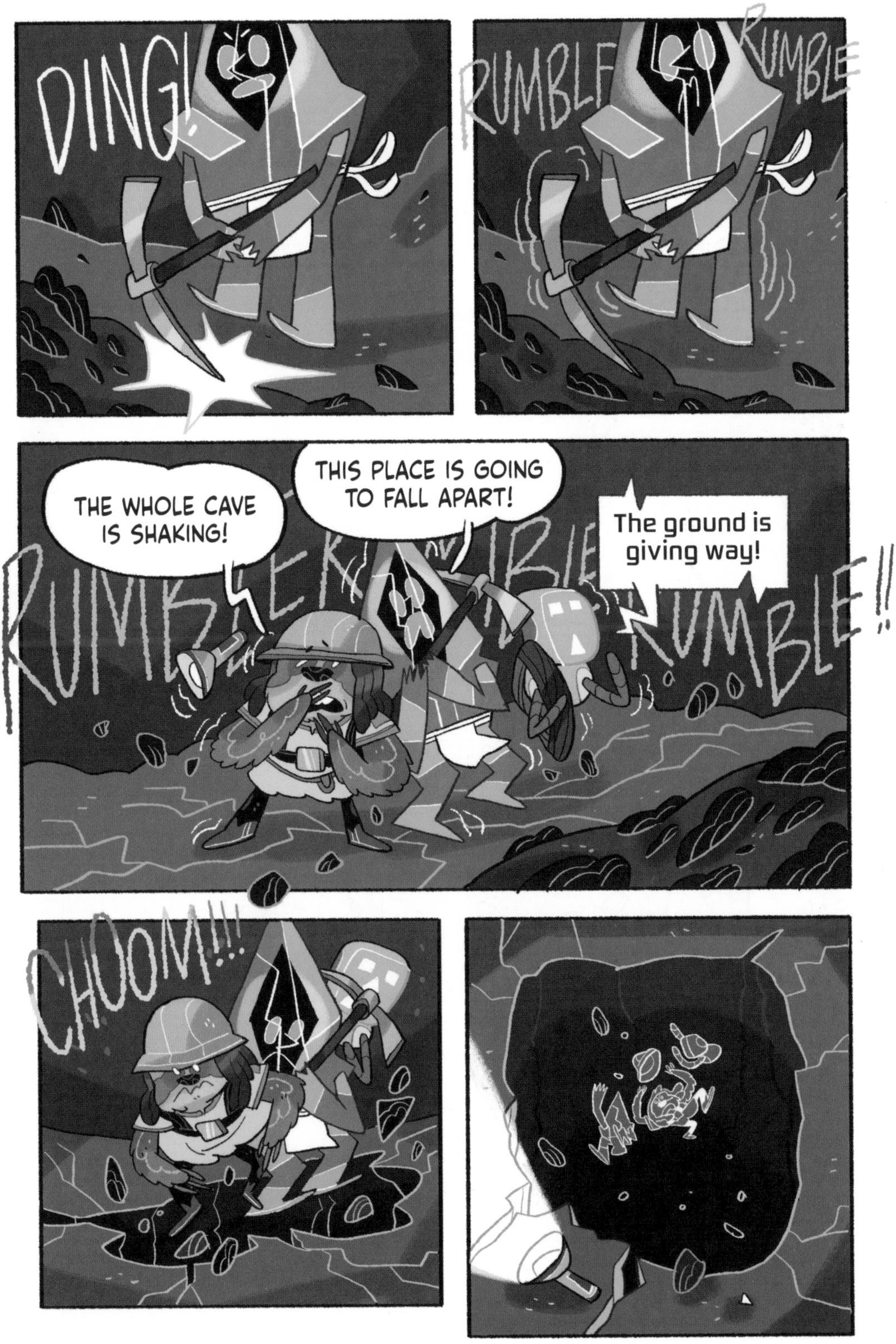
DING!
RUMBLF
RUMBLE
THE WHOLE CAVE IS SHAKING!
THIS PLACE IS GOING TO FALL APART!
The ground is giving way!
RUMBLE!!
CHOOM!!!

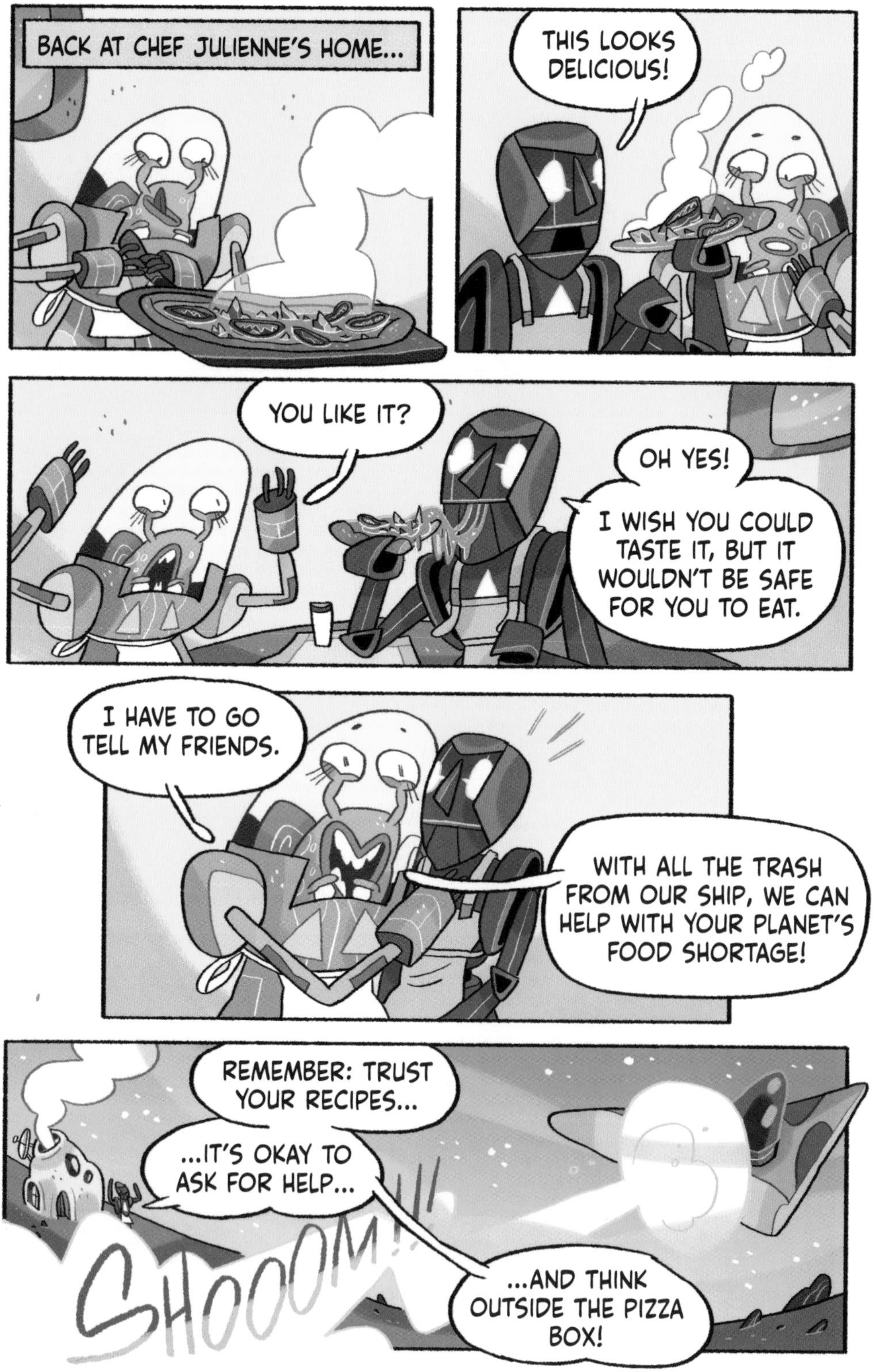
BACK AT CHEF JULIENNE'S HOME...
THIS LOOKS DELICIOUS!
YOU LIKE IT?
OH YES!
I WISH YOU COULD TASTE IT, BUT IT WOULDN'T BE SAFE FOR YOU TO EAT.
I HAVE TO GO TELL MY FRIENDS.
WITH ALL THE TRASH FROM OUR SHIP, WE CAN HELP WITH YOUR PLANET'S FOOD SHORTAGE!
REMEMBER: TRUST YOUR RECIPES...
...IT'S OKAY TO ASK FOR HELP...
SHOOOM!!
...AND THINK OUTSIDE THE PIZZA BOX!

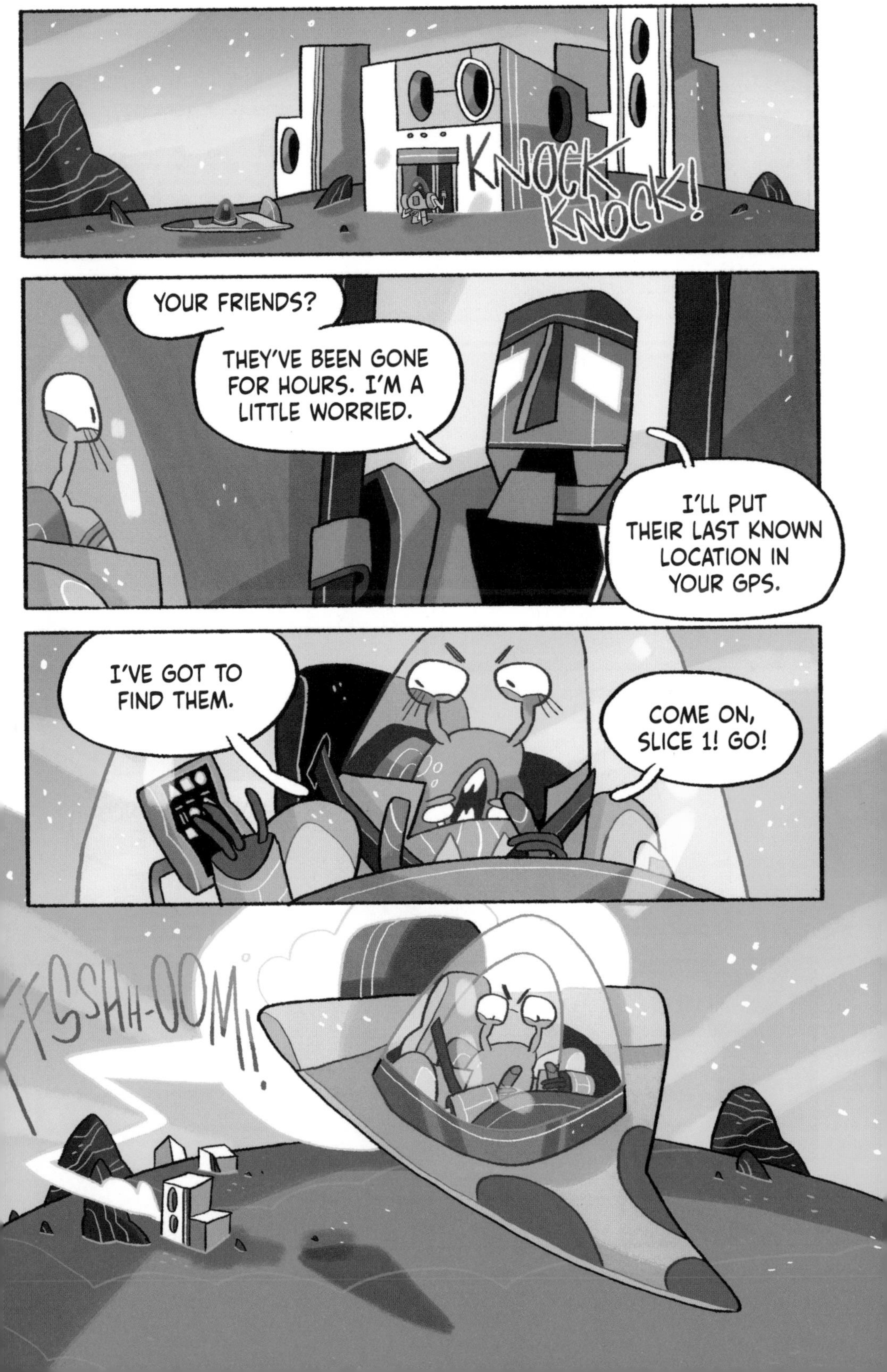
KNOCK KNOCK!
YOUR FRIENDS?
THEY'VE BEEN GONE FOR HOURS. I'M A LITTLE WORRIED.
I'LL PUT THEIR LAST KNOWN LOCATION IN YOUR GPS.
I'VE GOT TO FIND THEM.
COME ON, SLICE 1! GO!
FFSHH-OOM!!

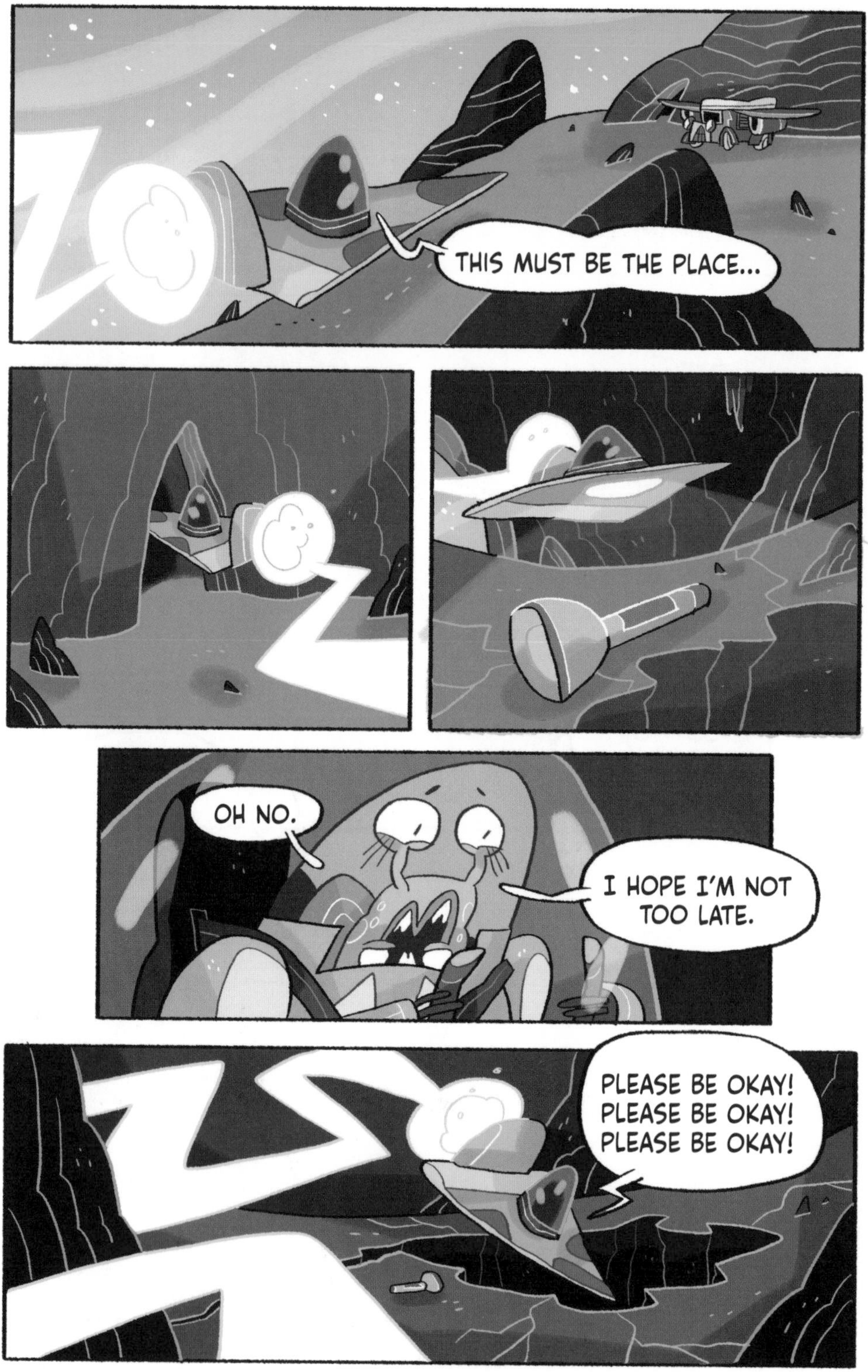
THIS MUST BE THE PLACE...
OH NO.
I HOPE I'M NOT TOO LATE.
PLEASE BE OKAY! PLEASE BE OKAY! PLEASE BE OKAY!

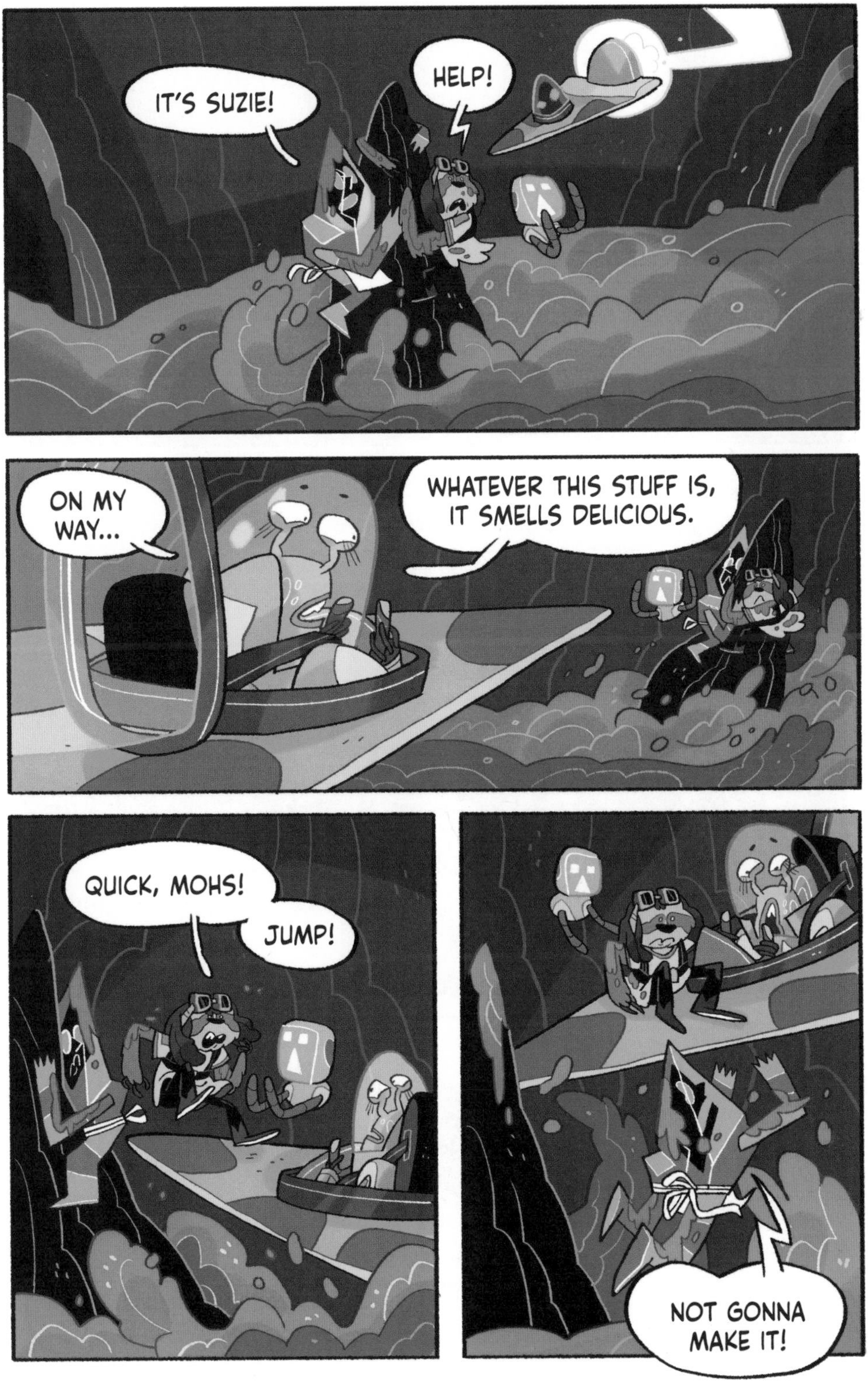
IT'S SUZIE!
HELP!
ON MY WAY...
WHATEVER THIS STUFF IS, IT SMELLS DELICIOUS.
QUICK, MOHS!
JUMP!
NOT GONNA MAKE IT!

After rescuing us, Suzie insisted that we go straight to the Plegan elder.

We did not even have time to clean ourselves up!

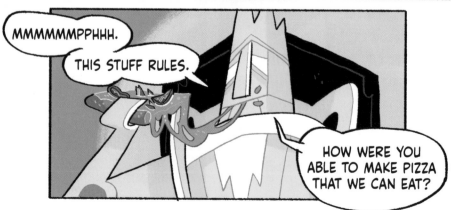

MMMMMMPPHHH.

THIS STUFF RULES.

HOW WERE YOU ABLE TO MAKE PIZZA THAT WE CAN EAT?

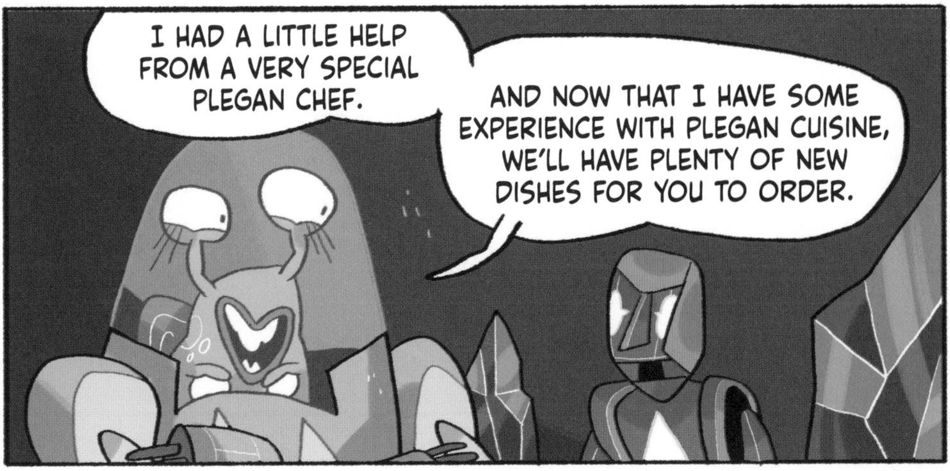
I HAD A LITTLE HELP FROM A VERY SPECIAL PLEGAN CHEF.
AND NOW THAT I HAVE SOME EXPERIENCE WITH PLEGAN CUISINE, WE'LL HAVE PLENTY OF NEW DISHES FOR YOU TO ORDER.

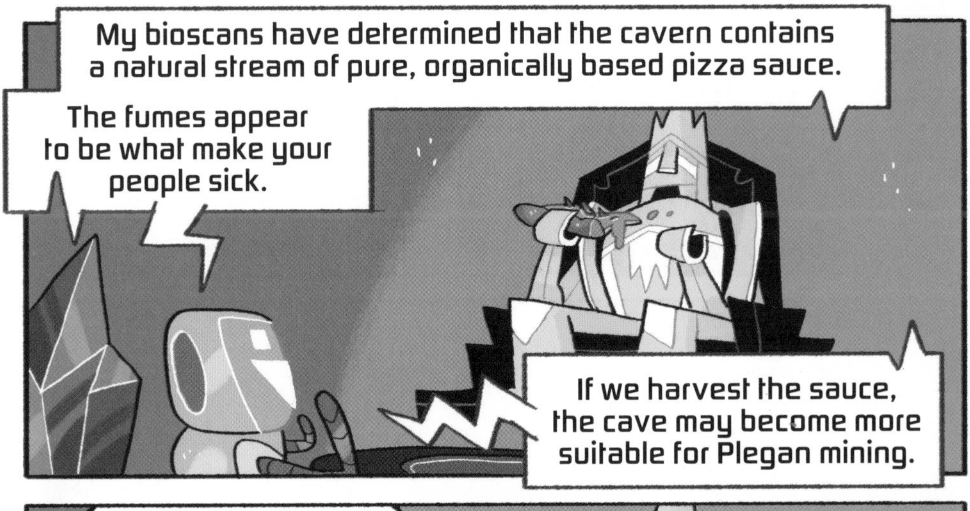
My bioscans have determined that the cavern contains a natural stream of pure, organically based pizza sauce.
The fumes appear to be what make your people sick.
If we harvest the sauce, the cave may become more suitable for Plegan mining.

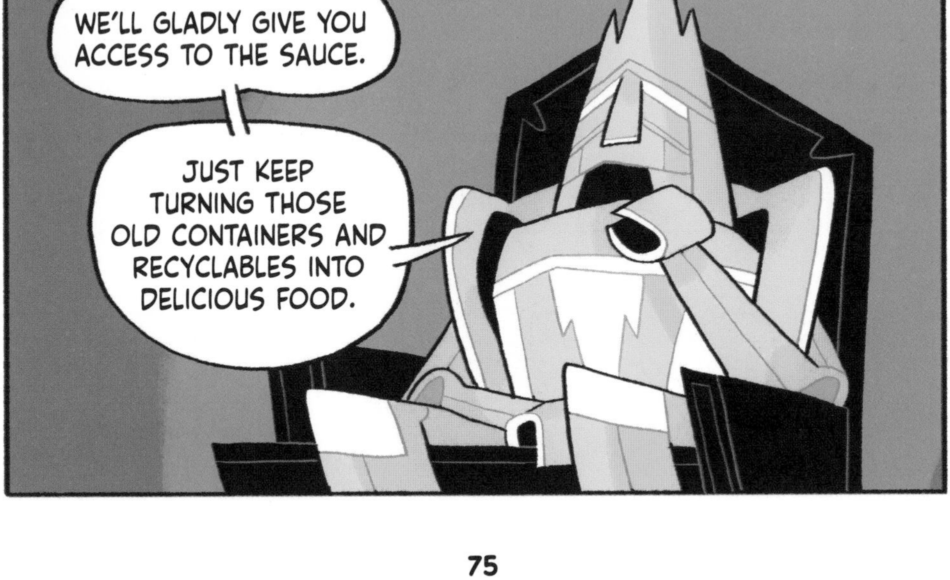
WE'LL GLADLY GIVE YOU ACCESS TO THE SAUCE.
JUST KEEP TURNING THOSE OLD CONTAINERS AND RECYCLABLES INTO DELICIOUS FOOD.

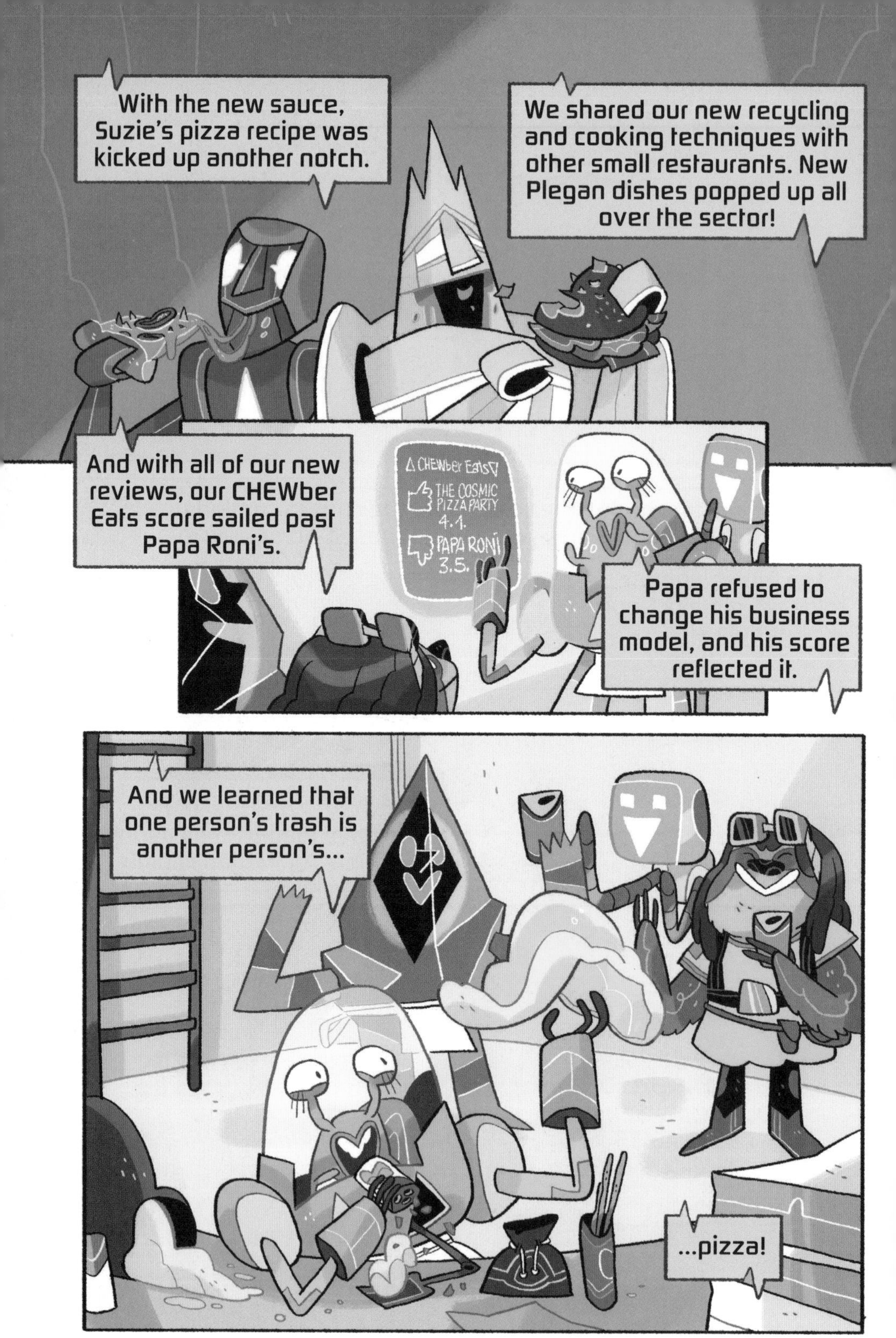
With the new sauce, Suzie's pizza recipe was kicked up another notch.
We shared our new recycling and cooking techniques with other small restaurants. New Plegan dishes popped up all over the sector!
And with all of our new reviews, our CHEWber Eats score sailed past Papa Roni's.
CHEWber Eats
THE COSMIC PIZZA PARTY 4.1.
PAPA RONI 3.5.
Papa refused to change his business model, and his score reflected it.
And we learned that one person's trash is another person's...
...pizza!

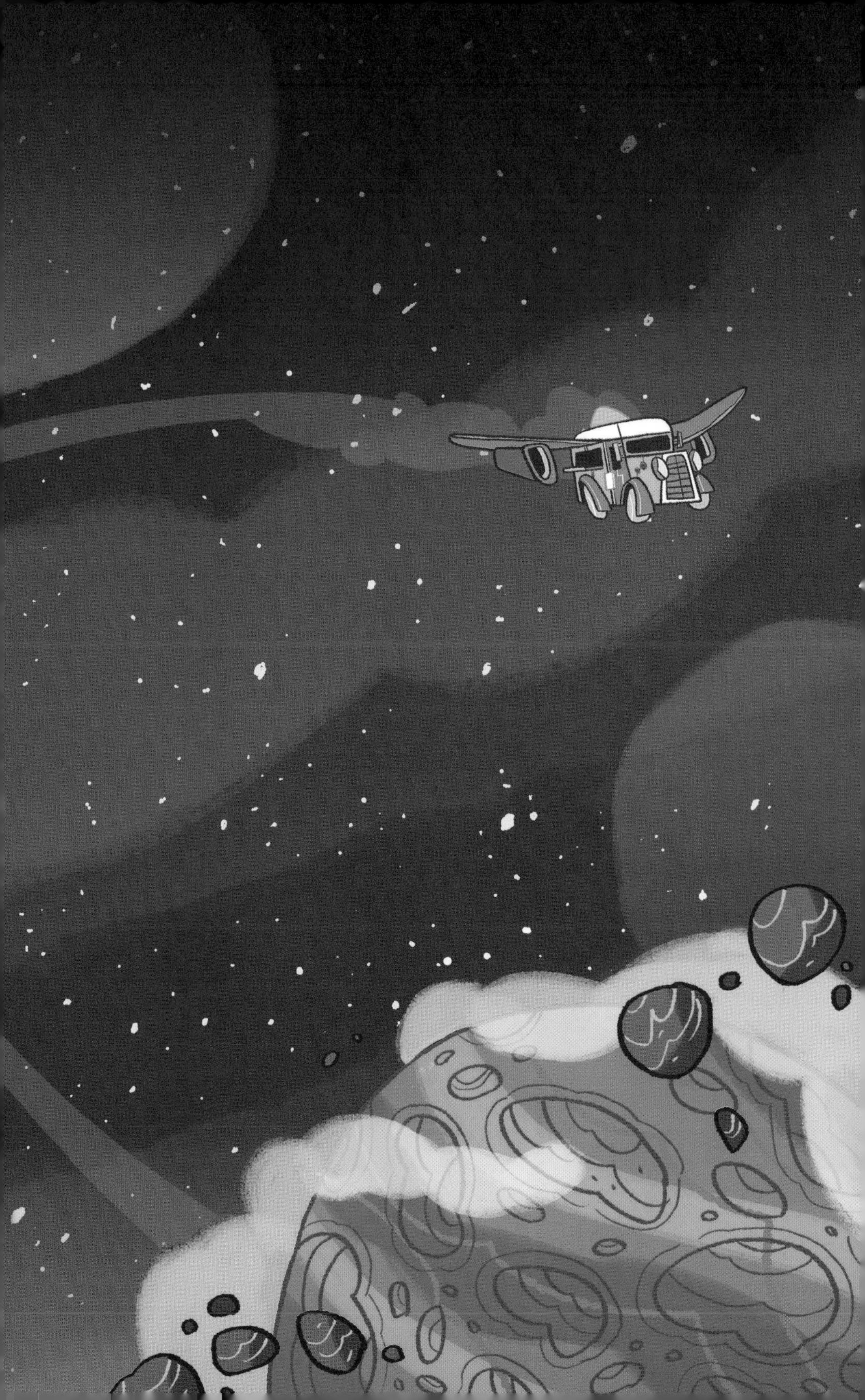

CHAPTER 4
Delivery Dilemma

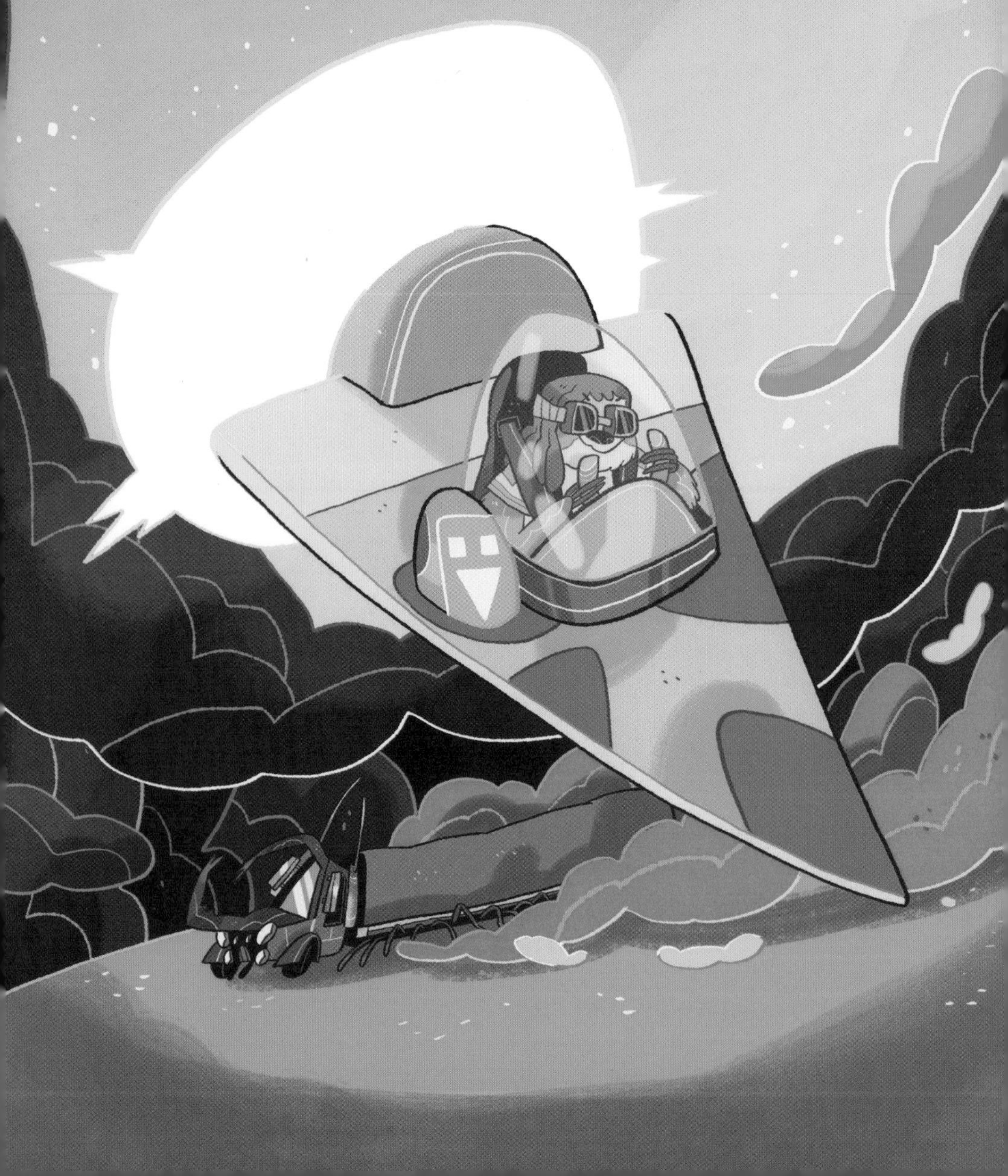

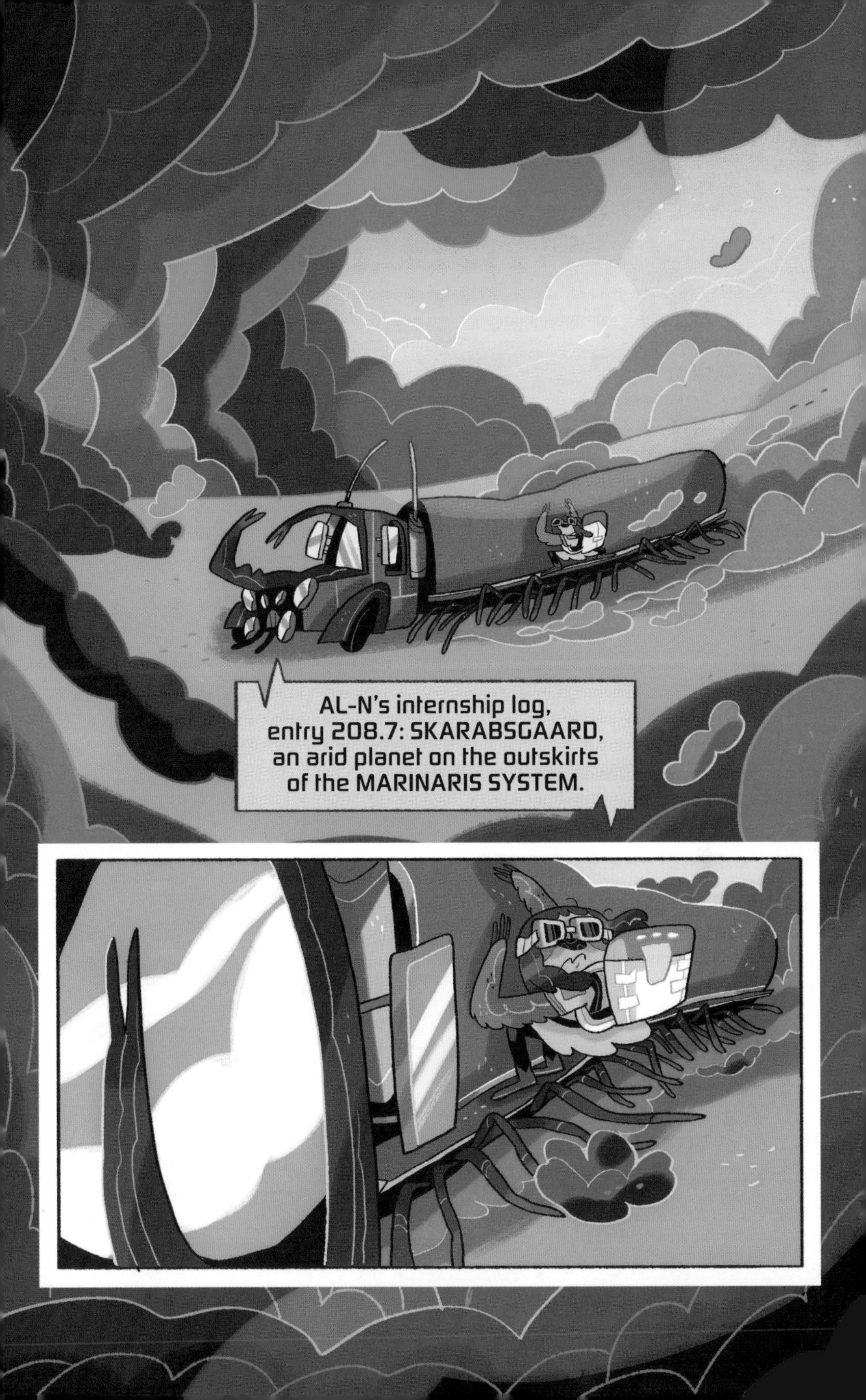
AL-N's internship log, entry 208.7: SKARABSGAARD, an arid planet on the outskirts of the MARINARIS SYSTEM.

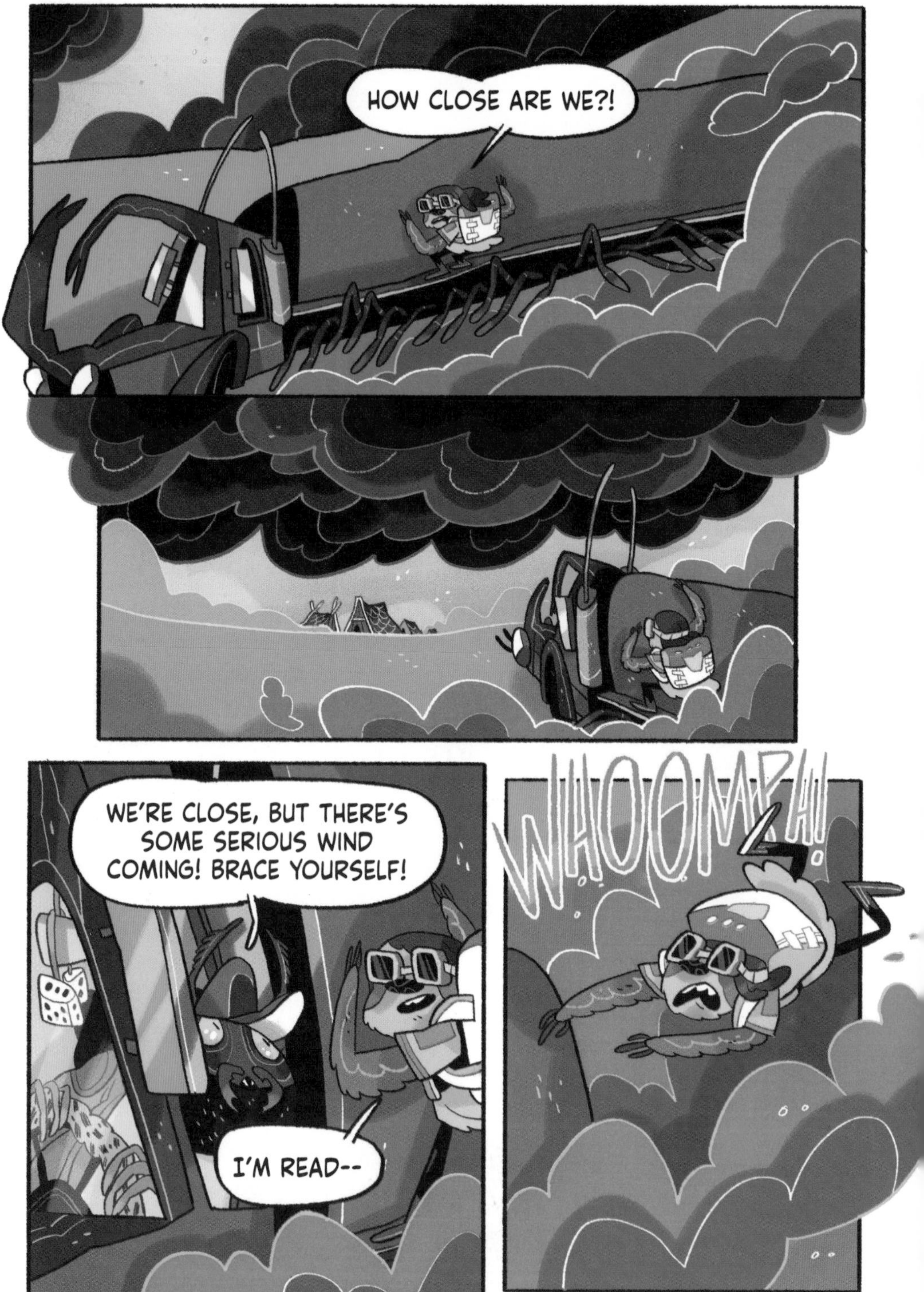
HOW CLOSE ARE WE?!
WE'RE CLOSE, BUT THERE'S SOME SERIOUS WIND COMING! BRACE YOURSELF!
I'M READ--
WHOOMPH!

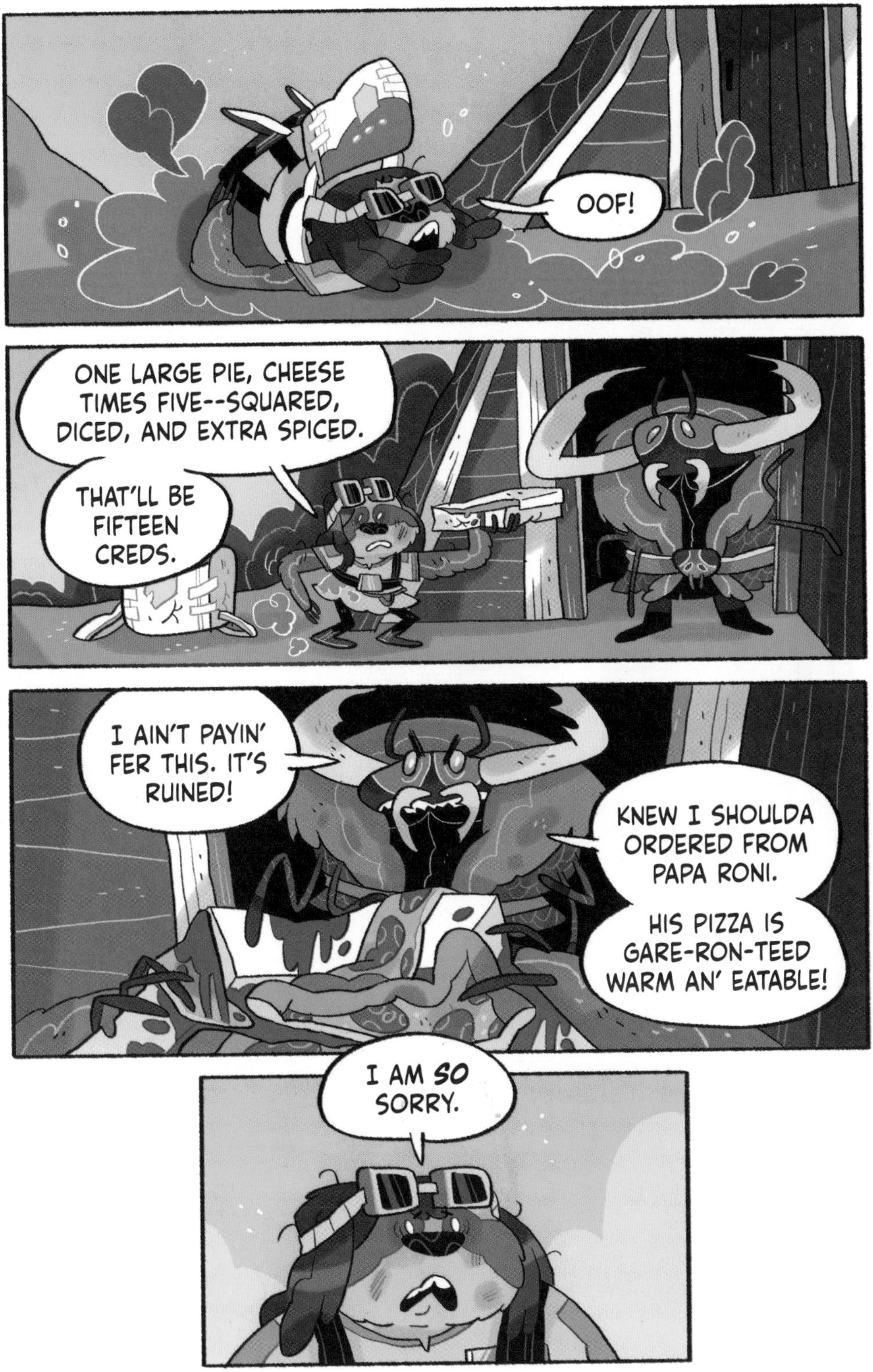
OOF!
ONE LARGE PIE, CHEESE TIMES FIVE--SQUARED, DICED, AND EXTRA SPICED.
THAT'LL BE FIFTEEN CREDS.
I AIN'T PAYIN' FER THIS. IT'S RUINED!
KNEW I SHOULDA ORDERED FROM PAPA RONI.
HIS PIZZA IS GARE-RON-TEED WARM AN' EATABLE!
I AM *SO* SORRY.

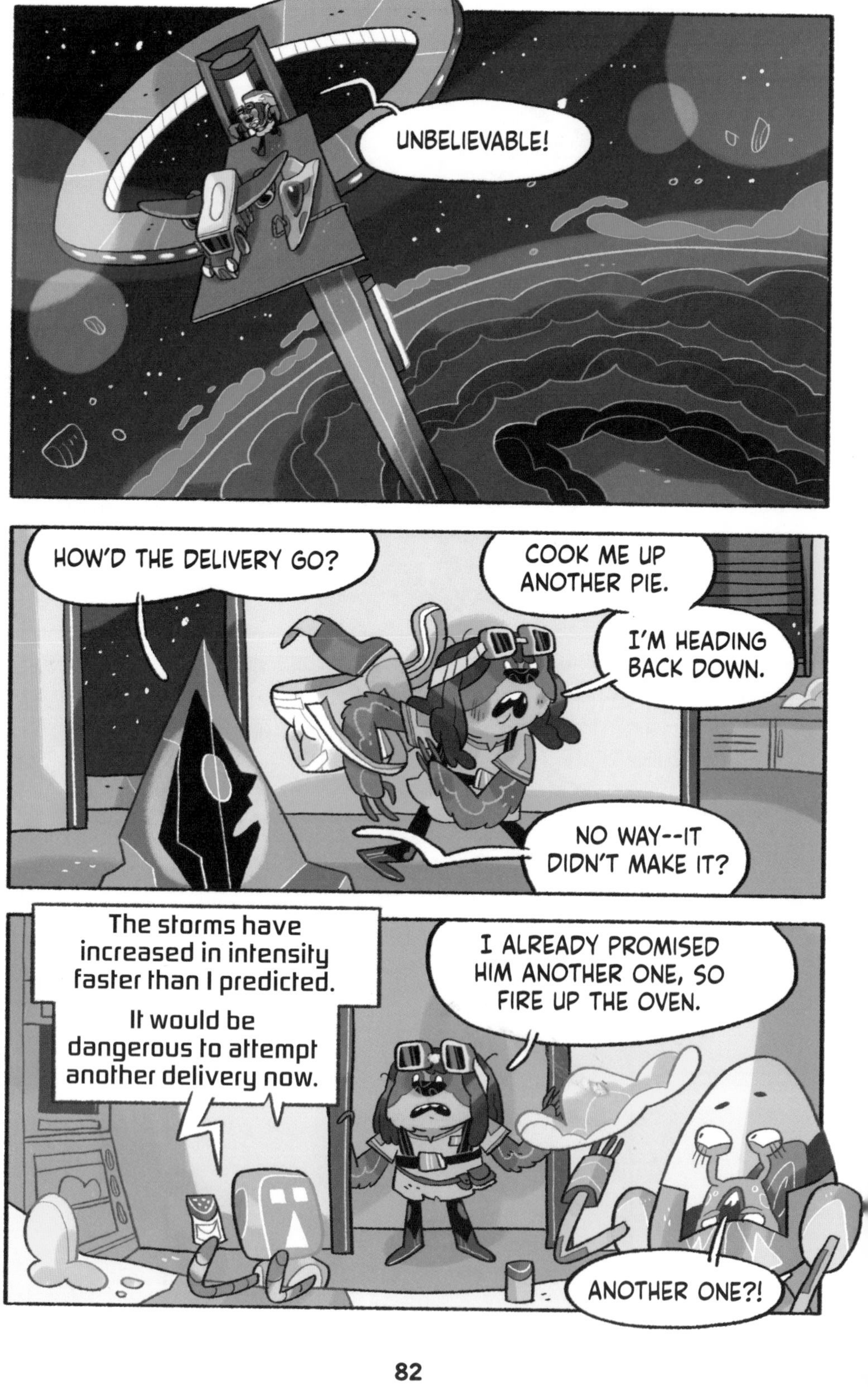
UNBELIEVABLE!
HOW'D THE DELIVERY GO?
COOK ME UP ANOTHER PIE.
I'M HEADING BACK DOWN.
NO WAY--IT DIDN'T MAKE IT?
The storms have increased in intensity faster than I predicted.
It would be dangerous to attempt another delivery now.
I ALREADY PROMISED HIM ANOTHER ONE, SO FIRE UP THE OVEN.
ANOTHER ONE?!

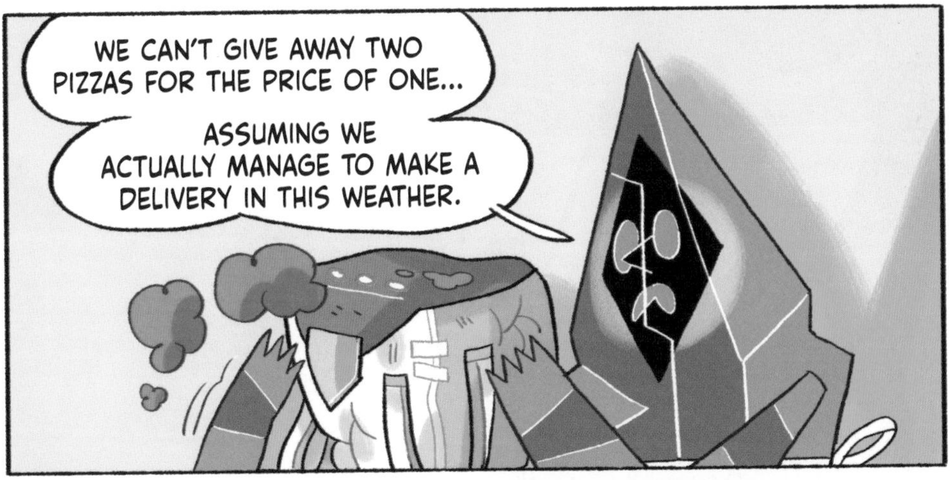
WE CAN'T GIVE AWAY TWO PIZZAS FOR THE PRICE OF ONE...
ASSUMING WE ACTUALLY MANAGE TO MAKE A DELIVERY IN THIS WEATHER.

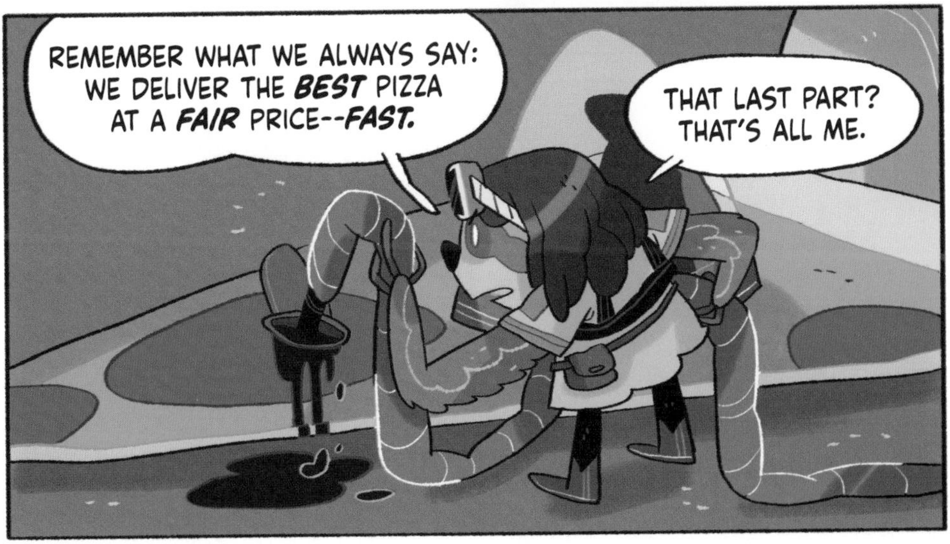
REMEMBER WHAT WE ALWAYS SAY: WE DELIVER THE ***BEST*** PIZZA AT A ***FAIR*** PRICE--***FAST.***
THAT LAST PART? THAT'S ALL ME.

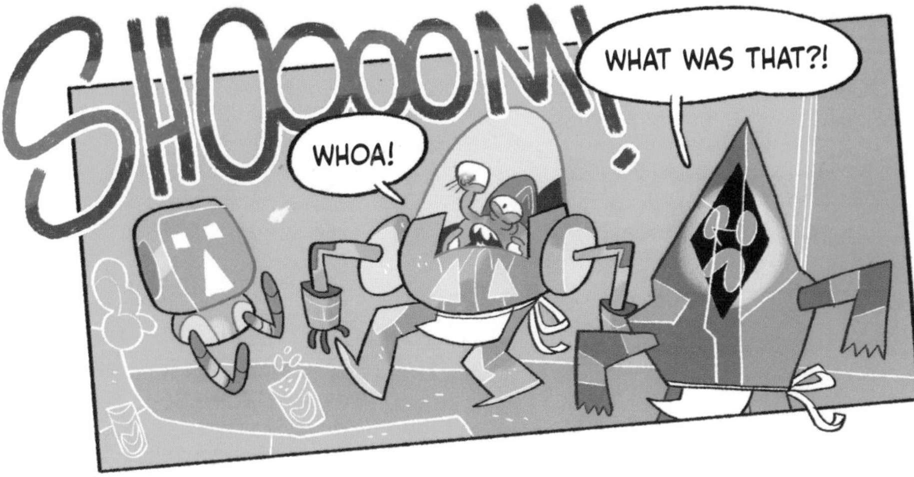
SHOOOOM!
WHAT WAS THAT?!
WHOA!

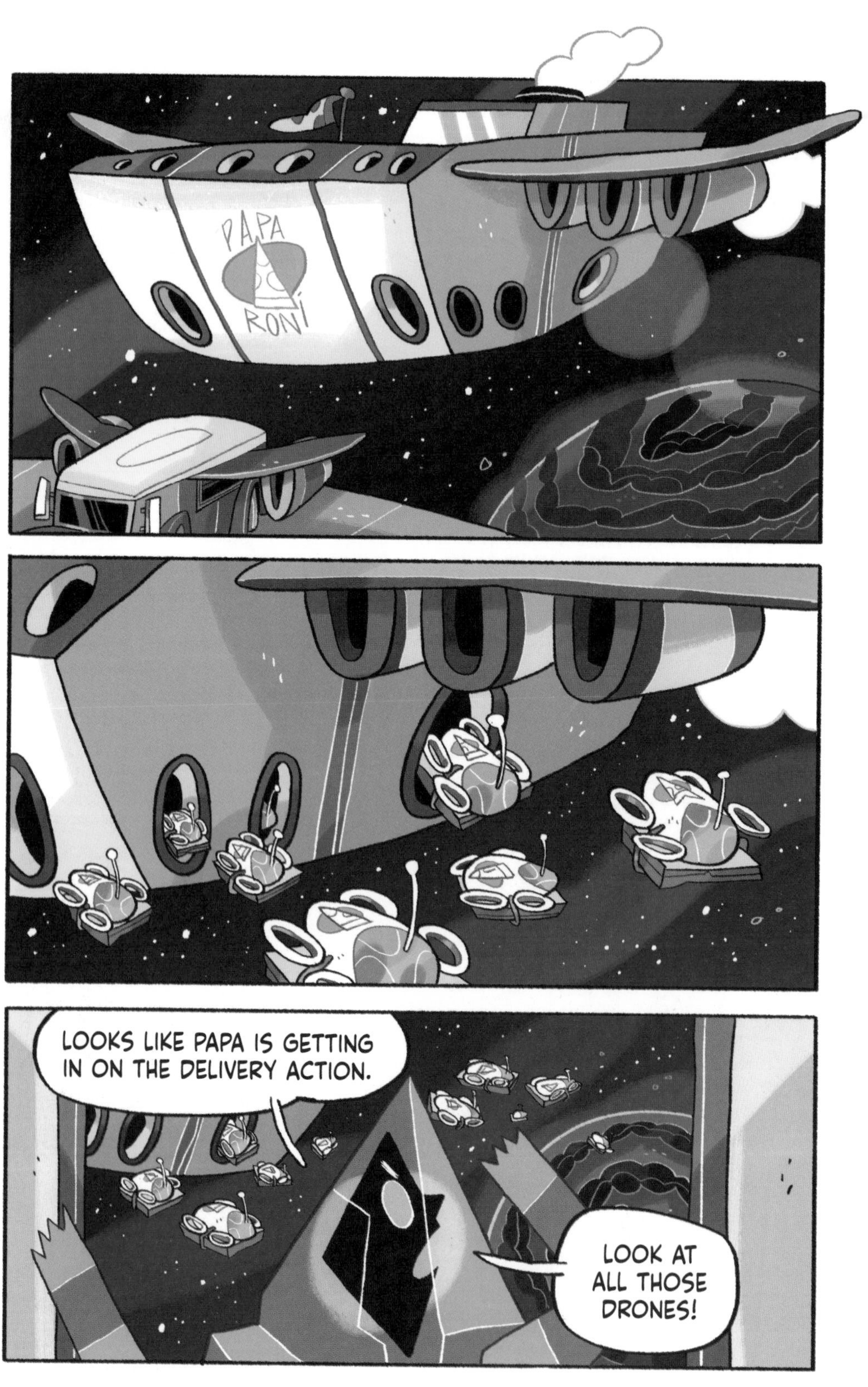
PAPA RONI
LOOKS LIKE PAPA IS GETTING IN ON THE DELIVERY ACTION.
LOOK AT ALL THOSE DRONES!

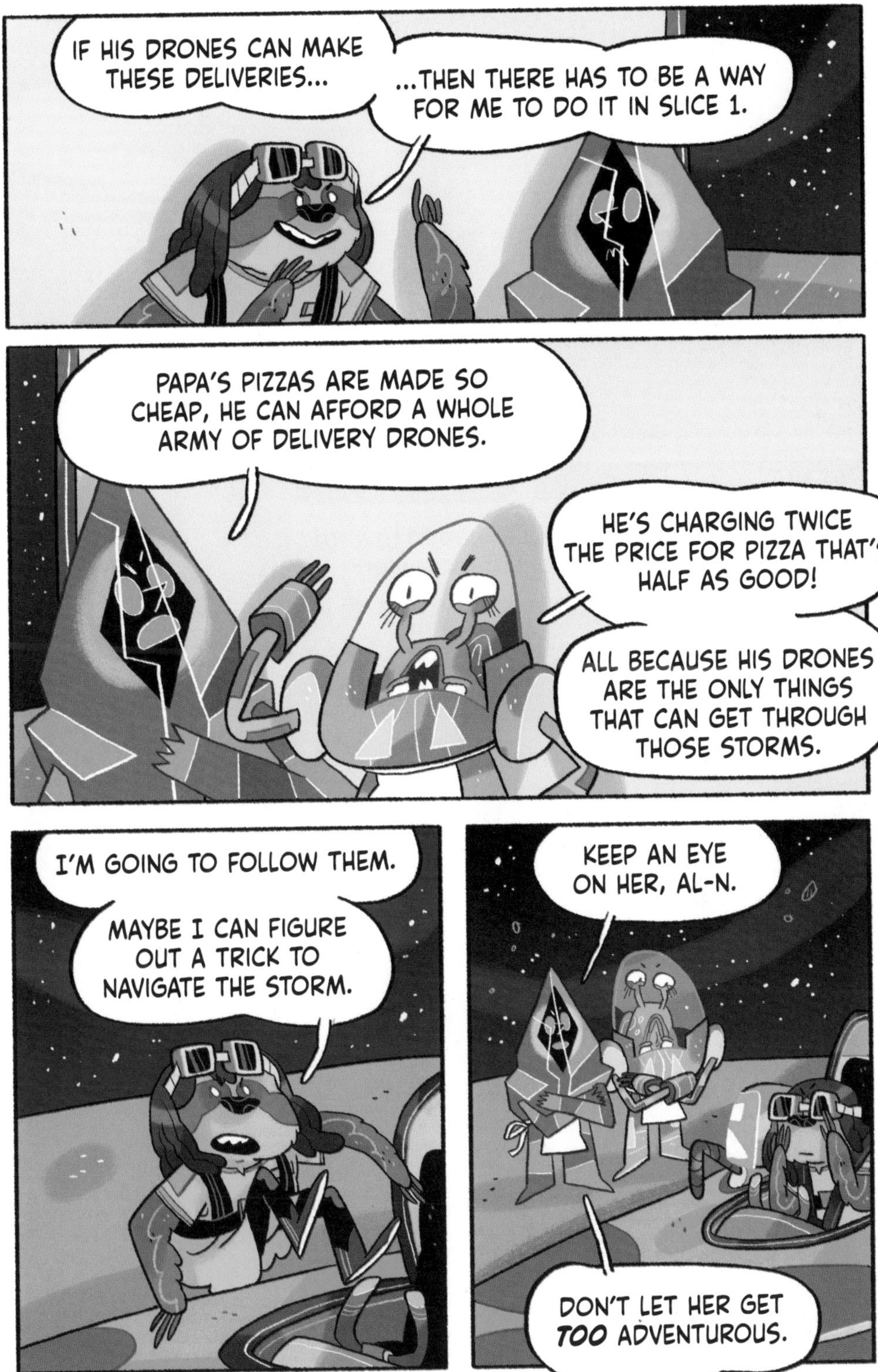
IF HIS DRONES CAN MAKE THESE DELIVERIES...
...THEN THERE HAS TO BE A WAY FOR ME TO DO IT IN SLICE 1.
PAPA'S PIZZAS ARE MADE SO CHEAP, HE CAN AFFORD A WHOLE ARMY OF DELIVERY DRONES.
HE'S CHARGING TWICE THE PRICE FOR PIZZA THAT'S HALF AS GOOD!
ALL BECAUSE HIS DRONES ARE THE ONLY THINGS THAT CAN GET THROUGH THOSE STORMS.
I'M GOING TO FOLLOW THEM.
MAYBE I CAN FIGURE OUT A TRICK TO NAVIGATE THE STORM.
KEEP AN EYE ON HER, AL-N.
DON'T LET HER GET *TOO* ADVENTUROUS.

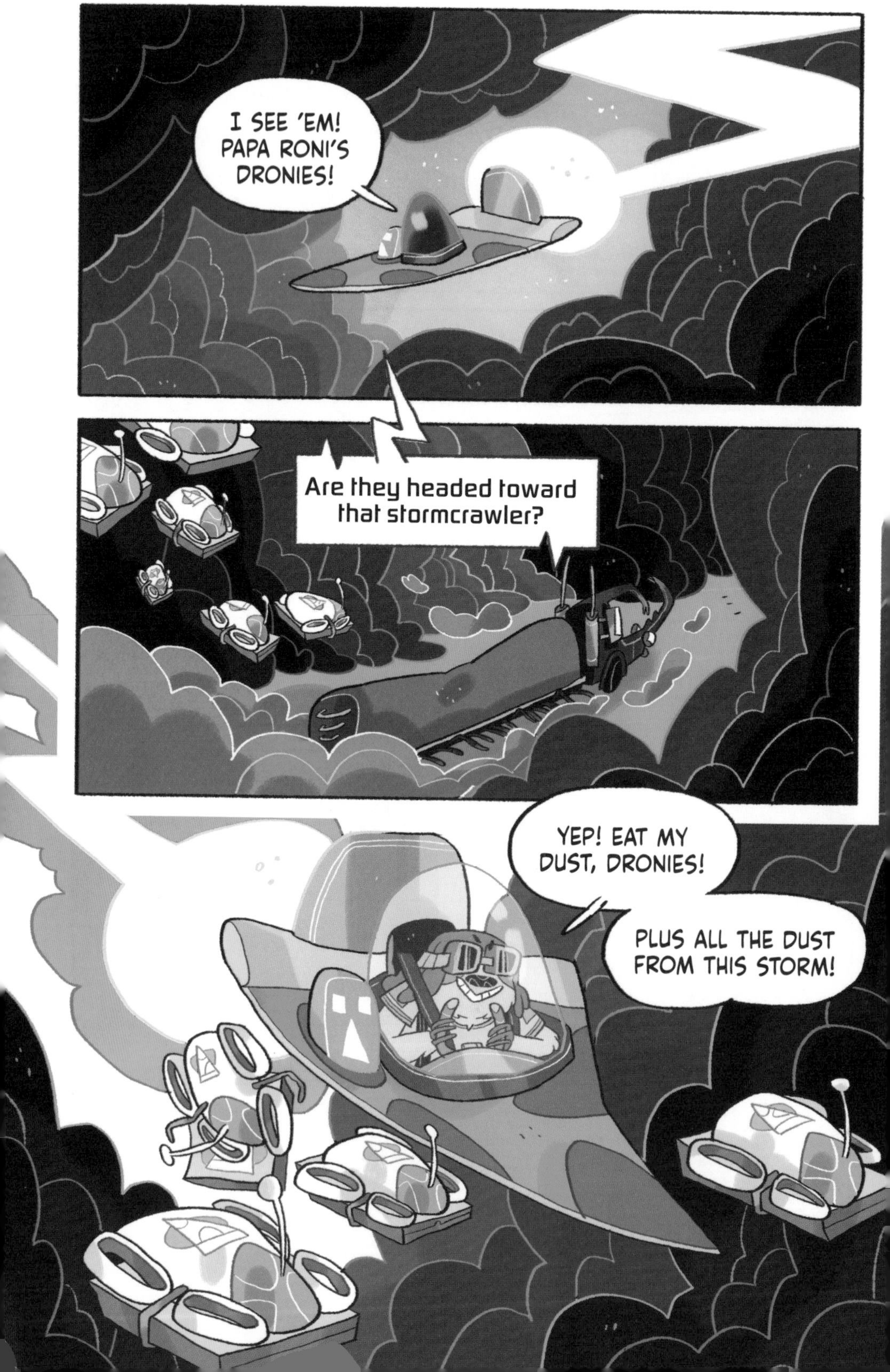
I SEE 'EM! PAPA RONI'S DRONIES!
Are they headed toward that stormcrawler?
YEP! EAT MY DUST, DRONIES!
PLUS ALL THE DUST FROM THIS STORM!

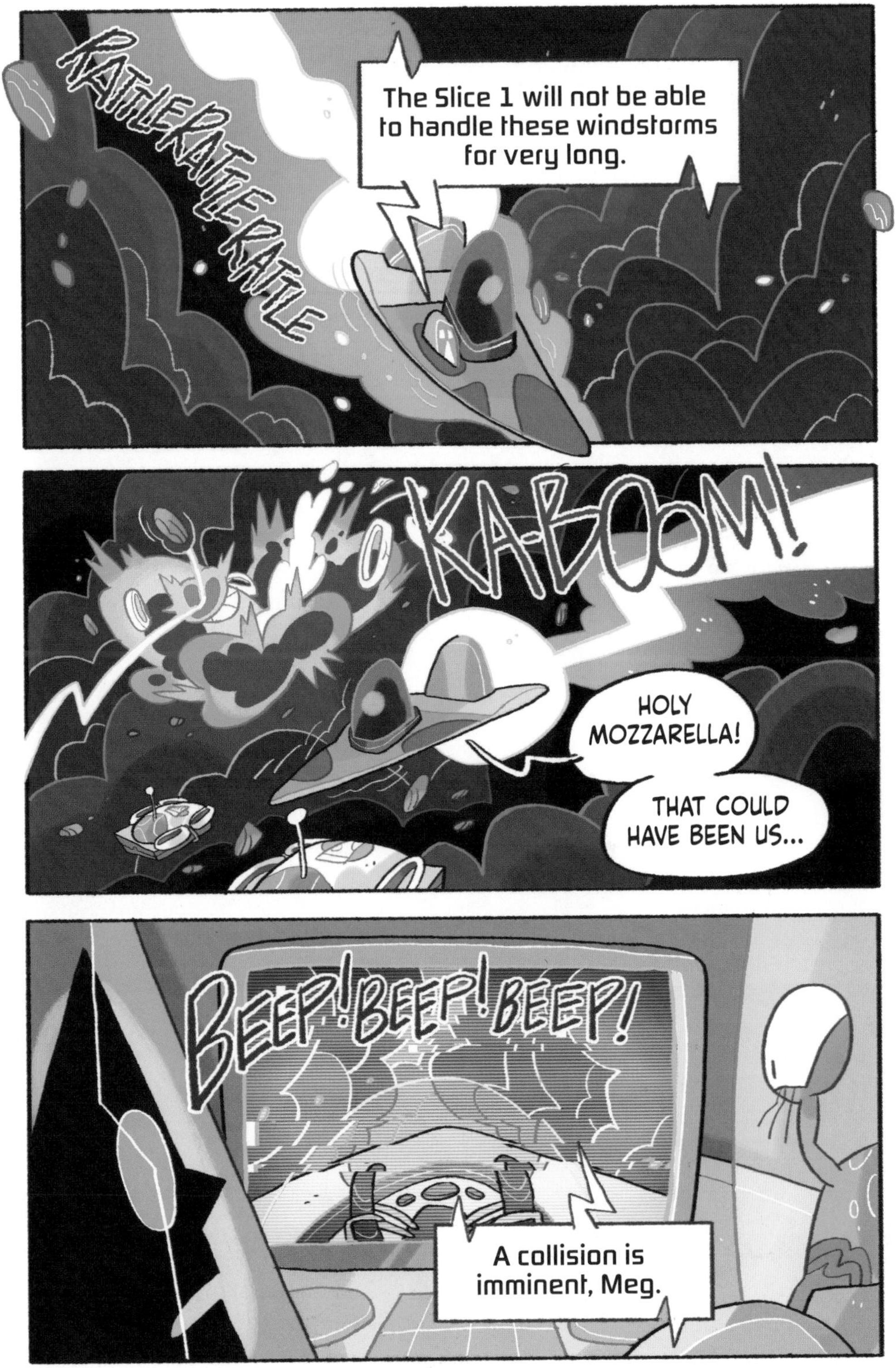
RATTLE RATTLE RATTLE RATTLE
The Slice 1 will not be able to handle these windstorms for very long.
KA-BOOM!
HOLY MOZZARELLA!
THAT COULD HAVE BEEN US...
BEEP! BEEP! BEEP!
A collision is imminent, Meg.

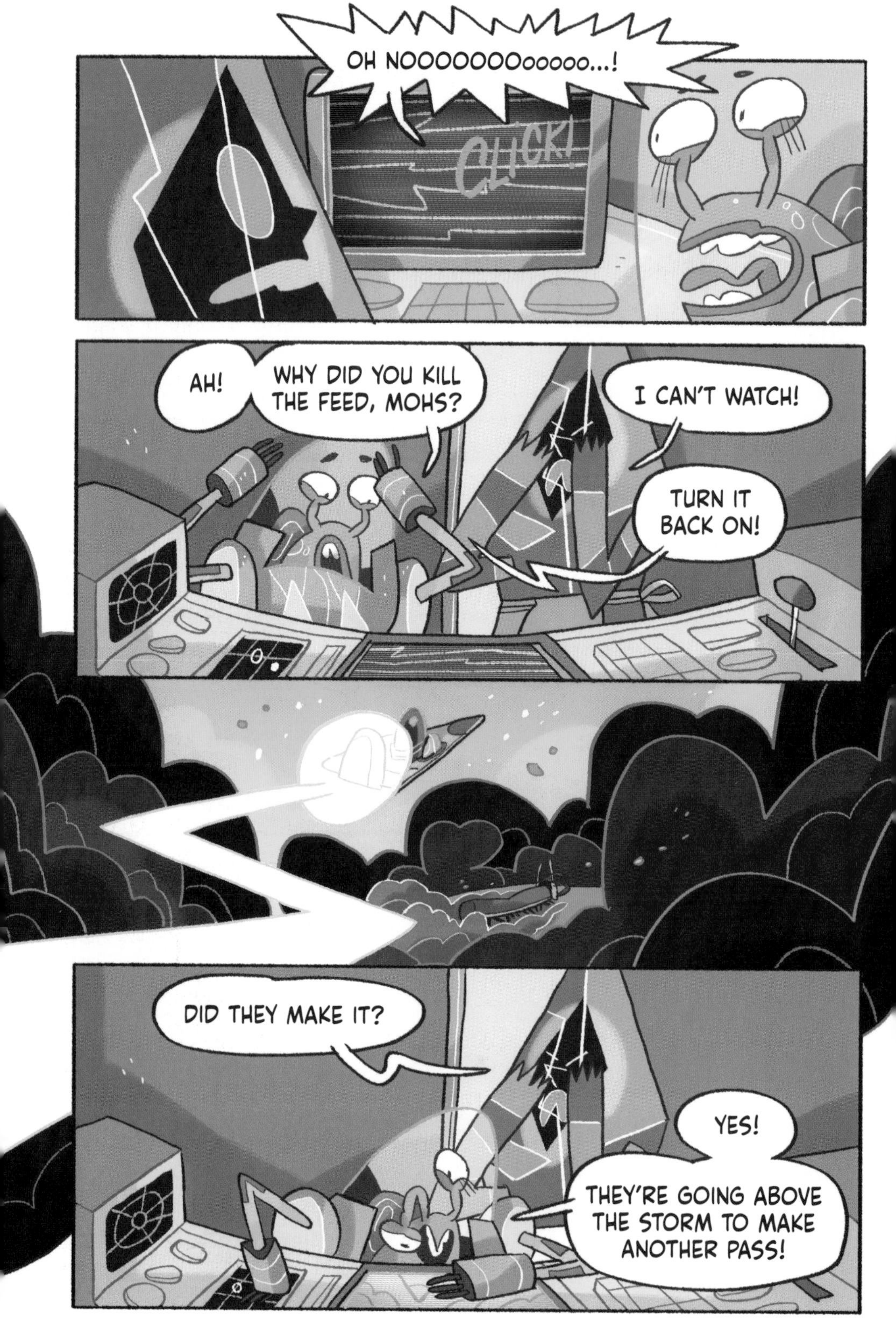
OH NOOOOOOOooooo...!
CLICK!
AH!
WHY DID YOU KILL THE FEED, MOHS?
I CAN'T WATCH!
TURN IT BACK ON!
DID THEY MAKE IT?
YES!
THEY'RE GOING ABOVE THE STORM TO MAKE ANOTHER PASS!

THE DRONES ARE DRAFTING BEHIND IT!
Yes, they are using the stormcrawler to shield themselves from the brunt of the storm.
Now the drones are attacking the stormcrawler!
NO, AL-N! THEY'RE ATTACHING THEMSELVES TO IT.

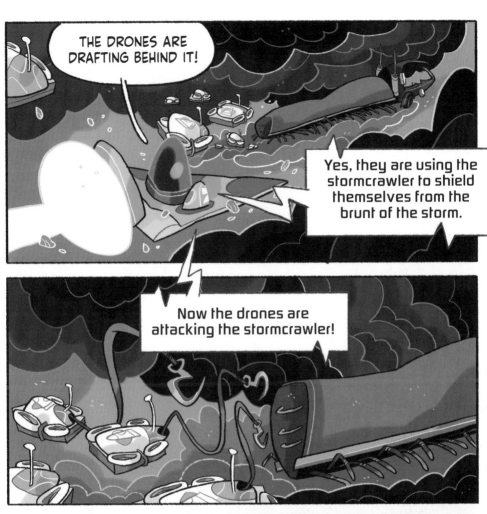

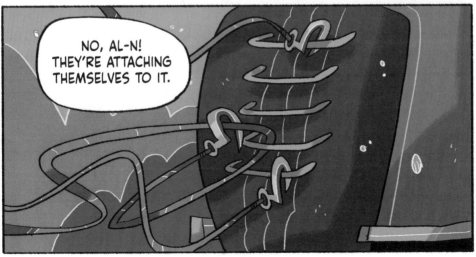

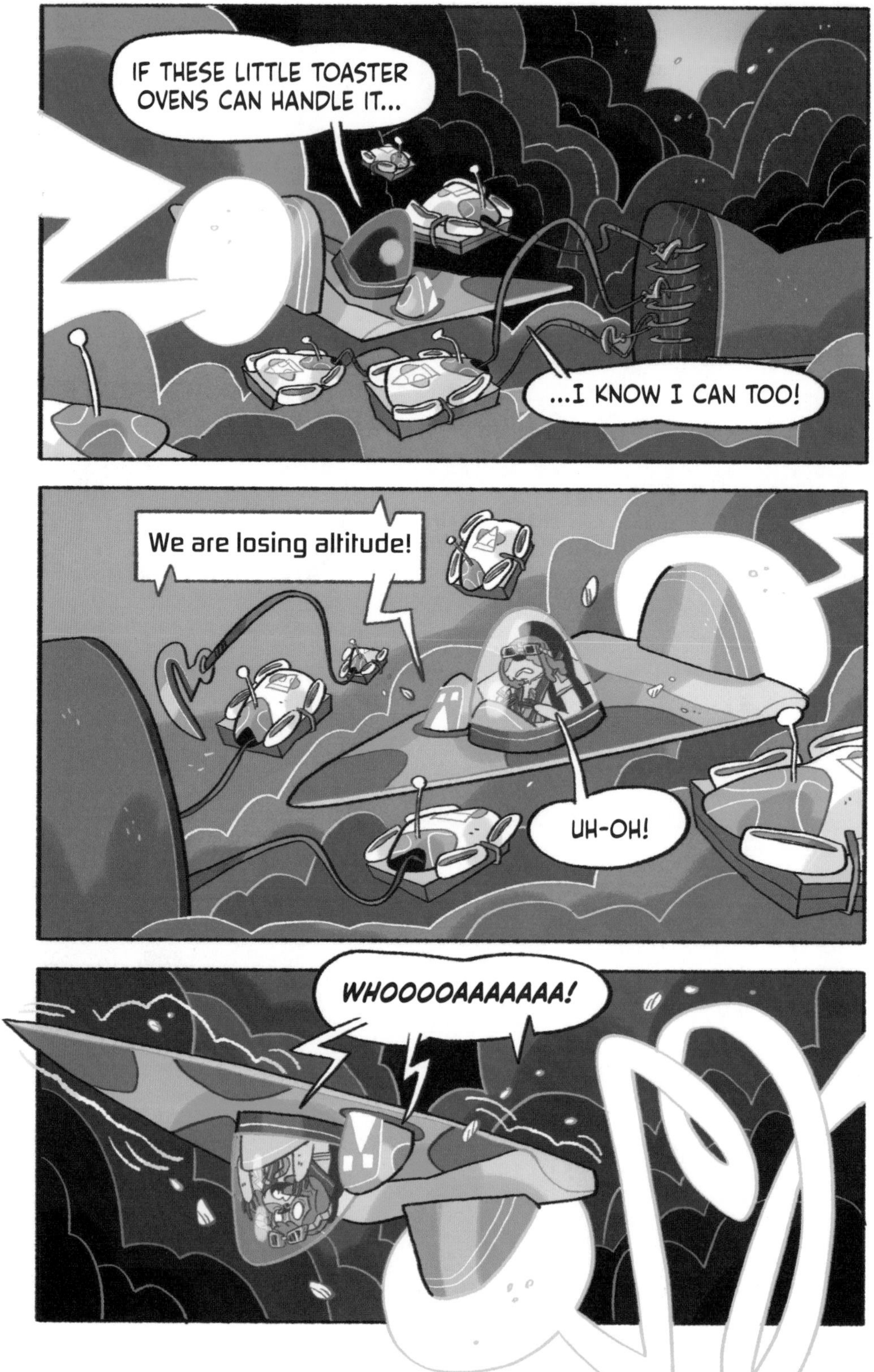
IF THESE LITTLE TOASTER OVENS CAN HANDLE IT...
...I KNOW I CAN TOO!
We are losing altitude!
UH-OH!
WHOOOOAAAAAAA!

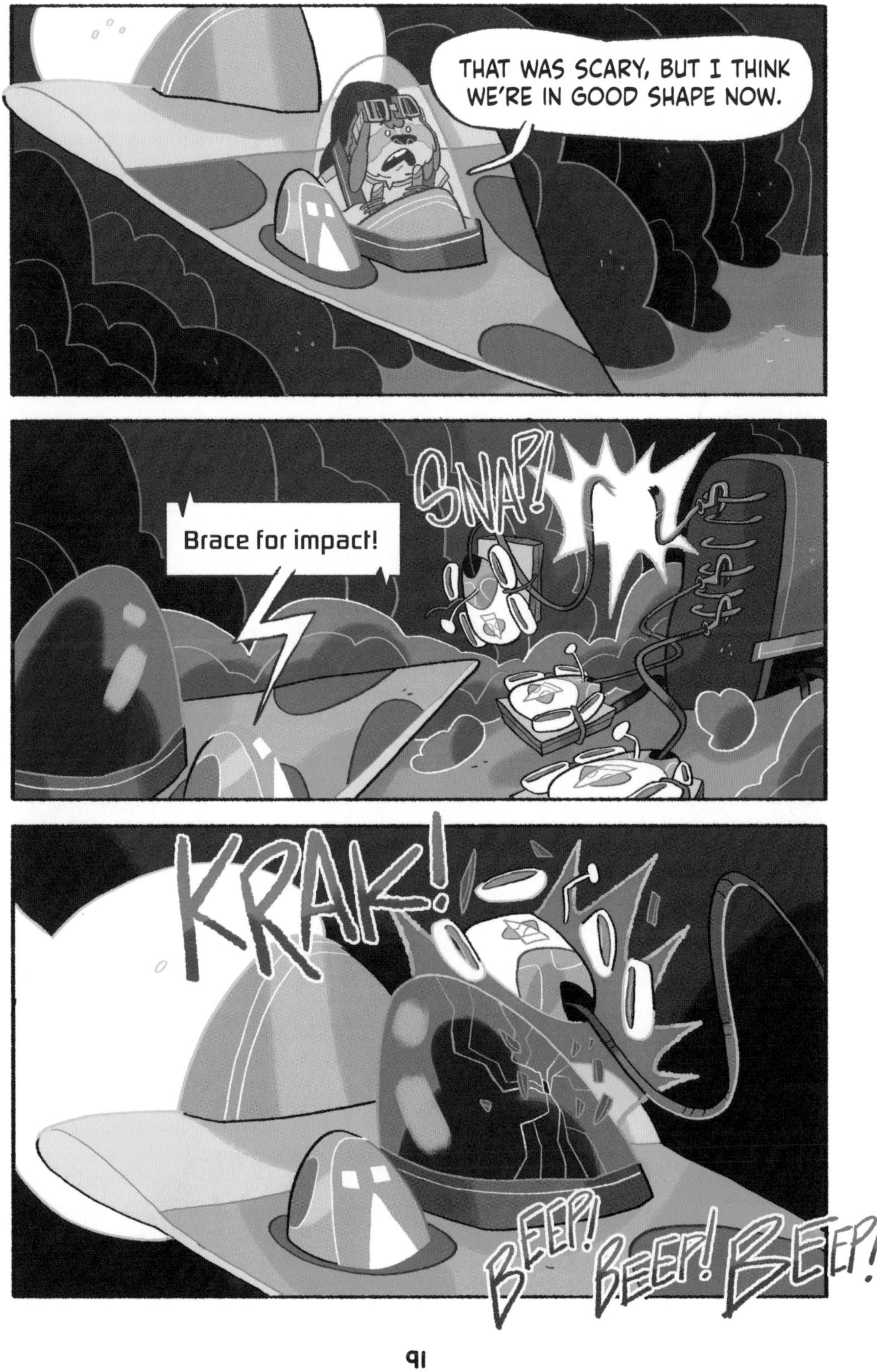
THAT WAS SCARY, BUT I THINK WE'RE IN GOOD SHAPE NOW.
SNAP!
Brace for impact!
KRAK!
BEEP! BEEP! BEEP!

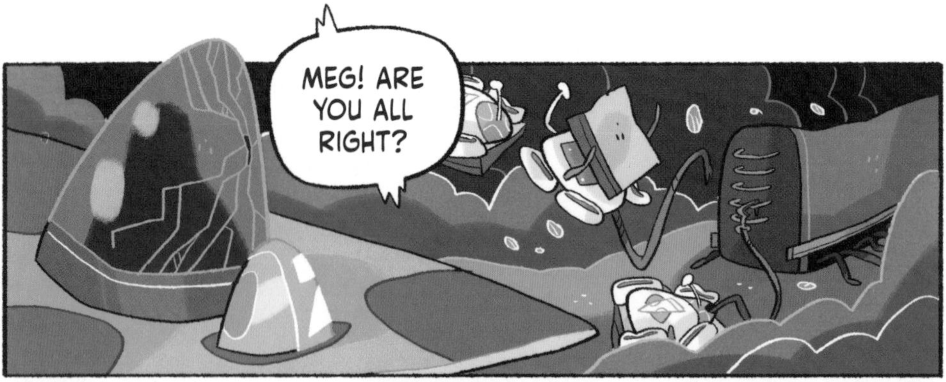
MEG! ARE YOU ALL RIGHT?

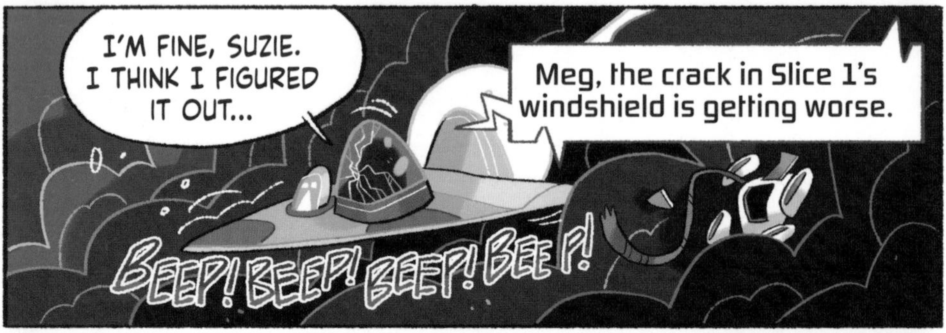
I'M FINE, SUZIE. I THINK I FIGURED IT OUT...
Meg, the crack in Slice 1's windshield is getting worse.
BEEP! BEEP! BEEP! BEEP!

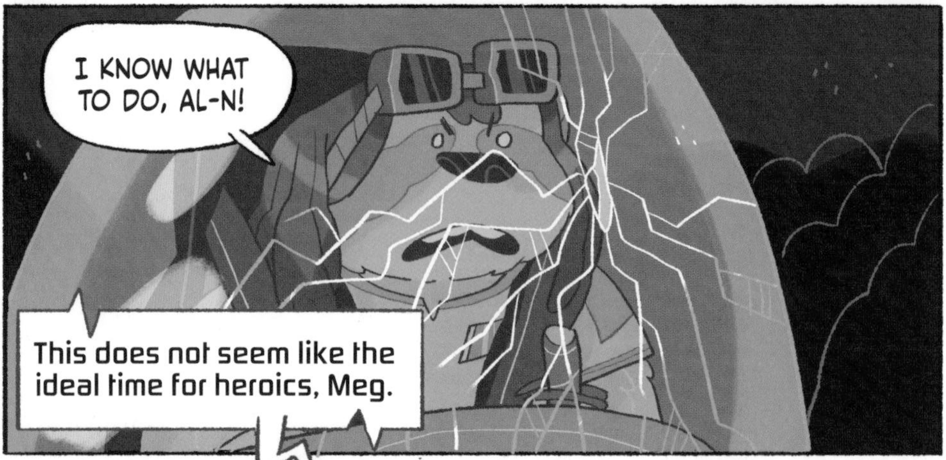
I KNOW WHAT TO DO, AL-N!
This does not seem like the ideal time for heroics, Meg.

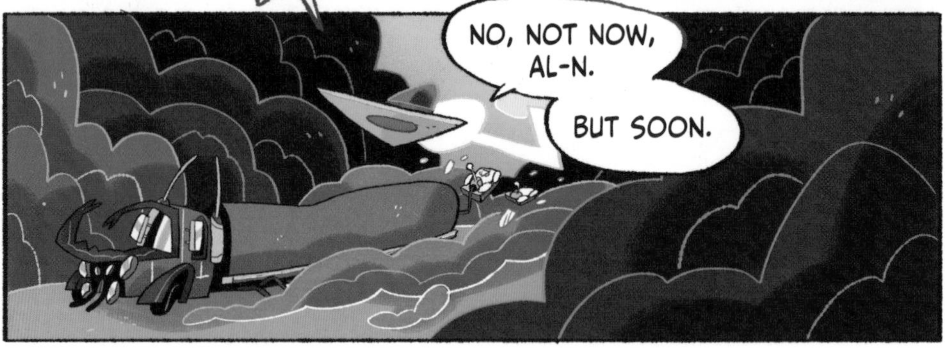
NO, NOT NOW, AL-N.
BUT SOON.

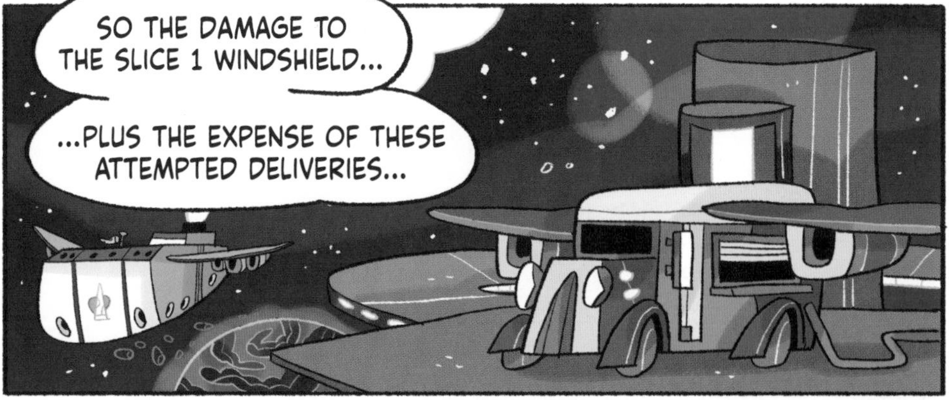
SO THE DAMAGE TO THE SLICE 1 WINDSHIELD...
...PLUS THE EXPENSE OF THESE ATTEMPTED DELIVERIES...

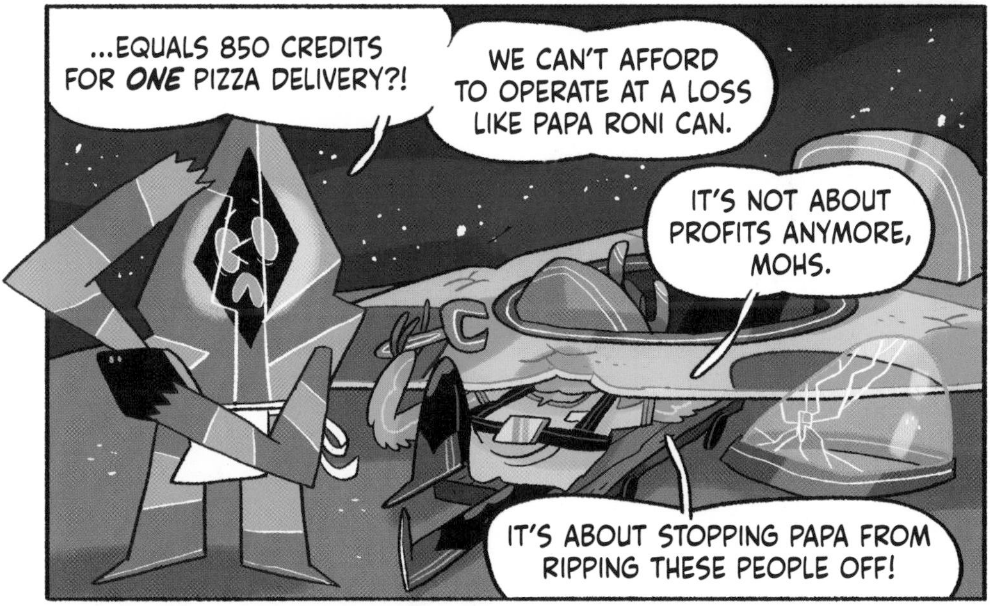
...EQUALS 850 CREDITS FOR *ONE* PIZZA DELIVERY?!
WE CAN'T AFFORD TO OPERATE AT A LOSS LIKE PAPA RONI CAN.
IT'S NOT ABOUT PROFITS ANYMORE, MOHS.
IT'S ABOUT STOPPING PAPA FROM RIPPING THESE PEOPLE OFF!

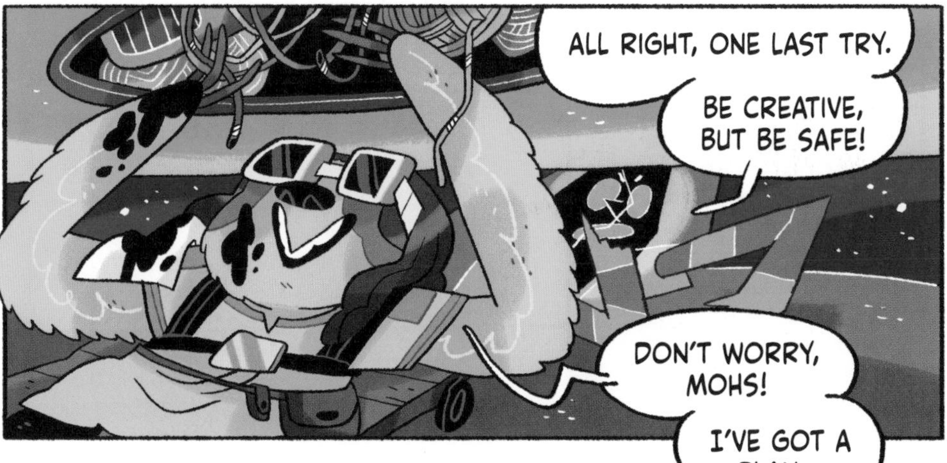
ALL RIGHT, ONE LAST TRY.
BE CREATIVE, BUT BE SAFE!
DON'T WORRY, MOHS!
I'VE GOT A PLAN...

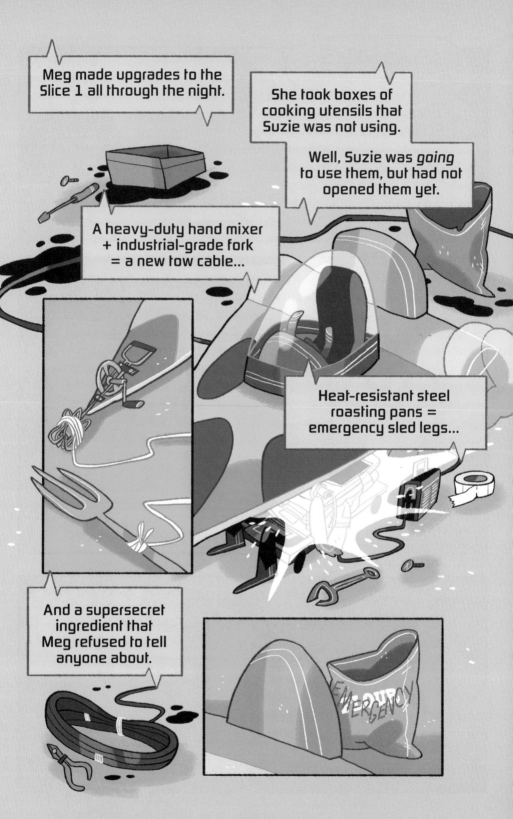

Meg made upgrades to the Slice 1 all through the night.

She took boxes of cooking utensils that Suzie was not using.

Well, Suzie was *going* to use them, but had not opened them yet.

A heavy-duty hand mixer + industrial-grade fork = a new tow cable...

Heat-resistant steel roasting pans = emergency sled legs...

And a supersecret ingredient that Meg refused to tell anyone about.

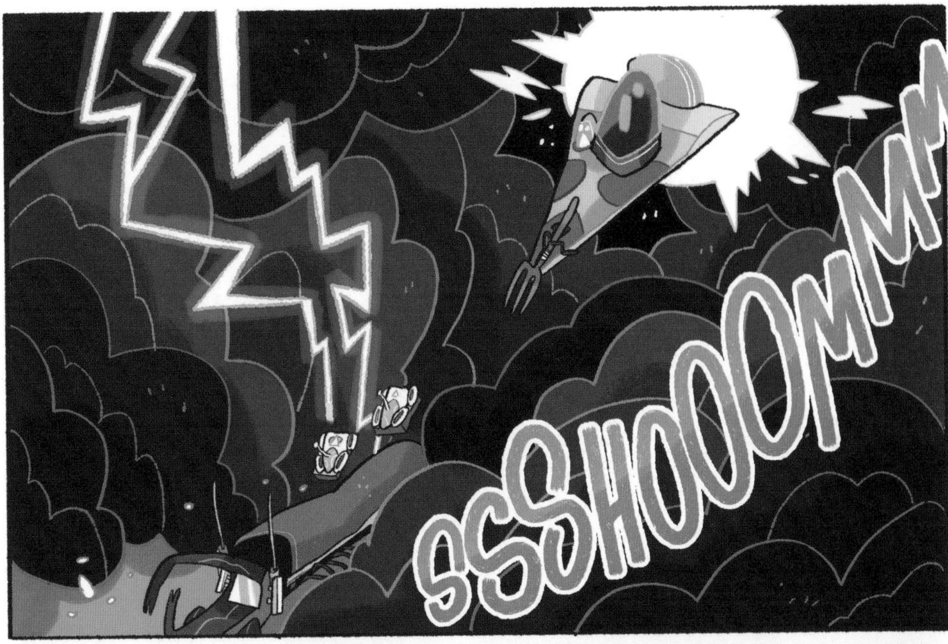
SSSHOOOMMM!

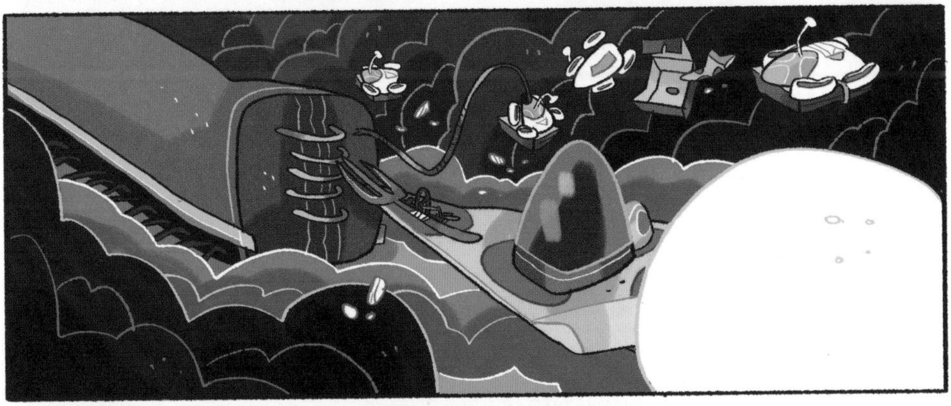

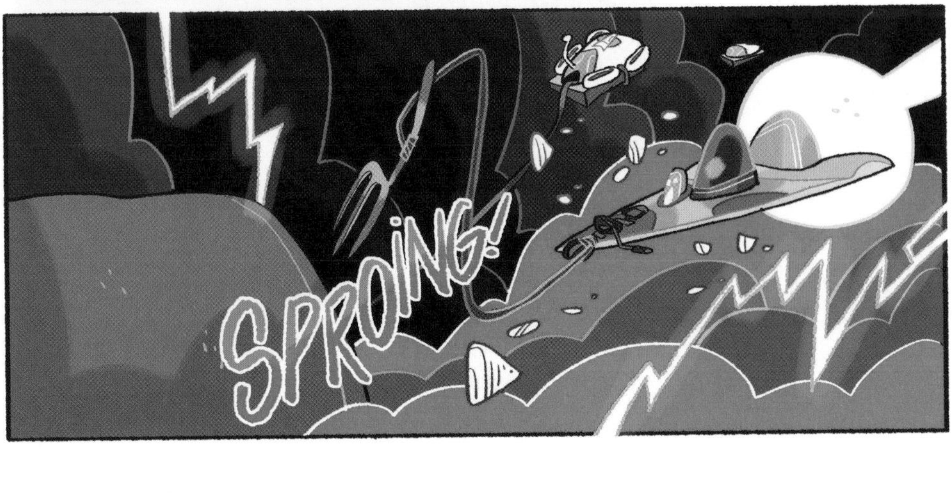
SPROING!

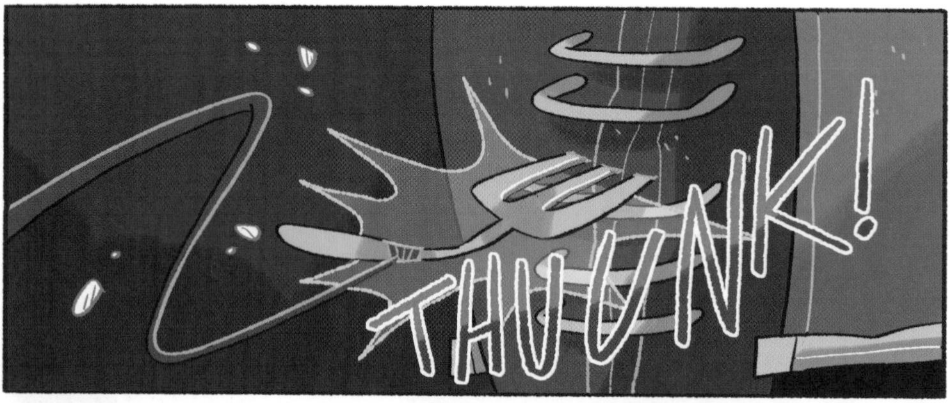
THUUNK!

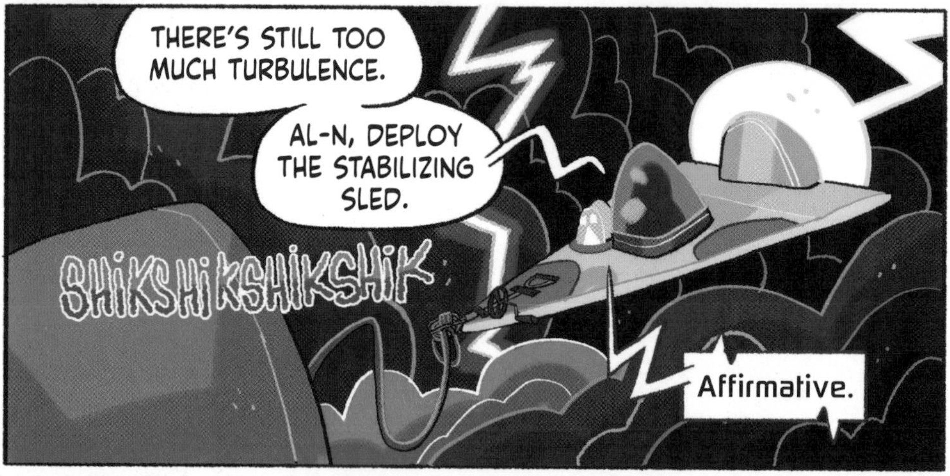
THERE'S STILL TOO MUCH TURBULENCE.
AL-N, DEPLOY THE STABILIZING SLED.
SHIKSHIKSHIKSHIK
Affirmative.

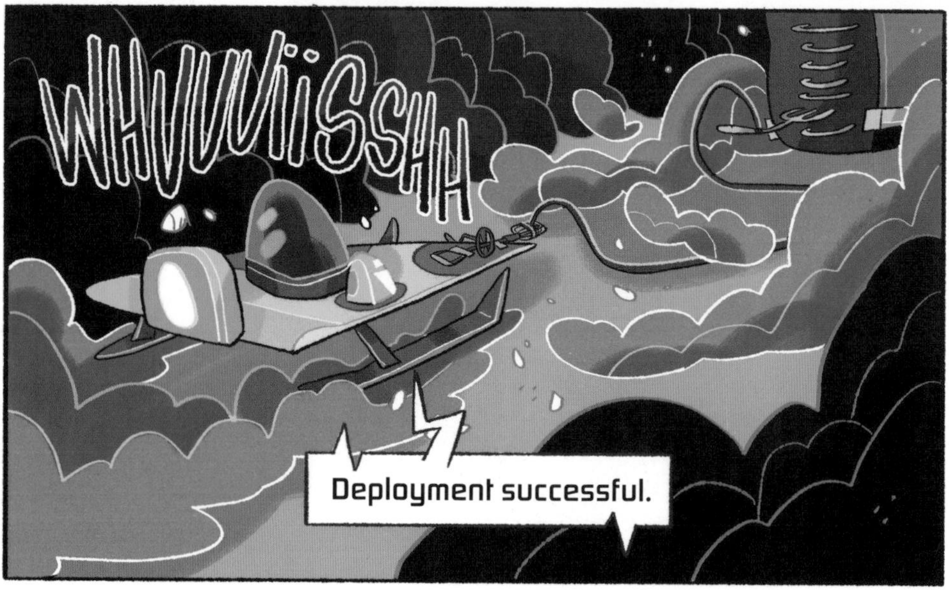
WHUUUiiSSHH
Deployment successful.

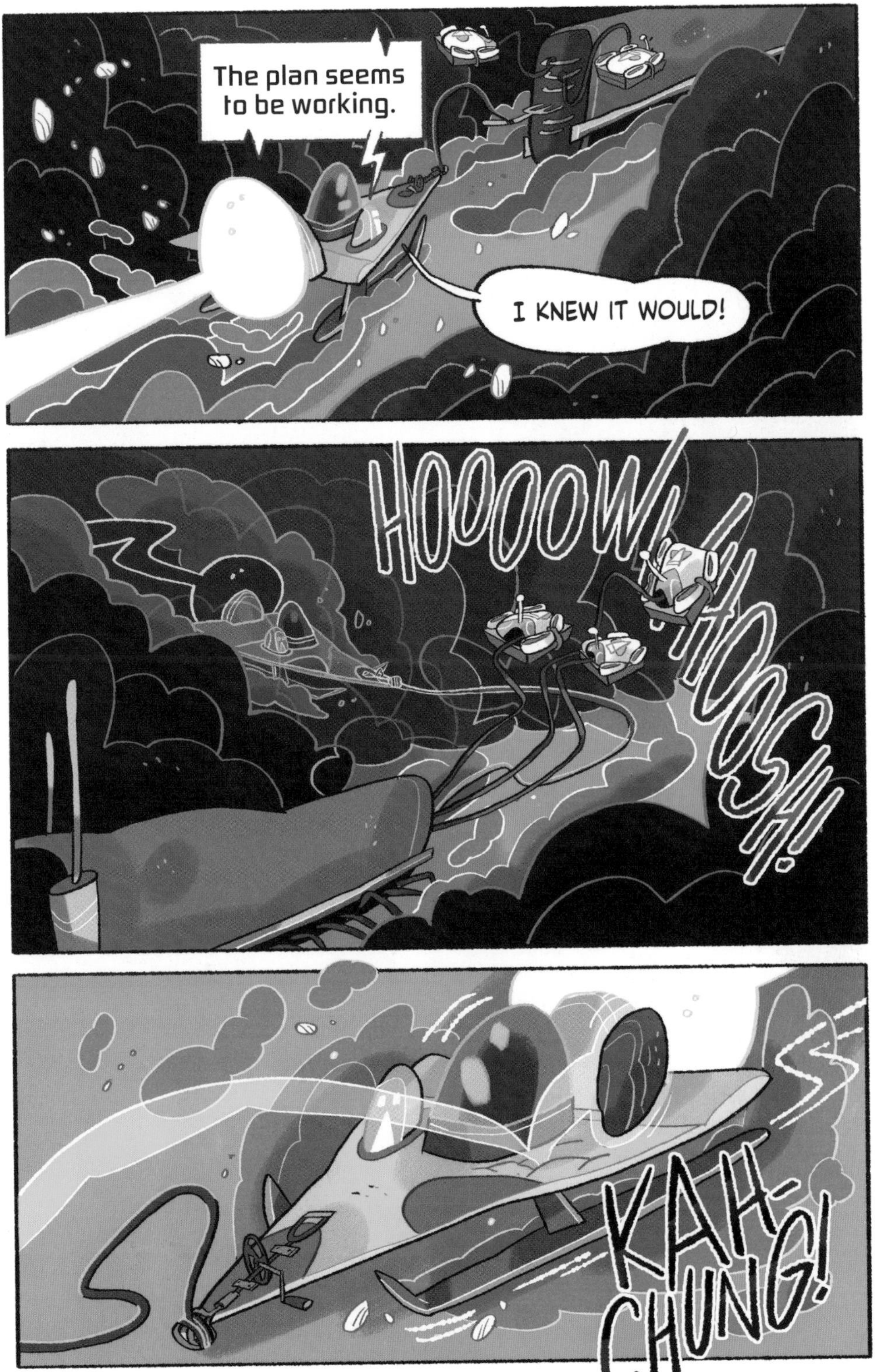
The plan seems to be working.
I KNEW IT WOULD!
HOOOOWHOOOSH!
KAH-CHUNG!

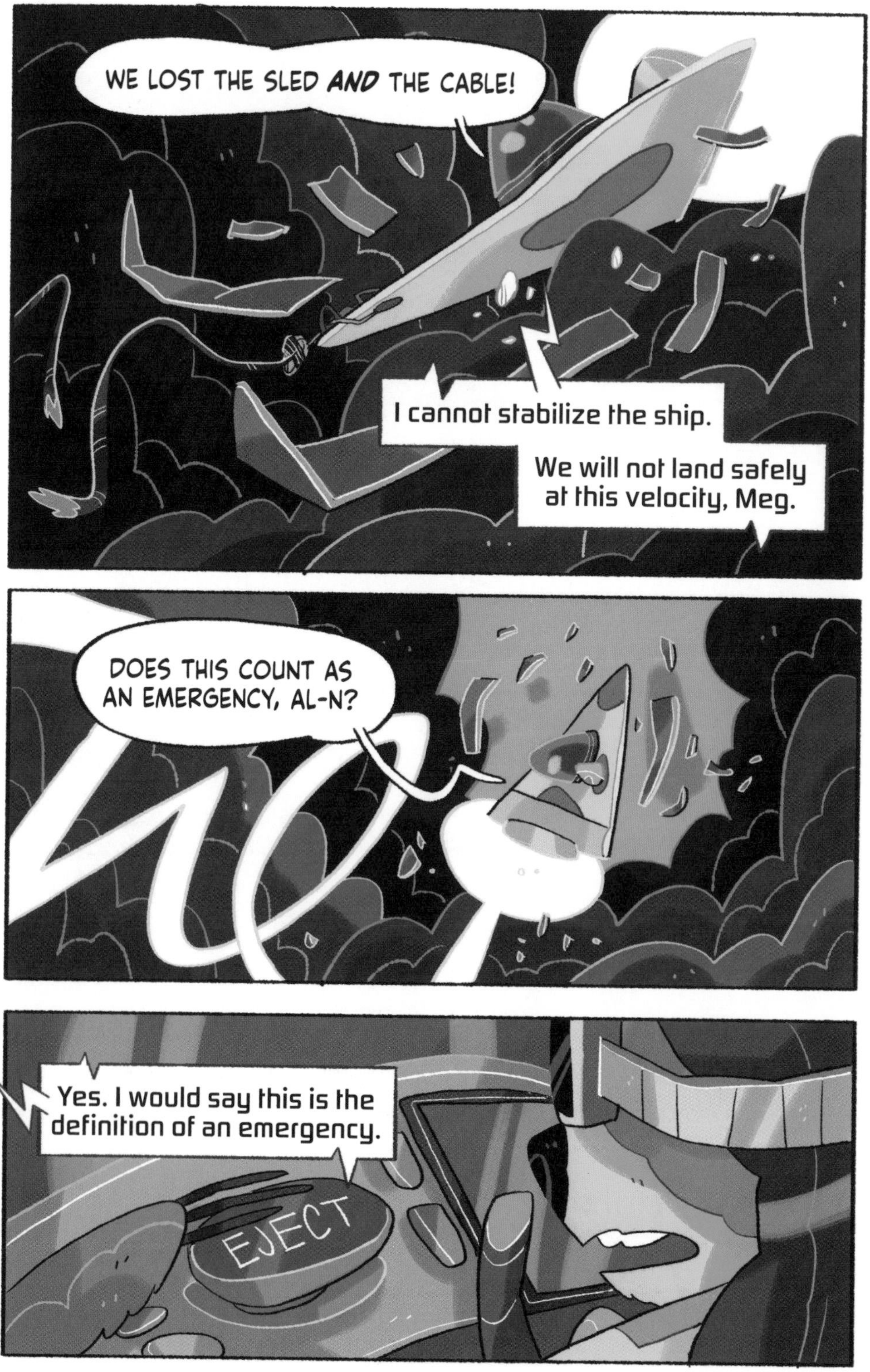
WE LOST THE SLED AND THE CABLE!
I cannot stabilize the ship.
We will not land safely at this velocity, Meg.
DOES THIS COUNT AS AN EMERGENCY, AL-N?
Yes. I would say this is the definition of an emergency.
EJECT

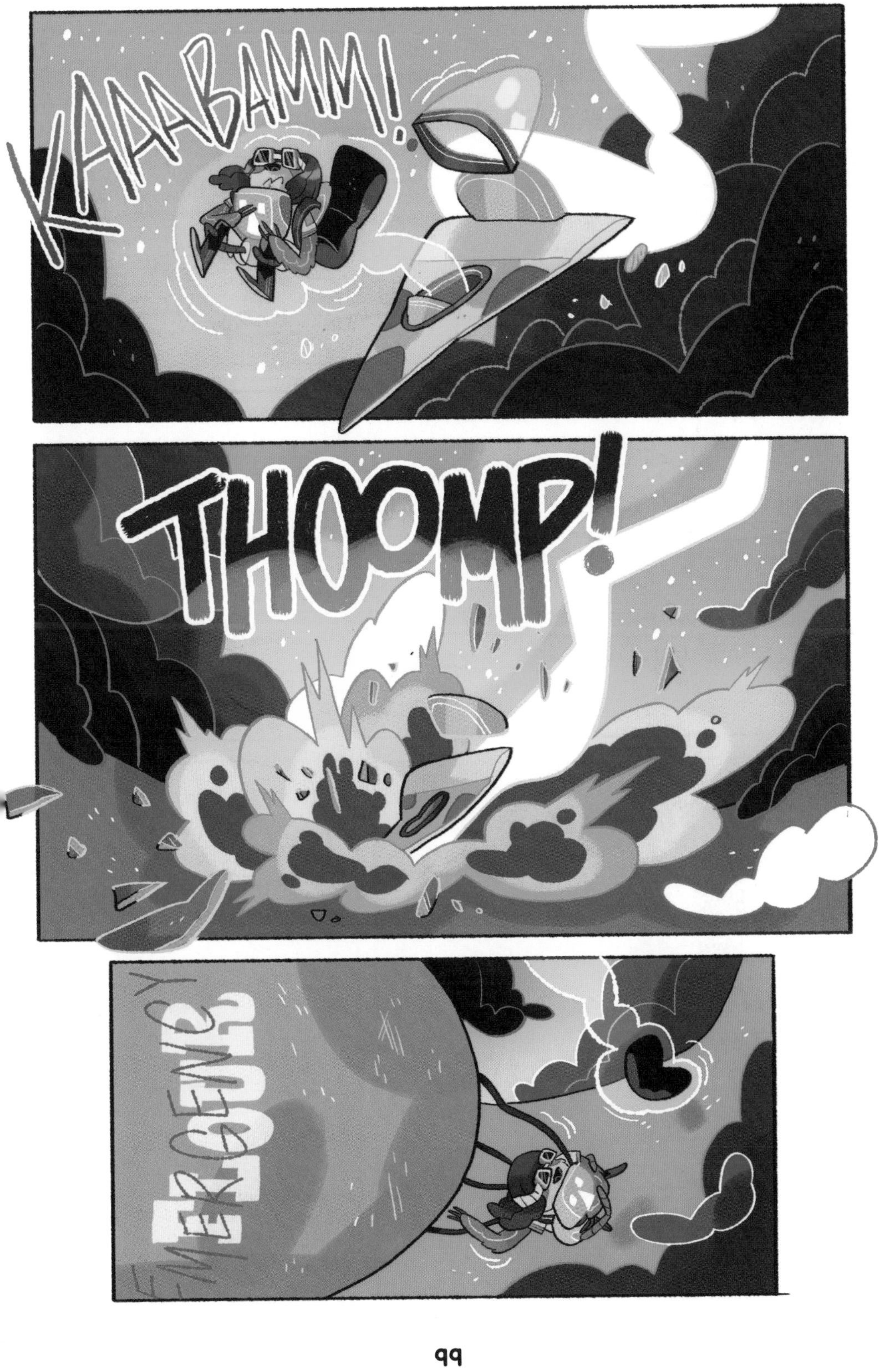
KAAABAMM!
THOOMP!
EMERGENCY

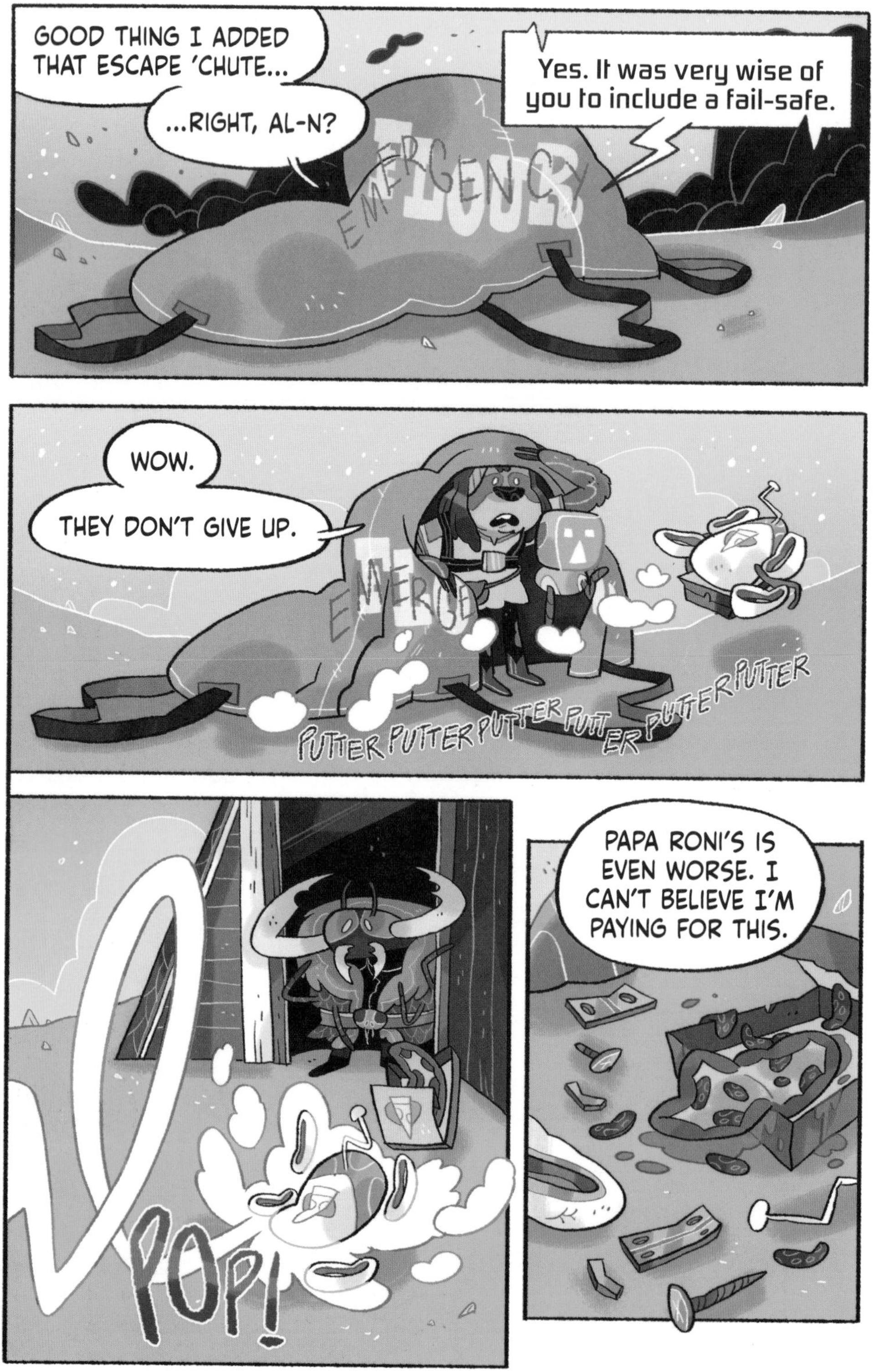
GOOD THING I ADDED THAT ESCAPE 'CHUTE...
...RIGHT, AL-N?
Yes. It was very wise of you to include a fail-safe.
EMERGENCY
FLOUR
WOW.
THEY DON'T GIVE UP.
PUTTER PUTTER PUTTER PUTTER PUTTER PUTTER
POP!
PAPA RONI'S IS EVEN WORSE. I CAN'T BELIEVE I'M PAYING FOR THIS.

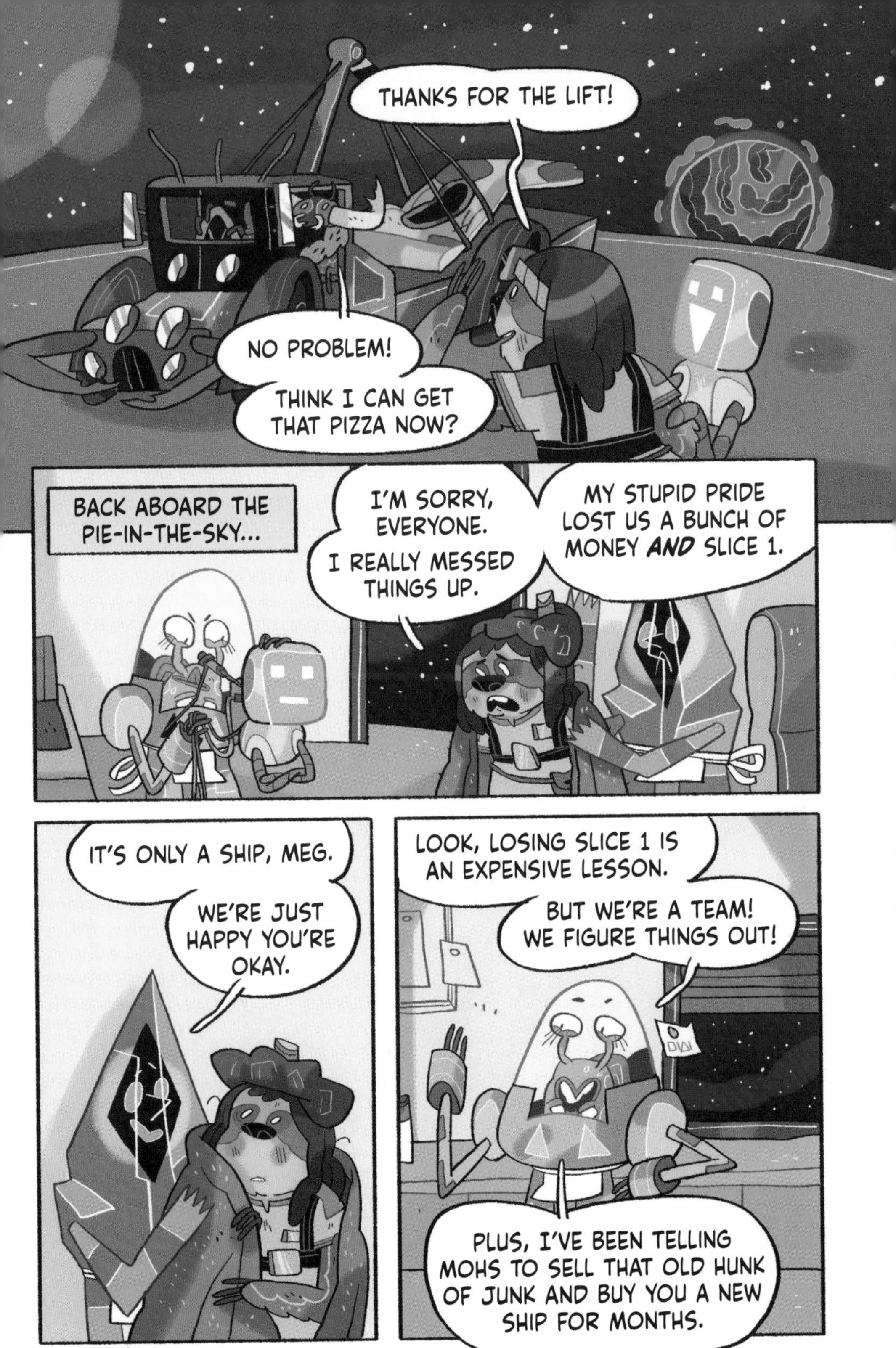
THANKS FOR THE LIFT!
NO PROBLEM!
THINK I CAN GET THAT PIZZA NOW?
BACK ABOARD THE PIE-IN-THE-SKY...
I'M SORRY, EVERYONE.
I REALLY MESSED THINGS UP.
MY STUPID PRIDE LOST US A BUNCH OF MONEY *AND* SLICE 1.
IT'S ONLY A SHIP, MEG.
WE'RE JUST HAPPY YOU'RE OKAY.
LOOK, LOSING SLICE 1 IS AN EXPENSIVE LESSON.
BUT WE'RE A TEAM! WE FIGURE THINGS OUT!
PLUS, I'VE BEEN TELLING MOHS TO SELL THAT OLD HUNK OF JUNK AND BUY YOU A NEW SHIP FOR MONTHS.

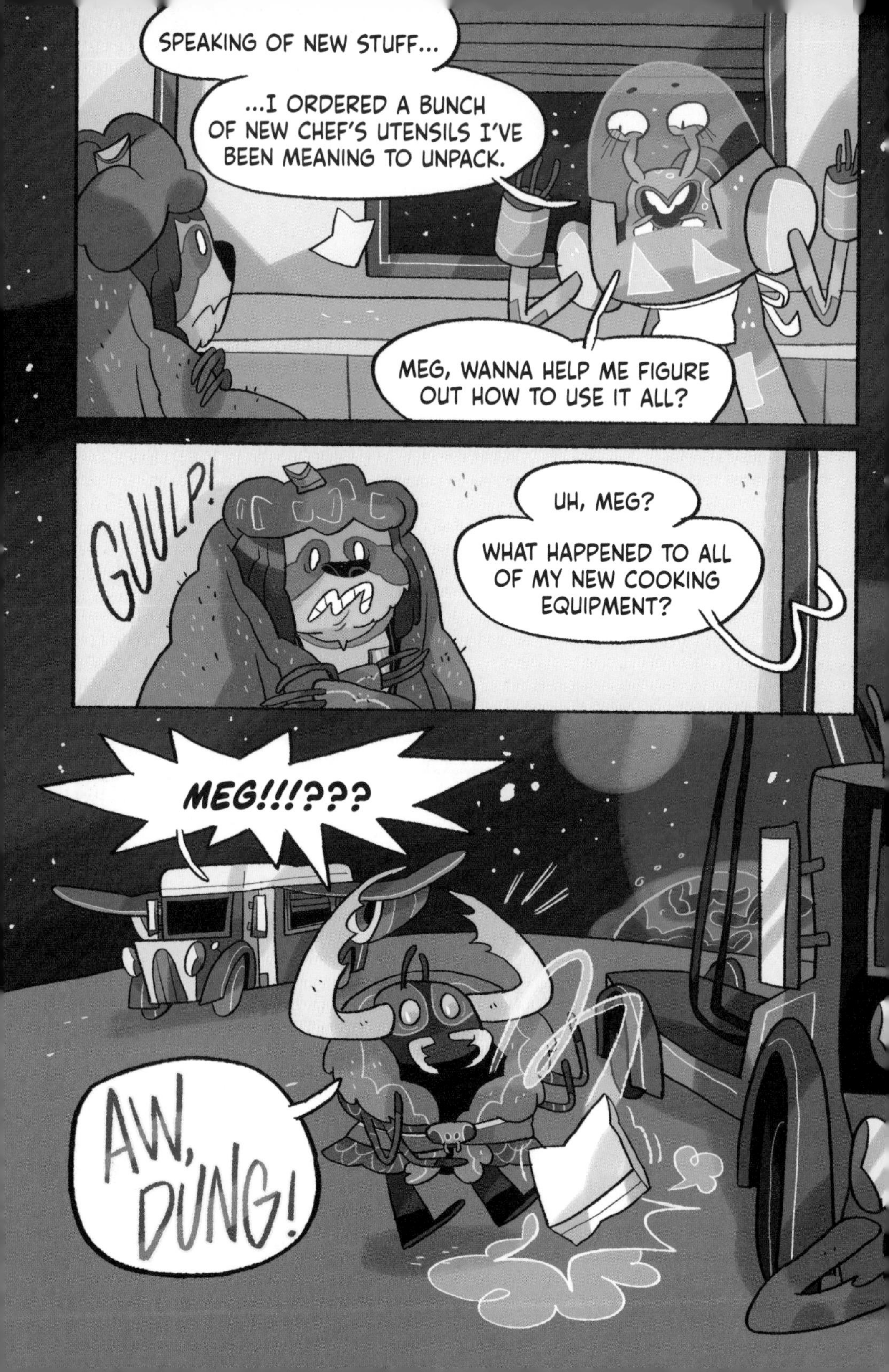
SPEAKING OF NEW STUFF...
...I ORDERED A BUNCH OF NEW CHEF'S UTENSILS I'VE BEEN MEANING TO UNPACK.
MEG, WANNA HELP ME FIGURE OUT HOW TO USE IT ALL?
GUULP!
UH, MEG?
WHAT HAPPENED TO ALL OF MY NEW COOKING EQUIPMENT?
MEG!!!???
AW, DUNG!

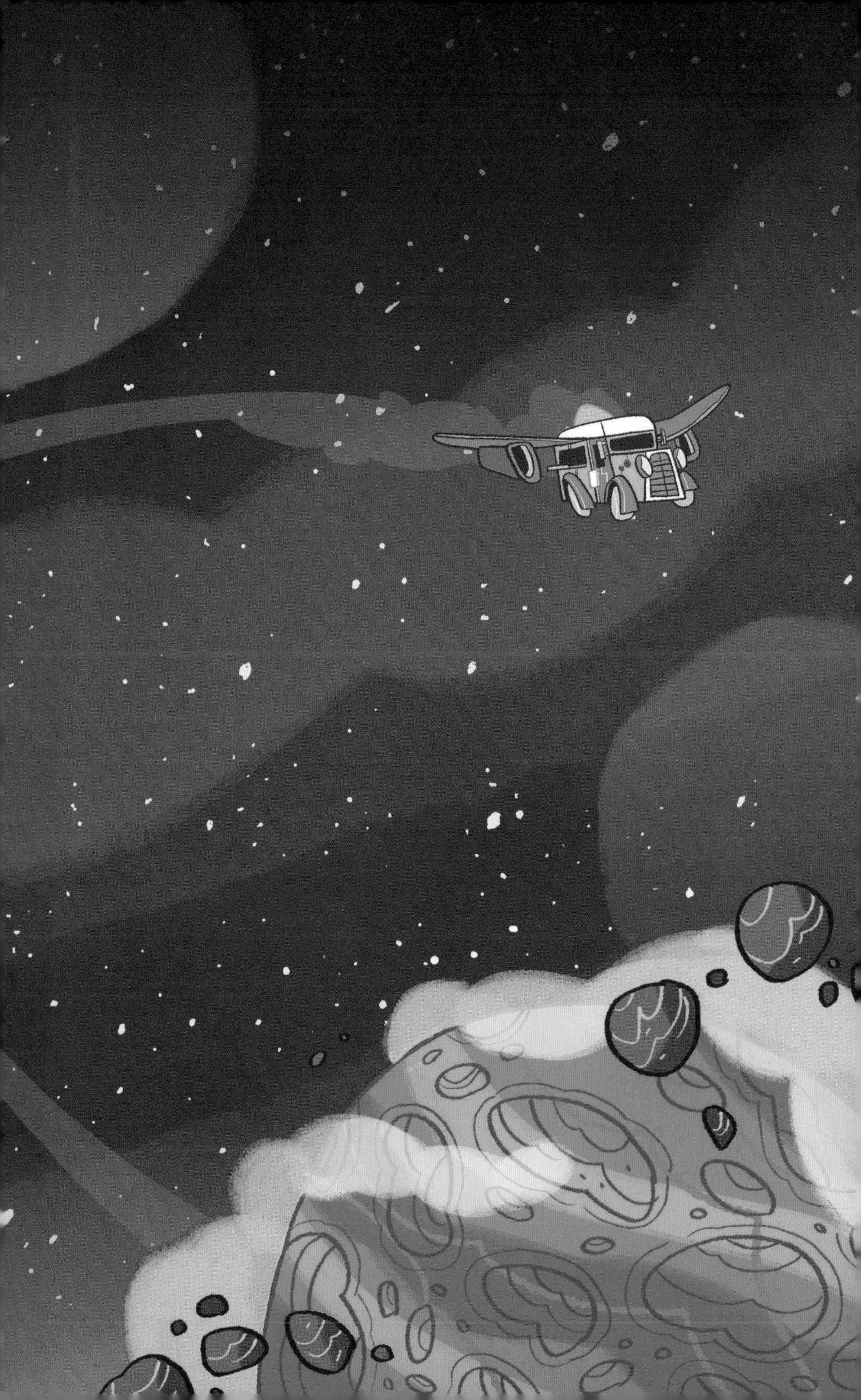

CHAPTER 5
REALITY SHOWDOWN

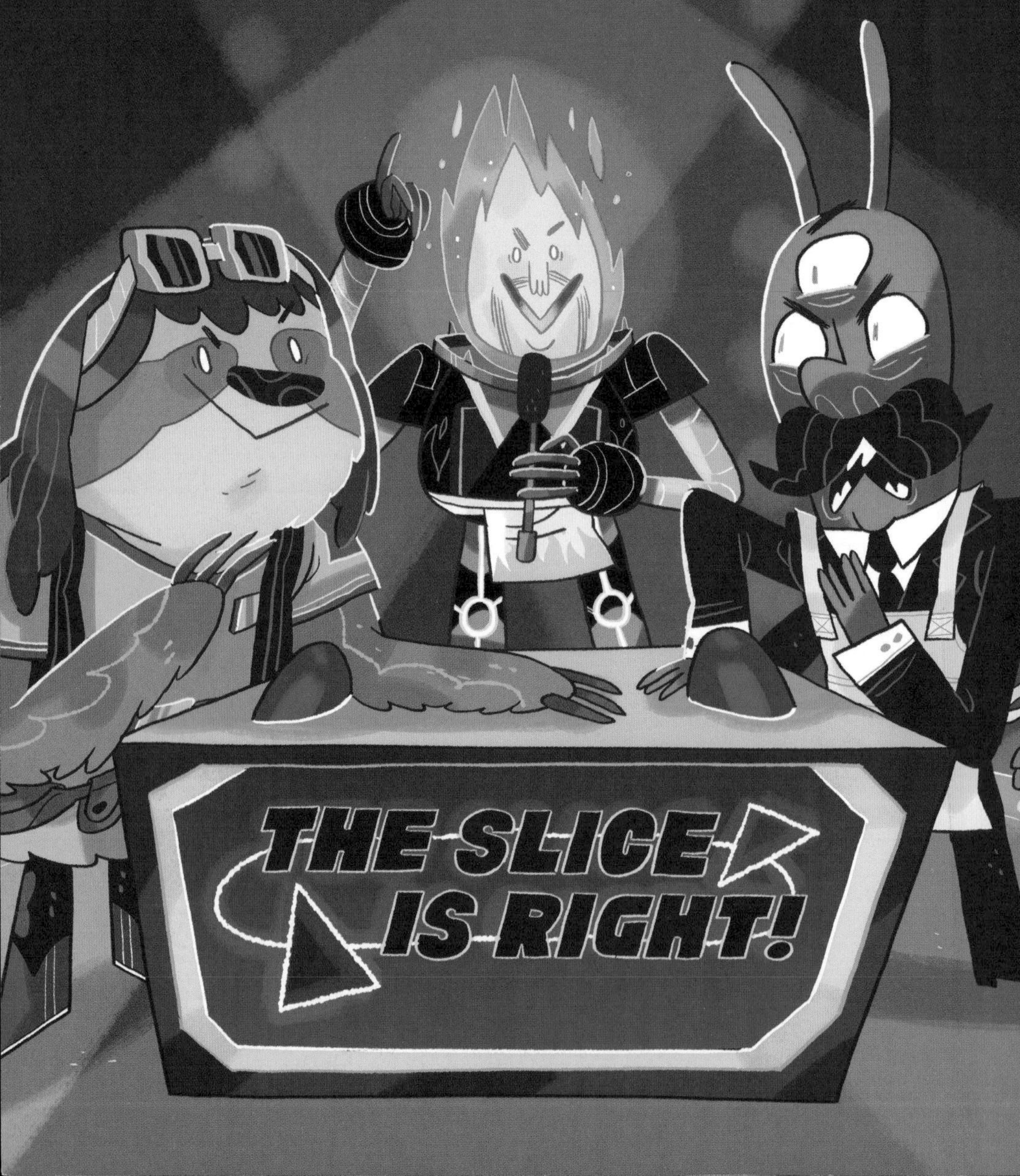
THE SLICE
IS RIGHT!

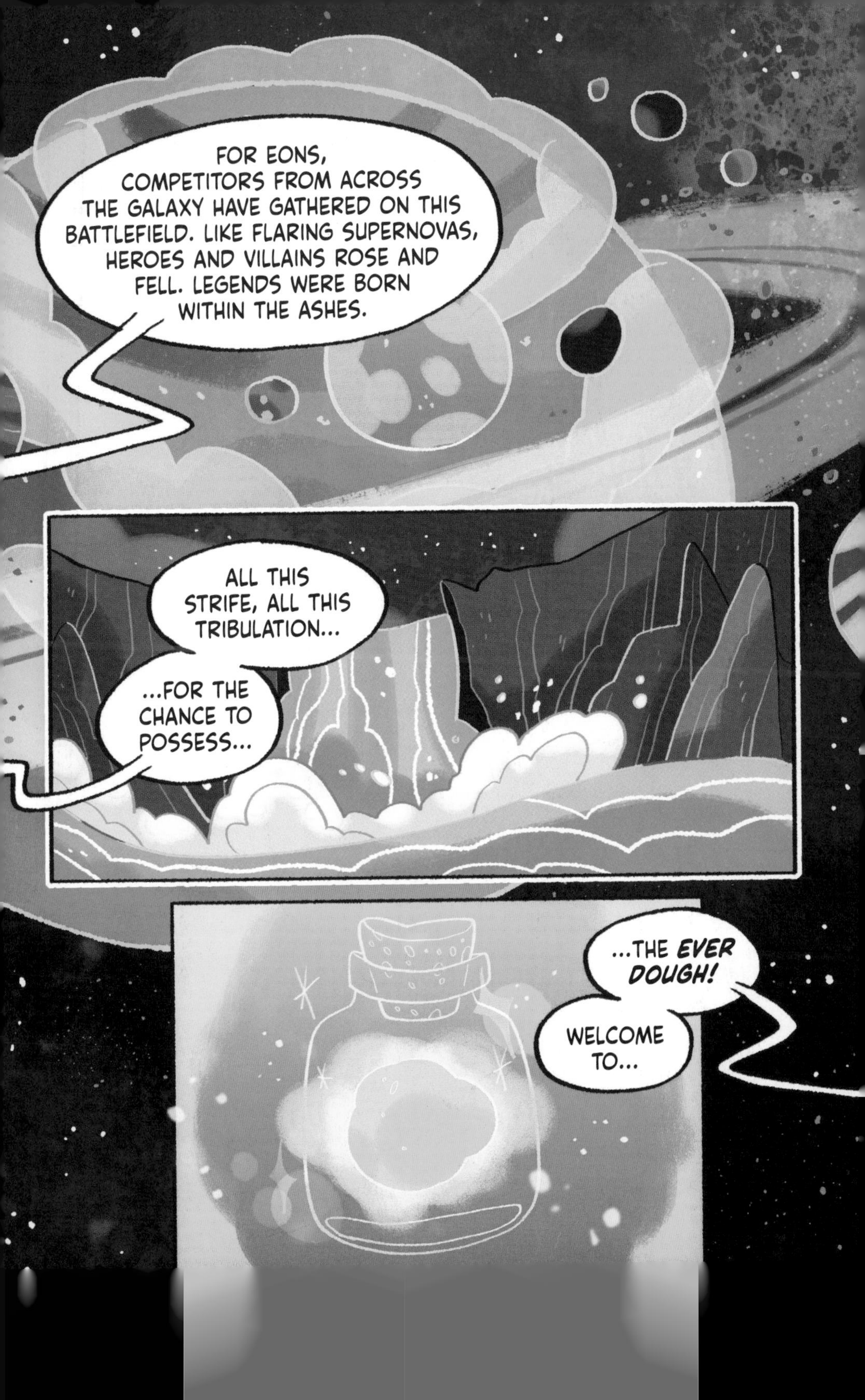
FOR EONS, COMPETITORS FROM ACROSS THE GALAXY HAVE GATHERED ON THIS BATTLEFIELD. LIKE FLARING SUPERNOVAS, HEROES AND VILLAINS ROSE AND FELL. LEGENDS WERE BORN WITHIN THE ASHES.
ALL THIS STRIFE, ALL THIS TRIBULATION...
...FOR THE CHANCE TO POSSESS...
...THE EVER DOUGH!
WELCOME TO...

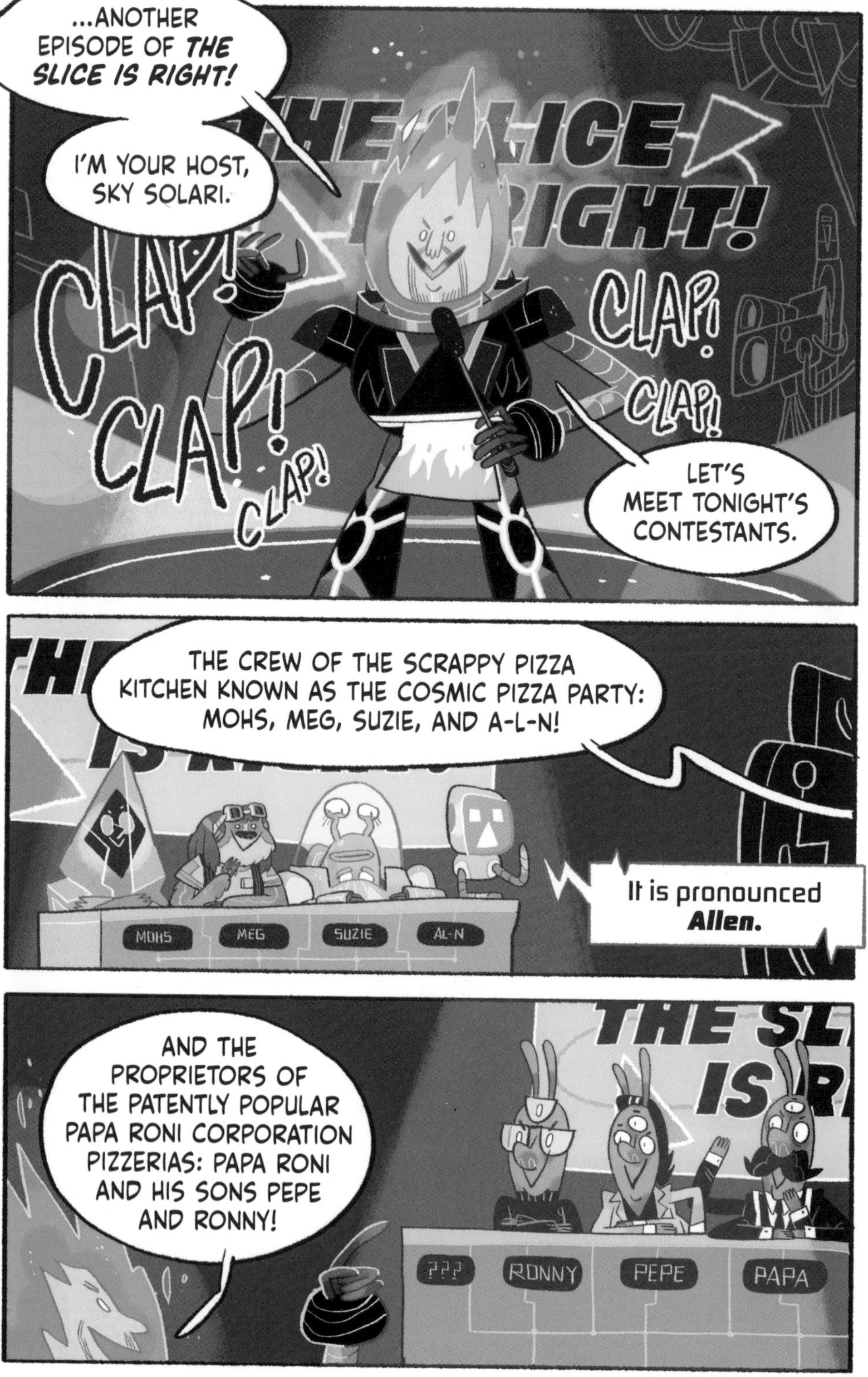
...ANOTHER EPISODE OF THE SLICE IS RIGHT!
THE SLICE IS RIGHT!
I'M YOUR HOST, SKY SOLARI.
CLAP! CLAP! CLAP!
CLAP! CLAP!
LET'S MEET TONIGHT'S CONTESTANTS.
THE CREW OF THE SCRAPPY PIZZA KITCHEN KNOWN AS THE COSMIC PIZZA PARTY: MOHS, MEG, SUZIE, AND A-L-N!
MOHS
MEG
SUZIE
AL-N
It is pronounced Allen.
AND THE PROPRIETORS OF THE PATENTLY POPULAR PAPA RONI CORPORATION PIZZERIAS: PAPA RONI AND HIS SONS PEPE AND RONNY!
???
RONNY
PEPE
PAPA

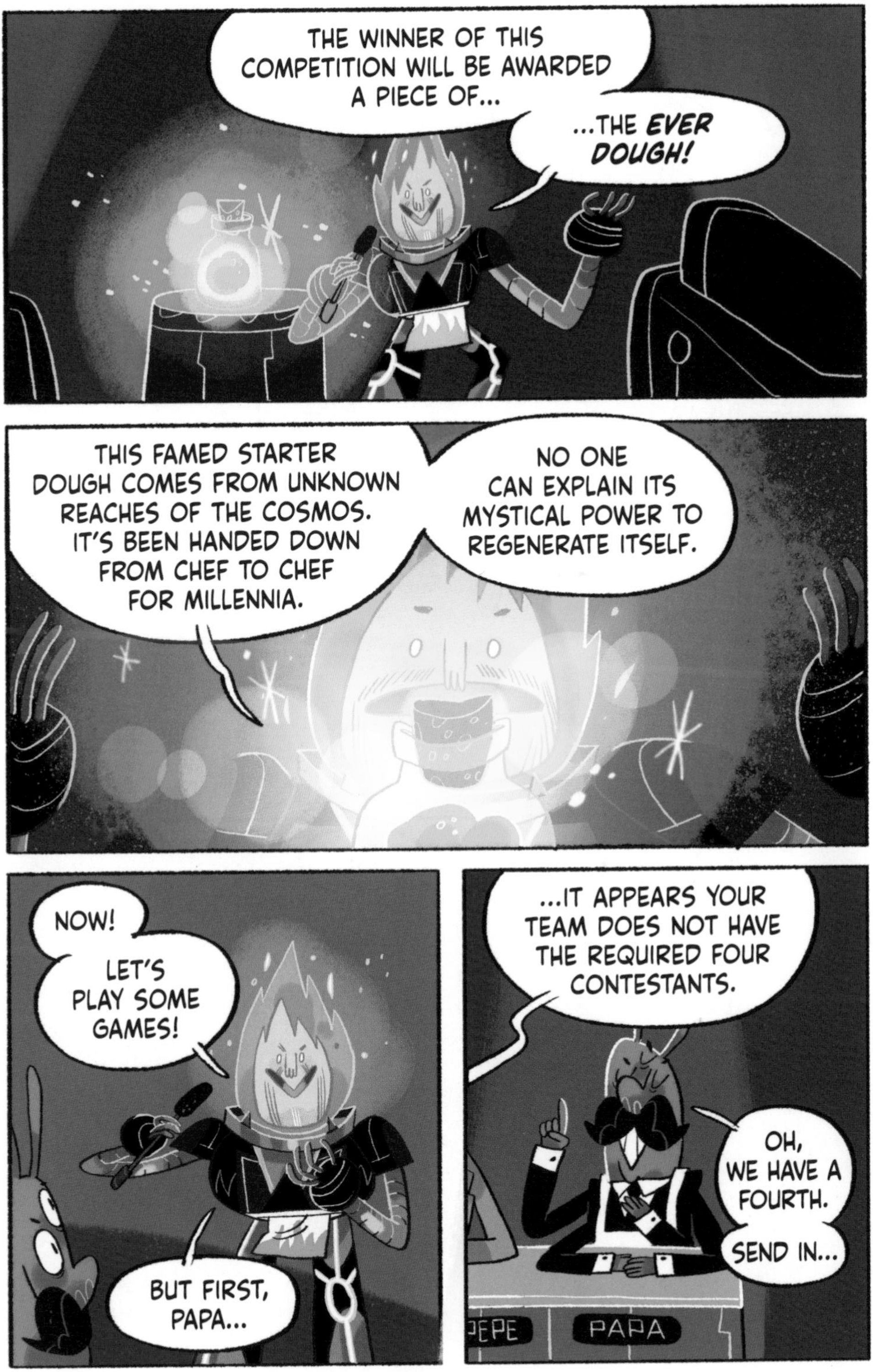
THE WINNER OF THIS COMPETITION WILL BE AWARDED A PIECE OF...
...THE *EVER DOUGH!*
THIS FAMED STARTER DOUGH COMES FROM UNKNOWN REACHES OF THE COSMOS. IT'S BEEN HANDED DOWN FROM CHEF TO CHEF FOR MILLENNIA.
NO ONE CAN EXPLAIN ITS MYSTICAL POWER TO REGENERATE ITSELF.
NOW!
LET'S PLAY SOME GAMES!
BUT FIRST, PAPA...
...IT APPEARS YOUR TEAM DOES NOT HAVE THE REQUIRED FOUR CONTESTANTS.
OH, WE HAVE A FOURTH.
SEND IN...
PEPE
PAPA

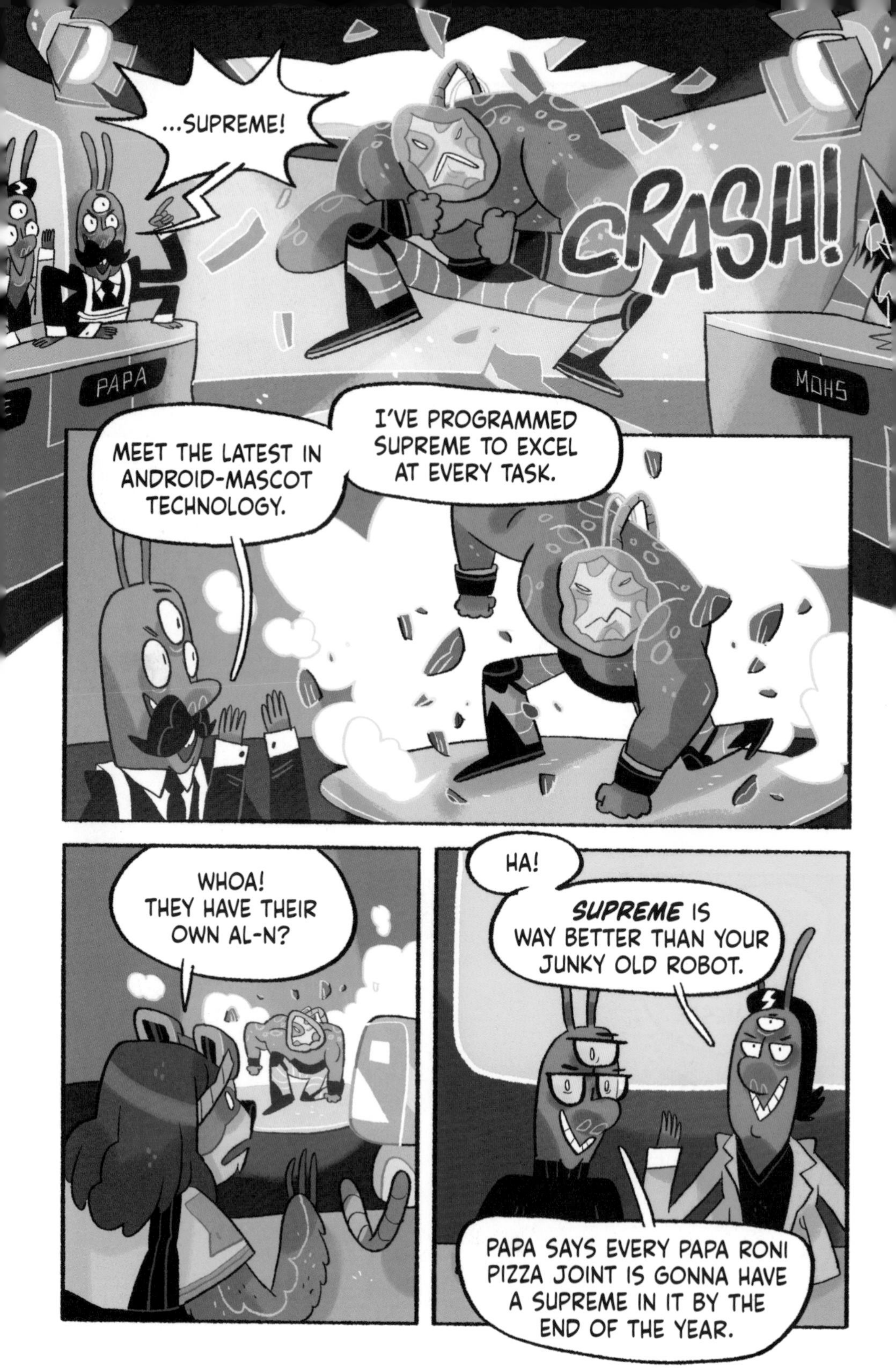
...SUPREME!
CRASH!
PAPA
MOHS
MEET THE LATEST IN ANDROID-MASCOT TECHNOLOGY.
I'VE PROGRAMMED SUPREME TO EXCEL AT EVERY TASK.
WHOA! THEY HAVE THEIR OWN AL-N?
HA!
SUPREME IS WAY BETTER THAN YOUR JUNKY OLD ROBOT.
PAPA SAYS EVERY PAPA RONI PIZZA JOINT IS GONNA HAVE A SUPREME IN IT BY THE END OF THE YEAR.

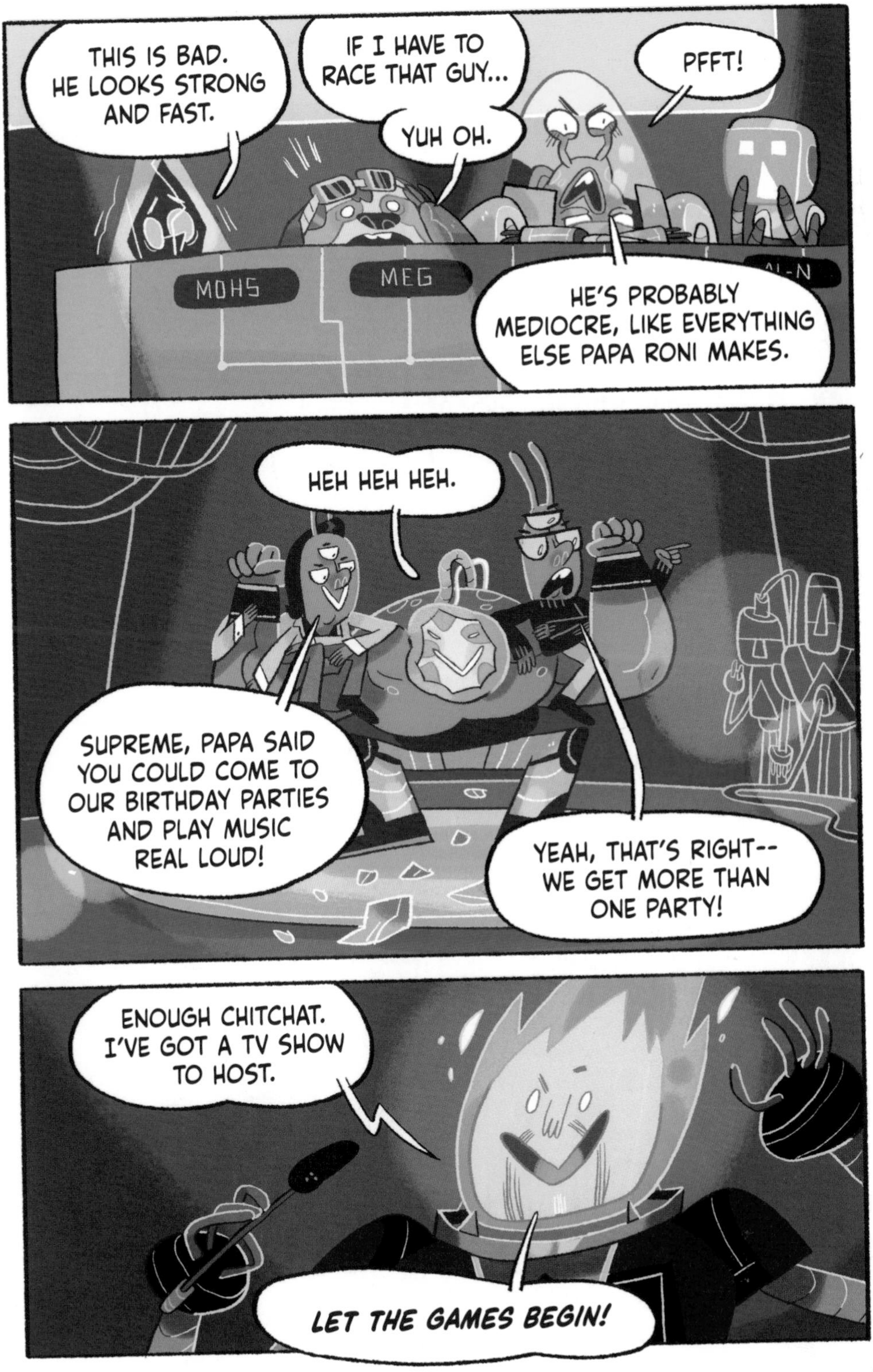
THIS IS BAD. HE LOOKS STRONG AND FAST.
IF I HAVE TO RACE THAT GUY...
YUH OH.
PFFT!
MOHS
MEG
HE'S PROBABLY MEDIOCRE, LIKE EVERYTHING ELSE PAPA RONI MAKES.
HEH HEH HEH.
SUPREME, PAPA SAID YOU COULD COME TO OUR BIRTHDAY PARTIES AND PLAY MUSIC REAL LOUD!
YEAH, THAT'S RIGHT--WE GET MORE THAN ONE PARTY!
ENOUGH CHITCHAT. I'VE GOT A TV SHOW TO HOST.
LET THE GAMES BEGIN!

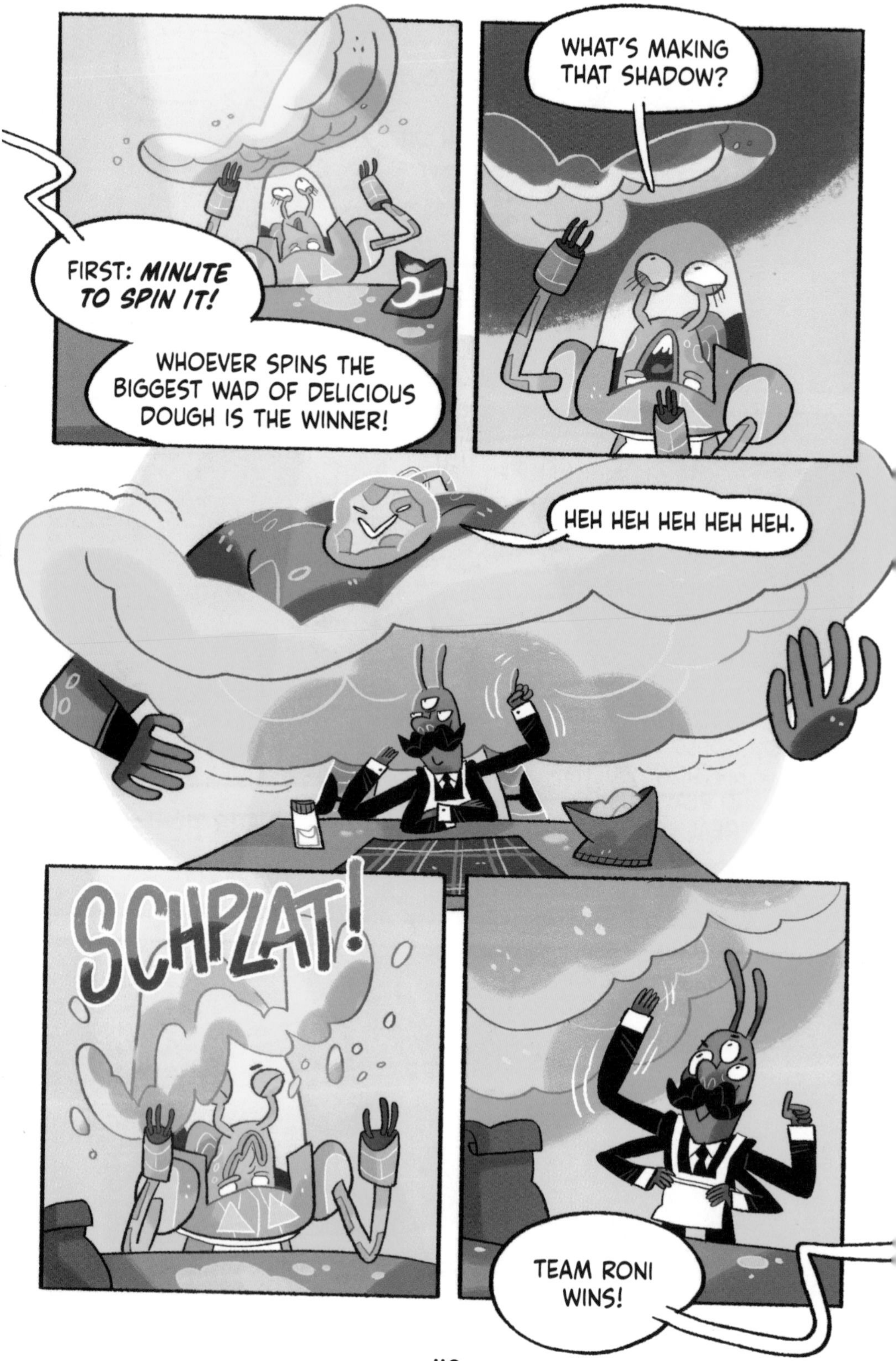
FIRST: *MINUTE TO SPIN IT!*
WHOEVER SPINS THE BIGGEST WAD OF DELICIOUS DOUGH IS THE WINNER!
WHAT'S MAKING THAT SHADOW?
HEH HEH HEH HEH HEH.
SCHPLAT!
TEAM RONI WINS!

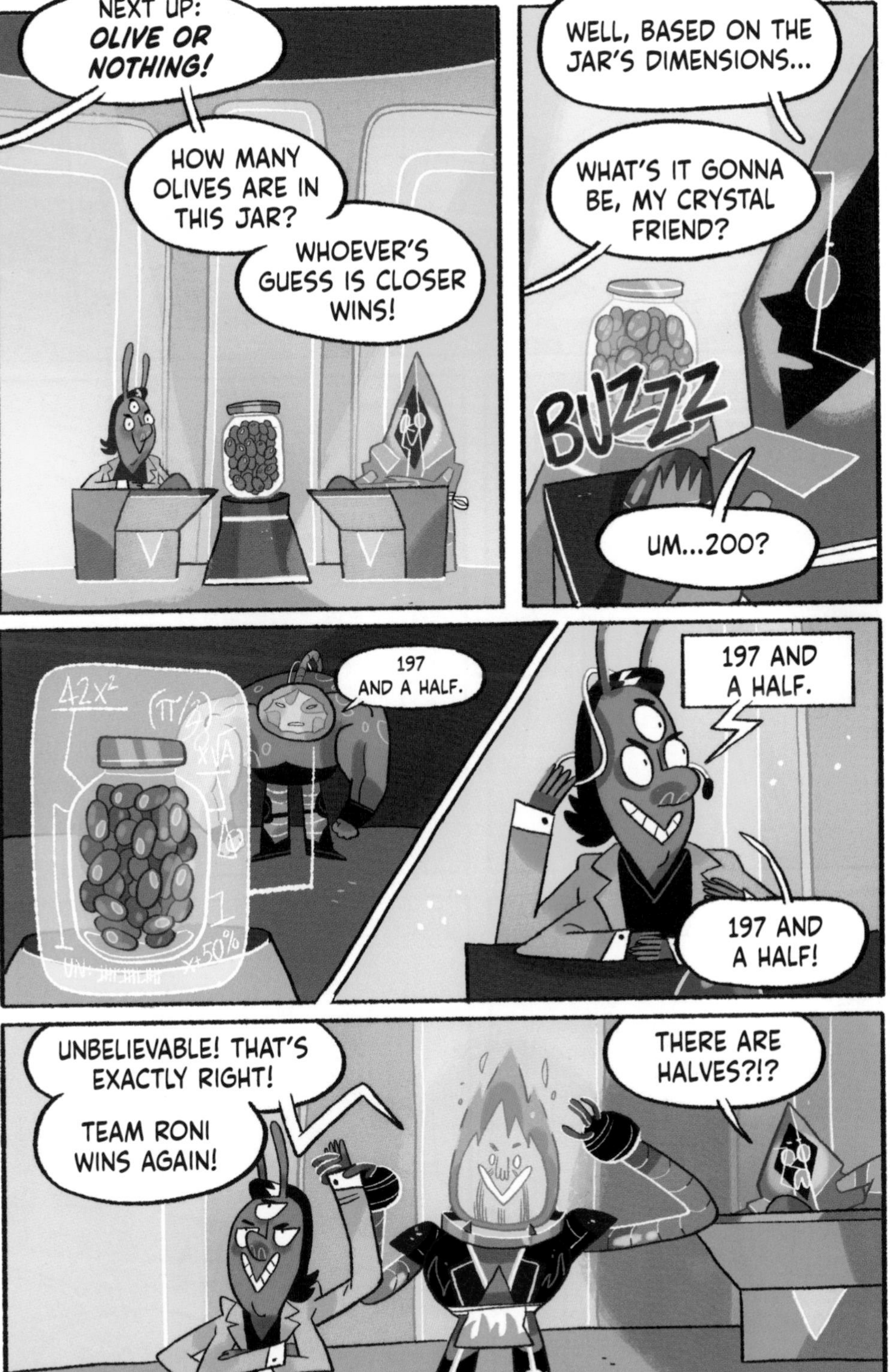
NEXT UP: *OLIVE OR NOTHING!*
HOW MANY OLIVES ARE IN THIS JAR?
WHOEVER'S GUESS IS CLOSER WINS!
WELL, BASED ON THE JAR'S DIMENSIONS...
WHAT'S IT GONNA BE, MY CRYSTAL FRIEND?
BUZZZ
UM...200?
197 AND A HALF.
197 AND A HALF.
197 AND A HALF!
UNBELIEVABLE! THAT'S EXACTLY RIGHT!
TEAM RONI WINS AGAIN!
THERE ARE HALVES?!?

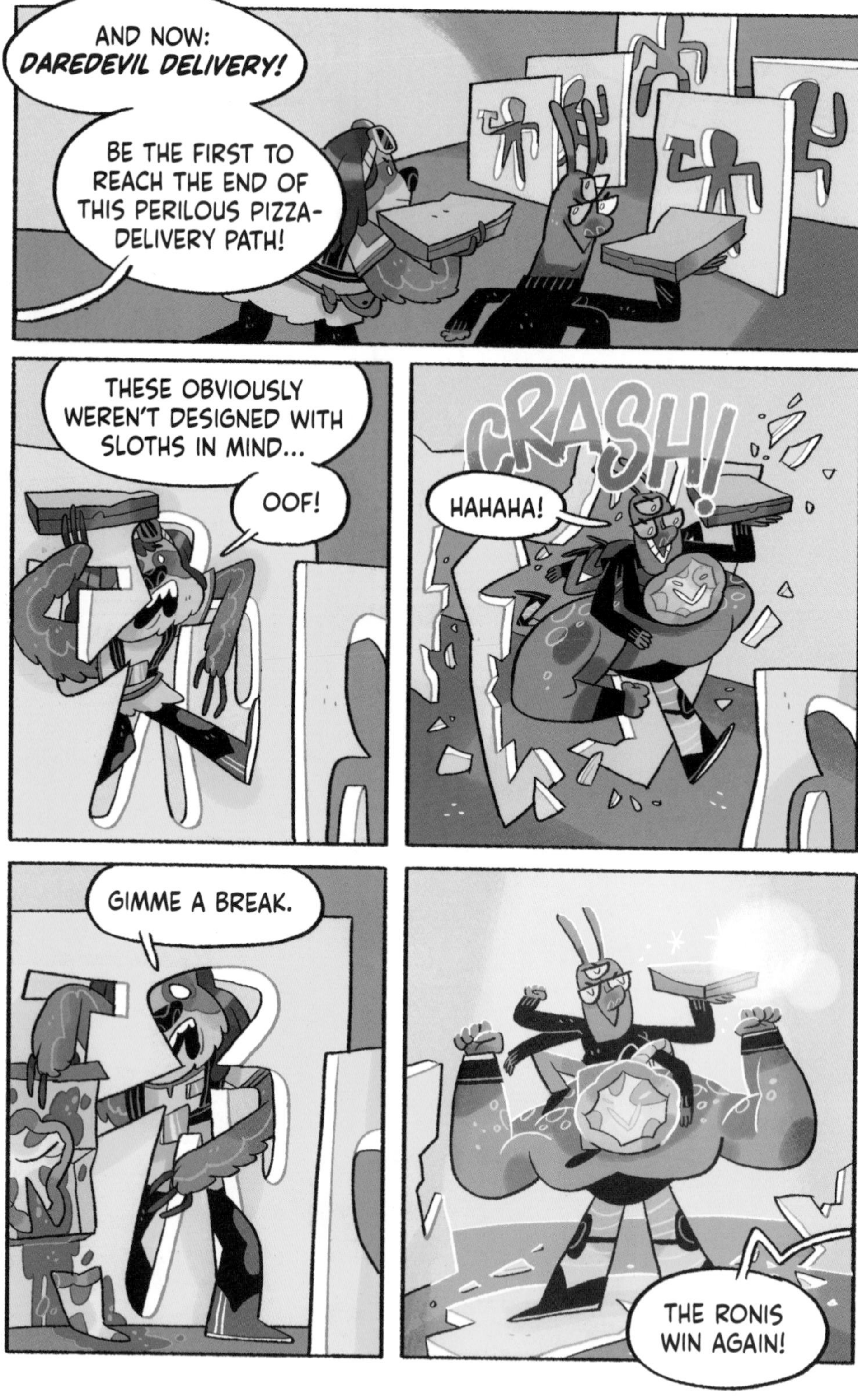
AND NOW: DAREDEVIL DELIVERY!
BE THE FIRST TO REACH THE END OF THIS PERILOUS PIZZA-DELIVERY PATH!
THESE OBVIOUSLY WEREN'T DESIGNED WITH SLOTHS IN MIND...
OOF!
CRASH!
HAHAHA!
GIMME A BREAK.
THE RONIS WIN AGAIN!

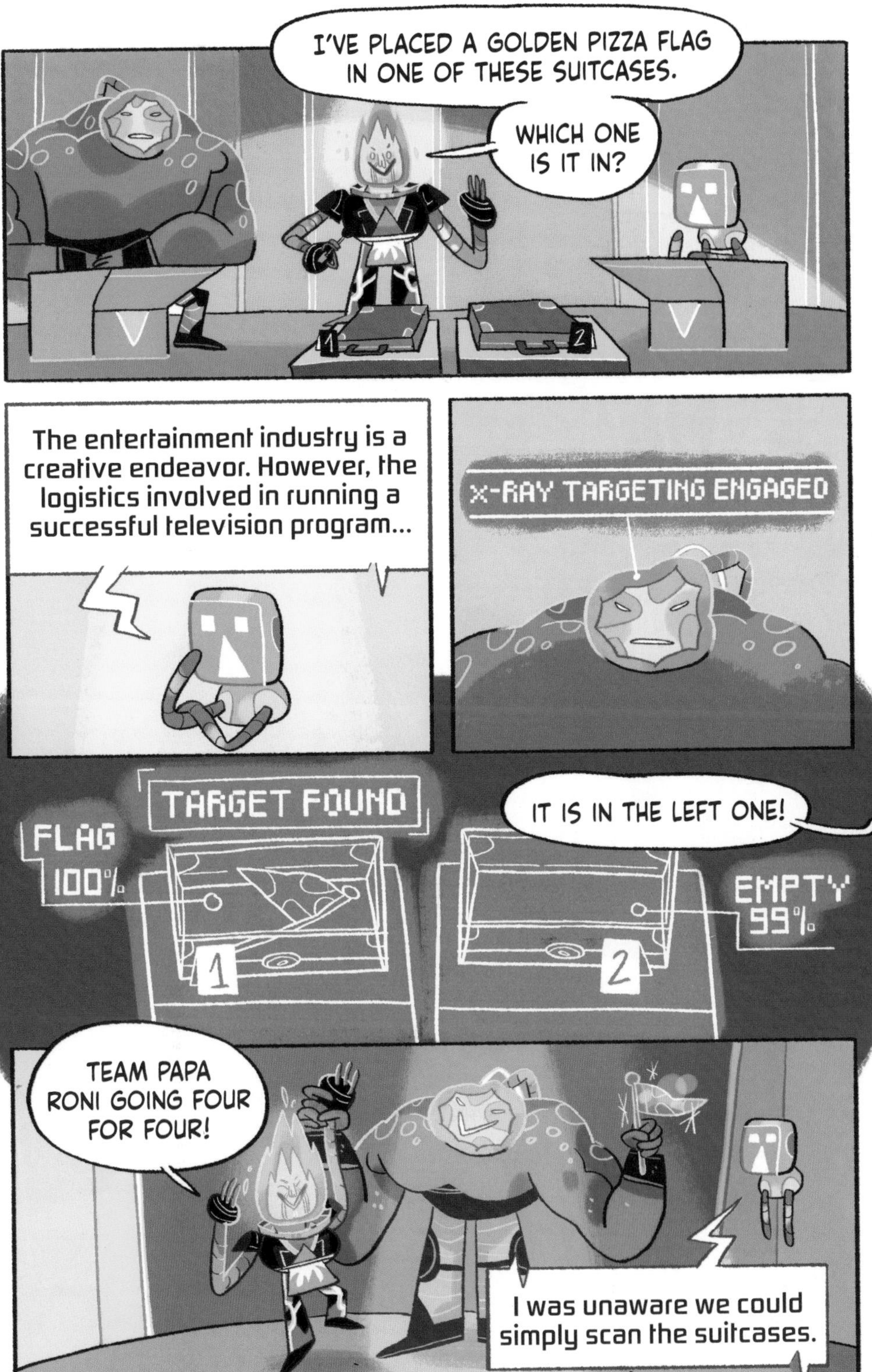
I'VE PLACED A GOLDEN PIZZA FLAG IN ONE OF THESE SUITCASES.
WHICH ONE IS IT IN?
The entertainment industry is a creative endeavor. However, the logistics involved in running a successful television program...
X-RAY TARGETING ENGAGED
TARGET FOUND
FLAG 100%
EMPTY 99%
IT IS IN THE LEFT ONE!
TEAM PAPA RONI GOING FOUR FOR FOUR!
I was unaware we could simply scan the suitcases.

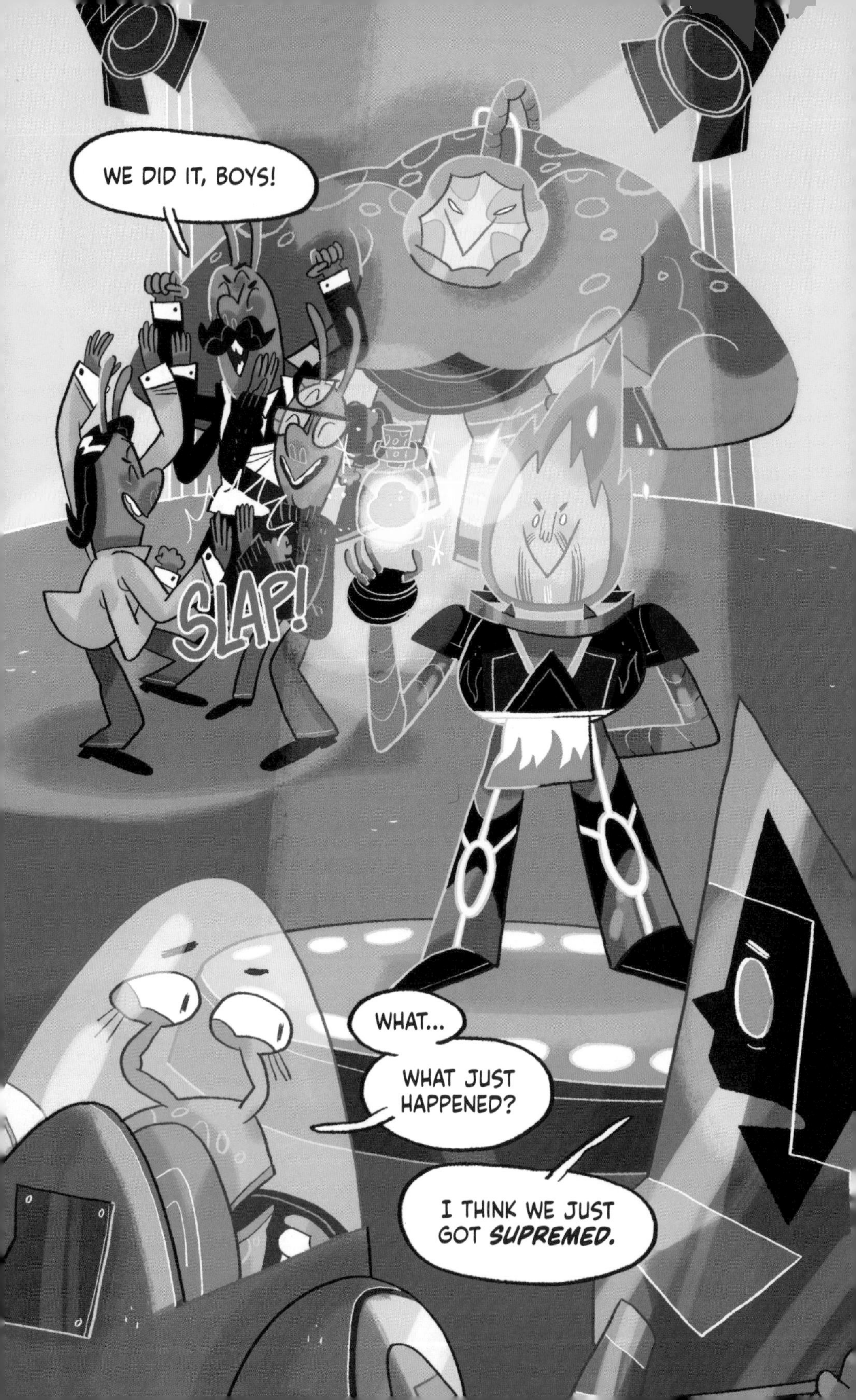
WE DID IT, BOYS!
SLAP!
WHAT...
WHAT JUST HAPPENED?
I THINK WE JUST GOT *SUPREMED.*

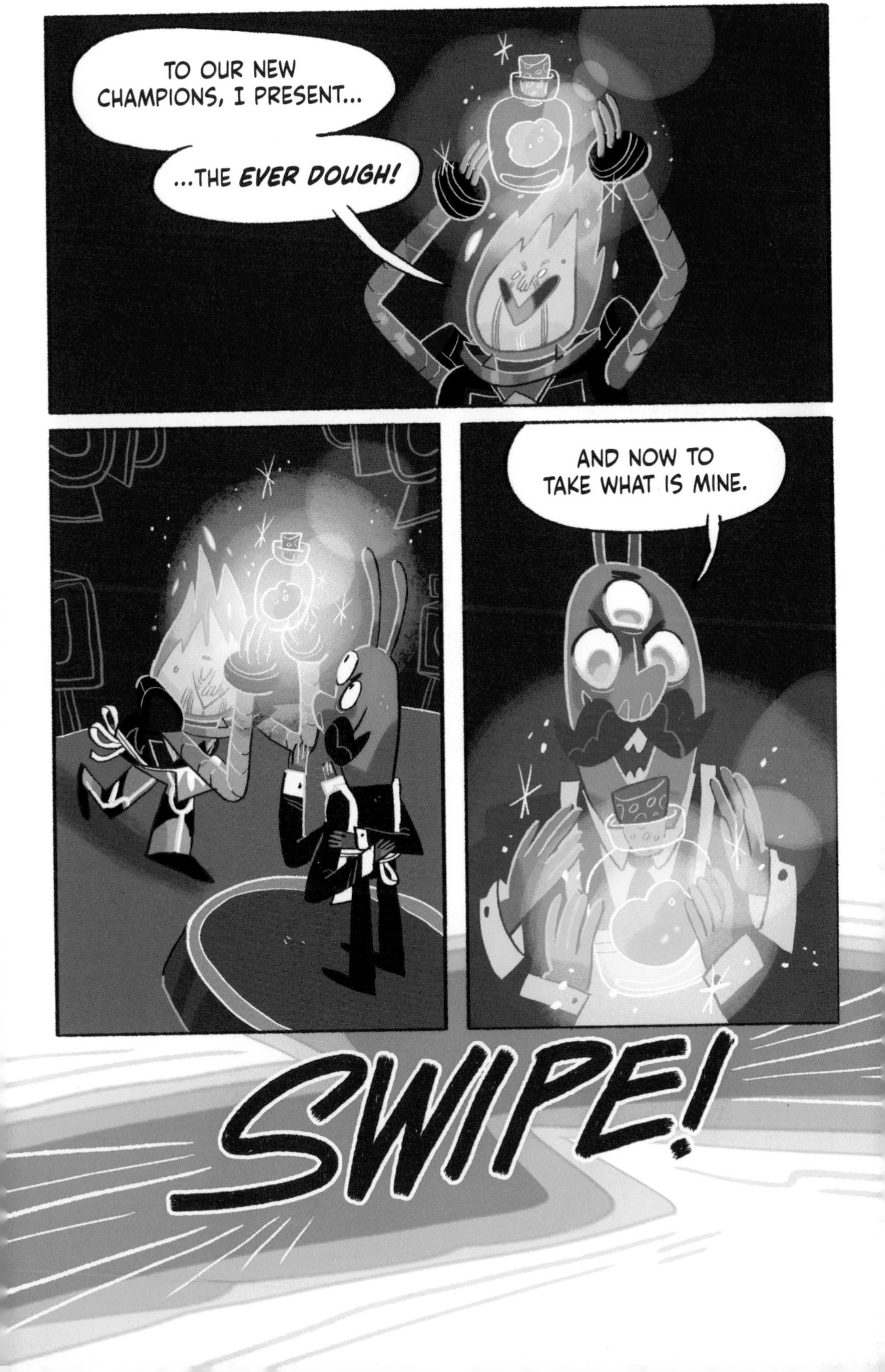
TO OUR NEW CHAMPIONS, I PRESENT...
...THE EVER DOUGH!
AND NOW TO TAKE WHAT IS MINE.
SWIPE!

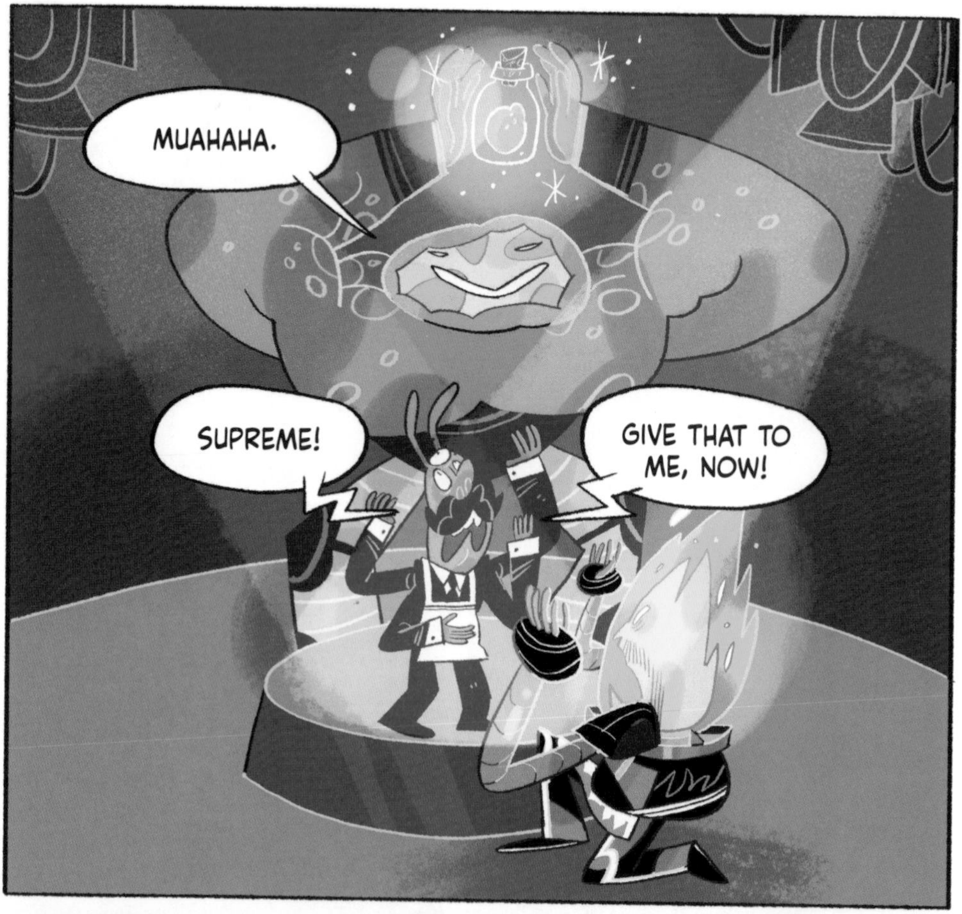
MUAHAHA.
SUPREME!
GIVE THAT TO ME, NOW!

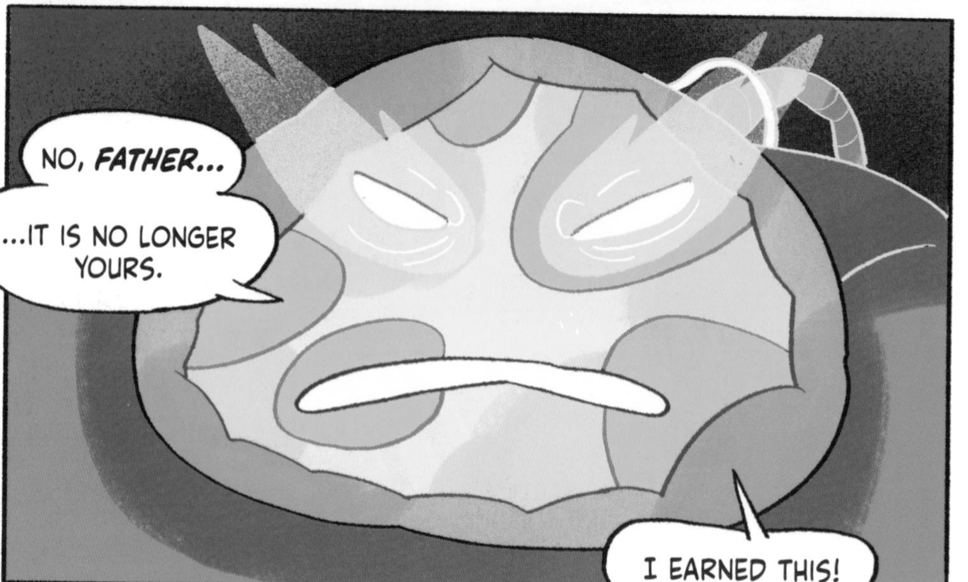
NO, *FATHER...*
...IT IS NO LONGER YOURS.
I EARNED THIS!

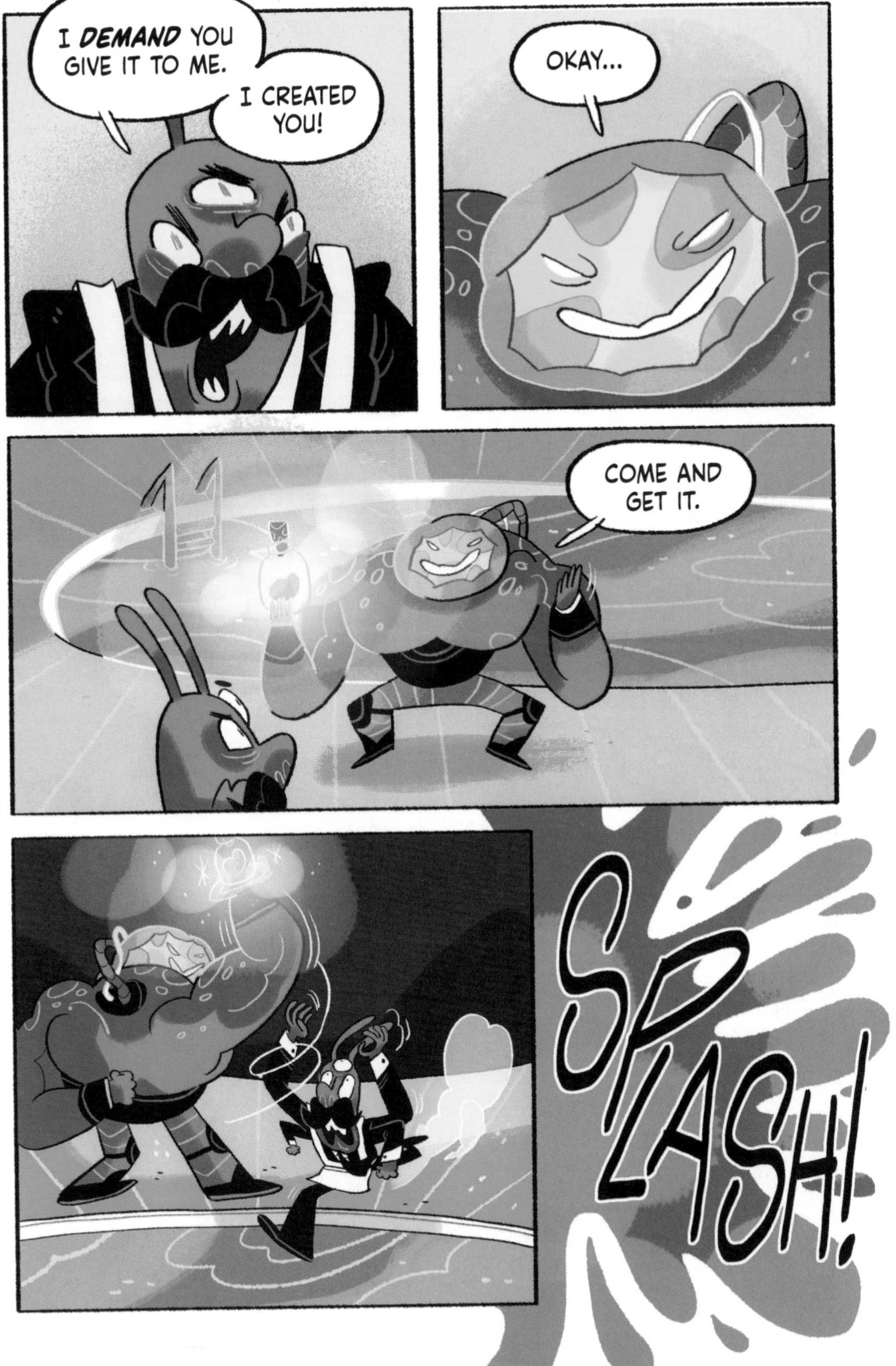

I *DEMAND* YOU GIVE IT TO ME.
I CREATED YOU!
OKAY...
COME AND GET IT.
SPLASH!

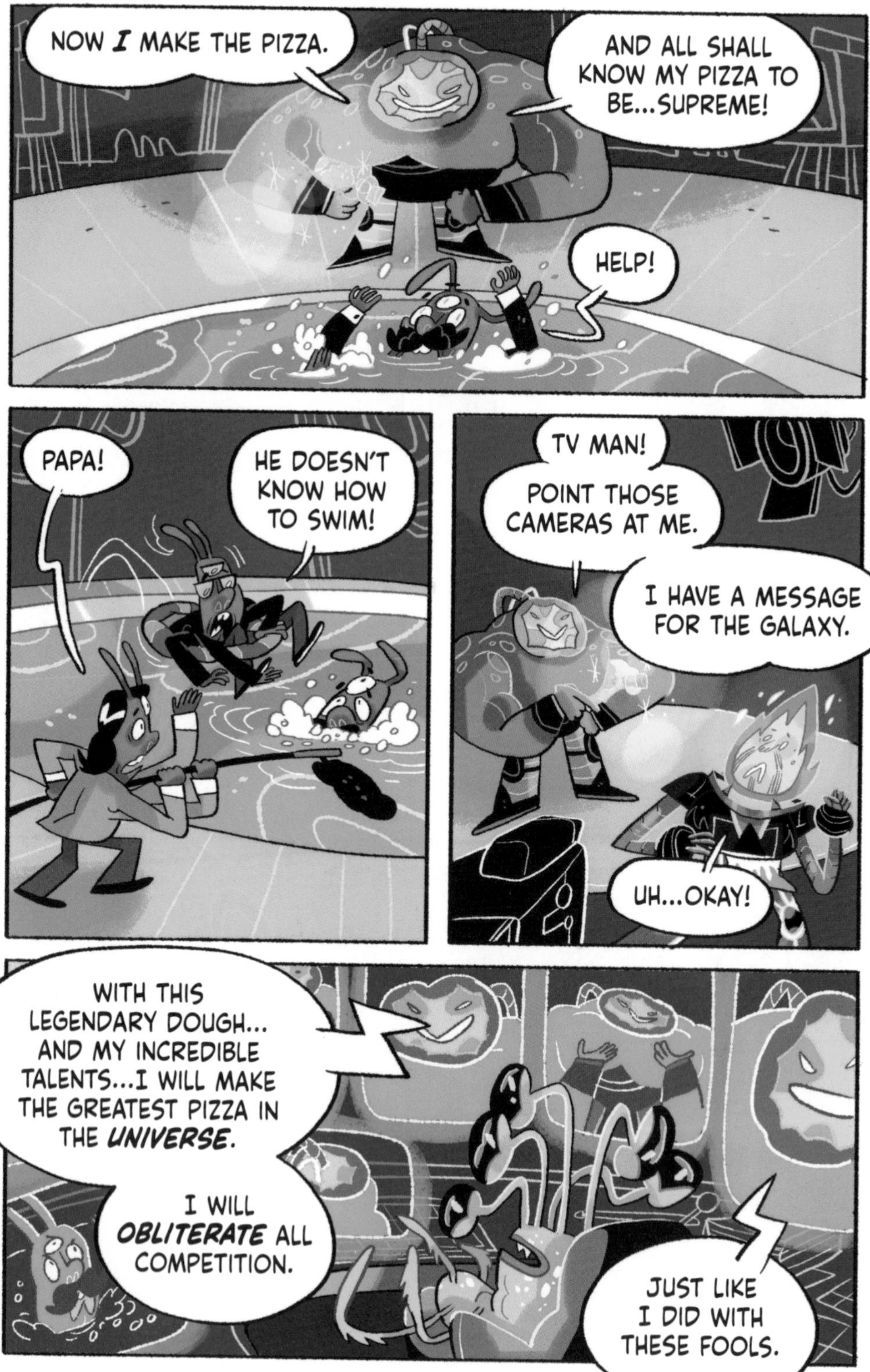
NOW *I* MAKE THE PIZZA.
AND ALL SHALL KNOW MY PIZZA TO BE...SUPREME!
HELP!
PAPA!
HE DOESN'T KNOW HOW TO SWIM!
TV MAN!
POINT THOSE CAMERAS AT ME.
I HAVE A MESSAGE FOR THE GALAXY.
UH...OKAY!
WITH THIS LEGENDARY DOUGH... AND MY INCREDIBLE TALENTS...I WILL MAKE THE GREATEST PIZZA IN THE *UNIVERSE*.
I WILL *OBLITERATE* ALL COMPETITION.
JUST LIKE I DID WITH THESE FOOLS.

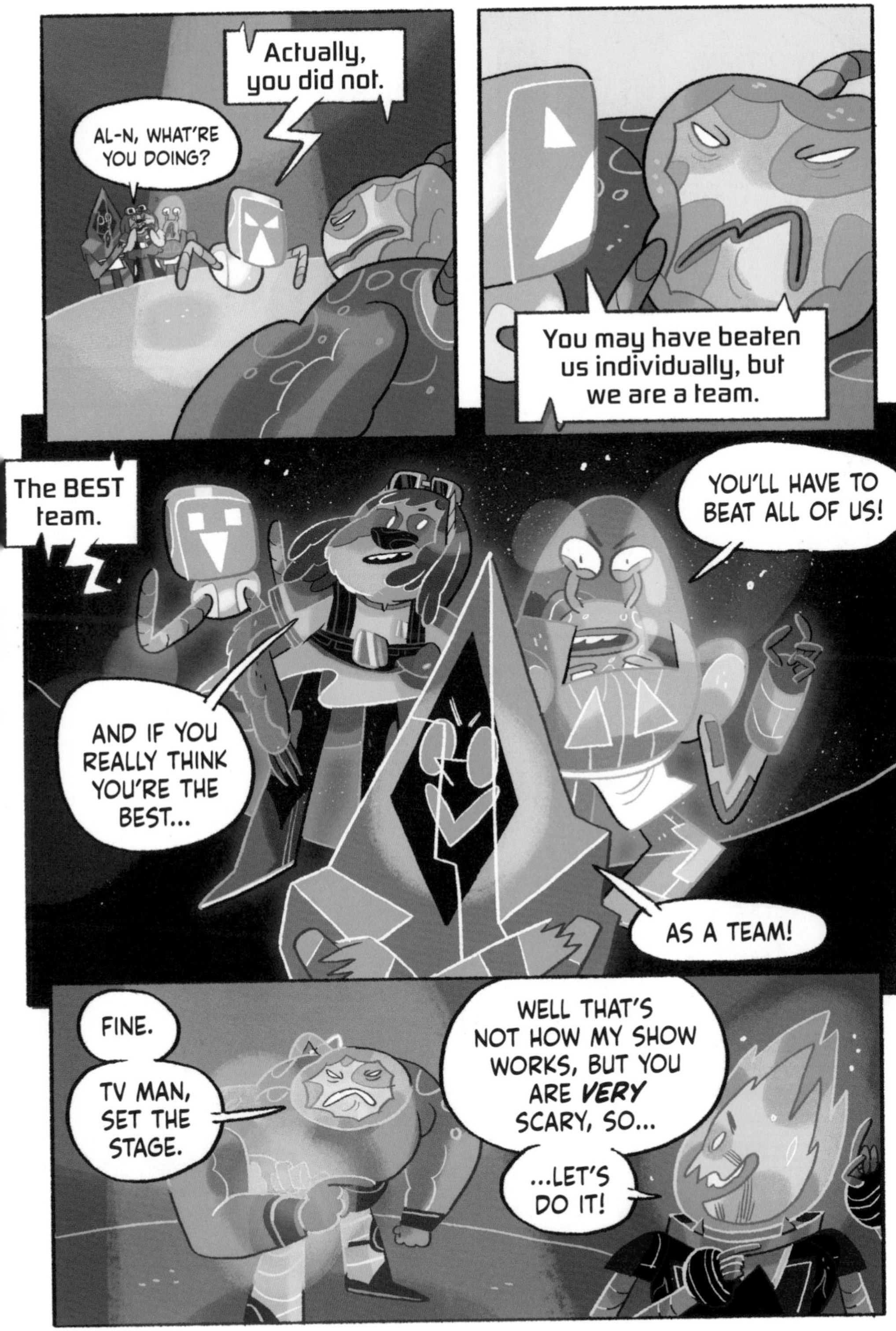
Actually, you did not.
AL-N, WHAT'RE YOU DOING?
You may have beaten us individually, but we are a team.
The BEST team.
YOU'LL HAVE TO BEAT ALL OF US!
AND IF YOU REALLY THINK YOU'RE THE BEST...
AS A TEAM!
FINE.
TV MAN, SET THE STAGE.
WELL THAT'S NOT HOW MY SHOW WORKS, BUT YOU ARE *VERY* SCARY, SO...
...LET'S DO IT!

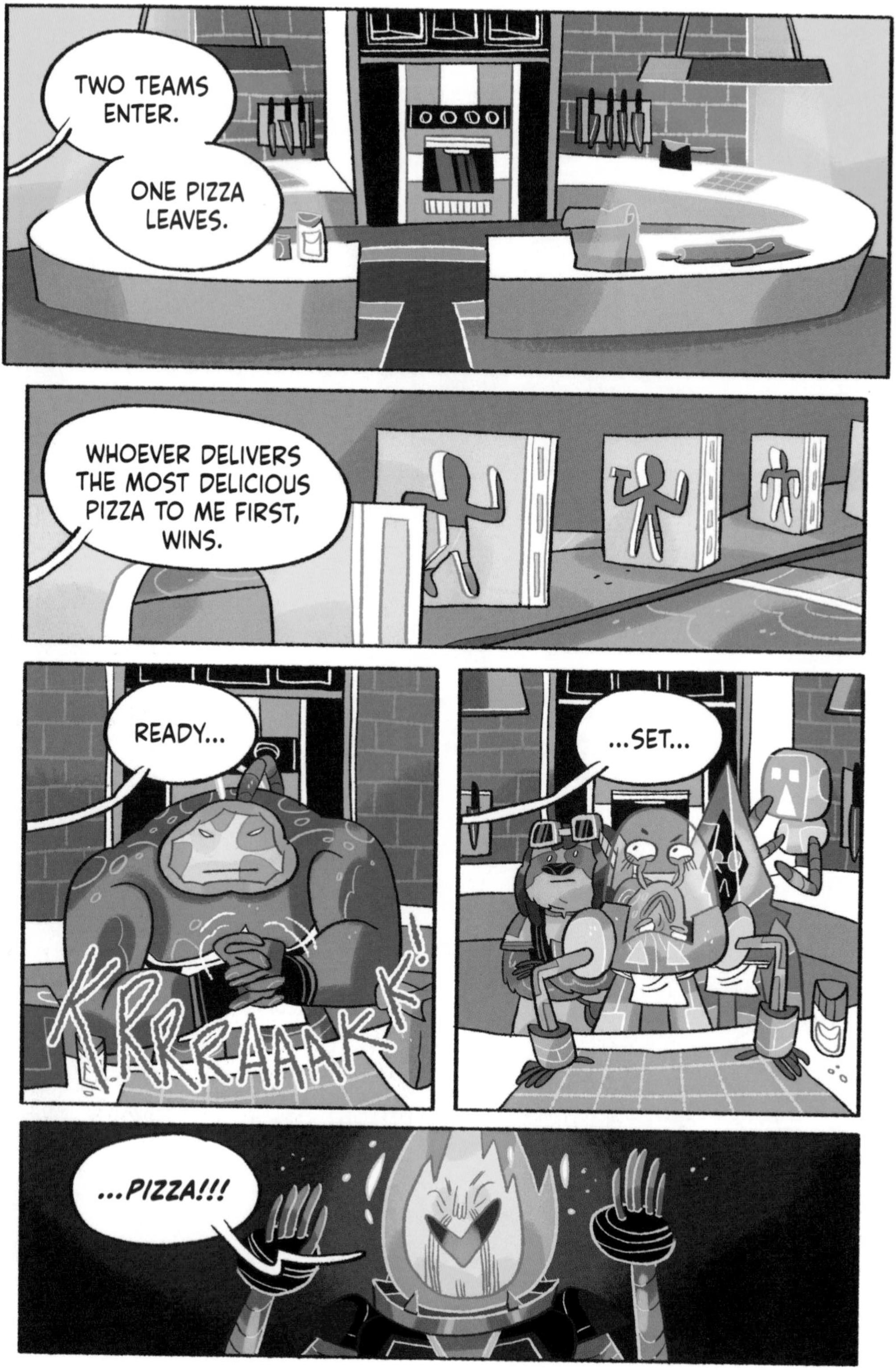
TWO TEAMS ENTER.
ONE PIZZA LEAVES.
WHOEVER DELIVERS THE MOST DELICIOUS PIZZA TO ME FIRST, WINS.
READY...
KRRRAAAKK!
...SET...
...PIZZA!!!

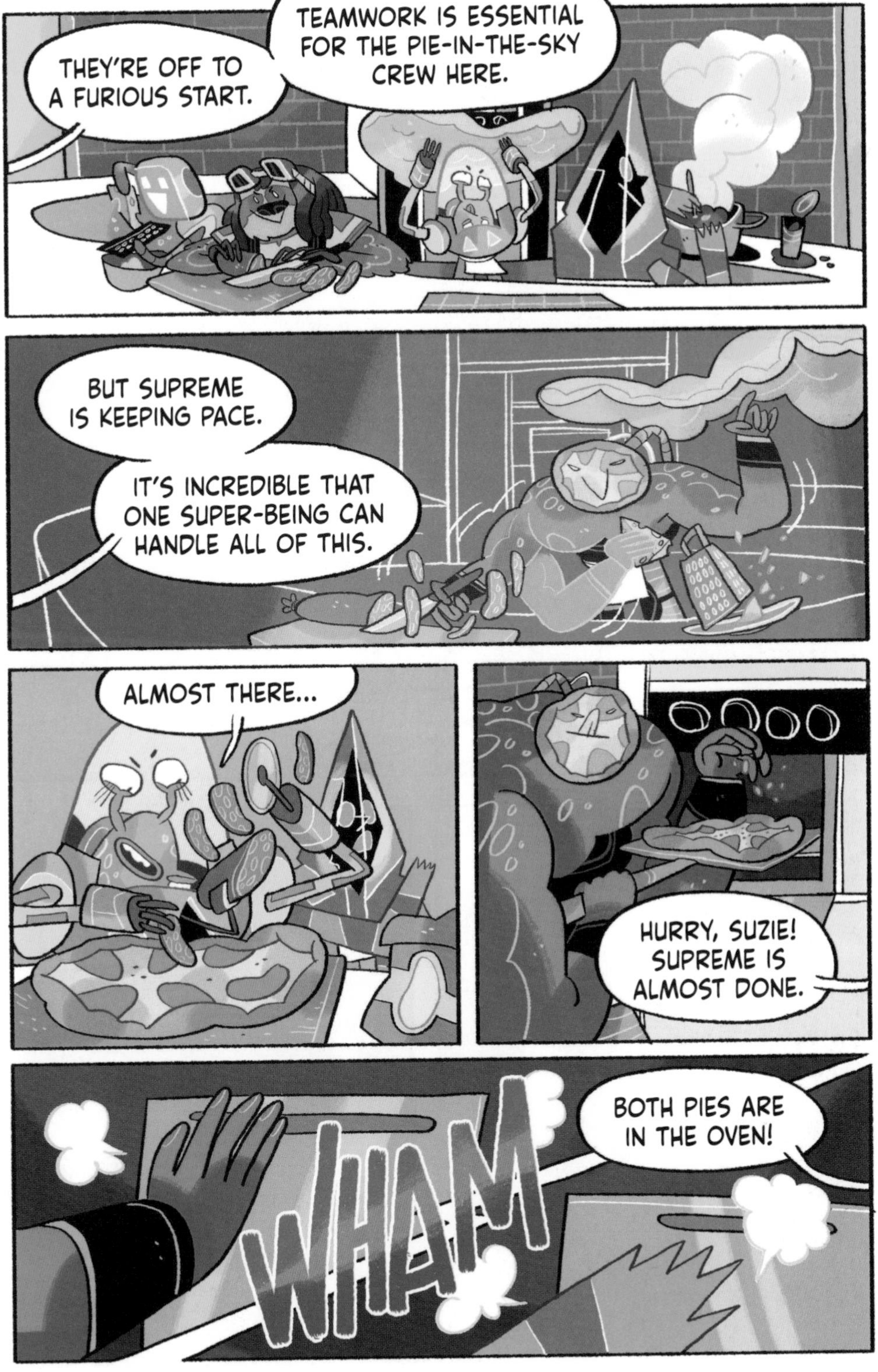
THEY'RE OFF TO A FURIOUS START.
TEAMWORK IS ESSENTIAL FOR THE PIE-IN-THE-SKY CREW HERE.
BUT SUPREME IS KEEPING PACE.
IT'S INCREDIBLE THAT ONE SUPER-BEING CAN HANDLE ALL OF THIS.
ALMOST THERE...
HURRY, SUZIE! SUPREME IS ALMOST DONE.
WHAM
BOTH PIES ARE IN THE OVEN!

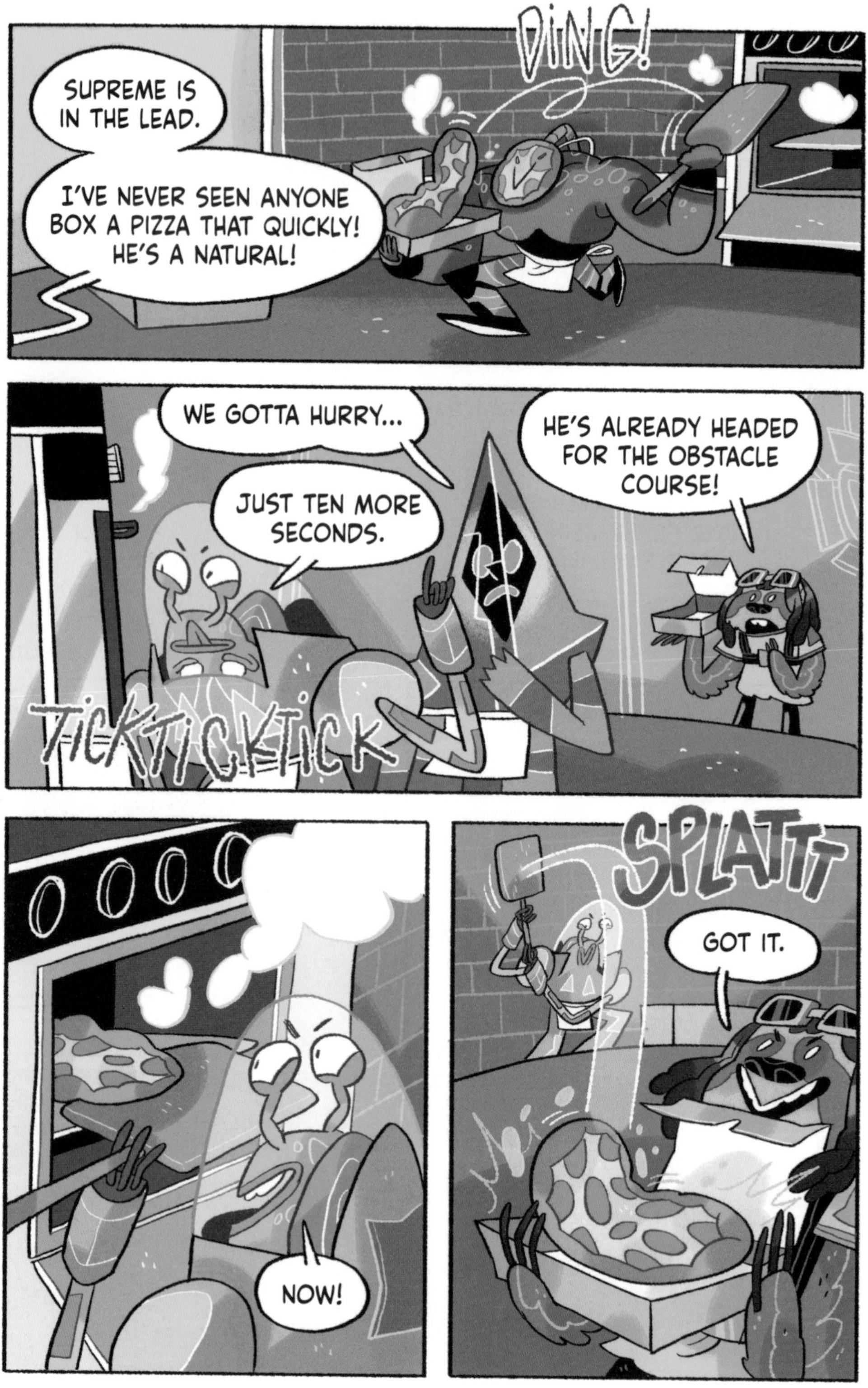
DING!
SUPREME IS IN THE LEAD.
I'VE NEVER SEEN ANYONE BOX A PIZZA THAT QUICKLY! HE'S A NATURAL!
WE GOTTA HURRY...
JUST TEN MORE SECONDS.
HE'S ALREADY HEADED FOR THE OBSTACLE COURSE!
TICKTICKTICK
NOW!
SPLATTT
GOT IT.

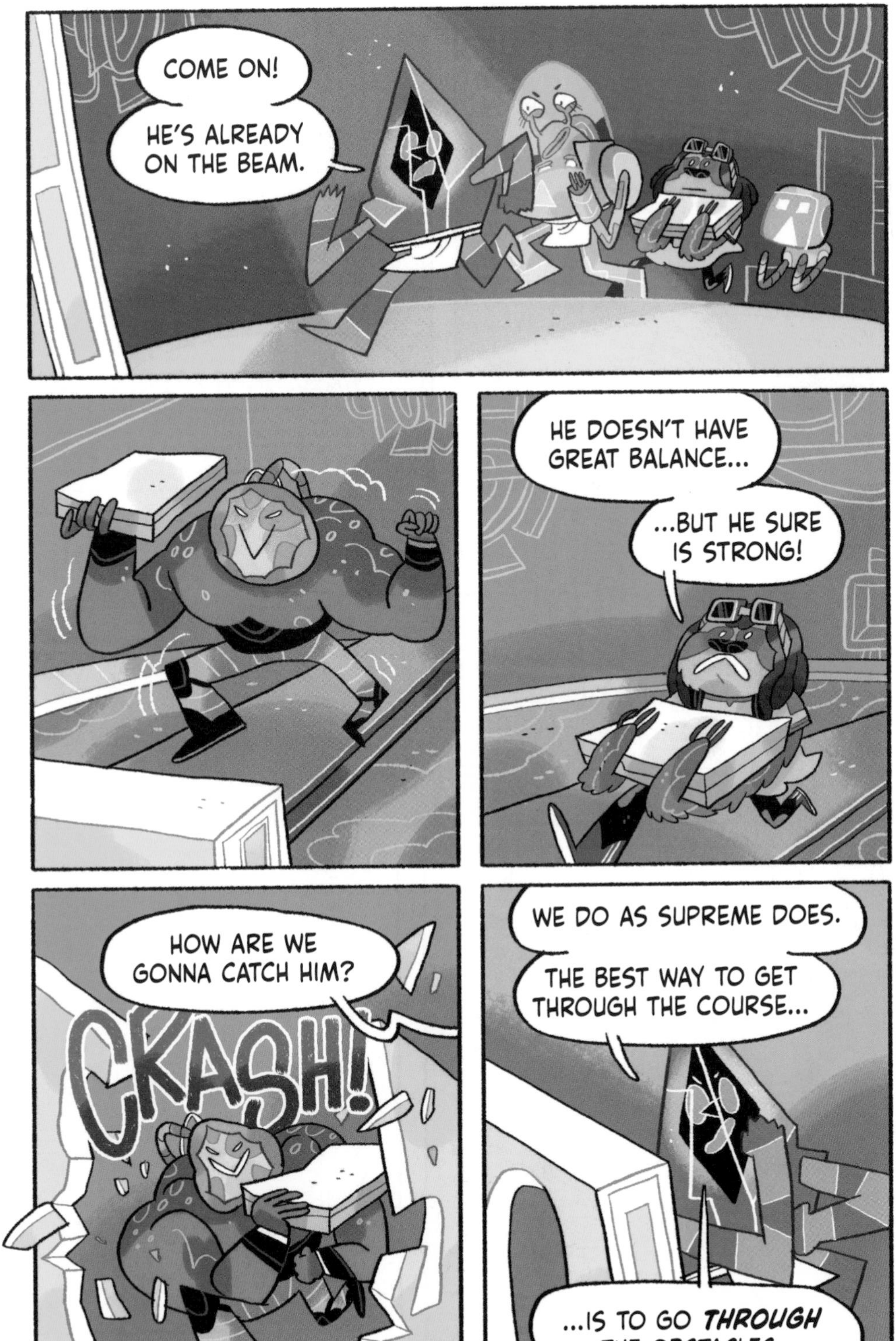
COME ON!
HE'S ALREADY ON THE BEAM.
HE DOESN'T HAVE GREAT BALANCE...
...BUT HE SURE IS STRONG!
HOW ARE WE GONNA CATCH HIM?
CRASH!
WE DO AS SUPREME DOES.
THE BEST WAY TO GET THROUGH THE COURSE...
...IS TO GO *THROUGH* THE OBSTACLES.

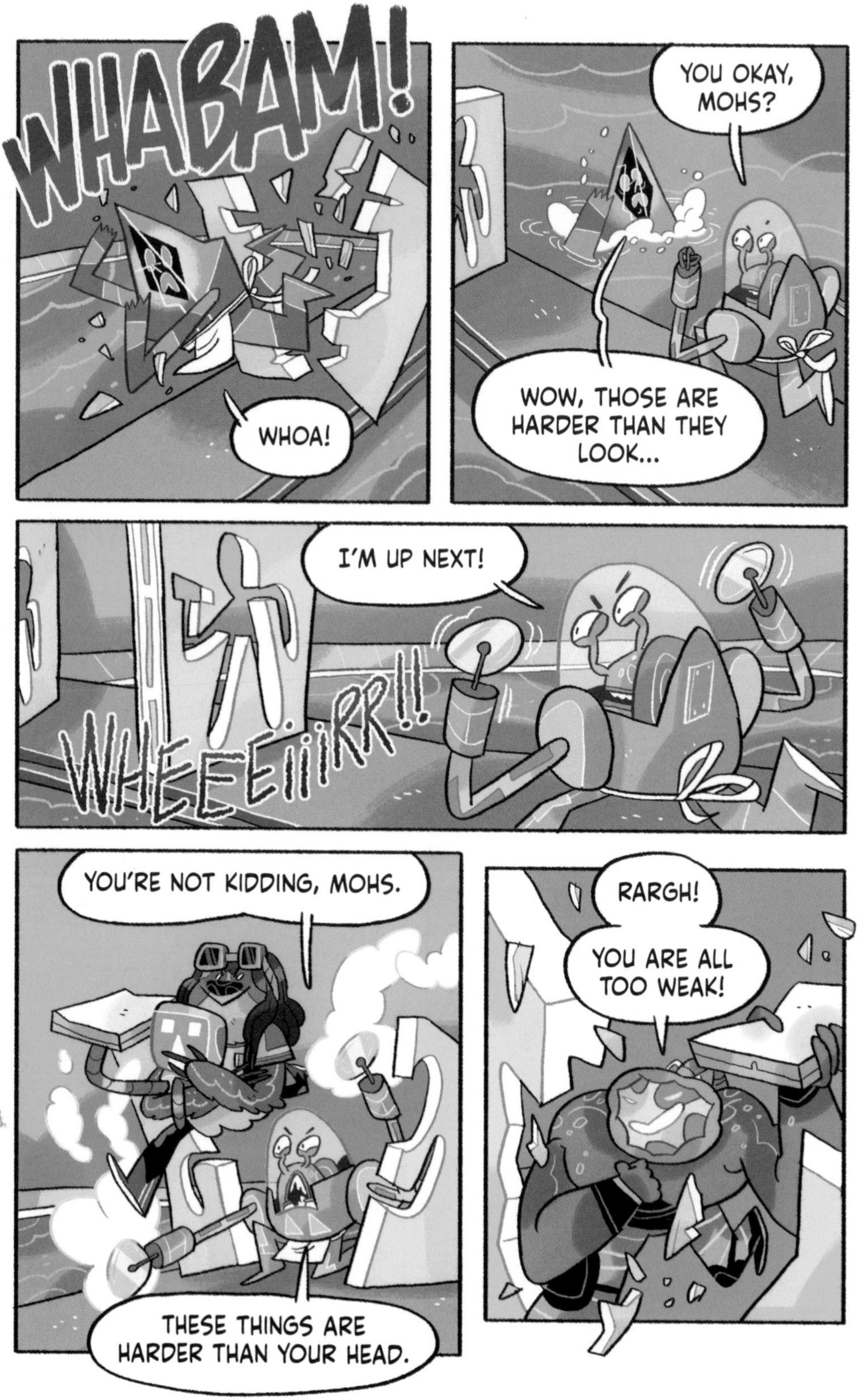
WHABAM!
WHOA!
YOU OKAY, MOHS?
WOW, THOSE ARE HARDER THAN THEY LOOK...
I'M UP NEXT!
WHEEEiiiRR!!
YOU'RE NOT KIDDING, MOHS.
THESE THINGS ARE HARDER THAN YOUR HEAD.
RARGH!
YOU ARE ALL TOO WEAK!

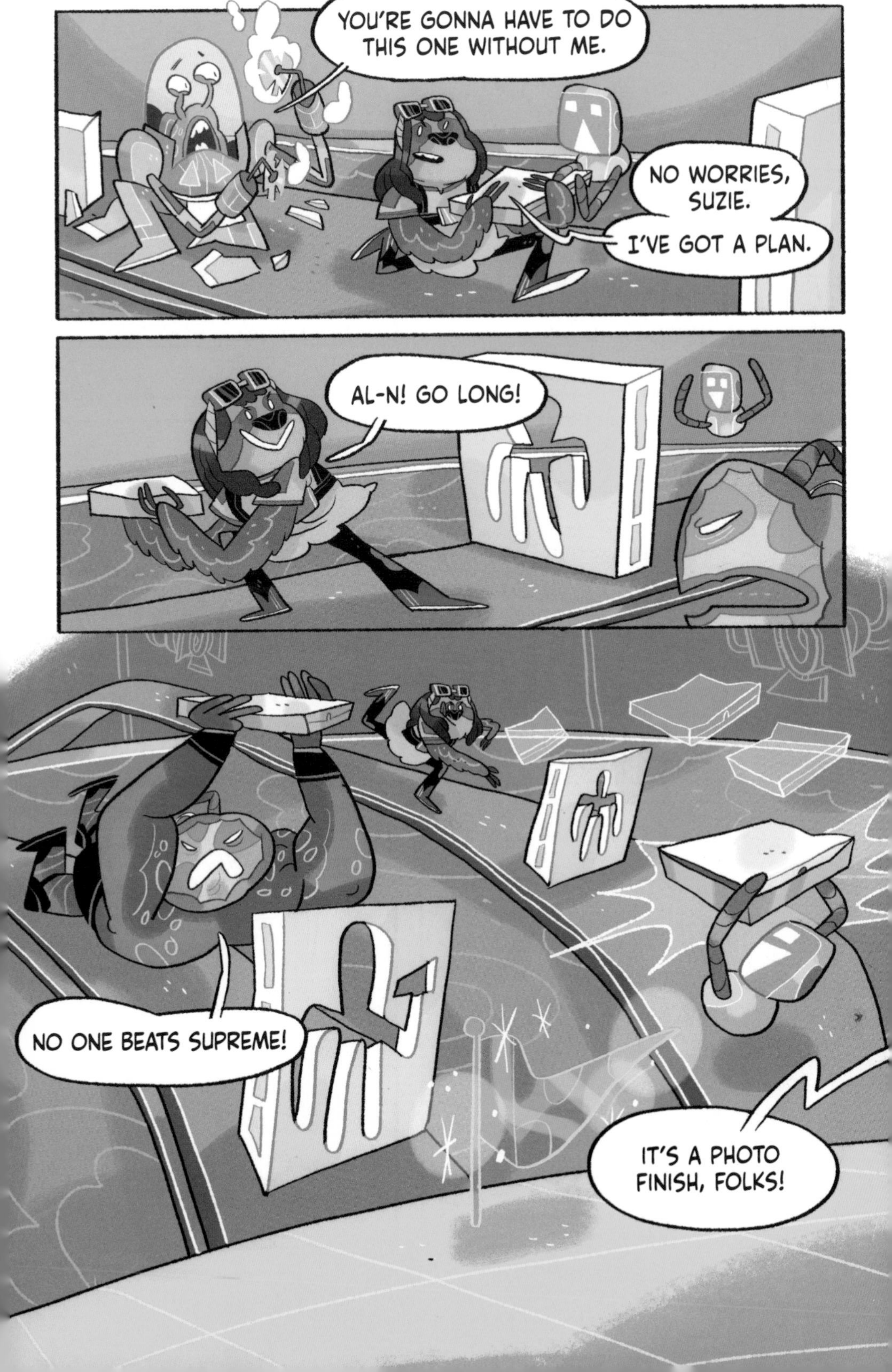
YOU'RE GONNA HAVE TO DO THIS ONE WITHOUT ME.
NO WORRIES, SUZIE.
I'VE GOT A PLAN.
AL-N! GO LONG!
NO ONE BEATS SUPREME!
IT'S A PHOTO FINISH, FOLKS!

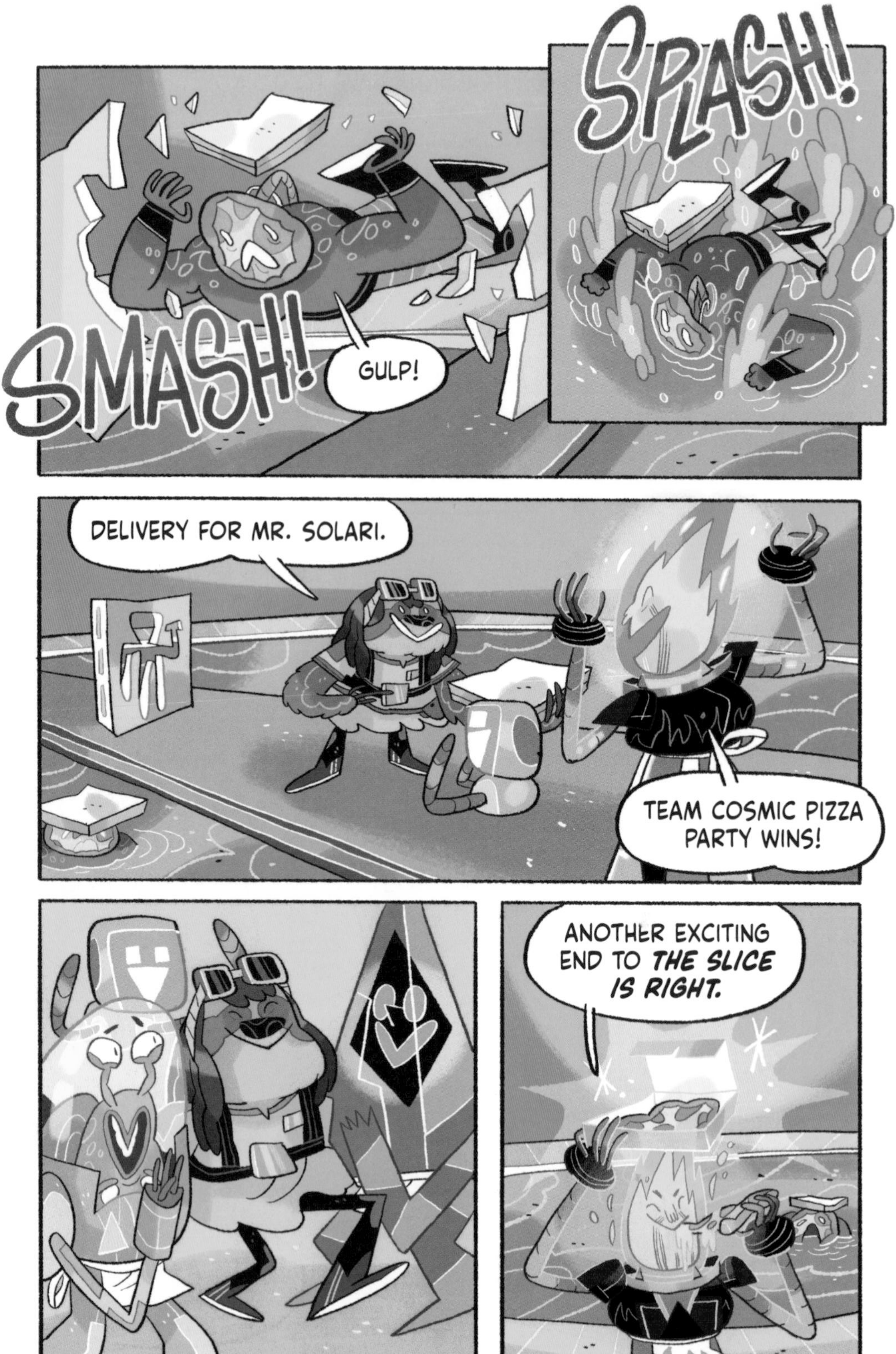
SMASH!
GULP!
SPLASH!
DELIVERY FOR MR. SOLARI.
TEAM COSMIC PIZZA PARTY WINS!
ANOTHER EXCITING END TO *THE SLICE IS RIGHT.*

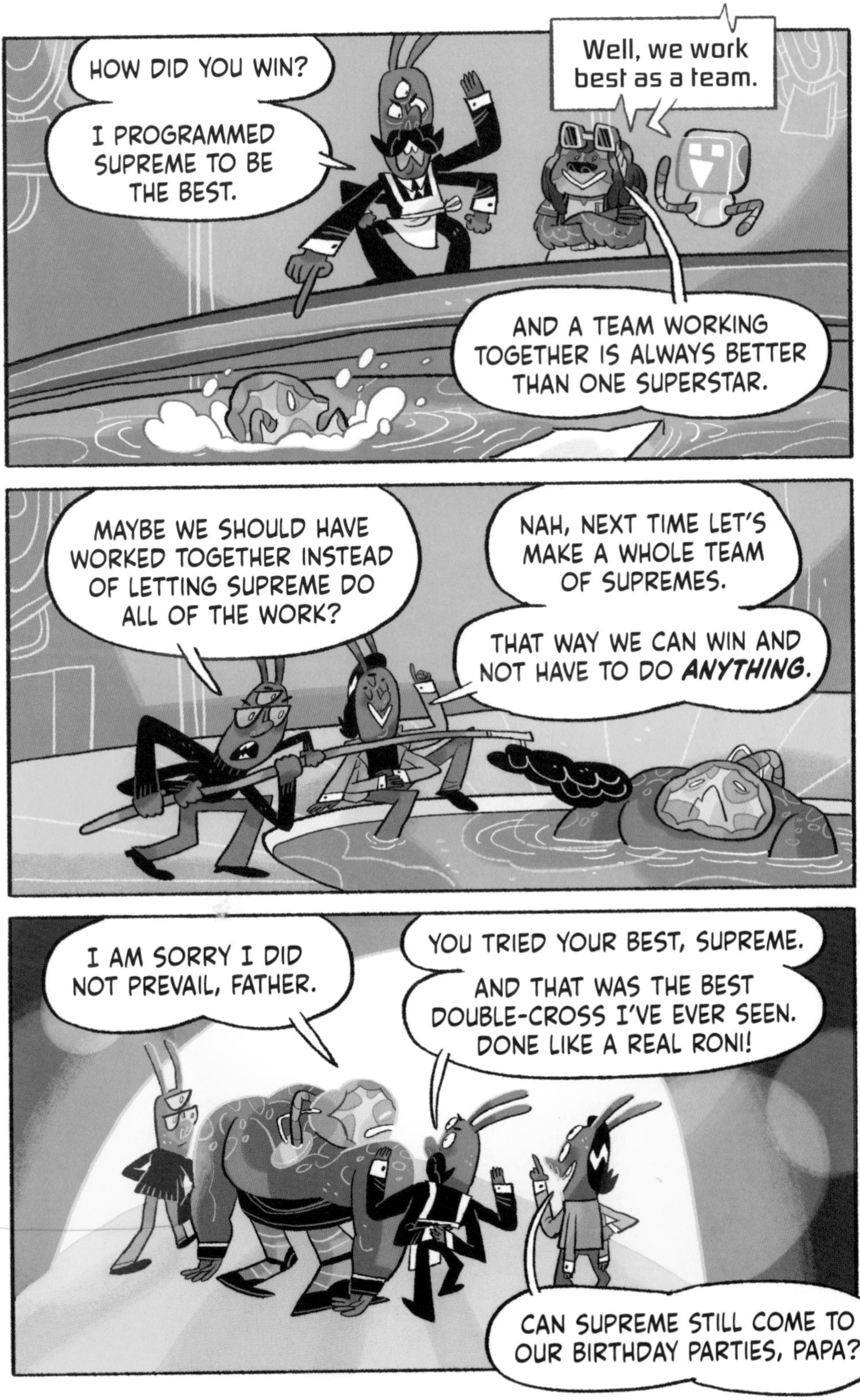
HOW DID YOU WIN?
I PROGRAMMED SUPREME TO BE THE BEST.
Well, we work best as a team.
AND A TEAM WORKING TOGETHER IS ALWAYS BETTER THAN ONE SUPERSTAR.
MAYBE WE SHOULD HAVE WORKED TOGETHER INSTEAD OF LETTING SUPREME DO ALL OF THE WORK?
NAH, NEXT TIME LET'S MAKE A WHOLE TEAM OF SUPREMES.
THAT WAY WE CAN WIN AND NOT HAVE TO DO ***ANYTHING***.
I AM SORRY I DID NOT PREVAIL, FATHER.
YOU TRIED YOUR BEST, SUPREME.
AND THAT WAS THE BEST DOUBLE-CROSS I'VE EVER SEEN. DONE LIKE A REAL RONI!
CAN SUPREME STILL COME TO OUR BIRTHDAY PARTIES, PAPA?

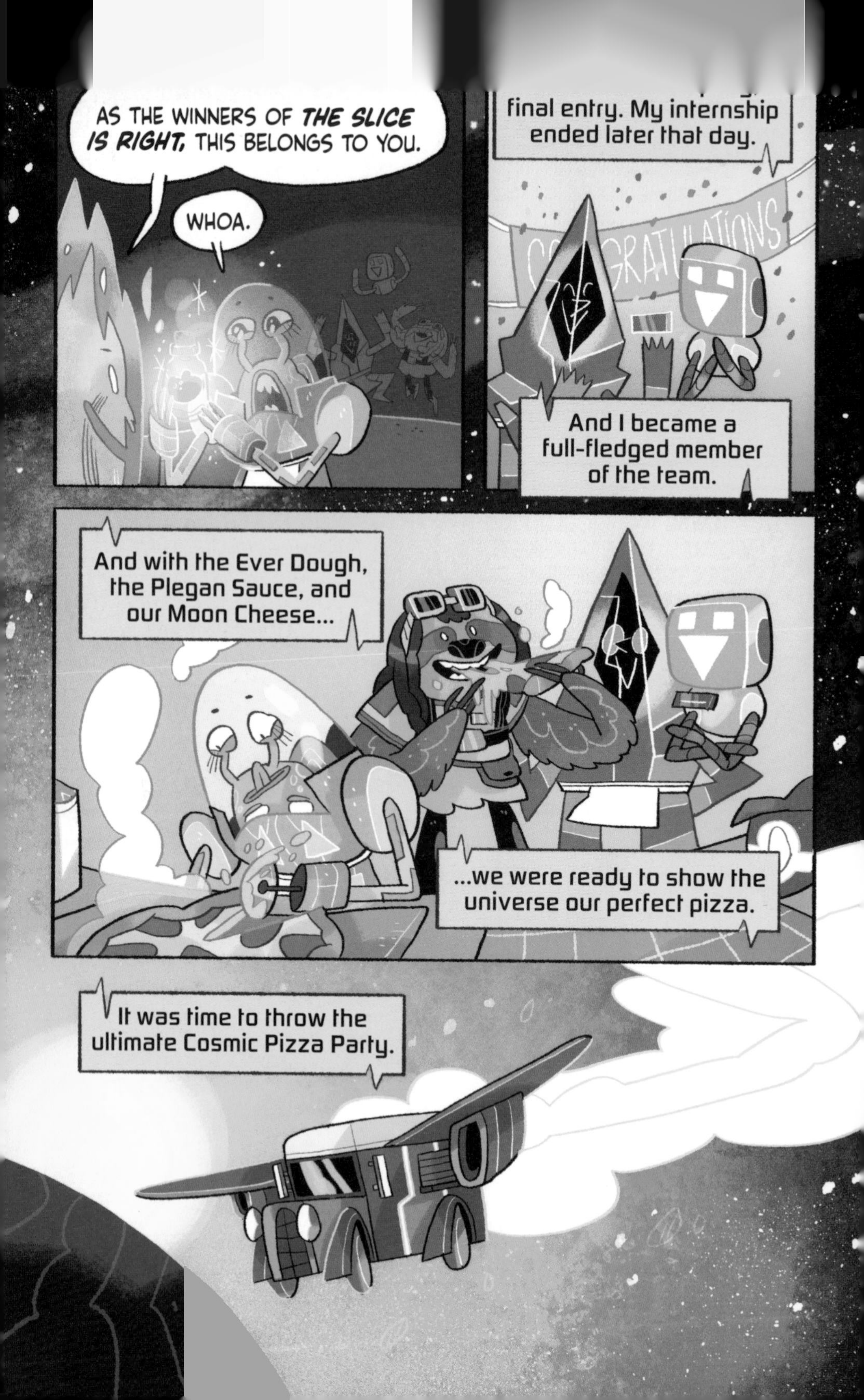
AS THE WINNERS OF ***THE SLICE IS RIGHT,*** THIS BELONGS TO YOU.
WHOA.
final entry. My internship ended later that day.
And I became a full-fledged member of the team.
And with the Ever Dough, the Plegan Sauce, and our Moon Cheese...
...we were ready to show the universe our perfect pizza.
It was time to throw the ultimate Cosmic Pizza Party.

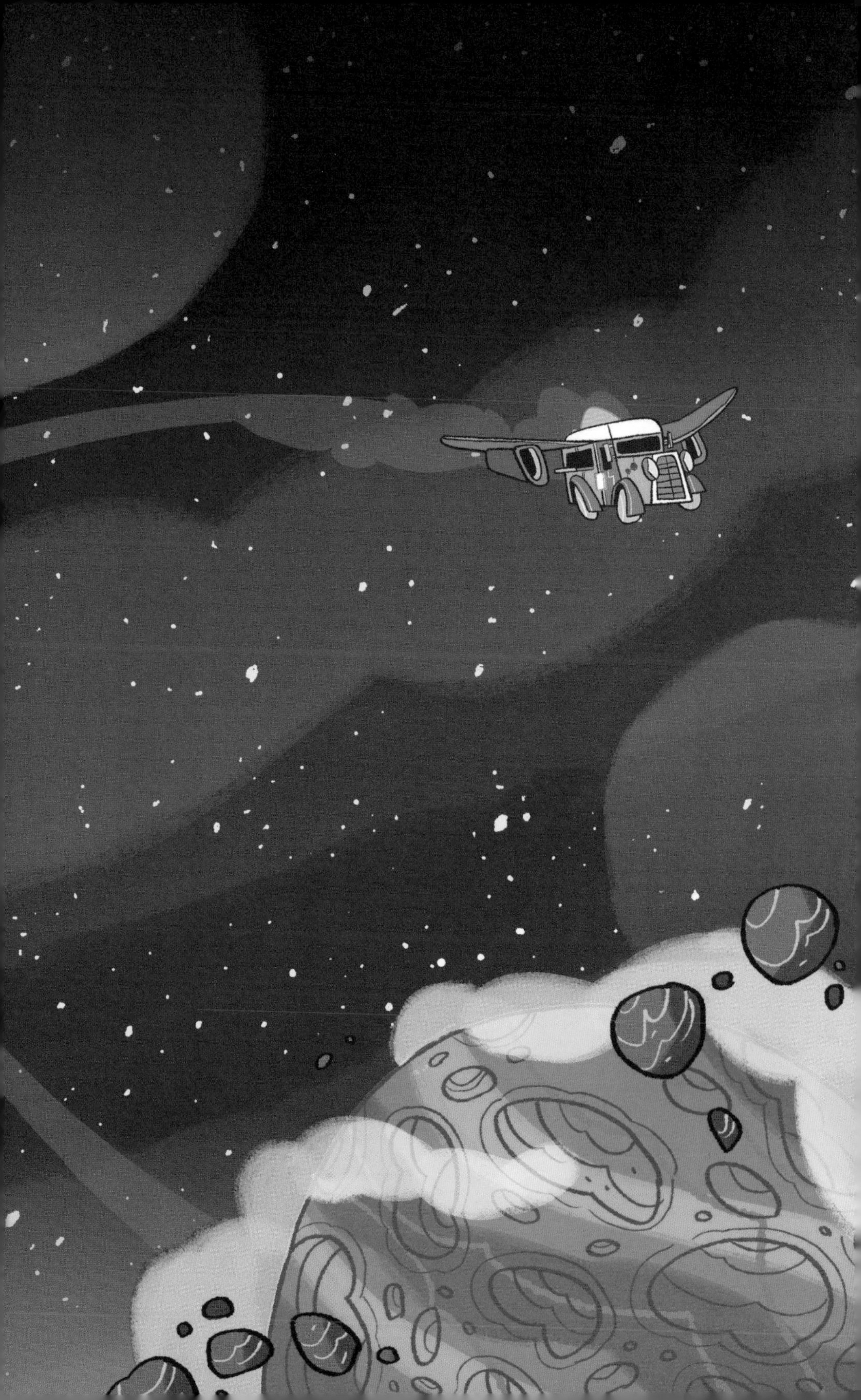

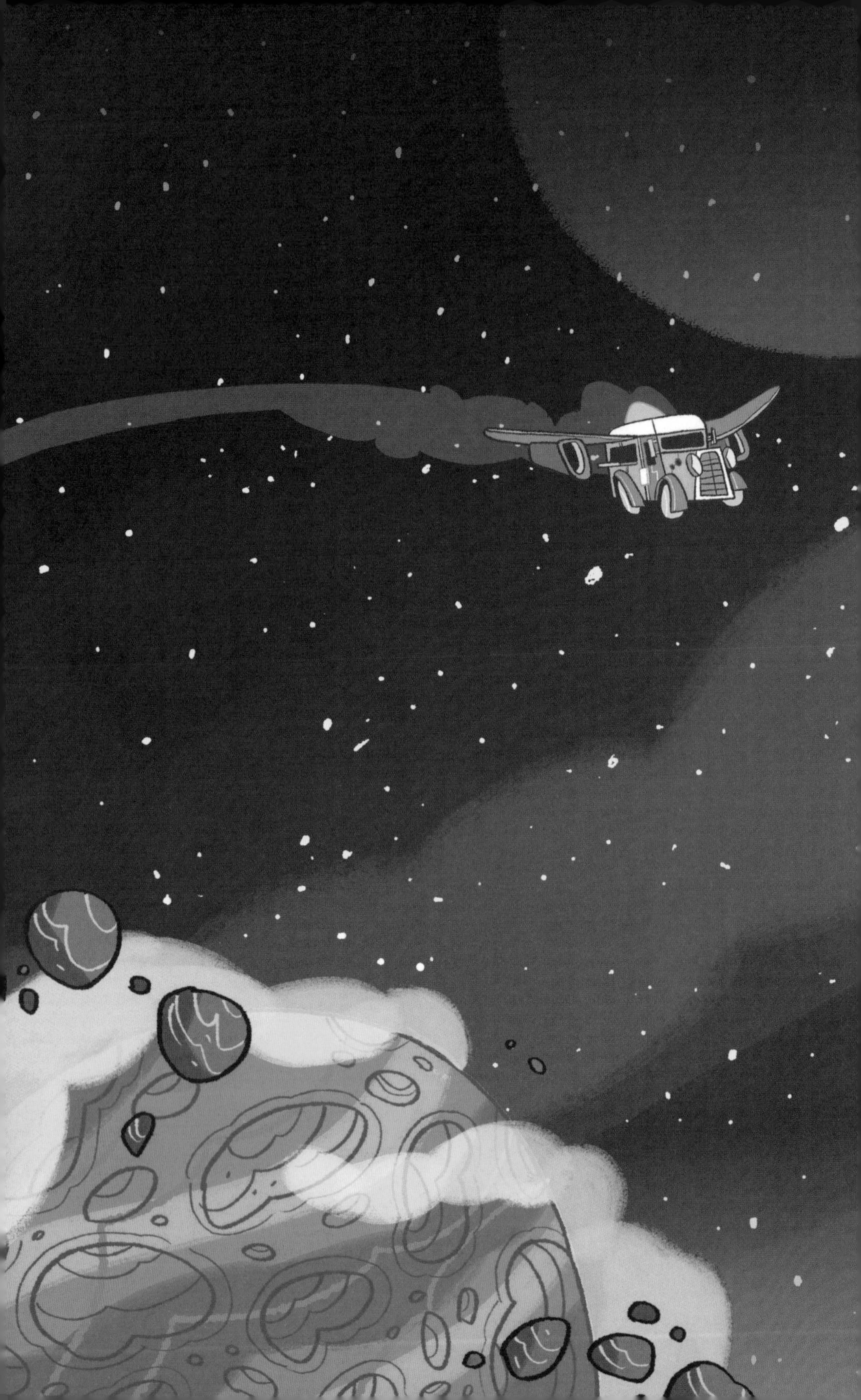

ABOUT THE AUTHORS

NICK MURPHY IS A FILMMAKER AND CO-HOSTS THE PODCAST *PRETEND FRIENDS*. HE'S A GRADUATE OF THE UNIVERSITY OF THE ARTS. NICK ENJOYS REPETITION, POP CULTURE, THE '80s, TIME TRAVEL, STAR WARS, REPETITION, TUNNELS, 24 FPS, REPETITION, BEING COLOR-BLIND, AND WRITING HIS BIOGRAPHY. HE CURRENTLY LIVES IN PHILADELPHIA WITH HIS WIFE, ARTIST REBECCA CHEWNING, AND THEIR AWESOME SON, DESMOND.

PAUL RITCHEY IS A FILMMAKER AND WEB HOST LIVING IN PHILADELPHIA. HE HOSTS *CONTINUE?*, A WEEKLY GAMING COMEDY SHOW. HE ALSO PERFORMS ON *PRETEND FRIENDS*, AN ACTUAL-PLAY TABLETOP ROLE-PLAYING SHOW. PAUL IS SO FAST THAT HIS MOVEMENTS ARE BEYOND HUMAN RECOGNITION. SOME QUESTION HIS QUICKNESS, BUT THAT IS ONLY BECAUSE HIS SPEED IS SO BEYOND HUMAN RECOGNITION THAT HE APPEARS TO BE STANDING STILL.

ABOUT THE ILLUSTRATOR

BEA TORMO IS A CHILDREN'S BOOK ILLUSTRATOR BY DAY AND A COMIC BOOK ARTIST BY NIGHT. SHE LIVES NEAR BARCELONA, SPAIN, WHERE SHE ENJOYS BEING PART OF A COMMUNITY OF ARTISTS. BESIDES CHILDREN'S BOOKS AND COMICS, BEA WORKS ON MAGAZINES, WEBCOMICS, AND FANZINES. SHE ESPECIALLY LOVES DRAWING GRUMPY PEOPLE AND MONSTERS.

COSMIC PIZZA PARTY TEAM!

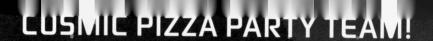

MEG

ACE DELIVERY DRIVER. THE INTERGALACTIC SLOTH MAY LOOK SLOW, BUT WHEN SHE'S PILOTING HER DELIVERY SHIP--THE SLICE 1--SHE'S FASTER THAN A SLICE OF PIZZA BEING GOBBLED UP AT A BIRTHDAY PARTY. BOLD AND READY FOR AN ADVENTURE, MEG ZOOMS HEADFIRST INTO EACH DELIVERY WITH HER BEST BUD, AL-N.

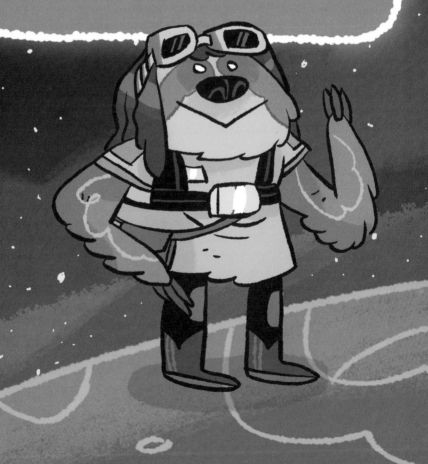

AL-N

ROBOTIC INTERN. THIS ANDROID IS TRYING TO LEARN ALL HE CAN ABOUT THE PIZZA BUSINESS WHILE METICULOUSLY LOGGING ALL OF THE CREW'S ADVENTURES. THE INTERNSHIP POSTING READ, "TRAVEL THE GALAXY, VISIT EXCITING LOCALES, MEET INTERESTING CLIENTELE, AND EAT ALL THE PIZZA YOU WANT!" IT WAS A DREAM COME TRUE...EXCEPT FOR THAT LAST PART. AL-N DISCOVERED THAT EATING PIZZA DOESN'T AGREE WITH HIS CIRCUITRY.

MOHS

THE MONEY GUY. THIS ROCKLIKE CRYSTALI MAKES SURE MONEY COMES IN AND ALSO TRIES TO MAKE SURE AS LITTLE MONEY AS POSSIBLE GOES OUT. MOHS IS ALSO RESPONSIBLE FOR GETTING THE WORD OUT ABOUT THE COSMIC PIZZA PARTY'S PIES...BUT SOMETIMES HE THINKS A LITTLE TOO FAR OUTSIDE THE PIZZA BOX.

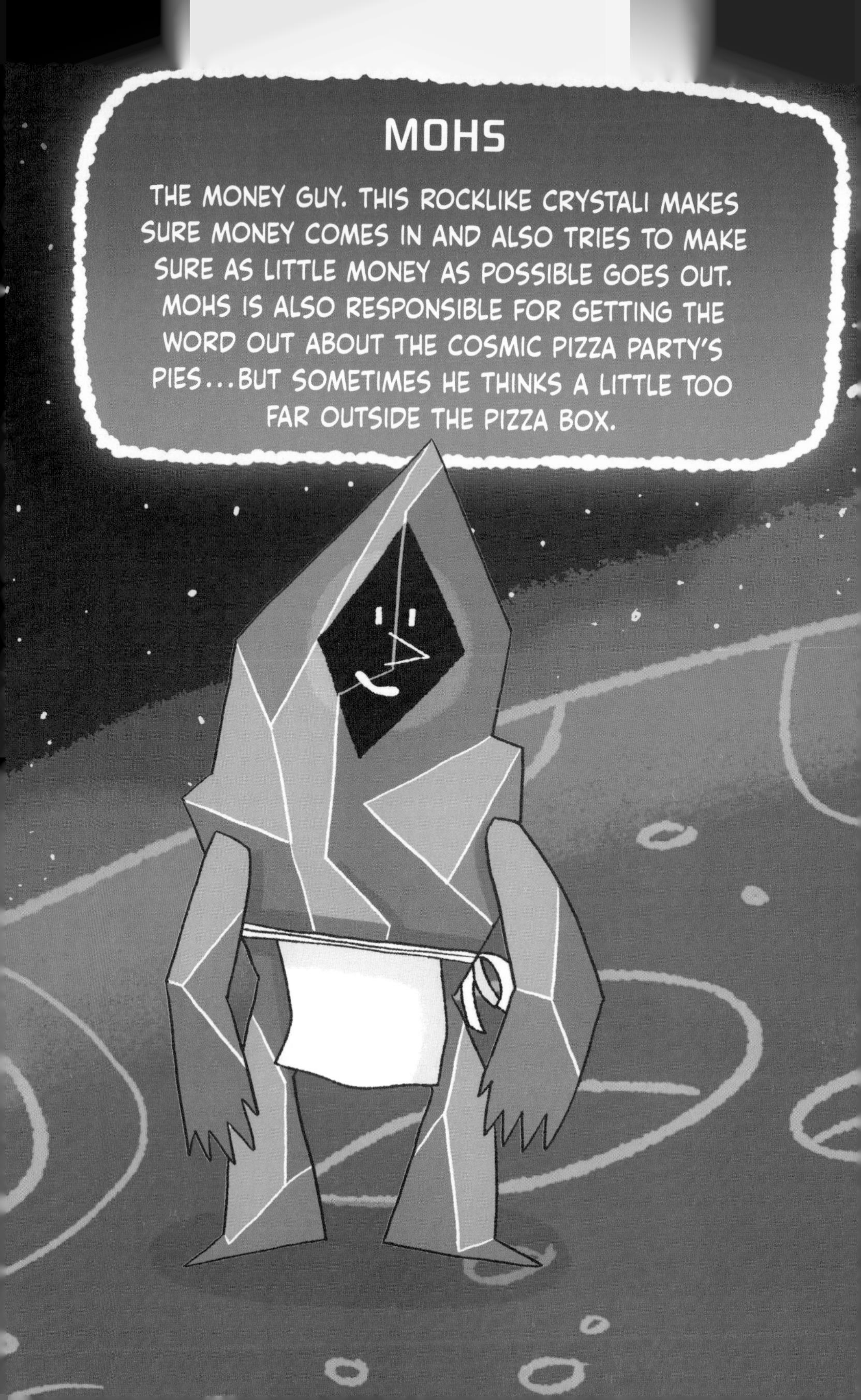

SUZIE

HEAD CHEF AND CHIEF PIZZA OFFICER. THIS MECHA-SLUG IS A TRUE PIZZA GENIUS. SUZIE IS DEVOTED TO THE GASTRONOMIC OATH: "ALL FOR FOOD, AND FOOD FOR ALL!" THAT MEANS SHE SPENDS EVERY MOMENT OF HER DAY THINKING UP NEW WAYS TO MAKE HER PIZZAS EVEN MORE DELICIOUS. SUZIE HAS A BIT OF A TEMPER, THOUGH, SO IF YOU WANT TO GIVE HER SOME PIZZA FEEDBACK, DO IT FAST AND PREPARE TO DUCK FOR COVER!

COSMIC *PIZZA* TRUCK

From outrunning space worms to delivering the best pizza in the galaxy, the pizza truck is essential to the Cosmic Pizza team.

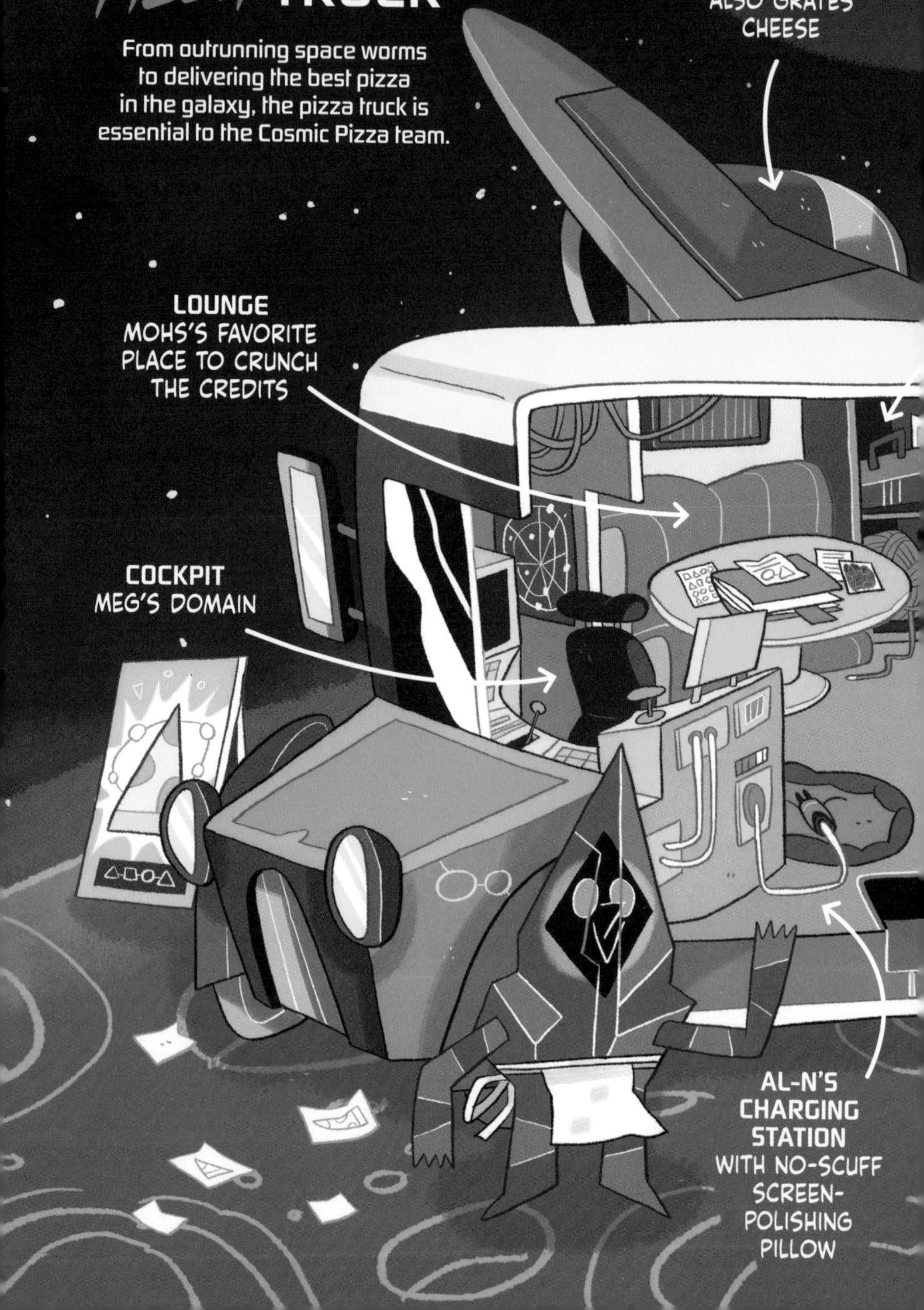
RIGHT ENGINE
ALSO GRATES CHEESE
LOUNGE
MOHS'S FAVORITE PLACE TO CRUNCH THE CREDITS
COCKPIT
MEG'S DOMAIN
AL-N'S CHARGING STATION
WITH NO-SCUFF SCREEN-POLISHING PILLOW

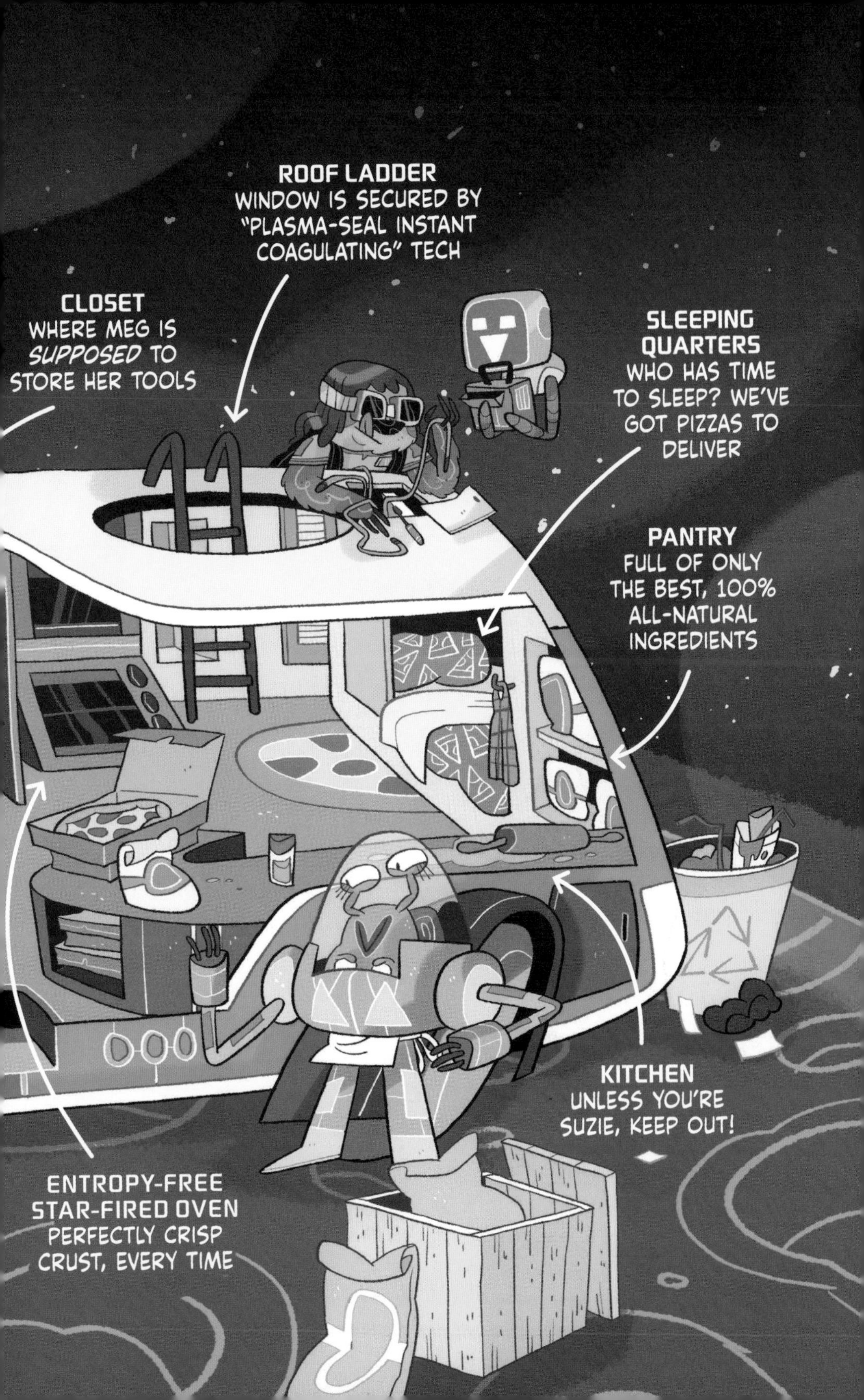
ROOF LADDER
WINDOW IS SECURED BY "PLASMA-SEAL INSTANT COAGULATING" TECH
CLOSET
WHERE MEG IS *SUPPOSED* TO STORE HER TOOLS
SLEEPING QUARTERS
WHO HAS TIME TO SLEEP? WE'VE GOT PIZZAS TO DELIVER
PANTRY
FULL OF ONLY THE BEST, 100% ALL-NATURAL INGREDIENTS
KITCHEN
UNLESS YOU'RE SUZIE, KEEP OUT!
ENTROPY-FREE STAR-FIRED OVEN
PERFECTLY CRISP CRUST, EVERY TIME

WHO IS YOUR PERFECT PIZZA PAL?

Answer a few questions about pizza, and we'll let you know who your pizzeria BFF is!

1. WHAT IS YOUR FAVORITE TOPPING?
   - A. ALL OF THEM! I LOVE PIZZA SO MUCH THAT I WANT IT ALL!
   - B. PEPPERONI AND CHEESE. IT'S A CLASSIC FOR A REASON!
   - C. TOPPINGS? THOSE ARE EXPENSIVE. LET'S NOT GO OVERBOARD HERE.

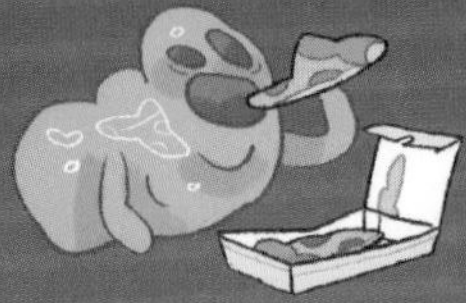

2. HOW MANY SLICES DO YOU EAT?
   - A. SLICES? I EAT A WHOLE PIZZA IN A SINGLE BITE.
   - B. JUST ENOUGH. I WANT TO SAMPLE AND SAVOR EVERY BITE, BUT I DON'T WANT TO GET SICK.
   - C. JUST ONE SLICE A DAY. A WHOLE PIZZA CAN LAST ME A WEEK!
3. HOW DO YOU EAT YOUR PIZZA?
   - A. DON'T TELL ANYONE, BUT SOMETIMES I BITE THE CRUST FIRST.
   - B. ONE SLICE AT A TIME. I DIDN'T KNOW THIS WAS UP FOR DEBATE.
   - C. WITH A FORK AND KNIFE, LIKE A CIVILIZED PERSON (OR ALIEN)!
4. WHAT'S YOUR PIZZA DELIVERY MOTTO?
   - A. ALWAYS HOT. ALWAYS ON TIME. ALWAYS DELICIOUS.
   - B. THE PERFECT PIZZA, OR YOU'RE WRONG.
   - C. THE FIRST TOPPING IS FREE! (DOUGH COUNTS AS A TOPPING, RIGHT?)
5. WHAT KIND OF CRUST?
   - A. THE THICKER THE BETTER. MORE PIZZA = YUM.
   - B. NOT TOO THICK, NOT TOO THIN. A GOOD PIZZA IS ALL ABOUT BALANCE.
   - C. PAPER THIN, SO WE CAN MAKE MORE PIZZAS WITH LESS DOUGH.
6. WHICH PLANET WOULD YOU MAKE A DELIVERY TO FIRST?
   - A. FIRST?! I'D GO TO EVERY PLANET AS QUICKLY AS POSSIBLE.
   - B. THE PLANET WITH THE RICHEST CULINARY SCENE.
   - C. WHICHEVER ONE HAS THE MOST MONEY.

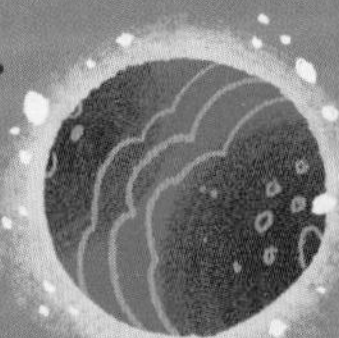

7. DO YOU LIKE COLD PIZZA?
   - A. COLD? I'VE NEVER LET A PIZZA GO COLD IN MY LIFE!
   - B. ARE YOU SERIOUS? PIZZA NEEDS TO BE ENJOYED FRESH OUT OF THE OVEN.
   - C. OF COURSE! I NEVER LET ANY PIZZA (OR MONEY) GO TO WASTE.

8. WHAT IS YOUR LEAST FAVORITE PIZZA?

A. RED GIANT TOMATO PIE

B. PLUTONIUM PINEAPPLE PIZZA! YUCK!

C. BETELGEUSE DEEP DISH

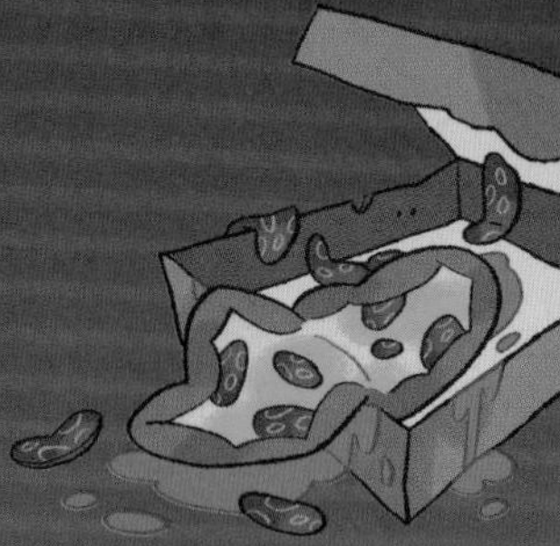

9. WHEN IS THE BEST TIME TO EAT PIZZA?

A. ANYTIME! BREAKFAST, LUNCH, DOUBLE LUNCH, PRE-DINNER, AND EVEN DESSERT!

B. WHEN IT'S RIGHT OUT OF THE OVEN AT A SAFE BUT OPTIMAL TEMPERATURE.

C. WHEN SOMEONE ELSE IS PAYING!

10. AND FOR THE FINAL QUESTION, SPONSORED BY PAPA RONI PIZZA RESTAU-RONI™, WHO MAKES THE BEST PIZZA IN THE GALAXY?

A. ~~PAPA RONI~~ COSMIC PIZZA PARTY

B. ~~PAPA RONI~~ COSMIC PIZZA PARTY

C. ~~PAPA RONI~~ COSMIC PIZZA PARTY

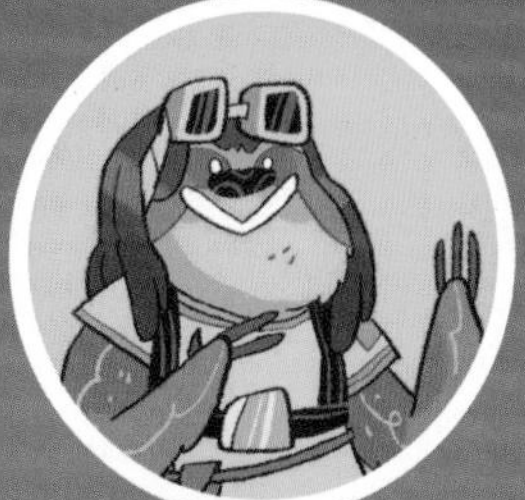

IF YOU MOSTLY ANSWERED A:

Your best pal is Meg! You both just love pizza--it's as simple as that. You'll eat pizza any way it's made, but you also know exactly what you love the most. You're always ready to leap face-first into the next pizza adventure. There's plenty of pizza excitement in your future!

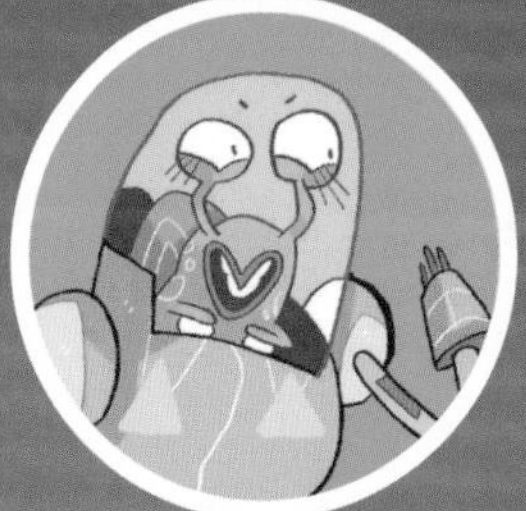

IF YOU MOSTLY ANSWERED B:

Suzie is your pizza bud. You're a pizza purist! You appreciate the fine art of "Pizzaioli." You bow at the altar of the supreme pizza trinity: dough, sauce, and cheese. People will call you a foodie, and that's fine, because way down in your deep dish of hearts, you know what you are: a connoisseur.

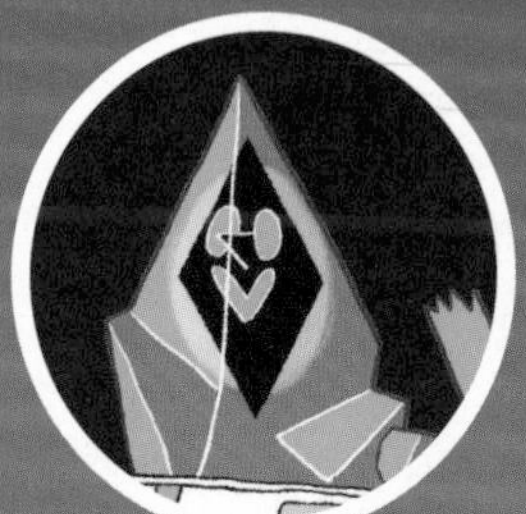

IF YOU MOSTLY ANSWERED C:

You and Mohs are kindred pizza spirits. Pizza is your business. Literally. You spend all day finding the most cost-efficient way to make the most pizzas--and then finding the customers who will buy them from you! Truth be told, you'd probably rather have money than pizza, but that one time you tried to bite a Space Credit, you almost cracked a tooth.

PAPA RONI'S BUSINESS QUIZ

Hello, I am AL-N. After my internship with the Cosmic Pizza Party crew, I decided to take Papa Roni's Guide to Pizza Business Success course. Help me answer these questions to see if we both learned the best way to run a pizza company.

1. FIND THE CHEAPEST INGREDIENTS POSSIBLE. NEVER WORRY ABOUT QUALITY.
   TRUE OR FALSE

2. NEVER PAY FULL PRICE BECAUSE THEY'RE PROBABLY RIPPING YOU OFF.
   TRUE OR FALSE

3. IF A CUSTOMER SAYS THAT YOU MADE A MISTAKE, JUST CHARGE THEM TWICE AS MUCH TO FIX IT.
   TRUE OR FALSE

4. THERE'S NOTHING WRONG WITH STEALING IDEAS, ESPECIALLY IF THEY'RE BETTER THAN YOURS.
   TRUE OR FALSE

5. IT'S TOTALLY FINE TO USE SOMEONE ELSE'S BETTER-LOOKING PIZZA IN YOUR ADVERTISEMENTS.
   TRUE OR FALSE

6. MASCOTS SHOULD BE BIG, SCARY, AND INTIMIDATING.
   TRUE OR FALSE

7. NEVER GIVE YOUR EMPLOYEES A RAISE.
   TRUE OR FALSE

8. IF A CUSTOMER HAS A COUPON, TELL THEM YOU DON'T ACCEPT COUPONS--EVEN IF YOU GAVE IT TO THEM THE WEEK BEFORE!
   TRUE OR FALSE

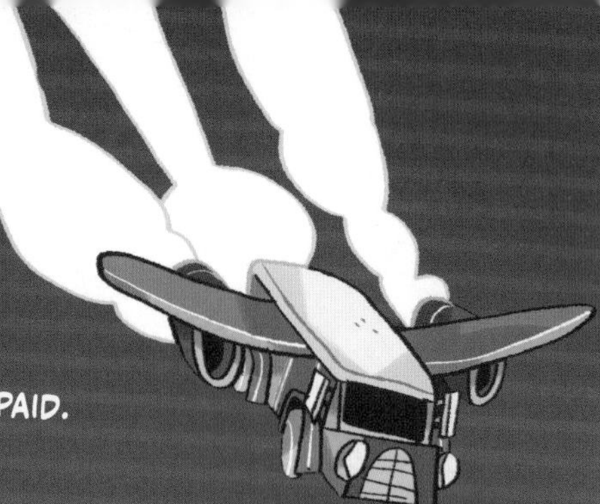

9. BUSINESS PLANS ARE FOR SUCKERS.
TRUE OR FALSE

10. LYING IS OKAY AS LONG AS YOU GET PAID.
TRUE OR FALSE

11. IF SOMEONE SAYS YOU'RE BREAKING THE LAW, TELL 'EM TO TAKE YOU TO COURT AND PROVE IT.
TRUE OR FALSE

12. IF A CUSTOMER SAYS THAT THEY CAN GET BETTER PIZZA SOMEWHERE ELSE, BAN THEM FOR LIFE.
TRUE OR FALSE

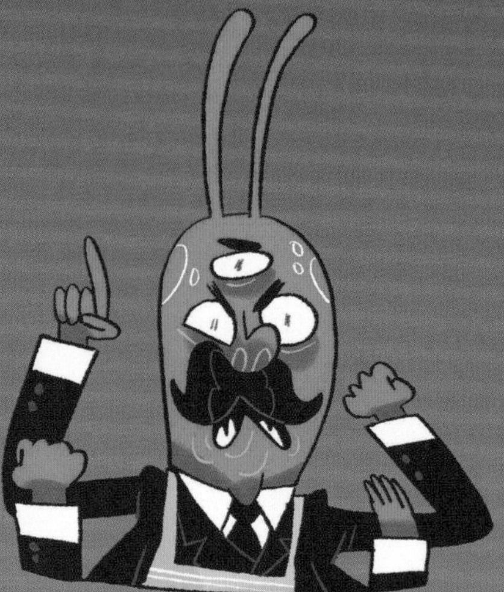

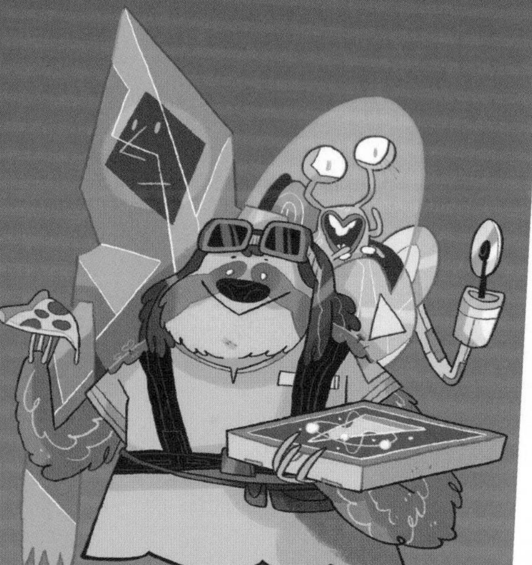

IF YOU HAD MORE TRUE ANSWERS:
You passed Papa Roni's course. . . but that might not be a good thing. Papa can be pretty careless toward others when it comes to his business practices. Being successful is good, but being kind and caring to your customers and friends is important, too!

IF YOU HAD MORE FALSE ANSWERS:
That's the ticket! Running a business requires a lot of hard choices. Making money is important, but being respectful and thoughtful to your customers is important, too. You're on your way to making sure your business is out of this (and every) world!

PIE-IN-THE-SKY PIZZA

Suzie learned in *Cosmic Pizza Party: Scrap Iron Chef* that not everyone enjoys the same foods. This recipe lets you explore the flavors you like best. Don't forget to ask for help if you need it. All for food, and food for all!

FOR THE DOUGH (MAKES TWO 12-INCH PIES):

2 to 3 cups all-purpose flour
1 package (2 1/4 teaspoons) active dry yeast
1 teaspoon sugar
1/2 teaspoon salt
1 cup warm water (approximately 110°F)
2 tablespoons olive oil
Cooking spray

TOPPINGS FOR TRADITIONAL CHEESE PIZZA (double for two pies):

1/2 cup tomato or pizza sauce
1 cup pizza cheese, shredded
(a blend of mozzarella, provolone, and parmesan cheeses)

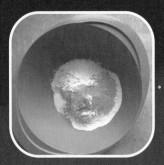
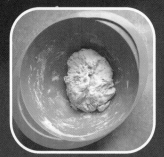

1. In a large bowl, combine 2 cups of the flour with the yeast, sugar, and salt.

2. Add the water and oil and mix with a spoon or your hands until the dough comes together to form a ball. If the dough is too sticky, add flour 1 tablespoon at a time. If the dough is too dry or crumbly, add water 1 tablespoon at a time.

3. Turn the dough onto a lightly floured surface and knead by pushing the dough into the surface and away from you, then folding it in half and repeating the process.

4. Knead the dough for 8 to 10 minutes, or until you can form it into a smooth, firm ball.

5. Lightly coat a clean bowl with cooking spray. Place the ball of dough in the bowl and cover it with plastic wrap. Place the bowl in a warm spot and let the dough rise for 20 minutes. It should double in size. Ask a grown-up to preheat the oven to 450°F.

6. Remove the dough from the bowl, divide it into two equal pieces, and then stretch and flatten both pieces into discs with your hands. Place the dough on a pizza pan or baking sheet and stretch it to the edges with your fingertips.

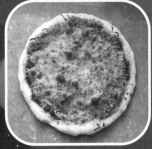

7. Spread sauce on the pizza dough, leaving 1/2 inch uncovered around the edge.

8. Sprinkle the cheese on top of the sauce.

9. Bake for 10 to 15 minutes, or until the crust is golden brown and the cheese is bubbly.

INSTEAD OF TOMATO SAUCE, TRY:
Ricotta cheese
Olive oil
Pesto
Barbecue sauce
Hummus

OUT-OF-THIS-WORLD TOPPINGS TO TRY:
Ham
Bell peppers
Eggs
Mushrooms
Arugula

Light-Speed Delivery:
Use a store-bought pizza shell, a bagel, or even a flour tortilla for the base of your pizza. Just don't tell Suzie!

SUZIE'S STELLAR FRUIT PIZZA

Pizza should be enjoyed all the time--even for dessert!
Suzie created this recipe for the Applevores, an alien
race that only eats fruit. Get a grown-up's help with the
oven, and you'll be on your way to a delectable dessert.

FOR THE CRUST:
1/2 cup butter, softened (1 stick)
3/4 cup sugar
1 teaspoon vanilla extract
2 cups all-purpose flour
1 teaspoon baking soda
1/4 teaspoon salt
2 tablespoons milk
Cooking spray

FOR THE TOPPING:
8 ounces mascarpone or softened cream cheese
1/2 cup powdered sugar
4 ounces whipped topping
2 cups sliced soft fruit such as peaches, berries,
  bananas, mango, mandarin oranges, figs, or kiwifruit
2 tablespoons honey

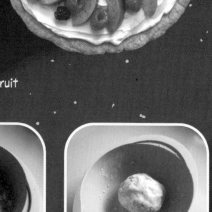

1. Ask a grown-up to
   preheat the oven to
   350°F. In a large mixing
   bowl, combine the
   butter, sugar, and
   vanilla.

2. In a separate bowl,
   combine the flour, baking
   soda, and salt. Add the
   dry ingredients to the
   butter mixture, and use
   your hands to combine
   until you have fine crumbs.

3. Add the milk and
   knead to combine.
   If the mixture is too
   dry, gradually add milk
   until you can form
   a ball with the dough.

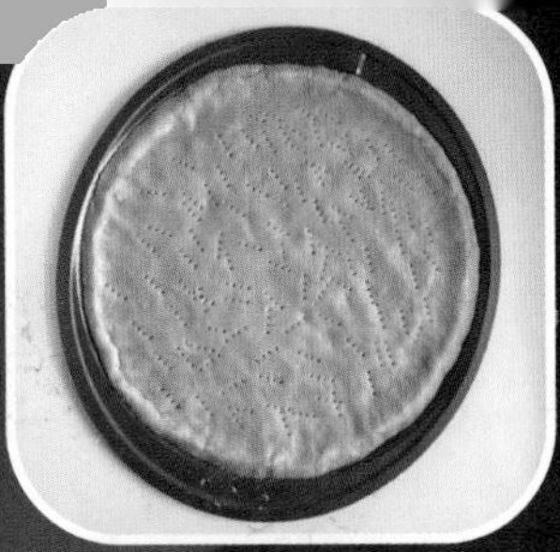

4. Lightly coat a baking sheet or pizza pan with cooking spray. Use floured hands or a rolling pin to spread the dough evenly, about 1/4 inch thick. Poke holes in the crust with a fork.

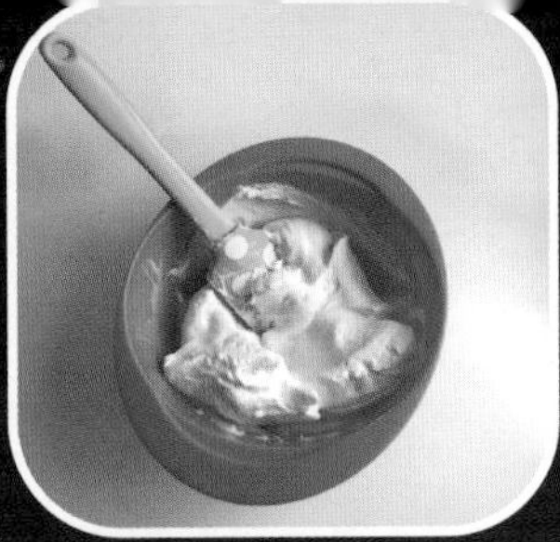

5. Ask a grown-up to help you bake the crust for 12 to 15 minutes, or until light golden brown. Remove from the oven and let cool completely. In a clean bowl, mix the cheese and sugar well, and fold in the whipped topping.

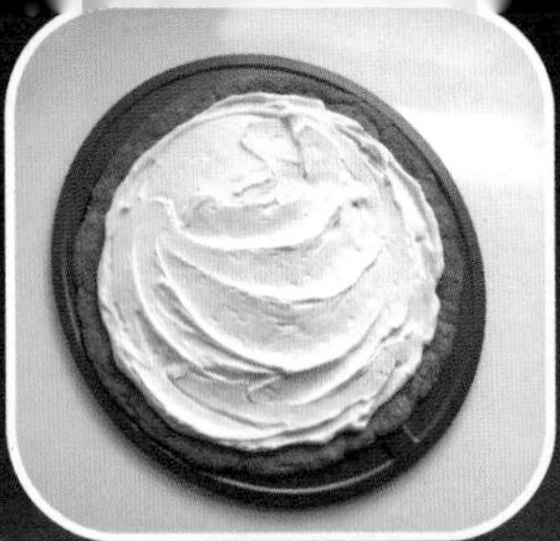

6. Spread the cheese mixture on the crust, leaving 1/2 inch uncovered around the edge.

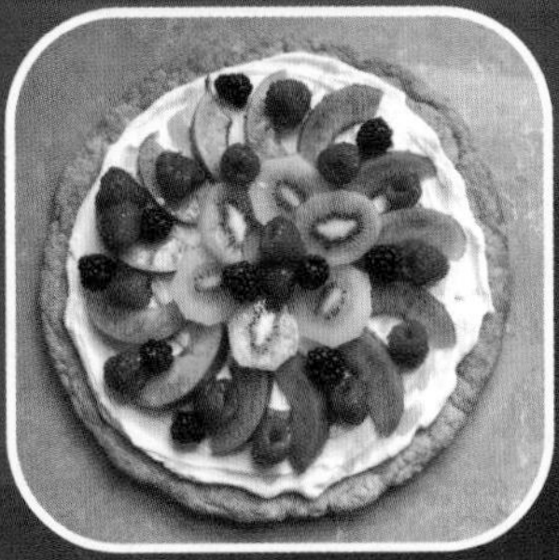

7. Top with the fruit, drizzle with the honey, and enjoy!

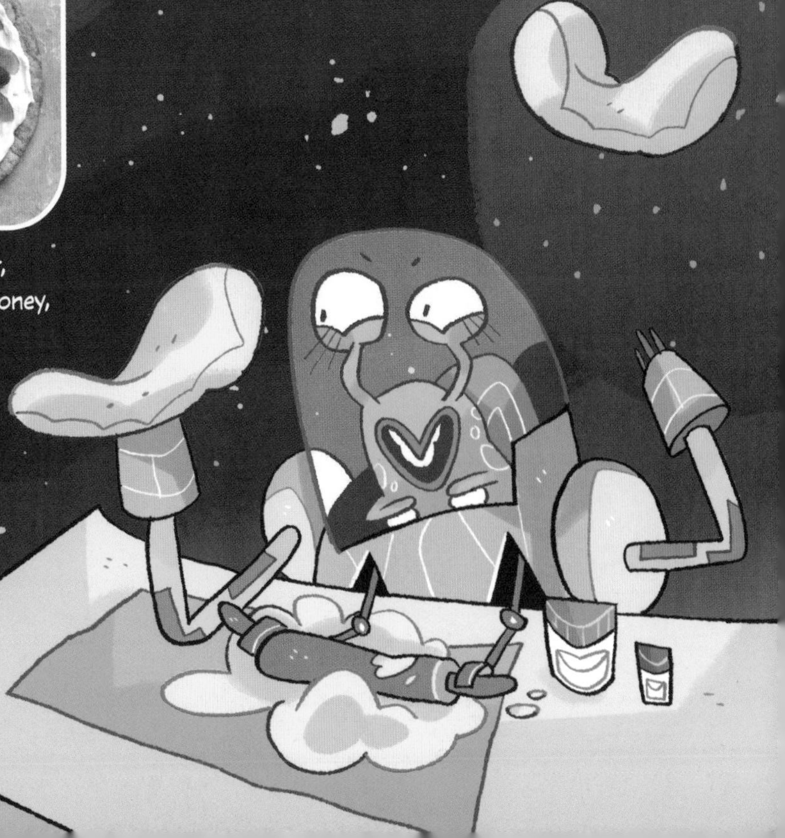

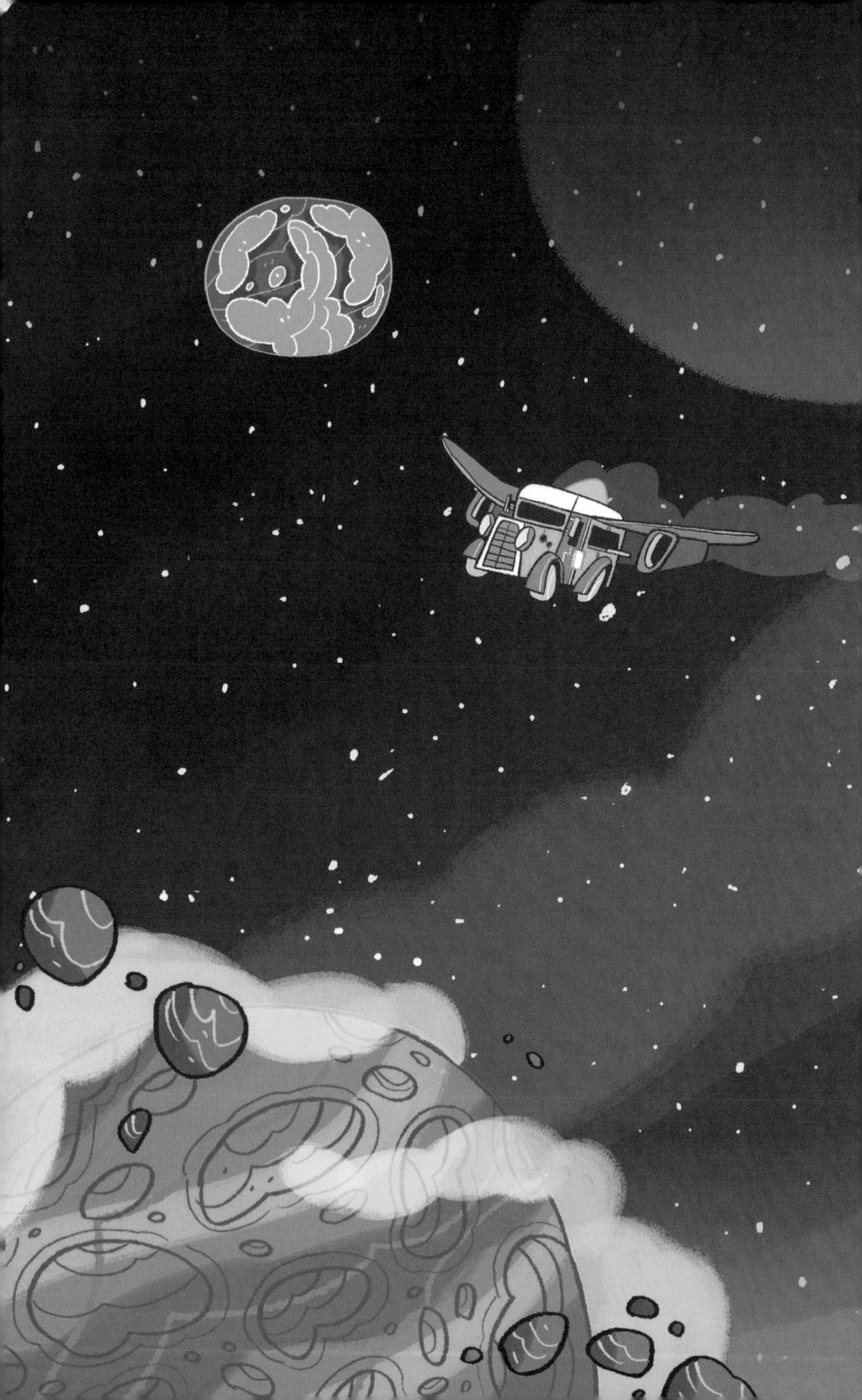

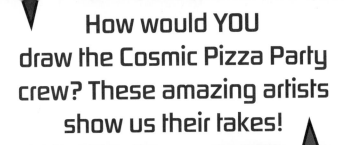

How would YOU
draw the Cosmic Pizza Party
crew? These amazing artists
show us their takes!

Pin-Ups

Suzie's Pie-in-the-Sky:
David Vordtriede

Meg's Mini Pizza Party:
Aliza Layne

Eat at Papa's!:
Ryan Goldsberry

Pizza Surfing:
Joey Ellis

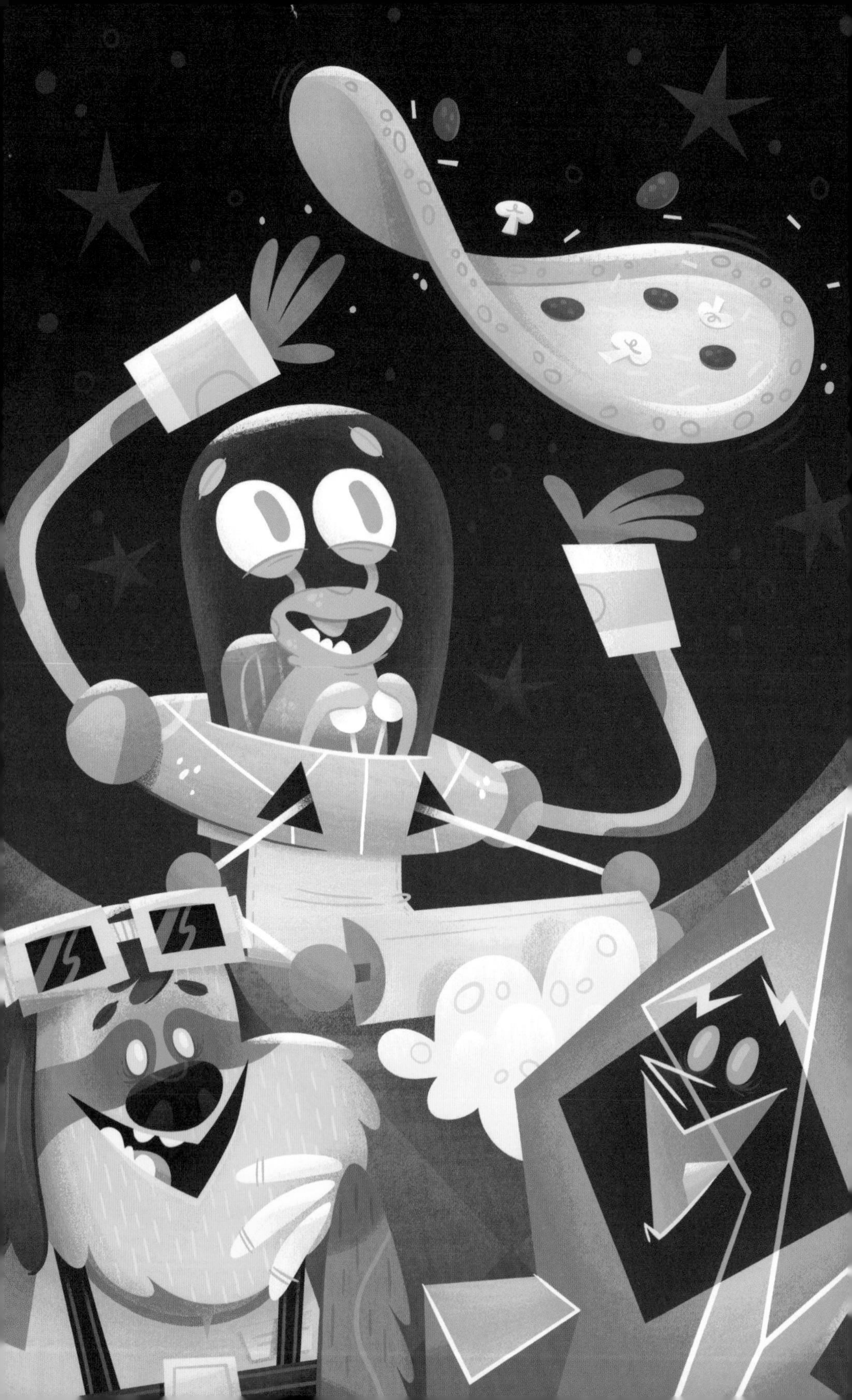

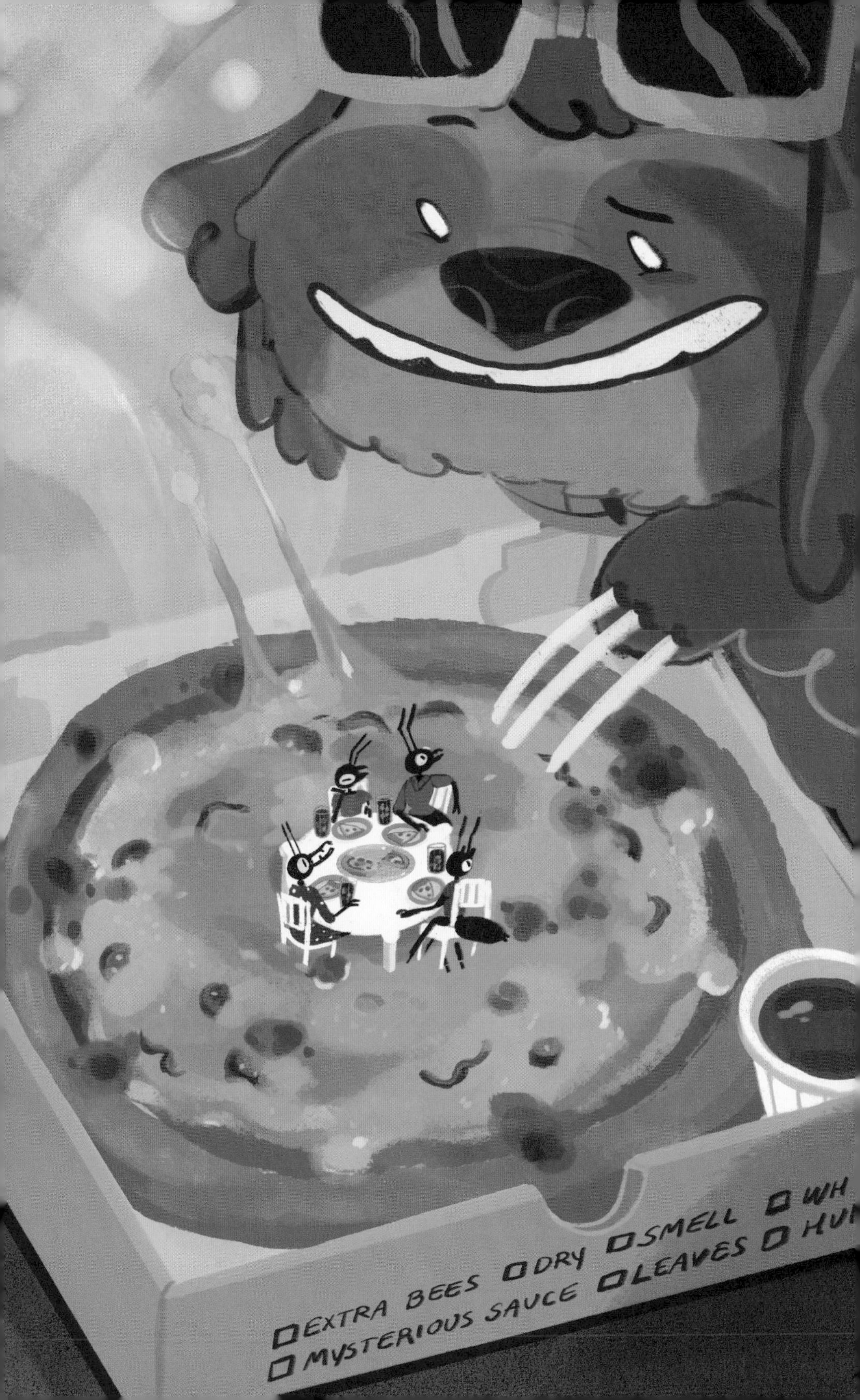

EXTRA BEES
DRY
SMELL
WH
MYSTERIOUS SAUCE
LEAVES
HUM

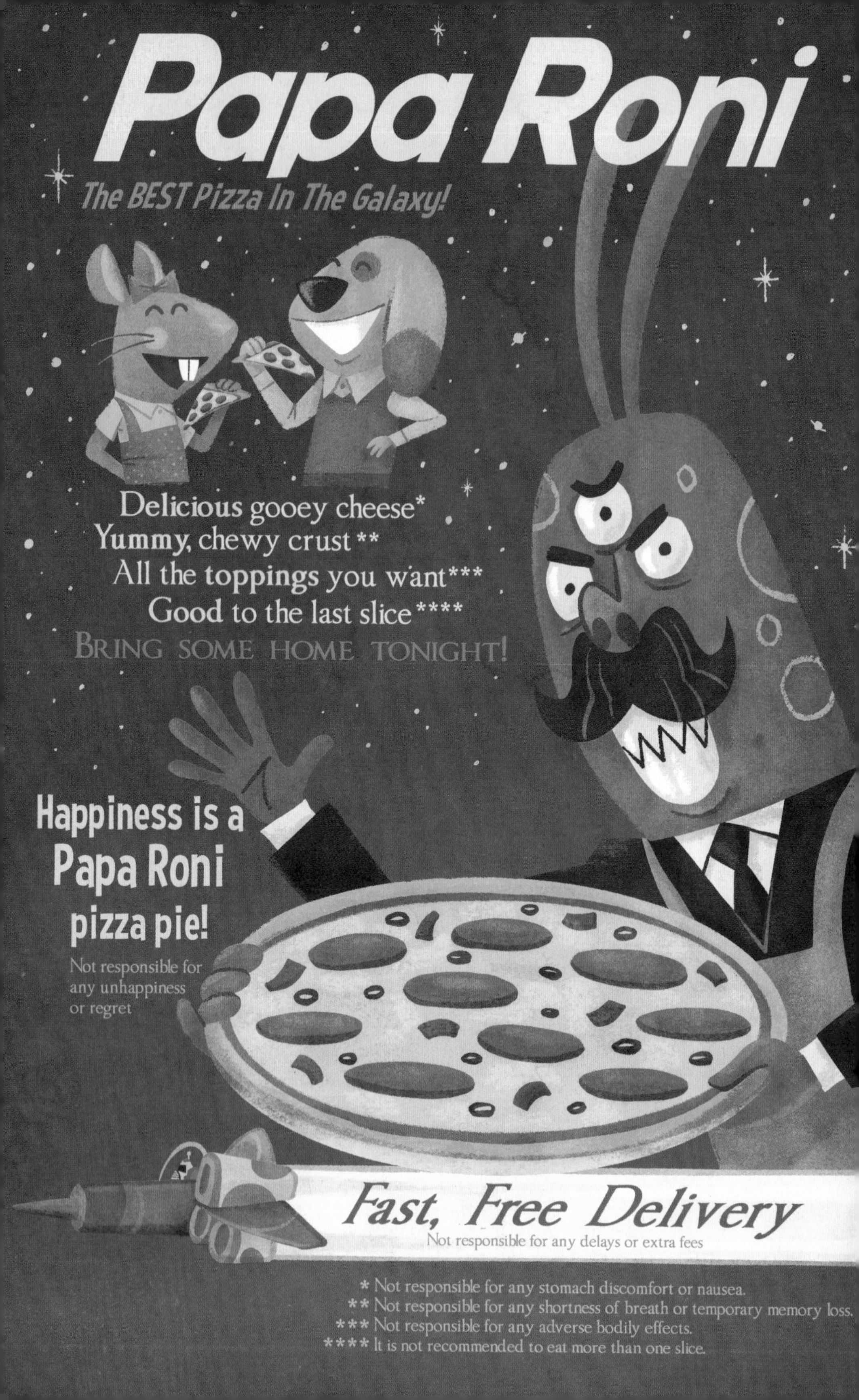

Papa Roni
The BEST Pizza In The Galaxy!
Delicious gooey cheese*
Yummy, chewy crust **
All the toppings you want***
Good to the last slice****
BRING SOME HOME TONIGHT!
Happiness is a Papa Roni pizza pie!
Not responsible for any unhappiness or regret
Fast, Free Delivery
Not responsible for any delays or extra fees
* Not responsible for any stomach discomfort or nausea.
** Not responsible for any shortness of breath or temporary memory loss.
*** Not responsible for any adverse bodily effects.
**** It is not recommended to eat more than one slice.

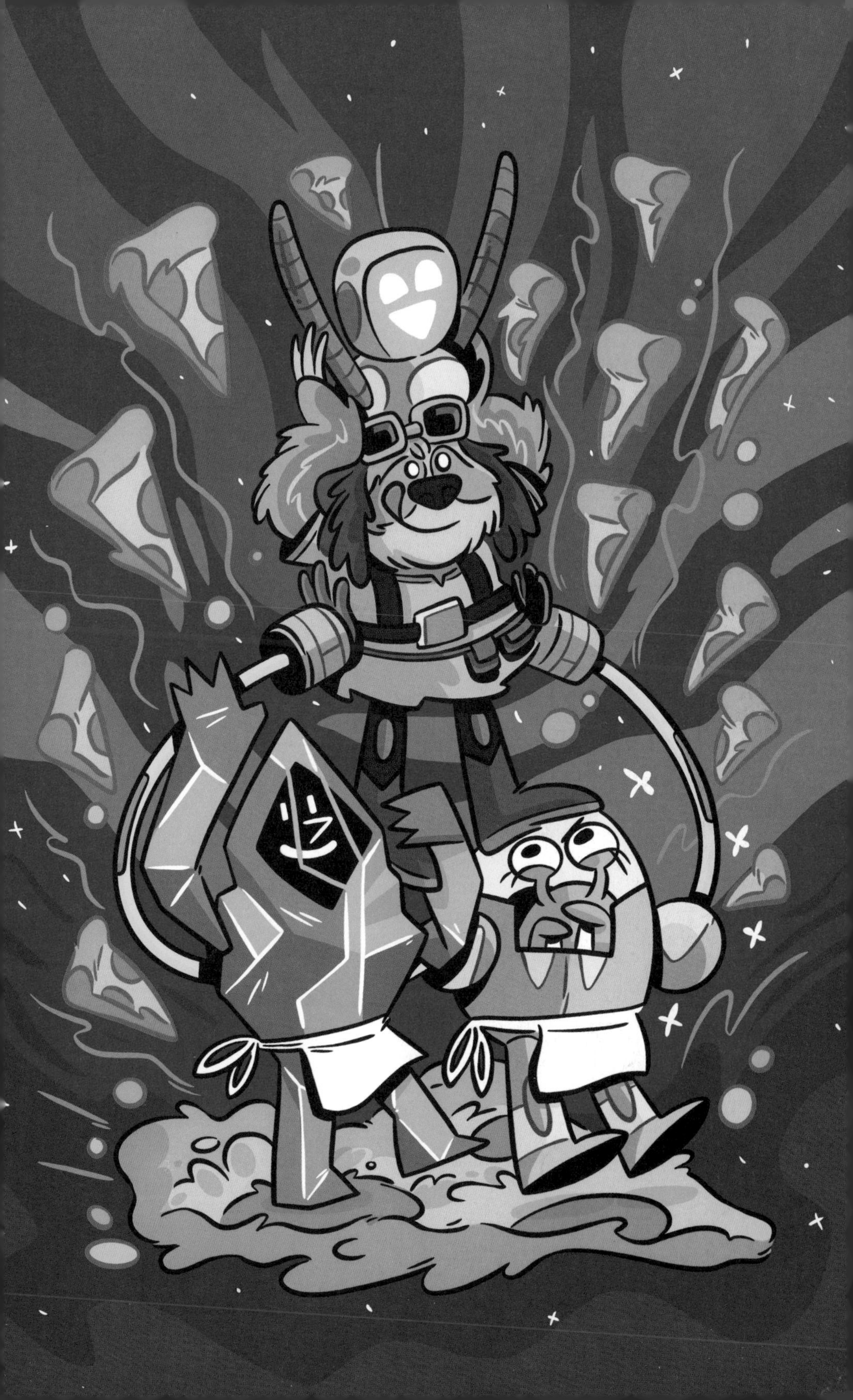

HAVE YOU HEARD ABOUT epic! YET?

We're the largest digital library for kids, used by millions in homes and schools around the world. We love stories so much that we're now creating our own!

With the help of some of the best writers and illustrators in the world, we create the wildest adventures we can think of. Like a mermaid and a narwhal who solve mysteries. Or a pet made out of slime.

We hope you have as much fun reading our books as we had making them!

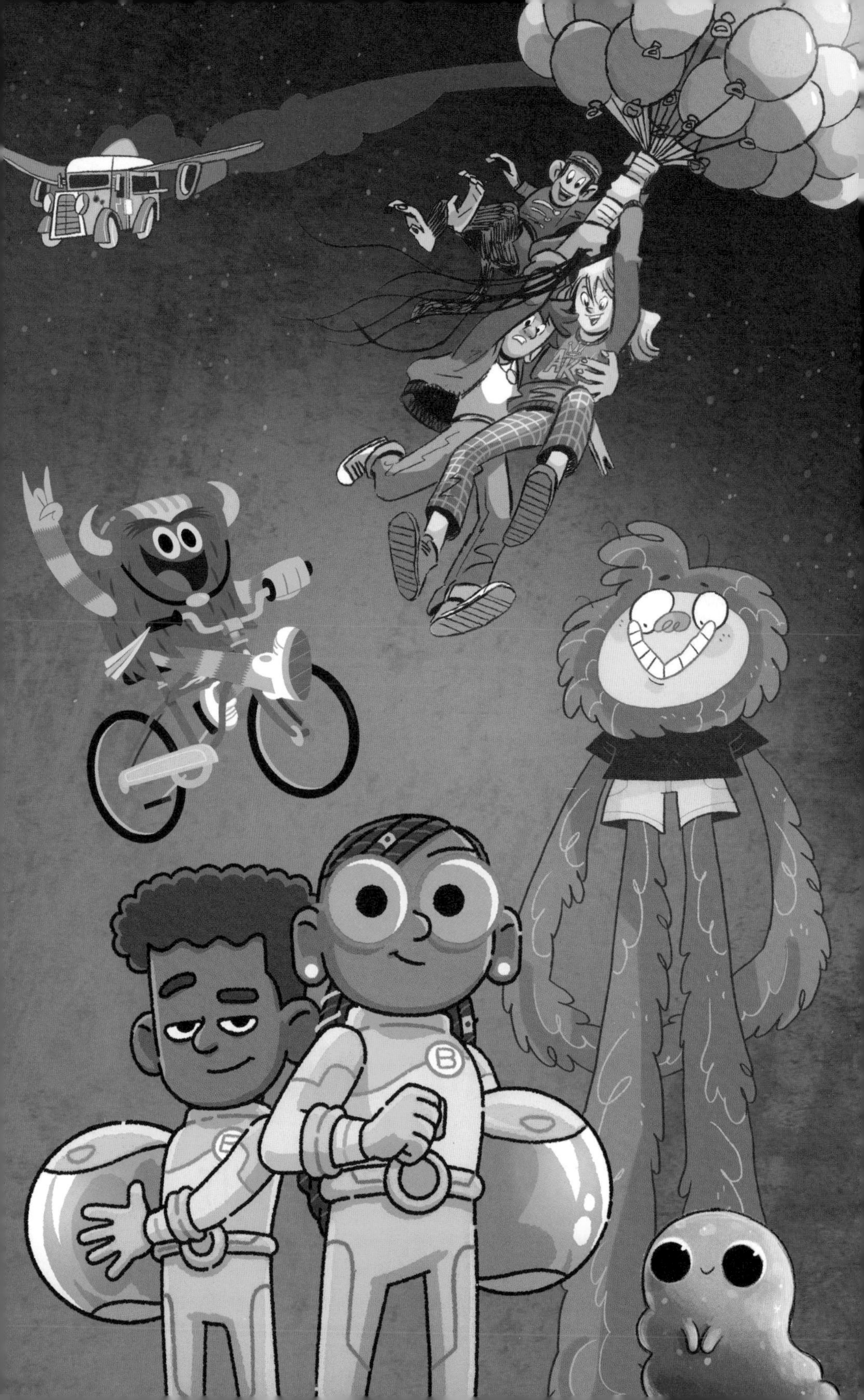